A Sound like Distant Thunder

Readers are encouraged to go to
www.MissionPointPress.com to contact
the author or to find information on how
to buy this book in bulk at a discounted rate.

MISSION POINT PRESS

Published by Mission Point Press
2554 Chandler Rd.
Traverse City, MI 49696
(231) 421-9513
www.MissionPointPress.com

ISBN: 978-1-954786-43-1
Library of Congress Control Number:

Printed in the United States of America

A Sound like Distant Thunder

A Steampunk Raj Novel
Book 2

J.R. SEEGER

Mission Point Press

Back Bay

Gymkhana

Bombay Harbor

Taj Mahal Hotel

St John's Church

ISLAND OF BOMBAY

"You may not be interested in war,
but war is interested in you."

— *Leon Trotsky*

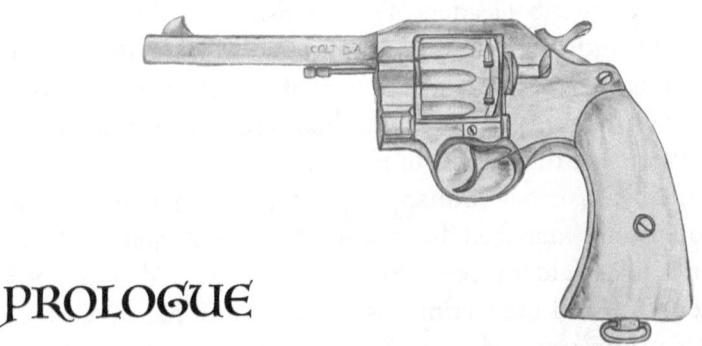

PROLOGUE

October 1913 — Waziristan, Tribal Areas, British India

FRANCIS BANKROFT AND ABDUL RASHID JOWZJANI WERE RIDING AT A FULL gallop, along with a third horseman who weakened and fell farther and farther behind. The Mahsud tribesmen chasing them were less than a mile to the rear and determined to prevent the two intelligence officers and their rescued diplomat from reaching the safety of the British garrison in Wana.

Francis realized he and Jowzjani should have taken more time to scout the camp of the rebel tribal leader known only as Mullah Mahsudi. But time was running out before the Indian Army took over and started punitive action against Mahsud and Waziri villages. Both he and Jowzjani were tired of the cat-and-mouse game with the mad mullah and his small band of insurrectionists. The Army would punish all for the crimes of a few. Bankroft and Jowzjani were acting quickly to prevent that collective punishment if they could.

Mahsudi used his clerical credentials, marginal though they were, to call for *jihad* or Holy War against the Indian Army in the tribal areas. As his first step in his Holy War, Mahsudi kidnapped the district commissioner for Waziristan. Joseph Macnaughton had been the commissioner for ten years, spoke excellent Pashtu, Afghan Persian and a number of different tribal dialects of the nomads who travelled along the Durand Line. He had a reputation for fair dealing with the maliks, or tribal leaders of the Mahsud and Waziri people. Mahsudi and his followers wanted two things: the end of government by malik and the end of British claim on their mountain territory. They saw kidnapping the commissioner as a way to set their effort in motion.

Usually, a tribal kidnapping meant formal and polite negotiations, managed by one of the tribal maliks. Most often a village elder received something he wished, a well or a better road, and the victim was freed without harm.

This time was different. Mahsudi threatened to kill the commissioner if the British government did not leave the tribal areas. The governor in Peshawar garrison thought this was just an excuse to murder a government official. His Indian Army counterparts agreed. They dispatched a squadron of the Frontier Force from Miriam Shah along with Bankroft and Jowzjani and a squad of Gurkhas working with Bankroft. The Army officers in charge were determined to punish Mahsudi and his men. Bankroft persuaded the officer in charge to give him a week to recover the commissioner. If he was unsuccessful in that time, the troops would march into Waziristan to start burning villages and killing tribesmen in what the Indian Army often referred to in uncharacteristic accuracy as "butcher and bolt."

Now, the rescue operation was in danger. It did not look to Bankroft that they would make Wana before the tribesmen caught them. Something needed to be done and done soon. As he crested a small hill, he pulled up. The sky was turning from grey to light blue. It would be dawn in minutes. As he peered through his binoculars, he could see the dust from their pursuers on the western horizon. Jowzjani rode up to him and said, "Baba Jan, Macnaughton cannot keep up. We have to stop them now before they catch us."

"I was thinking the same, my friend. I make twenty horsemen after us."

"Perhaps twenty. Perhaps less. Certainly, no more."

"Good. Here's what we must do. You stay here with Macnaughton. I will go downslope. When you see me start shooting, you begin as well. If we can take them by surprise, we should be able to take them down by a few and terrify the rest. These tribesmen want an easy payday. They may be willing to kill for *jihad*, but, in my experience, they will not want to die for *jihad*. My only request: no matter what, don't shoot me. I may be among them sooner than either they or you expect."

As he slid down from his horse, Bankroft pulled his rifle from the scabbard attached to his British Army saddle. He handed the rifle to his Uzbek colleague. "Use my Mauser as well as your Enfield. Make every shot count." As he prepared to confront their pursuers, he pulled from his saddle what looked to Jowzjani like a small blanket.

Jowzjani had worked with Bankroft for over ten years. He knew Bankroft's plans were often confusing, but they always worked. He dismounted and pulled out an Enfield carbine. It would be a near-run thing, but Jowzjani was confident they would survive to tell another tale around the campfire. Macnaughton finally rode up, caught his breath, and croaked, "We need to keep going. They will overtake us and kill us!"

Bankroft took a moment to compose himself and apply his rarely used mesmerism skills. He reached up and touched Macnaughton on the thigh. As he made contact, he said in a calm voice, "Commissioner, you need to stay with my colleague. All will be right. You need to dismount and keep our three horses safe. Please take them down the hill toward the road to Wana." As he spoke, he pointed downslope along their route. He handed the reins of his horse to Macnaughton and Jowzjani did the same.

In the half-asleep, half-awake manner of the mesmerized,

Macnaughton eased down from the saddle and said, "I will take the horses down the hill. All will be right." Leading the horses, Macnaughton walked slowly in the direction Bankroft had indicated.

Jowzjani looked toward Bankroft and realized his British partner had disappeared. He said to himself, "I need to ask someday how he does that."

The Mahsud tribesmen approached the small hill at a full gallop. They knew their prey were close. They would overrun the three and, at the instruction of Mullah Mahsudi, they would kill them at this spot, and take their horses and their weapons. Mahsudi would have a new plan ready for them when they returned with their war booty. The leader of this troop of fifteen horsemen, Akbar Khan, smiled as he thought of the praise that he would receive when he returned laden with weapons and, perhaps, even some English gold. His long black beard and long hair kept barely controlled by his black turban flowed with the wind from the ride. The sun was just creeping over the horizon in front of them. It would be full light when they killed the Britishers.

As if by magic, a shimmering ghost rose straight out of the desert floor. The grey cloak shed sand as he rose. The lead Mahsud tribesmen were not entirely sure he was human. A Djinn perhaps? He seemed both visible and invisible in the morning light. As he appeared out of the desert sand, Bankroft's heavy Colt automatic pistols barked. Akbar Khan fell off his horse, a round through his forehead. Khan's deputy dropped from his saddle with a rosette of blood forming on his chest. The next two riders received similar wounds from the heavy .45 caliber automatics. Bankroft killed four riders before Jowzjani realized that Bankroft was even among them.

Jowzjani recovered quickly. He shot three more riders as

fast as he could work the bolt action on his Enfield rifle. The high-powered rifle rounds hit the men, raising dust from their chests and knocking them to the ground. Perhaps not dead, but certainly no longer interested in hunting the three British agents.

In seconds, Bankroft was surrounded by horsemen reaching for their Khyber knives. Whether djinn or man, they realized he was bringing death to their host. Two more shots from each of the automatics and the two closest men were dead. Another round from Jowzjani dropped one of the last riders in the column. Bankroft holstered his two automatics and drew a heavy Colt revolver from his shoulder holster. Another pair of .45 caliber rounds hit men as they charged him with drawn Khyber knives. In less than a minute, twelve men who assumed they were predators had become prey.

The remaining three riders split off in multiple directions to escape the bloodbath. Later, they would explain that their stallions started to smell the human blood. Waziri stallions were hard to control in the best of circumstances. In the chaos of this bloody dawn, the horses panicked and ran in every possible direction away from the noise of Bankroft's pistols. Perhaps the remaining Mahsud tribesmen couldn't control their horses. Perhaps they had decided that today was not the day to be a martyr for Mullah Mahsudi's cause. It hardly mattered. They followed their horses' lead and rode away from the ambush site. As they were leaving, Jowzjani used Bankroft's bolt action Mauser to take one last, very long shot. He watched as one last rider fell. "At least 600 yards. I must have one of these rifles," was all Jowzjani said as he stood up and waved at Bankroft.

Bankroft was busy checking the dead for any intelligence they might reveal. He did not expect to find any written material. Few in Waziristan could read. What he did find was a single gold coin in each of the dead men's belt pouches. German gold.

Death at the Afghan Church

October 1913 — Bombay, British India

ELIZABETH BANKROFT LEFT THE TAJ HOTEL JUST AS THE SUN WAS STARTING to set into the Arabian Sea. She picked up a carriage in front of the hotel and told the driver to take her to the Afghan Church in Navy Nagar, near what was known to all the drivers as "Zero Point," the historic center of the English colony city. The turbaned Sikh driver looked back at the young lady who seemed barely old enough to be allowed out of the house. She was properly dressed in a shalwar kamiz and dupatta, but at least in his family, the idea of a woman traveling alone in a port city like Bombay seemed foolhardy. Still, she was going to a church on a late Saturday afternoon, so she must be an honourable woman. There could be no harm in taking her to the church. He snapped the reins, and the coach took off. A fare was a fare, after all, and at least he wasn't taking some English dandy from the Taj to the red-light district of the city where he might get robbed for his troubles.

Elizabeth was not going to church. She was a newly

minted British Intelligence officer meeting one of her local reporting agents, code named Z-1. For nearly a year, Elizabeth had visited Bombay as an agent handler and direct observer of the city. During her regular visits, she stayed in the Taj Hotel, Bombay's premier location, and ranged about the city sometimes as herself and sometimes using multiple disguises. On Elizabeth's last trip, just before monsoon in June, Z-1 reported a number of German engineers regularly visiting Bombay. They travelled on British-flagged liners from White Star and Cunard. The engineers would board the liners in Cairo or Durban, disembark in Bombay for one or two days, and return to the liner in time for its departure for Singapore and Hong Kong. Z-1 was used to passengers and merchant mariners spending their time and money at the gin shops in Lal Bazaar near the harbor. When they finally ran out of money, they would come to his shop to sell valuable stones, gold from the colonial mines in Africa and Australia, or even their pocket watches. What Z-1 found curious about the Germans was instead of visiting these sailor's haunts, they visited the Taj Hotel, the Victoria rail station, and the Royal Navy docks north of Apollo Bunder.

Z-1 visited the Sea Lounge at the end of each day for tea and on one of those trips, he observed the Germans. He did not think these visits at all normal. Elizabeth countered that she could imagine refined Europeans spending time viewing architecture and art and enjoying tea at the Taj Sea Lounge overlooking the harbor. After all, why would German engineers spend time walking through the crush of small streets in Lal Bazaar, risking pickpockets or worse. She stayed in the Taj herself, choosing not to go to the standard colonial hotel, Watson's Esplanade. During one stay, she did see German travelers in the lounge enjoying tea and using their binoculars to view the harbor. Z-1's comment to Elizabeth was simple: "Men are men wherever they come from and Lal Bazaar draws men like flies to honey." At this meeting,

Elizabeth hoped Z-1 would have more information on the Germans.

While riding to the Church of St. John the Evangelist, known to the locals as the Afghan Church, Elizabeth thought about this man, code named Z-1. He was a Russian Jew in exile. Z-1 escaped with his family at the turn of the century after one of the Tsar's pogroms. In the past ten years, Z-1 had made a good life for himself in this most cosmopolitan and mercantile city of British India. He bought precious and semi-precious stones from travelers and then sold them to the Ismaili jewelers living in the Muslim section of the city. He was known in the community as a man who always paid a fair price and expected a fair price when selling to the jewelers. He recognized that reputation was more important than a single success, no matter how profitable. For this reason, Europeans, Indians, and even the occasional Persian came directly from the harbor to Z-1's offices with their jewels. Along with a reputation as a reliable businessman, Z-1 was considered the most reliable source in the city for the Indian Army Intelligence Bureau.

Elizabeth liked Z-1 for his sense of humor, for his commitment to his family and for his commitment to his adopted country. They met in quiet parks in the late afternoon after he closed the shop for the day. He always brought a metal tiffin filled with wonderful food made by his wife. Over tea and pastries, Elizabeth had a chance to improve her Russian-language skills. He was like an adopted uncle who quoted Russian poetry and liked to play chess. It became clear over time that he liked Elizabeth because he could reveal his darkest concerns about his family with no concern that she would reveal those secrets.

Z-1 worried constantly about what life would be like for his son and daughter in a city that was not their own. He wondered if Russian exiles, and especially Russian Jews, would ever be accepted as British citizens. He told Elizabeth many times, "What I do for this country is a small thing compared to what this country has done for me. My family has survived, even thrived, in this place. My son is attending a good local college and will attend the Bombay school of art. My daughter is married to a well-respected German from Hamburg who is working for the German consulate. They have a wonderful baby boy. Life was unforgiving when we were in Russia. Now, we have a place where we can grow old and enjoy children and grandchildren. What little I do for you when I report snippets from the docks is a small repayment of the great benefit my family has gained."

Each time they met, Z-1 always came back to the same concern, "Will any of us ever be considered British citizens? Will we ever have documents that allow us to travel? My daughter has German travel documents only because she is married to a German trader. What if they leave? Will I never see my grandchild?"

Most of the skills Elizabeth learned at The Viceroy's College, the British Indian school for spies, focused on debriefing contacts who were either unwilling to talk or unlikely to tell the truth unless it was for their own gain. The school taught her ways to control men's minds so that they would report truthfully whether they wanted to or not. When meeting Z-1, Elizabeth used more of the skills she learned from her Scottish tutor Mrs. Edwards about how to be polite company, rather than anything taught at the school for British spies. She learned from Mrs. Edwards to be a good listener, a careful observer of human frailties, and, when needed, how to be a friend. Above all, Z-1 needed a friend in Bombay and Elizabeth was ready to be that friend.

Elizabeth had not expected any positive gains from her efforts, but it turned out that the closer she became to this sixty-year-old man, the better his reporting. Elizabeth had already established a reputation for accurate and timely reporting. Most of those reports were from Z-1. In the past month, Elizabeth realized that she had an obligation to this man who was central to her professional success. She needed to identify how she could obtain British citizenship or, at the very least, British Indian travel documents. It became a goal that she was determined to accomplish before the end of the year. It might not be the right thing to do as a professional, but from Elizabeth's perspective, it was the moral thing to do.

The carriage dropped Elizabeth off at the crushed-stone sidewalk leading to the large Anglican church. The church was surrounded by old trees and a lush Indian garden. Her approach was in deep shade and she barely heard her carriage leave. The long series of monsoon rains had turned the standard gardens into something just short of a jungle. The scent of jasmine and freshly mown grass around the promenade along with the ever-present sweet smell of plant and animal decay filled the air. If asked how this part of Bombay smelled, Elizabeth would have said, "Green, deep green, jungle green."

Elizabeth would have known her way even in the middle of the night because of her regular visits during the Sunday services and because this was a favourite meeting location for Z-1. There were a series of stone benches that surrounded the church. Their meeting would be at one of the benches on the far side of the church. Elizabeth smiled at the thought of meeting with her "uncle," the stories he would tell of his financial successes during the week and at least one humorous story he would relate about some foreign traveler. Then, as he talked business, they would share the small snacks that Z-1's wife would have made for them. Yes, this was work and their joint commitment to providing intelligence to the Crown was important, but Elizabeth was coming to learn that a successful espionage career would mean that she had to and would want to commit to personal relationships with her sources.

As she turned the corner of the church toward their meeting place, Elizabeth heard a voice, more of a whimper, cry out, "No. No more." She could see Z-1 on the ground being kicked by a man wearing the uniform of a British sailor. Next to him, looking on as if he was giving specific directions to the sailor was a man dressed in formal European clothes. As soon as she saw what was taking place, Elizabeth shouted, "Stop that immediately!"

The sailor and the European looked up, surprised to see anyone and especially a woman interrupt their effort to beat a man to death. While a woman might not stop them, she would certainly be able to call for the local police patrol and she would be a reliable witness to their attack. They looked at each other and ran in opposite directions leaving Z-1 a crumpled mass on the ground.

Later that night in her hotel room, Elizabeth realized she had a hazy recollection of what happened next. She was furious. Her focus was on the two men and she literally saw red as the blood rushed to her head. Who would attack a man as gentle as Z-1? A white-hot anger boiled up and overtook her normal, calm persona. The sailor had a good fifty yards on her and was in excellent physical condition. Elizabeth had no doubt he assumed he could make good his escape in the maze of streets surrounding Zero Point. Before she had even considered what she had to do, Elizabeth used the Tibetan skill of *lung gom pa,* controlled the air around her and covered the distance in bounding leaps. In the mountains, this meant Elizabeth could cover one hundred yards in a few seconds. At sea level, she was able to overtake the sailor in a single leap. One second, he was well on his way to escape and, the next, he was confronted by a young woman standing in front of him. In the receding light, the sailor was surprised, but not worried. After all, she was just a woman, and a slight woman at that.

He drew his long, sharp sailor's knife and said, "Girlie, let me pass. This is not your trouble."

Elizabeth raised her right hand in what looked like an

appeal to prevent his passage. As she did so, she projected her *chi* in a manner that sent a force directly through the sailor's chest. He flew back as if struck by club. As he rose to his knees, he waved his knife and said, "I don't know how ya did that, girley, but now you will have to pay."

This time, she flicked her left hand and the sailor's knife flew out of his hand and tumbled yards away on the freshly mowed lawn. Inside the sailor's head, he heard a loud voice cutting into his brain. It said, "How dare you touch a man like that! You are a sailor for the Crown."

First, the sailor put his hands to his ears. He had to make the noise stop. Along with the voice, there was a siren noise that made him deaf and blind. He could barely draw breath. He decided to attack Elizabeth headlong. Perhaps action and violence would make the pain stop. As he ran toward Elizabeth, she used a basic martial arts skill taught at the College to sidestep her attacker. He tumbled and then stood up again. He was closer this time, so the sailor was certain he would get his hands around her throat. That might end the pain and allow him to escape.

As he closed the distance and reached for her neck, Elizabeth put her open hand on his chest. She said in a voice that even she would not have recognized, "This is about the ladder of consequences. IT IS MOST DANGEROUS at the top of the ladder." The sailor collapsed as if every bone in his body had melted. Later, the police would report that the sailor's arms, legs and ribs were broken as if he had been beaten mercilessly with steel rods.

Elizabeth ran back to her friend. Elizabeth held him in her arms as he struggled to stay conscious. Z-1 repeated a mumbled, "I told them nothing, little one. I told them nothing."

Elizabeth started to cry. She could feel Z-1's life force leaving his body. There was nothing to be done to save her friend. The beating had been too severe. She reached into a concealed pouch in her dress and recovered a small opium tablet. The least she could do for Z-1 was make his last moments on earth pain-free. She pressed the tablet into his mouth and then held Z-1 in her arms until he died.

After he died, Elizabeth forced herself to check to see if there was anything in Z-1's pockets that might reveal his role as an agent of Empire or that would explain why he was at the meeting. There was nothing. She looked at the tiffin sitting on the bench. Perhaps there was something there? She walked over to the tiffin and quickly found the concealment cavity built into the bottom tray in the brass container. A small, hand-written report came out. She placed it in another pouch hidden in the long shirt of her shalwar kamiz.

Next, Elizabeth walked over to the dead sailor. As expected, his body matched his uniform. Here was a man used to life at sea. Rough, scarred hands, wrinkled skin, hard leather boots, and a thick blend of wool and cotton in navy blue. Elizabeth examined his single trouser pocket. A few Indian rupees and a small, folded note. She opened the note. In the fading light, she could see instructions telling him to be at the church at sunset. Wrapped inside the note were two small gold coins. Coins minted by the German Empire.

As she stood next to the sailor, she quieted her mind and focused on the second man she had seen attacking Z-1. Where did he go? As she focused, Elizabeth's mind seemed to stretch out far beyond her body. The last time she had practiced this art known by the Tibetans as the illusory body, her master guru Naismith had helped her control the travel. This time, she was on her own and her flight up and away from the crowded streets of Bombay was less controlled. Still, her search was not in vain. She finally saw the man in the formal clothes stepping onto a steam-powered motor launch near the Gymkhana on the west side of the island. In no time at all, the steam launch had passed the breakwater and was heading north up the coast. Elizabeth was puzzled. As far as she knew, there was nothing up the coast for miles.

A Sound like Distant Thunder

As she watched, the launch turned out to sea. Where was it going? Elizabeth could barely control her search. Her ability to use the illusory body was based on a level of emotional control. After the death of Z-1, it was hard to maintain that control. Still, she struggled to push her mind farther and farther out from the coast into the dark ocean. Suddenly, she saw the launch stop next to a shadow sitting still in the water.

A whale? No, it was too large to match the whales that rarely visited into the Arabian Sea. And no animal or fish would sit still as a boat approached. As she looked more carefully, she realized it must be an aeroplane floating in the water. It was a biplane with the lower wing just above the water with small pontoons hanging into the water on opposite ends of the wing. An enormous upper wing was attached to the boat-shaped fuselage by a series of metal struts. On the upper wing were eight engines riding above the wing on their own framework. Each engine had a large propeller, much like the propellers that Elizabeth had seen on the Royal Navy airships. The propellers faced the rear of the craft. Hoses from each of the engines ran down the wing, along the frame and into the body of the craft. Elizabeth had read that the Royal Navy was experimenting with what they called sea planes, which were simple craft designed to serve as scouts for the fleet. Gasoline powered engines meant their range was limited. The illustrations she had seen were nothing like this craft which was almost half the size of the giant military airships operating in India.

As she willed her illusory body to circle this strange craft, Elizabeth saw a hatch open on the grey hull. A man in a blue navy sweater, hardly appropriate for the Indian weather, raised a lantern. With the light of the lantern, Elizabeth could just make out a forward position with a machinegun. The man in the suit jumped from the launch to a ladder that took him up the side of the long, wide hull toward the man with the lantern. As they met, the man turned toward the boatman in the steam launch. He pulled out a pistol and fired three shots into the boatman. The boatman fell overboard and disappeared into the sea while the launch rocked in the waves.

Elizabeth concentrated and finally her mind penetrated the darkness. In the rear of the aircraft was another position with another machine gun! As she circled the strange craft with her illusory body, she could see a black iron cross on each wing and again on the twin tail at the rear of the aircraft. A military aircraft of the German Empire. So, this was some sort of flying warship.

It was sitting too low in the water to imagine it would ever fly in the same way as the airships or even the flying boats of the Royal Navy. Still, what else could it be? It seemed too fragile to serve as a ship and yet too large to serve as an aeroplane. As she watched, the man in the sweater extinguished the lantern, walked along the outside deck and then took a position behind an enormous wooden ship's wheel in the same cockpit as the forward machine gun position. Suddenly the propellers on the aircraft began to turn and eventually increased pitch until all Elizabeth could hear was their sound. It was entirely puzzling because she could not hear an engine noise like she had heard from steam, gasoline or even diesel engines. The ship moved slowly at first and then picked up pace. The wake of the ship created silver waves in the jet-black water. Elizabeth watched as this ship increased its speed. It seemed to skim the water and turned out to sea. If this was an aeroplane it was a strange beast because it did not really fly. Rather it seemed to ride just at the surface of the water.

Soon, the strange craft disappeared into the inky night. The last thing she saw was a trail of exhaust from the engines. Elizabeth's mind, her illusory body, returned to the church courtyard and inhabited her real body. She wasn't entirely certain what she had seen, but she knew, along with the death of Z-1, she needed to report this strange German warship in Indian waters.

It took Elizabeth an hour to walk from the Afghan church back to the Taj Hotel. She could have taken a cab, but she needed to be completely alone with her thoughts. A walk through the dark city streets would help. The hustle and bustle of the crowd of the business capital of British India had no effect on Elizabeth. As she walked with her head down, men on the street seemed to part to let this woman pass. Later, men interviewed by the police described a specter walking the streets away from the church. A woman in shalwar kamiz, but with what seemed to be a ghostly aura around her. The police dismissed the reporting simply because they were not interested in hunting ghosts. They were interested in hunting a man or men who might have done so much damage to the two bodies in the churchyard.

When Elizabeth arrived in her room, she immediately stripped off her "work clothes" and rolled out a small prayer carpet on the wood plank floor. As she sat in her one-piece underwear, she tried to use the calming mantras that both Guru Naismith and her mother had taught her. The mantra seemed to start working and her breathing would slow and then her memory of Z-1 and the memory of the shock on the face of the dying sailor came rushing back into her head. She would focus on her breathing and try again, only to have an image of Z-1's wife intrude her thoughts asking "And what will we do now?" Elizabeth knew that she had nothing to do with Z-1's death. Or did she? Her mind was a jumble of thoughts, fear, and anger. While the life of an intelligence officer was complicated, she never expected it to be quite so painful.

Eventually, Elizabeth gave up her attempt to wash the adrenaline out of her body. Instead, she walked over to the window in her room and stood there watching ships rocking at anchor in Bombay harbor. She stayed there until dawn. Then, she packed her suitcase and checked out of the hotel. The death of Z-1 might be only part of the story and she needed to be sure that her superiors knew at least that part from her own lips.

Interactions

December 1913 — Baghdad

JAMES O'CONNELL SAT ACROSS THE TABLE FROM HIS SON. THEY WERE enjoying a special Advent dinner served by the household staff made up of Chaldean Christians. While not precisely the holiday dinner that he remembered from his youth in Dublin, James O'Connell had to admit it was a far better meal than he had enjoyed in his time serving in one or another of the British consulates around the Arabian Sea. The Protestants in the British diplomatic service did not celebrate the saints' days or Advent quite like the Irish in Ireland or the Germans in Germany. The Germans had smuggled food and drink through Ottoman channels and around the eyes of Muslim clerics who would not approve. He had poured a properly chilled German hock in two glasses and sitting on the table was a beautiful German smoked ham. Potatoes and greens were from the kitchen garden that his staff maintained. It was well and truly a feast.

Michael had matured in the two years they had been living

together in Baghdad. His skin had tanned and with his grey eyes and black hair, he looked like he belonged to one of the many cultures of the Ottoman Empire, perhaps a Circassian or a Georgian or a Chaldean Christian. With a growing skill in Baghdadi-accented Arabic, his son had become a respected member of O'Connell's intelligence team serving the Kaiser. At only seventeen, Michael was considered by the Germans too young for the advanced responsibilities. James ignored his German masters and integrated his son completely into the world of espionage.

Under James' tutelage, Michael became an adept agent handler. He regularly disappeared into the streets of Baghdad, Kut, and even Basra to collect information from the O'Connell network reporting on both British and Ottoman activities in the Arab world. His age was a significant benefit since none of the British travelers in the region had any interest in what appeared to be just another inquisitive Arab boy. That was not the case with the Arab police and the Ottoman intelligence chiefs in the region. Michael had to take care that he was not wrapped up in the regular police sweeps looking for Arab nationalists or Islamic extremists backed by the Wahhabi tribesmen of Arabia. Boys were always targeted, mostly because they were easier to catch and far easier to intimidate during torture. So far, they hadn't focused on Michael as he collected intelligence on all sides of the ethnic and sectarian conflict. Some of this information James delivered directly to the German, some he kept at hand for a future moment when either the Ottomans or the Germans would jettison their Irish colleagues. A deep understanding of the Arab leadership in Iraq and the Arabian Peninsula would prove useful one day. James was as sure of that as he could be of anything in the shadow world of espionage.

As he drank a second glass of the white wine known as hock, James thought about his decision nearly three years ago to change sides and work for the Germans. The German understanding of how the Irish viewed British control over Ireland was a start-point for his defection to their cause in the Middle East. However, it was his commitment to his son's future that made the real difference. As he savoured the sparkling wine, he thought about how fate brought them to this point.

James O'Connell had well and truly loved his dear wife, Afarin Shirazi. His love overwhelmed his knowledge that marrying what the British establishment would view as a "local" would limit his career opportunities in the Intelligence service, both in India and in Britain. When he first met Afarin at a dinner party in the consulate in Aden, he was dumbstruck. The daughter of a Persian oil merchant and a distant member of the Qajar Persian dynasty, she was dressed in a blend of oriental and Parisian fashion that complemented her beauty. She spoke perfect English, perfect French and beautiful Persian. To James O'Connell, she seemed to be a character described in the best of the love poetry of Hafez or Khayyam. When he met her father, James knew there would be few obstacles to marrying this beauty. Cyrus Shirazi was a Zoroastrian who had what could only be called a flexible view on inter-faith marriages. Instead, he saw the marriage as an excellent link between his community in Persia and the British Empire.

When he returned as a married man to India for a staff assignment with the Military Intelligence Bureau in Calcutta, the only thing that he found was prejudice against his wife and his baby son. The British community could understand a man having local mistress, after all that was just part of being a colonial administrator. They could not imagine why a British officer would marry a local, even a local as beautiful as Afarin. At first, O'Connell attributed the prejudice to the British community in Calcutta. It was, after all, the center of the British government in India, filled with mid-level Army officers and senior civil servants striving to reach the heights of the Raj bureaucracy. They could not afford to show any understanding. Understanding might be interpreted as sympathy for the locals and that would never do.

In response to the prejudice, O'Connell requested reassignment to the British community in Bombay. The Intelligence Bureau agreed. His Arabic would be of greater use in a cosmopolitan city with trading links across the Arabian Sea. Traders from the ports of call from Arabia, Mesopotamia and Persia stopped in Bombay. A perfect place for a man of O'Connell's skills to build and sustain a regional intelligence network. As cover for his reassignment, they sent O'Connell as a member of the Royal Navy Logistics offices in Bombay supporting the Indian fleet. They promoted him to the rank of Lieutenant Commander to give him more than enough reason to travel to the various ports of call in the Arabian Sea and enough rank to argue his way on both Royal Navy and Merchant Marine ships.

Even with the large and commercially successful Zoroastrian community in Bombay, known locally as Parsis, the O'Connell family faced prejudice in the British military community living in and around the district known as Mazagoan. He moved the family to an apartment nearer to the Parsi community in Cumbala Hill on the Western side of the island. For a time, it made a difference and they were happy.

However, in the end, prejudice resulted in the greatest tragedy of O'Connell's life. During a late monsoon, Afarin came down with cholera. O'Connell was on a mail ship returning to Bombay from travel to Karachi. Afarin was taken by O'Connell's household staff to the British Hospital in the Navy Lines. The British doctors refused to treat "a local." O'Connell returned to find his beautiful wife barely alive. By the time he found a Parsi doctor able to treat her, Afarin was dead. O'Connell was left with a ten-year-old son and a deep hatred of the prejudices that remained from the era of Queen Victoria. His efforts to create a normal life for his son were unsuccessful. English boarding schools refused what the administrators called an Anglo-Indian. The British Indian schools were committed to the elite of the Empire. O'Connell's rank was not sufficient. He did his best in Bombay to create a stable household for his son. The Parsi community helped him find the best teachers in the city. Those teachers included some of the most respected scientists of the Raj. It mattered little to the British community. The Parsis were still locals and their commitment to science and arts could never reach the quality expected of a British educator. O'Connell realized over the years that in the stratified society of the Raj and, especially in the class structure of the British homeland, Michael O'Connell would never find the success he deserved.

In British India, Michael would always be considered Anglo-Indian, the son of an Irish civil servant and a local. Michael's intelligence and his father's link to the Indian intelligence service would provide him with opportunities, but only up to a point when the prejudice would take over. James knew he could easily succeed in structured Edwardian society. He was certain that his son would not. The first mark against him was he was Irish. The second mark against him was he was the son of a British officer and a Persian princess. The final mark was he was born in India. No one in the British Empire would support him outside of the Raj. It wasn't fair, but James knew it was as true as the fact that the sun rose in the East and set in the West.

Months ago in Aden, the unchecked remarks of a foolish Royal Navy subaltern handed James the opportunity he wanted to give Michael a different life. The subaltern had described a secret calculating device on board the *HMS Skirmisher* resting in Aden harbor. James met with the ship's executive officer and used his mesmerism skills to convince the executive officer that his captain should host a small reception for the senior British officials in Aden. While attending the reception on the fantail of the cruiser, James used other espionage skills to steal the instruction manuals for this new device. Later that same month, O'Connell approached the German diplomatic mission in Baghdad and offered the plans for this Royal Navy analytic engine. The Germans were delighted. The analytic engine was a computing machine that could enhance accuracy in navigation, naval gunnery and the improved German torpedoes. They immediately accepted O'Connell's offer to continue to work for the German Empire.

After his role in preventing the capture of a German intelligence team in Afghanistan, the German intelligence service brought both O'Connells back to Baghdad on permanent assignment. In less than a year, James O'Connell used his skills as an Arabist and as a trained intelligence officer to build a network of sources from Baghdad to Damascus and Beirut. By the end of their first year in the employ of the Kaiser, the intelligence supervisor in Baghdad recommended sending Michael back to a German University or to the Prussian Military Academy in Berlin. The premier German orientalist, Max von Oppenheim, met both James and Michael during a tour of the Middle East to assess both O'Connells for more advanced work for the German Empire. In a one-on-one meeting with James, he offered to take Michael back to Germany for higher education at his alma mater in Cologne. Once Michael had completed his studies, Oppenheim said he would place Michael on his staff in Berlin.

James did not want to annoy his new masters. He had demurred based on Michael's age. German boys did not go to university until they were nearly eighteen. Michael was only sixteen. James had some months before he could determine where Michael would receive a higher education. He knew for certain that the Germans might be polite to Michael, but they were at least as prejudiced as the English about families of mixed European and Asian heritage. James' goal was to get Michael an advanced degree in Ireland, specifically at Trinity

College. It might be a Protestant university, but it was considered the best in Ireland and would prepare Michael for a future in a new Irish republic, when the island broke free of the English Crown. Michael's complexion and hair colour would simply be accepted as part of his Irish heritage that was so common among the diverse society of Dublin. All James needed was a little money and, perhaps, a little help from the Germans to get a place for Michael. James already had a plan to explain why it would be in the German interest to send "one of their spies" back to the United Kingdom. It still meant treason.

Treason. James often wondered how he would explain his decision to Michael when it came to the point of conflict between the British Empire and the German Empire. It would be a tale that began with events well before Michael was born.

"Father, you looked as if you were miles away. Are you troubled?" Over the past year, Michael's voice had transformed from a squeaky youth to an adult tenor. In his father's eyes he remained the child he had raised, but he was fast becoming a man. His experience over the last two years as a courier and agent handler, as well as his continuing education at the hands of his father, had sharpened his observational skills and his ability to sense trouble. That was what he sensed now.

"My son, I was thinking about our work here in Mesopotamia. I am very proud of your successes over the last year." He raised his glass of sparkling wine and toasted his son.

Michael sipped the hock and said, "Father, you should not worry about explaining why we are working for the Kaiser and not the British King. I have known for some time that we were no longer allied with Calcutta. I never had any great loyalty to the English in India. The English killed mother after all. And then as I grew up, they treated me badly. I was never given a chance to show my skills even when I was at

The Viceroy's College, that special school for spies. The boys picked on me and called me names. The instructors seemed to have little time for me. They sent me to study Russian even though it was clear I had proficiency in Arabic and Hindi. Their focus on protecting their control over India meant they didn't really want to hear what any of us who have lived in India thought about India."

Michael paused to reflect and took a sip from the German wine. "There was only one student I cared about, a young girl named Elizabeth but even she embarrassed me at one point in the Circle of Decision. I had to live with that embarrassment for the rest of the term with boys pointing to me as the one who couldn't win a fight with a girl. The Germans may not be any better, but at least they let us do our job without interference. Perhaps there will come a time when we must leave them as well, but for now, I find the work stimulating. So, please do not worry." Michael smiled his most personable smile. He knew he had to settle his father's mind and he hoped to do so with his comments and his smile.

James wondered how skilled his son had become in reading thoughts. To test him, he commented using telepathy. The message said, "Can you hear what I am saying?"

Michael responded back quickly, "Of course, Father. I thought you knew I always had this skill." James switched back to speaking rather than telepathy and said, "Michael, you are well and truly a marvel."

Michael smiled and said, "Thank you, father." What he was thinking in his most guarded recesses of his mind was, "And you have no idea how far I will go with these skills. I already know your capabilities and have long surpassed them."

A Sound like Distant Thunder

Rawalpindi, December 1913

Christmas at the Bankroft household on the Rawalpindi Mall was one of the few times that the entire family gathered together. The rule of the household was no work talk during the holidays. Amusing anecdotes, observations related to culture or natural philosophy were acceptable, but no work discussions. In years past, Elizabeth always wondered why her parents enforced such a strict rule. After working for the Indian Military Intelligence Bureau for a full year, she now knew why. Long ago, her father quoted an Afghan saying: "The walls have mice and the mice have ears."

Francis Bankroft spent 1913 "up country" working as the senior intelligence officer for the *Piffers*, the Punjab Irregular Frontier Force. The *Piffers* were based in Abbotabad on the border of the Northwest Frontier. Throughout 1912 and into 1913, Francis assumed multiple guises as he moved from Rawalpindi to Abbotabad to Peshawar. He ranged up and down the Afghan border with a small cadre of trusted agents and a squad of Gurkhas. While there were moments when he chafed at the restrictions placed on him by his conventional military masters, Francis acknowledged that it was far easier to work a few days in disguise and then return to the barracks. In his previous assignments he was required to live in disguise for weeks and even months waiting for that terrible moment when he might be uncovered as a spy. In the past year, his greatest pleasure was riding the mountain trails with his Uzbek partner Jowzjani, meeting with tribal leaders on the frontier. After a few days on the frontier, he returned with reports of which of these tribal leaders would be allies of the Raj and which would be adversaries. The work also allowed him more regular visits to Rawalpindi and time with his wife.

There were times when he returned to their house in Rawalpindi to find Mary not at home. She made two additional forays into Mesopotamia in 1912 and early 1913 to determine what had happened to James and Michael O'Connell and, more importantly, what had happened to the plans for the Royal Navy analytic engine. While the intelligence service was convinced that O'Connell had stolen the plans when he defected to the Germans, there was no way to prove that accusation. The plans could easily have been stolen and transported by nearly any source who might have been on board *HMS Skirmisher* when the ship docked at the port of Aden. O'Connell's disappearance at the same time might be coincidental. For most of her travels, Mary still had trouble accepting O'Connell was a traitor.

It was on the last trip to Baghdad in November 1913 that she collected the most disturbing of reports. Both O'Connells were working as mercenaries supporting the Kaiser's efforts to establish greater control of the Ottoman regions of Kurdistan, Mesopotamia and Arabia. Part of their treacherous mission was to identify British collection efforts and, if possible, to counter those intrigues. The report caused Mary great pain. It was the first time she had to accept the fact that even Britons could become traitors. It was especially difficult because she would have to let her daughter know that one of her classmates from The Viceroy's College, Michael O'Connell, was now working against the Crown and for the Kaiser. Mary decided that she was not going to ruin Christmas holidays. Unfortunately, sooner or later, Elizabeth would have to know.

Conrad Bankroft returned from his army assignment guarding the Bolan Pass. He came with tales of adventure and trinkets from Afghanistan to give as Christmas presents. Now a senior lieutenant, Conrad was battalion adjutant. The job involved far less risk and more time in garrison. Conrad was not pleased with the new role which he said was "paperwork, paperwork, and then more paperwork." Francis told Conrad that if wanted to command a company in his regiment, he had to succeed at a staff assignment first. Boring it might be, but it would raise his profile in the regiment and that would result in promotion and command. Unlike his previous holidays where he could describe adventures chasing bandits into Afghanistan, Conrad's stories were now more about playing polo or hunting wild game with rifles or on horseback with lances. Elizabeth did her best to look interested, but to her it sounded dreadful. As she looked into her brother's eyes and peered ever so gently into his sub-conscious mind, she learned that he thought it dreadful as well. One of the new skills she had mastered was what writers and circus performers might call "mind reading." Elizabeth found over the holidays that mind reading was not always a good thing when the mind you were reading was a family member.

While Conrad had no such training, he did see a new level of maturity in his sister's eyes that he had not seen on previous holidays. He realized that his little sister was no longer a child. Early on during the holiday, his father told Conrad that Elizabeth was working for military intelligence. He was incredulous at first. After all, this was a girl who told him that she intended to be a scientist and the first female graduate of Cambridge University. He had expected that fantasy to disappear when she found a man to marry and a family to raise. Instead, she was a spy? It seemed so unlikely, but when Elizabeth met him alone at the train depot in Rawalpindi, dressed in a felt campaign hat, a white cotton shirt, leather belt holding up her jodhpurs and knee-high riding boots, he accepted his little sister was no longer a child.

Elizabeth returned to The Viceroy's College in 1912 after her sojourn in Afghanistan and completed her one-on-one tutorials with her mentor, Guru Marian. During these months, Marian taught her advanced espionage tradecraft as well as how to refine the skills of Tibetan mystics. Mesmerism, levitation, and the illusory body, called by her tutor "remote viewing," were key to her tutorials. Guru Naismith reviewed Marian's weekly reporting and, at the end of term, admitted to Elizabeth that she was the most skilled pupil he ever had at The Viceroy's College. Elizabeth officially graduated with her class in December 1912. Along with the coveted cream-coloured scarf with the three embroidered stripes given to the female graduates, Elizabeth received a formal commission, albeit a secret commission, as an ensign in the Intelligence Service of the British Indian Army.

After brief holiday in Rawalpindi, she spent the early months of 1913 on short assignments. At first, as a junior intelligence officer, she received basic tasking that required travel from Rawalpindi to Karachi. Each assignment required Elizabeth to uncover and report on the activities of the Russian exile community. During these early assignments, Elizabeth was paired with more senior officers in the intelligence service. The long train rides between the two cities gave her a chance to write her reports and to consider the lessons these informal mentors taught her about her new trade. By early summer, she was dispatched on her own to expand the network into the port city of Bombay.

There was little to report on the exile community in Bombay. Russian Jews who escaped the Tsar's pogroms against Jewish communities were displaced throughout the Ottoman world and all the port cities of British India and even as far as Hong Kong. Still, it was a chance to hone her skills and use her Russian. While working in these port towns, Elizabeth also improved her street language skills in Persian and Hindi. She found these languages useful as she passed through the communities, appearing one day as a British woman, the next as a lesser princess from Jaipur, and the next as a Bombay washerwoman.

The only report that did attract attention from the Indian Military Intelligence Bureau and in the Military Intelligence Department in the War Office was from one of her Russian exiles, Z-1. His reporting on German travelers in India puzzled these intelligence mandarins, even if Elizabeth could not understand why they were interested in European travelers. When two of these travelers killed Z-1, Elizabeth finally began to understand the significance of the reporting. It was also when she killed a man. When she returned to Rawalpindi for holidays, Elizabeth spent some time with her mother explaining the events, describing her feelings and telling her mother about the confrontation with the British sailor.

Mary Bankroft had expected this conversation, but honestly not as soon as it happened. The espionage trade was filled with dangers and when you added in the natural dangers for women in India, there were more than enough reasons for her to worry over her daughter's new role in the British intelligence service. Well before Elizabeth revealed her concerns, Mary heard from the head of The Viceroy's College, Guru Naismith. How he found out about Elizabeth's encounter near the Afghan church was anyone's guess, but he did. Naismith used his telepathic skills to warn Mary about her daughter's actions. Naismith's voice came to her just before she retired for the night. He said, "Mary, Elizabeth was just in a confrontation in Bombay. She is well, but two things happened. First, she lost an agent for the very first time. That is traumatic enough. But she also killed a man for the first time. She used powers I never taught her. Powers I didn't know she had. She projected a force that crushed the man. I have looked at the police reports. It was as if all of the bones in his body were dissolved."

Mary responded, "Master Guru, what shall we do?"

"Mary, when Elizabeth returns for the holidays, give her time to talk about these events. Also, I need you to probe whether Elizabeth understands the power that she unleashed. If so, I will need to engage her. She needs to learn how to manage that power. If she does not understand what she did, if she just responded in anger and doesn't realize that she has a new power, then we have time to begin a new level of education. Either way, I need you to teach her how to meditate to wash the negative energy out of her system and come to terms with her actions in Bombay."

Mary nodded and said, "I understand, Master Guru. I will obey."

When Mary finally had a chance to sit down with her daughter for a quiet chat, Elizabeth broke down in tears. She asked, "Mother, was I the reason Z-1 was killed? Was it something I did?"

Mary could see her daughter was filled with emotion. Her aura shimmered in bright orange. The only way to handle this was to calm Elizabeth and then talk through all of her worries. After all, she was still a teenager who was now deep inside the world of espionage. Elizabeth was walking a trail that Mary walked but only after several years of service to the Crown. She said, "Elizabeth, if you will let me, I will help you focus."

"Mother, focus is not what I need. I need answers!"

"Dear, sometimes in our trade there are few answers, and those answers only raise more questions. If you can focus, at least we can start to understand what questions to ask."

"Mother, I'm not sure I can return to this work. It seemed like a fun little game at first. Now, I realize it is a matter of life and death. And, I was the one causing death."

Mary decided whether Elizabeth wanted to focus or not, she had to do so. Mary put a hand on Elizabeth's shoulder and stared into her eyes. She concentrated on Elizabeth's aura and said, "You can focus, dear. You need to try."

At one level, Elizabeth knew what her mother was trying to do and it upset her. On another level, she felt her mother's voice help her relax and that felt very good. She gave into the voice and slid into the "waking dream" state that she knew her mother intended to induce. "I will try."

"Excellent. Now, you need to decide what is most important."

"Z-1's death. Did I cause it?"

"Did you bring those men to the meeting?"

"No. I did not. They were at the meeting before I arrived."

"Did you force Z-1 to work with you?"

"No, mother. I did not. He was working for the Crown well before I arrived. We just seemed a better fit than my predecessor."

At this point, Mary realized her daughter was holding herself responsible for everything that happened. She was too young and had too little experience to know that sometimes the world was unfair. She said, "Then you hold no blame, Elizabeth. In this trade, there are risks. Even when you do your best to manage the risks, there are going to be events out of your control. You are not responsible for everything that happens."

"Mother, perhaps I am not ready to be an agent for the Empire."

Mary smiled at the comment. It was just what you would expect from someone at her age facing such an enormous challenge. She said, "You should relax. You need to know that you are ready to be an agent for the Empire. You are already an agent for the Empire. The Empire needs you. Consider this as you rest." Mary slid her hand up Elizabeth's neck to her temple and pressed gently. Her daughter slipped into a dreamless sleep.

A Visit to the Archaeologists

December 1913 — Baghdad

FOR THE FIRST TIME, MICHAEL O'CONNELL SAT ALONE IN THE OFFICE OF THE senior intelligence officer for the Kaiser. The German mission in Baghdad was in one of many 19th century brownstone houses in the foreign quarter where the Ottoman government tolerated diplomats, scientists, businesses and, of course, spies. Michael scanned the room as he waited for the German officer to invite him to sit down. In an effort to mitigate the eventual summer heat, the room had a fifteen-foot-high ceiling. To Michael's right, large casement windows could open to catch any breeze. The windows were bordered by embroidered drapes that could be used to keep out the heat and the dust. Behind the officer's desk was a life-sized portrait of the Kaiser in military uniform. Flanked on either side of the Kaiser were prints of German military successes during the Napoleonic Wars and the more recent Franco-Prussian War. To his left hung a six-by-eight-foot map of the Ottoman Empire, flanked by two cavalry sabers.

Standing to the right of the desk was a German civilian. Surrounded by militaria, the civilian was dressed in what could only be described as high-status Arab clothes. His dress included a white silk thobe and headdress matched with a khaki-coloured, three-buttoned suit coat. Michael had heard of this man before. He was Wilhelm Wassmuss, Arab and Persian expert and agent provocateur based in Bushehr, Persia.

In contrast to Wassmuss, Colonel Manfred von Trier was everything Michael imagined a German officer would be. He was in full uniform of a German hussar. His sword, scabbard and holstered pistol were hanging on a leather belt on a carefully polished coat tree. Michael judged the colonel to be slightly older than his father, somewhere between 50 and 60 years old. At one point, he had certainly been an athlete, but Michael could see that von Trier was beginning to pick up weight. Not portly, at least not yet. His hair was cut so short that Michael could see his pink scalp. Matching his German military presence, von Trier had a scar that ran from his jaw to his left ear, just missing his left eye. Based on the depth and width of the scar, Michael could see the wound was not from some frivolous duel in Prussia but from some battlefield of the last century. As he concentrated, Michael used his growing synesthesia skills to identify the colonel's aura. A halo of purple surrounded the colonel. This was a man of immense confidence in his own views. He was not one who would tolerate informality. Michael prepared himself for interrogation.

The colonel spoke in formal English with a slight German accent, "Herr O'Connell, please have a seat."

Michael was relieved. He had been prepared to stand for the entire audience with von Trier, and this small invitation suggested that the colonel might not dismiss his skills out of hand. It was interesting that the colonel intended to proceed in English. It argued that he had some advanced education in Britain. It also meant Wassmuss was fluent in English as well as Arabic and Persian. Once Michael sat down, he prepared both brain and body so that if he was given a chance to speak, he would use a light touch of mesmerism to gain some advantage. He bowed slightly and simply replied, "Thank you, sir."

In his best parade-ground voice, the colonel shouted to his aide de camp, "Coffee for three if you please."

Behind him, Michael heard a voice respond, "Absolutely, Excellency."

The coffee arrived, served by a Baghdadi in a white servant's uniform. The three men spent a moment preparing the Turkish brew to their liking. Michael simply stirred the coffee with the provided spoon; Wassmuss swirled his coffee after putting a sugar cube in his mouth, and the colonel added two spoonfuls of brown sugar and stirred. The clinking of the spoons on the edges of the tall, cut-glass cups was the only sound in the room except for a ponderous ticking of a large clock sitting in the center of von Trier's desk. Michael thought about how the colonel had stage-managed this entire interview so that he maintained both a sense of control and superiority. This was not the first time that he had faced an older man focused more on himself than on Michael. Again, Michael was relieved. He was also slightly distracted as he thought about how he might recruit the Baghdadi to report on his master. That would be an interesting challenge.

Michael had heard the colonel was a man with a reputation for the audacious. As a cavalryman, Michael was certain that these were the colonel's traits. That would make him so much easier to manipulate than a man who was cautious and used to being on the receiving end of a verbal or physical lash. Step one was to let the colonel think he was controlling the conversation. Step two would be to ingratiate. Step three would be to mesmerize. The only question for Michael now was: What was he to do with Wassmuss?

"So, young O'Connell, I have read your file. You have been very successful in your work for us. The first report comes from your interlocutor at the Rawalpindi airship station. You accepted his authority immediately and did not question him. That was a very good sign. Liemann also remarked that you were willing to take on hardship without complaint. Again, very good. The rest of your file is based on your reports and your father's comments about your skills. I have dismissed his comments as simply the remarks of a proud father. Your reporting, on the other hand, demonstrates excellent operational skills. There are some in my command who would have dismissed you as too young to work for the Empire. I am not one of those men. I have known men your age who have been brave and steadfast on the battlefield. I believe you are one of them."

While he remained seated, Michael bowed his head to show both the colonel's authority and a feigned modesty. He knew precisely how good he was and had no doubt that the Germans involved knew it as well. From his perspective, Michael was obedient for two reasons: first, his father had asked his assistance and, second, because both he and his father were hoping to leverage their assistance to get back to Ireland and work with the Irish independence movement. The Germans promised to help in this effort and, so far, there was nothing to suggest they were not sincere. He could imagine the Kaiser would like very much to dismember the United Kingdom. Almost as much as family O'Connell.

Michael noted that the German had spoken carefully but comfortably in English without the slightest hesitation. He decided to take a small bit of control in the conversation. He spoke in unaccented German, "Thank you, Herr Colonel. I am pleased to hear that I have been of some service."

The colonel smiled and said, "Your file does not say you speak German."

"Sir, I do my best, though I would not want my file to suggest I am fluent. My skills in German do not match yours in English."

Michael was not surprised to see the colonel act like a cat that had just had his back scratched. He was pleased to hear yet another soul remark on his brilliance. Wassmuss did not react at all. The colonel switched back to English, "We shall proceed in English."

Michael responded back in English, "Sir, as you wish."

"Herr O'Connell, I have a mission that I wish you to handle. I do not think it will be too challenging for you, but it is of great importance to our efforts here. I have heard that you are quite comfortable in disguise as an Arab. Apparently, you speak Arabic with a Baghdadi accent, something that I understand to be quite distinctive. Is that true?"

"Sir, I am quite comfortable in street Arabic. I doubt I could hold a conversation in Arabic with a Muslim cleric or an Ottoman officer, but I mix very well with what you might call…" Michael paused for effect, "the man on the street." It was time to see if Wassmuss would say anything. "Of course, I have none of the skills of Herr Wassmuss. He is known throughout the region as the real expert."

Wassmuss did not take the bait. He only offered a slight bow. Michael couldn't decide if the bow was an acknowledgement of the compliment or an acknowledgement of the beginning of a duel.

The colonel continued, "Excellent. This is what we need. A man who can disappear into a crowd of Arabs but has the education and wit of a European. How good are your engineering skills?"

On this point, Michael needed to be careful. His tutors had made him proficient in basic mathematics, but just enough to allow them to keep their jobs in British India. His classes in the first year of The Viceroy's College had been heavy on basic engineering, but mostly so that he could accurately draw maps including roads, bridges, and tunnels. Hardly an engineering background. He decided that it would be useful to answer truthfully. He said, "Sir, I am schooled in basic mathematics and can accurately read an engineering diagram and commit it to memory. My skill in drawing maps and other scientific illustration is excellent. I am not a trained engineer and would not be helpful if the mission requires military engineering skills. I hope you are not upset by my honesty." Michael used his growing mesmerism skills as he related the truth. He would have been surprised if the colonel did not respond in a positive manner. Even Wassmuss seemed to be taken in.

"Young man, I am used to those who are willing to exaggerate their capabilities to please me. I have nothing but admiration for a man who knows what skills he has and what skills he is missing. I simply want to know if you can observe and report engineering activities."

"Sir, I have demonstrated that skill in previous reports on British ships entering Basra Harbor. I believe I can accomplish any mission that requires these skills."

Von Trier nodded and Michael noted in his eyes that he was slowly allowing Michael to control what he knew and what he cared not to know. Whatever the mission was, Michael was certain that he would be the man tasked to complete it.

The colonel stood up and walked to the wall map. He said offhandedly, "Please join me at the map." When Michael arrived, the German was pointing to a spot not far from Baghdad. Wassmuss was behind them both, which made Michael uncomfortable.

"The British are one of many sets of foreign scientists conducting archaeological digs throughout the Ottoman Empire. We are doing the same in Egypt and the Sudan as well as in Greece, Cyprus, and Crete. There are real discoveries to be made in these ancient lands, but there are also good reasons to send intelligence officers under the guise of archaeologists. We have noted the British are working on ancient sites that are close to our work with the Ottomans on the Kaiser's project of creating a Berlin-to-Baghdad railway." For effect, the German pointed to multiple locations on the map between Constantinople and Baghdad.

He continued, "Once completed, it will be an engineering marvel that will tie the East and West with a single set of steel rails. Germans and Ottomans working on economic development with German engineering and Ottoman manpower. The wealth of the East will no longer have to be loaded on British ships and carried to Europe by British companies. We are already building an Ottoman Army using our weapons, our training, and even our military leadership. They will protect this line and future trade. The rail system will be just one more means of tying our two Empires together with our sister Empire based in Vienna." The colonel paused and looked at Michael.

Michael assumed a posture and expression that argued he was well impressed. "It will make the Suez Canal obsolete and challenge the wealth of India. It will also mean that visitors to the Holy Land or, for that matter, to the Holy sites of Islam, will no longer need to travel by anyone's ship." It was an exaggeration, but he hoped it reinforced his commitment to this absurd scheme that would have to carve tunnels and bridges through hundreds of miles of mountains and desert terrain.

The colonel walked up to Michael and said, "Herr O'Connell, you have grasped the strategic importance. It will mean a German Empire like none since the days of the Holy Roman Empire." He smiled and continued, "Now, we certainly know that it is no coincidence that the British archaeologists are watching us. What we need to know is: How serious is their collection? Who is conducting the collection? And, if possible, what are their intention? With that information, we can decide … with our Ottoman counterparts, of course, what we intend to do about these spies."

Michael thought for a moment. This would be an excellent opportunity to hone his skills and, if he understood it correctly, line his pockets with German gold. He did not want to appear too enthusiastic, at least for the moment, so he asked, "Sir, do you not have German archaeologists monitoring the British?"

"Our best intelligence officers under archaeologist cover are being used in Egypt and Crete. The Germans here are good archaeologists but terrible spies. The Ottoman security personnel working the construction sites along the rail line are easily duped by the British. I need someone who can pose as a local and watch what the British are doing. The British rarely notice the actions of the locals. They believe them to be too stupid and too poor to be anything but laborers. I suspect you can make good use of those failures."

Michael smiled and said, "Sir, it will be an honor to work for you on this project and a pleasure to work under the noses of the British."

The colonel nodded and said, "Excellent." He turned back to the map and said, "Your first target needs to be here, at Carchemish. The site is run by an Oxford professor and known British spy named Hogarth. The digging season is already underway. There are several other British academics on site already. I want you to find out who they are, why they are there and what they know. I need to know quickly because I have reporting that two of these archaeologists are about to depart for Palestine. I need to know why."

Michael did a short bow and said, "Sir, I have my orders. I will begin immediately."

With that and before the colonel could offer any instruction that might limit Michael's flexibility, he turned to go. As an afterthought, he turned to the colonel, who was headed back to his desk. Michael said, "Sir, this is a larger mission that my previous assignments. Have you authorized a budget for this project? I don't want to end up spending more money than you would approve."

Von Trier looked up from his desk and said, "I have already approved a budget of one thousand marks to be drawn in Ottoman dinars or British gold sovereigns. You can go to Lieutenant Reisen today and draw the full amount." In an aside which Michael later assumed was an effort at humor, the colonel said, "And, please do not let anyone murder you over such a princely sum."

Once Michael O'Connell left the room, the Colonel turned to Wassmuss. "Herr Wassmuss, what do you think of this agent of ours?"

"Sir, I believe he will accomplish the mission you have given him. However, you need to realize he will never be an agent for anyone. He only works for himself. And, I must add, he has well-developed mesmerism skills. I watched as he tried to work those skills on both of us. I hope you were aware of this after my warning."

"Indeed, my friend. But it doesn't really matter to me who he thinks he works for so long as he completes the mission. After all, if he completes the mission, we may actually help him and his father on a new mission in their island homeland. If he fails, then it is not too difficult for this young man and his father to have some sort of accident here."

Wassmuss nodded. "Mesopotamia is a dangerous place."

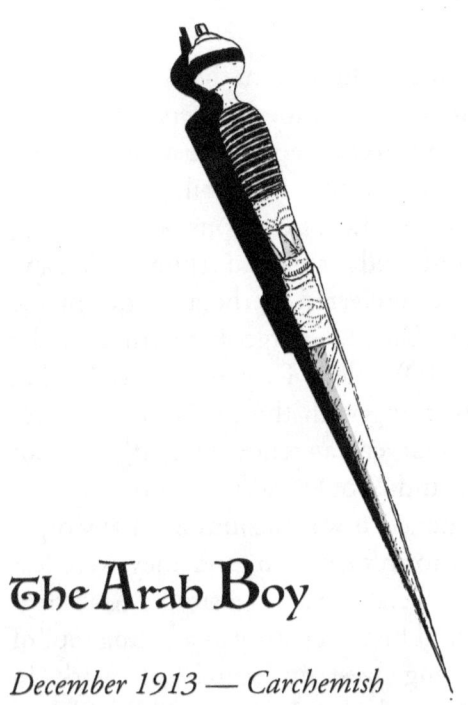

The Arab Boy

December 1913 — Carchemish

THE ARCHAEOLOGY SITE AT CARCHEMISH STARTED IN EARNEST IN **1911** WITH a series of trenches dug into the desert sand to find a vanished ancient city. There were remains visible above ground, of course, but those included ruins of temples and the city walls. Most of those buildings were from the Roman occupation of a commercial city on the Euphrates. While there were many British archaeologists interested in temples and the likely artifacts that went with them, during the digging seasons of 1913, Leonard Wooley, the on-site manager of the excavation, was just as interested in the lives of the people who lived in ancient Mesopotamia. The British Museum certainly wanted artifacts, but they also wanted context. And, it was through that context that the ancient, over 2000-year-old-Hittite city was identified by name as Carchemish.

Research continued year-round both in the desert and in the museum in London. The excavation season at Carchemish started in May and ran through the hot summer months into

the winter. At the beginning of the season, the British archaeologists tasked local leaders to hire the laborers who would
do the digging and run the large screens. The archaeologists
would sort meaningful artifacts from the spoil.

In 1913, one member of the excavations was a young,
recently graduated Oxford student named Thomas E. Lawrence. The Germans were interested in the activities of the
head of the excavations, David George Hogarth and the
on-site manager, Leonard Wooley. They were certain that
both individuals were working with the British intelligence
service. Michael chose to target Lawrence. Hogarth was not
at the dig in late 1913 and Wooley seemed too senior to
target. In Michael's experience, it was the juniors of any organization who had access to information, and they were less
careful in their speech. Especially around a simple Arab boy.

Michael worked to build his cover story as a young, out of
work Baghdadi wandering west in search of work in
Damascus or Beirut. After the story was established and
after Michael actually *became* that young, out of work Baghdadi named Ali, he identified a caravan headed to Jerablus.
Michael was not in the least interested in the work that he
had to accomplish to keep his new identity. In fact, Michael
would be the first to admit he hated building this cover. It
meant being dirty, thirsty and tired all the time. The camels
and donkeys in the caravan were unwilling to bear their over-
loaded burdens. They were sickly and covered with ticks and
saddle sores. Michael had to use a switch to drive them on
when they stopped. Even when they walked together, he was
engulfed in the dust from their hoofs and the smell of their
long-haired coats. Pebbles from the road filled his sandals and
blistered his feet. Each night, he had to help set up the tents,
collect firewood and then sleep next to the animals as the
caravan masters slept in their tents. He knew it was all part of
the job, but it was misery. However, by the time the caravan
reached that destination, every member of the team knew

of Ali's fictious tale of woe: having lost father and mother to plague, his bad treatment by his elder brother and his desire to make his fortune.

This made the next step in his effort much easier as he looked for a job that would give him direct access to his targets. Michael quickly found a job in one of the shops in Jerablus where the English regularly traveled for supplies. Michael presented himself as a young Arab with a smattering of English and a willingness to work hard and ask few questions. After one week, his patience delivered results.

In the middle of December, Michael was working one of the food stalls when a tall Arab arrived. He was dressed in a fine embroidered jacket, white overshirt and trousers tucked into leather boots. What captured Michael's attention was the large knife tucked into one of the Arab's boots and the wooden grip of an equally large revolver tucked in a bright red cummerbund wrapped around the man's waist. Haj Wadid, the majordomo, cook, and all-around factotum for the Carchemish dig was in town shopping for supplies. Michael served Haj Wadid a mix of carefully worded admiration and the necessary addition of mesmerism. Michael was not surprised when the senior Arab at Carchemish or, as he called himself, the *Kaimakhan*, the governor of Carchemish, offered — actually ordered — Ali the orphan Arab boy to follow him to the site.

Michael was responsible for the donkey caravan during the day's walk from Jerablus to the digs at Carchemish. Haj Wadid walked in front as was befitting his role as leader of this parade of supplies. Michael worked back and forth along the caravan to keep the laden donkeys along the desert track. Periodically, he would spend time with Haj Wadid, asking questions that fit his role as an inquisitive, clever Arab boy. Haj Wadid was happy for a new audience and offered far more than Michael expected.

He said, "You know that before I was the Kaimakhan of

the site, I worked for the British in Aleppo. I was the major-domo for that most exalted master of the British. In fact, I went to prison when I fought and killed men who did not honor my master's authorities." Michael looked up at the tall Arab. Clearly there was more to the story than he was offering, most probably parts that were less chivalrous but he allowed Haj Wadid to continue with an exclamation of awe.

"When the Turks finally released me, I obtained the job of Kaimakhan for the work here in Carchemish. It is a site as old as time. Many great leaders have lived here for thousands of years. The British are uncovering the secrets for the world."

"Secrets? Master, what secrets?"

"Ah, Ali. They are too complicated for a young man to understand. Ancient secrets, perhaps as ancient as time itself. And there are those who would steal those secrets from us."

"Master Haj Wadid, is it dangerous? Do I walk to my death?"

Haj Wadid laughed. "No, little one. You do not join us in a fight to the death. But we are against the Germans who are building the great railway between the Sublime Porte, through Damascus and on to your town of Baghdad. The Germans do not understand the importance we place on the ancient world. They just see dirt and stones. They need both for their railroad, so they try to steal them from the site. If you can believe it, last year the German in charge tried to steal the dirt and stones from the ancient city wall!"

"What happened?"

"As the Kaimakhan, I had to defend the walls by myself. My British masters had left me in charge. Alone, I kept the German and his workers from tearing down the walls. After days and nights facing death, Master Lawrence brought the Turkish authorities to the rescue. The German was chastised, I was praised and we have had little trouble since. Well, until the revolt."

Michael could see Haj Wadid was enjoying himself and

demonstrating his skills as a storyteller. He had paused the rest of the story just at its most dramatic point and was waiting for Michael's response. Michael gave him what he asked for and said, "What revolt, master?"

"Well, you have to understand that the Germans are not in the least bit interested in their workers. They used a local malefactor to get their workforce. The proof of the malefactor's actions was he hired only Kurds. Ali, you probably already know Kurds are dangerous folk. They are easily angered. They were cheated by this mountebank. When the Germans were unwilling to accept the fact that they had been cheated as well, there was a revolt of the workers. The reputation of yours truly and his British masters was such that they came to us to ask for assistance. Master Wooley and Master Lawrence both speak our language, perhaps not well, but they understand us. The Germans pursued the Kurds and began to fire at our position on the city walls. Well, that would not do. I returned fire. I made sure I did not kill the Germans, but I did make them retreat. Once again, my British masters sent communications to both Ottoman *vali* and the director of antiquities. They came and sorted it out. Of course, they praised us for our actions and made the Germans apologize. The revolt ended and all was well because of Haj Wadid."

Michael needed time to think before the caravan arrived at the site. He said, "Master, I must return to the donkeys. They will wander if I do not do my duty."

"That is an honourable thing to say, Ali. Do your duty." Haj Wadid continued leading the caravan as Michael run along the side of the donkeys, encouraging them to keep pace. Bathed in the dust from the donkeys' hooves, Michael had time to consider the most likely aspects of Haj Wadid's story. While in Jerablus, he had seen Germans from the rail construction walking the streets, cursing the locals if they got in the way. It reminded him of his observations of the British colonial administrators in India. They saw themselves as overlords and the locals as sub-human. Michael could imagine that, in an effort to save face, the Germans would report that Wooley and Lawrence were spies or saboteurs. Michael would have to see for himself if the two British archaeologists were anything but scientists. If they were just that as he expected, he would have to manage the German hierarchy's expectations without pointing directly to the foolish way Europeans treated locals. It would be a challenge to create a truthful report while keeping the Germans happy. Perhaps if Wassmuss was still there when he returned, he might be able to tell more truth and less fiction. If not, then it would be more fiction than fact.

The donkey caravan reached the archeological site at sunset. As they passed through the south gate of the ancient city, Michael was captured by the stone gate, the towers on either side, and the dramatic bas-relief sculptures that the archaeologists' work revealed. Michael felt strange as he walked past the images of the various gods of the Hittites. He couldn't quite decide what happened as walked past the gods. Whatever it was, he could see why the archaeologists were so dedicated to the site and to their understanding of the world of the past.

Haj Wadid shouted, "Boy, I know it is easy to be distracted, but we have work to do. *Yahlah, Ali!*"

Michael did his most obsequious bow and said, "Yes, Master."

Haj Wadid instructed Michael to take the supplies to what the Arab majordomo called *beyt-e-inglesi,* or the Englishers' house. As he unloaded the donkeys, Michael saw the young British archaeologist that the Germans identified at Thomas E. Lawrence. Lawrence was dressed in a pair of baggy khaki pants, a white shirt and heavy boots. He wasn't wearing any headgear and his fine, sand-coloured hair was whipped by the wind. He was an inch shorter than Michael and looked to be only a few years older. Michael noticed the stunning blue eyes of this young man. As he shifted the supplies into the kitchen, he heard Lawrence speaking in Arabic. He spoke with confidence even though his grammar and some of his vocabulary were archaic. He was joking with the Arab workers and Michael suspected they were laughing as much at this *feringi* as with him. After his time in Afghanistan, Michael knew the looks and the aura of a warrior. Lawrence offered neither sign. Clearly, he was a scholar, not a fighter.

As he continued to work in the kitchen, Lawrence approached him. "Are you a new boy?"

"Yes, master. I am working in Jerablus and the Kaimakhan asked me to help him."

Lawrence laughed, "Ah, the Kaimakhan of Carchemish. We all must do as he requires."

"Yes, master. I will unload the supplies and take the donkeys back tomorrow morning."

As he watched Lawrence, Michael thought the young man a bit too clever for his own good, but he was pleased that the young British archaeologist was so easily convinced of his cover story. And, why not? There were nearly a hundred men and boys working on the site. Pickmen, spade men, and boys as basket carriers. Michael was just one of those Arab boys. Suddenly another boy walked up to him and began to give him orders.

He pointed to the last bags that Michael had unloaded. "Take these to the house. They don't belong here."

Michael nodded and did as he was told.

"Are you dumb? Can you not speak?"

Michael wondered what was bothering the young man. He knew that he could easily make the young man uncomfortable using his mesmerism skills. It was simply not the time. Michael carefully picked his words. He used his Baghdadi accented Arabic and said, "I can speak. I am Ali. I work for Haj Wadid."

"When you come into the house, you work for me."

Michael did not understand what was going on. He could read the young Arabs emotions and saw the boy's aura. It was bright orange. Anger? Jealousy? Did he see Michael as some sort of threat? Before he could answer, Lawrence intruded. "Dahoum, this boy is from Jerablus. He just got here with the donkeys. He doesn't know how we work. He has been hired by Haj Wadid. Why are you being so mean?"

"He doesn't act like a village boy." This comment worried Michael. What did he do to undermine his cover?

Lawrence said sarcastically, "And what exactly does a village boy act like, Dahoum?"

Dahoum looked at Michael and responded, "He works too hard. He is not from Jerablus where young boys are all *sujlu*. His accent is from Baghdad."

Michael puzzled over the boy's use of the Turkish word for felon or criminal. Did he think that a local boy would not understand the Turkish word? Michael relaxed slightly. The comment meant that this Dahoum was doing his best to get Michael dismissed. As he looked at Dahoum, which was really a nickname that meant pitch dark or dead of night, he could see the aura shifting from orange to red. This boy was angry! Based on this assessment, he turned to Lawrence and said, "Master, I meant no harm. I am just working for Haj Wadid. And your manservant is correct, I am not from Jerablus. I am a Baghdadi. Orphaned. Some day, I will make my fortune in Damascus. For now, I am just working so I can feed myself." He bowed slightly to both Lawrence and Dahoum.

Lawrence looked bemused. Michael could see he didn't understand Dahoum was jealous of a new boy arriving in Carchemish who wasn't a basket carrier. Lawrence said, "See, Dahoum? He is just a traveler in this world of ours. The Prophet instructs us to offer hospitality to all travelers, does he not?"

"Yes, Lawrence." Dahoum was already sulking as he responded. He returned to the expedition house with no further comment.

With Lawrence's demonstration of innocence and little in the way of diplomatic tact, Michael thought the Germans were quite wrong about this Englishman. He seemed an unlikely spy. Still, he was easy enough to manipulate. Michael would get the reports that the Germans wanted without any risk of hard work so long as he could stay at the site for a few more days. As Lawrence returned to his work, Haj Wadid arrived at the kitchen acting like the master for all he surveyed. "Ali, do you know how to use a knife?"

"Master, I have worked in a kitchen before. Yes, I can use a knife."

"Then you must begin chopping vegetables. It is too late for you to return to Jerablus. If you want to eat tonight, you must work."

Michael smiled and nodded. "Yes, master. I want to eat and I will be happy to work tonight."

The next day Michael began to assemble the donkey train for its return to Jerablus. He had not identified any reason to stay, but he expected Haj Wadid to invite him to return the next time they needed supplies. Michael was not entirely disappointed. While life at Jerablus was hardly luxurious, life at Carchemish was worse. He spent the night on the roof of the kitchen shed, covered by a single blanket on a cold winter night.

Lawrence walked up as he was assembling the donkeys. "Ali, what are you doing?"

Since Lawrence was alone, Michael decided to elicit as much as he could from the young archaeologist. He revealed a more refined, Baghdadi dialect and said, "Sir, I have made the delivery as you asked. I must return the donkeys back to Jerablus."

Lawrence looked at the lean young man who was trying to be so helpful. He said, "I will have another boy take them back. I will be working on mapping the site and the area for the next few days. I wish to have you help me. My best boy, Dahoum, is busy working on photographic film we completed today. I will need someone to carry the equipment and make notations. You can write, Ali?"

"Yes, sir. I can write and read well. I have not always been such a wretched person." Michael was afraid that he might have been too direct, but he noticed Lawrence's aura was a blue-green. He had accepted the story without question.

"Then we shall leave later this morning. We may have to stay in the desert overnight, so bring your abaya and your water skin."

"As you wish, master."

As he walked away from the expedition house, he heard a young Arab voice say, "Lawrence, why are you taking Ali with you?"

"Dahoum, Ali is smart, but not as smart as you. I wish to use him for map making."

"I do not trust him, Lawrence."

Michael heard Lawrence let out a small chuckle. He said, "Dahoum, you must not be jealous of every boy I talk to. There is no one who can replace you here at the excavation. As you know, we are leaving soon. I can't spare you for this simple task when you must prepare for the trip. Do not fear."

"Lawrence, you are English. You have come to stay for a time, but you will leave. We must stay. You have your country, but I have no country. I will only have Ottoman masters when you leave."

At that point, Michael was out of earshot. He already knew that the workers feared what would happen when

Lawrence and Woolley departed and the Ottoman military returned. Michael realized their fear would be a useful way to gain the confidence of this young man. More importantly, he needed to determine where Lawrence and Dahoum were going. He was able to answer that question later that morning.

Later that morning Michael was waiting with two donkeys when Lawrence and Woolley came out from the expedition house. Woolley smiled and spoke in formal Arabic, "Welcome to our family, Ali. I hear that you will be traveling with my colleague today."

Michael was immediately on his guard. Woolley's aura was a green tinged with orange. He couldn't be sure whether that was because of Lawrence's planned excursion or because of his addition to the excursion. He decided to be his most obsequious. He bowed deep and kept his eyes on the dirt before Woolley's boots. He said, "It is an honor, master."

Woolley turned to Lawrence and said in English, "Are you sure you want to take someone with you on this job? I know he is just a boy, but these Arab boys have a natural curiosity. He might be more of a risk than assistance."

"Professor, I need someone to carry the loads and write down the measurements while I am observing. Dahoum is busy with the latest photographs. We have to finish this portion of the work soon if we are going to meet our travel deadline for the PEF. We both know that we have a rendezvous with Newcombe in Gaza. I can't complete this final piece of the survey on my own. The other men and boys have been here quite a long time and if there are Ottoman spies in our midst, they are the most likely. And, this one is a Baghdadi. How likely is it that the Ottomans are going to use someone from the city where they are already trying to cope with Arab unrest?"

"All good, my friend. But be careful."

"Professor, I am always careful." Lawrence patted the small automatic pistol in a worn leather holster. He turned to Michael. He spoke in his curious Arabic, "Ali, we are ready?"

"Master, I have loaded the equipment you requested as well as food and water for tonight and two blankets. Is that satisfactory?"

Lawrence smiled and said, "Most satisfactory."

Michael watched as Lawrence and Woolley walked toward the dig. He wondered what job was drawing Wooley and Lawrence to Gaza. Clearly there was more to this young archaeologist than he had expected. The good news was Michael was also careful and he had the advantage of knowing that his skills were far better than this young student from England.

A Daydream in the Desert

THEY TRAVELLED ON FOOT SOUTH TOWARD JERABLUS ALONG THE SAME TRACK that Michael had walked with Haj Wadid. After a half hour, Lawrence looked back at the distant earthen walls of the ancient city. As he looked in the other direction, he could see the Germans working on the roadbed for the Berlin-to-Baghdad railroad. He turned to Michael and said, "Here is where we stop."

Michael nodded and began to unload the equipment from the donkeys. He said, "Master, is this where we will spend the night? If so, I will gather wood for a fire."

Lawrence reached into his trouser pocket and pulled out a large, silver pocket watch on a worn leather lanyard. "Ali, it is just before noon. It is not clear that we will spend the night. We will work first and if we need wood, we will have time before dark. For now, I need you to set up the two tripods. There is a table that sits on the one tripod. I will set up the barrel level on the second one."

Michael knew what a barrel level was and how it was used,

based on his classes in The Viceroy's College, but he wasn't sure if this was some sort of trap laid by Lawrence to determine his skills. He said, "Barrel level? Master, do we have a rifle with us?"

"Ali, I forget you have not worked with me before. It is a telescope that can be leveled and then used to measure distances. It has other names. We simply call it a barrel level because the telescope looks like the barrel of a gun."

Michael thought the description of a theodolite too simplistic, but he nodded and said, "As you say, Master."

Once they were set up, Lawrence started using the theodolite. Michael used the chains and the datum rod so that Lawrence could take measurements. It appeared to Michael that the focus of Lawrence's attention was more on the railroad roadbed than on the ruins of earthworks along this track.

After an hour of work Michael asked, "Master, what are we mapping?"

"It is part of the old city. Perhaps Roman but probably where the workers in the original fortress lived. We are interested in the fortress, of course. But we are also interested in the people who lived so long ago. The old city extends out toward where the Germans are building the railroad."

Lawrence had opened the discussion of the Germans, so Michael used a gentle nudge of mesmerism to elicit the information that he needed. "Master, why do you have such trouble with the Germans?"

Lawrence smiled and said, "The Germans can be so self-important. They don't treat their workers well and they encourage the Ottoman bureaucrats to put obstacles in our way. It is just a game, Ali. Just a game and I intend to play it so that we win."

Now Michael used additional mesmerism techniques including focusing on Lawrence's eyes and changing his tone and demeanor. "Win?"

Lawrence's voice changed as he became more and more

under Michael's spell. "We just want to be left alone to do our work. If the Germans want to claim control of the area, then they must cooperate with us. We still have a formal Ottoman *firman* from Constantinople that says we can work the site. There is nothing more to it than playing a game of local control." Lawrence paused. He seemed reluctant to continue, but Michael's mesmerism had taken hold. He continued, "Of course, we want to know the construction techniques the Germans are using in building this railroad of theirs. Any information on this is good information."

Michael thought for a moment. Lawrence was already beginning to come under his mesmerism spell. It seemed unlikely that the archaeologist was lying. The tales of Haj Wadid, exaggerated though they might be, were consistent with Lawrence's statement. It was also clear that Lawrence and Wooley had a more professional interest in the railroad. He decided to deepen the spell. He concentrated on Lawrence, looked into his blue eyes and asked another question, this time in English. "Lawrence, why Carchemish?

Lawrence answered as in a dream. "We want to see the world of the past. Mesopotamia is so old. From the beginning I have been interested in the ancient, the unknown ancient. Dr. Hogarth and Dr. Woolley are such experts and they have taught me so much."

"What have they taught you?"

"That ancient history can be mirrored in modern history. The Arabs here have the same pattern of life as the ancients. Yesterday, they were caught between Romans and Persian Empires. Today, they are caught in conflicts between the Ottomans, the Germans and us. They only want to be treated as honorable men, not as servants. When you treat them like people, they work hard. If you treat them like slaves, they work only as much as they must work. And, the Turks and the Germans barely know Arabic. When you don't speak the language, it is easy for the locals to deceive you."

Michael thought for a moment. He knew from personal experience how colonialists treated local peoples. Woolley and Lawrence seemed to be exceptions. If their skills were ever used in war, those skills could be dangerous to any adversary. Carchemish was hardly a hotbed of rebellion and the English archaeologists were no danger to the Ottomans and only an annoyance to the German engineers building the railway. He needed to deliver something to his masters that would be more than this. He changed subject. "Master Lawrence, why are you in a rush? Do you leave soon? Do you return to England?"

The dream state induced by Michael relaxed Lawrence and he felt that he wanted — no, needed — to answer. He was no longer talking to an Arab boy. He was talking to a colleague back in Oxford. He answered dreamily, "We are leaving before the end of the month. Wooley, Dahoum and I are going to Gaza to work with the military. It is officially a survey funded by the Palestine Exploration Fund focusing on Old Testament sites." Lawrence smiled as if thinking of something from his youth. "It is called Zin in the Bible. Now we simply call it the Southern Desert of Palestine. I think the survey is more about what the Army wants than anything to do with the Old Testament. Newcombe is a soldier, so that's Newcombe's business. Wooley and I will get a chance to survey archaeological sites."

"Who is this Newcombe?"

"Captain Newcombe. I suppose he is a Royal Engineer."

"Do you know more?"

"No more. The entire project was established through Dr. Hogarth. It should be another paid adventure. If the Army wants to pay instead of the PEF or the British Museum, I say, why not?"

Michael was pleased. He had accomplished far more than he expected when he was living in Jerablus waiting for a contact with the British. He had established that the Carchemish archaeological site was nothing more than what it claimed to be except for an interest in the railroad construction. Now he knew that the British were going to use archaeology as a cover for a military survey in Palestine. Wooley and Lawrence might be just pawns in this game or they might be spies. Either way, it was clear that Lawrence and Wooley were both attuned to Arab culture and could be a problem in the future. This would be an intelligence coup he hoped would gain the praises of the Germans.

There was no time to delay. Using his best mesmerism voice, he impressed a mental suggestion on Lawrence. "Now we must go back. Our survey work for today is complete." Michael touched Lawrence slightly on the elbow. He shifted to his more obsequious voice and said, "Master, are you alright? You seemed far away?"

Lawrence shook his head. He said, "I must have been day-dreaming, Ali. I think we are done for the day. We must get back to Carchemish."

"As you wish, master. I will load the donkeys."

That night, once everyone was asleep, Michael saddled a donkey and rode south toward Jerablus. Once there, he returned to a small cache hidden in an abandoned house further south. Ali, the orphan boy disappeared and a wealthy Baghdadi named Mohammed Akim Pasha would walk the streets of Jerablus, purchase an Arabian stallion, and ride to Baghdad. There was no time to lose.

Dispatched!

January 1914 — Rawalpindi

AS WITH ALL CHRISTMAS HOLIDAYS IN THE BANKROFT HOUSEHOLD, THE END of the year meant the departure of loved ones and a return to work. One day into the new year, Conrad was the first to return to his regiment on the Bolan Pass. Elizabeth traveled in the carriage with Conrad to the Rawalpindi rail station. The train was waiting on the platform when they arrived. It was a new, streamlined locomotive painted forest green much like the trains Elizabeth had seen before when she visited England. The locomotive and tender were pulling a half-dozen cars, two each for first, second and third class. Before departing their quarters in Rawalpindi, Francis provided the money so his son could travel first class as far as Tank in the Northwest Frontier. From there, he would have to travel by horse to Ft. Sandeman on the Bolan Pass. Francis said, "My son, enjoy what little luxury you can while you can. Once you transfer at the Scouts cantonment in Tank, you will be back to hardship."

A Sound like Distant Thunder

Conrad said farewell to his sister with a brief embrace and a handshake. Elizabeth looked with pride at her brother in his khaki uniform, Sam Browne belt with revolver, and cork helmet known as a topee. He was wearing a wool duffel coat against the cold on the stone platform. She said, "Take good care, Conrad. Best wishes for successes in 1914!"

For the first time in his life, Conrad had to offer a similar farewell. "Sister dear, please do the same. I always expected you to become an academic not an adventurer. Clearly, I was wrong. You are now in a very dangerous profession. Be safe, my dear. Now, farewell." He lifted his leather Gladstone bag in his right hand and his carpet bag in his left, turned and walked to the first-class carriage. Elizabeth waited on the platform until the train whistle announced the departure and the carriages slowly left the station. The steam from the train pistons and the smoke from the locomotive crawled down the platform. Elizabeth disappeared into the cloud and headed home.

Next of the Bankrofts to depart was Francis Bankroft. He was summoned to the Rawalpindi cantonment two days after Conrad departed. He returned with a mission. He told his wife first and then Elizabeth. "We are going to have a mission together. First, I must prepare the battlefield."

Mary rolled her eyes and said, "Francis, please speak clearly and avoid your military speeches."

Francis smiled and said to his daughter, "Well then, I suppose I have been well and truly chastised."

This was the first time Elizabeth had been included in such a family meeting and did not know that this banter was the opening gambit to a discussion of missions. She decided to intervene, "Mother and Father, please just tell me what we are going to do."

Francis relented and said, "The colonel wants us to move to Constantinople. I will be assigned as one of the military attachés to the Sublime Porte. That will be our reason for living in the city. Our work in the city will be to build a network of agents focusing on the new government. It is known as the Committee of Union and Progress. My work will be focused on the military and one of the CUP leaders, Enver Pasha. The Ottomans and the Russians have nearly gone to war twice in the last year. The Tsar's forces are growing more powerful both on land and sea. These Young Turks who are running the Ottoman government have been building closer relations to the Germans. Our own ambassador hasn't helped much in building a good understanding of the CUP. Last year, he claimed that the Young Turks are all Jews who are working against England. Whitehall in London is in an uproar. The colonel received instructions from the viceroy to send one of his own to the Sublime Porte to determine what is really going on. He decided that a family of intelligence officers would be a perfect solution. When you two arrive, you will be responsible for building networks focused on Arabs, Persians and Russians living in the city. So, the Bankrofts will move to Constantinople!"

Mary was astonished by the scope of the mission. "And, precisely why were we not involved in this discussion with the colonel?"

Francis raised his hands in mock surrender. "I warned him that you would ask. His direct response to me was as follows: 'You need to travel to Constantinople immediately.' Then he said, 'I have something they need to accomplish before they can join you. He said nothing else. You are to receive your briefing soon.'"

Mary nodded. There had been other missions in the past where she had access to something that Francis did not know and the same was the case with his various missions on the frontier. If the colonel wanted to keep the missions separate, it was his prerogative. She said, "Well, we must prepare you for your diplomatic endeavor." She walked up to her husband and pulled on the lengthy beard that he had grown while on the frontier. "This will have to go. After that, we need to engage the tailors at S. Mohammed Shah on the Mall to have a proper set of uniforms made. Your normal khakis simply will not do. I will also call in the tailor to have several new suits made. Your traveling suits will be satisfactory for the voyage, but we simply can't have you wandering about Constantinople looking like some Sufi beggar."

Francis knew this was Mary's way of coping with another lengthy separation. He said, "I am in your hands, my dear. You are the daughter of a brigadier after all. I am merely a major in service to the Crown."

Elizabeth was excited about the possibility of visiting the seat of the Ottoman Empire. She said, "And Father, you must not forget your Colts!"

Mary smiled and said, "Elizabeth, you never need to mention the Colts. Your father might forget his pajamas, but he would not forget his pistols or his binoculars."

"Too right, my dear."

Francis Bankroft left Rawalpindi on 18 January by way of the airship *HMFS Resolve*. The airship was scheduled to travel from Rawalpindi to Karachi on a show of force tour along the Indus River. Francis was their only passenger. Once in Karachi, Francis would transfer to the Royal Navy light cruiser *HMS Yarmouth,* returning home from nearly a year on station in the Arabian Sea. The cruiser would dock in Alexandria and Francis would take a local steamer to Constantinople. He would be at the British Mission in two weeks to present his credentials issued by the viceroy. Mary and Elizabeth bid farewell at the airship docking station inside the Rawalpindi cantonment with hugs, promises to keep in touch, and wishes of good luck.

Once her husband departed, Mary began the process of packing and shutting down the household inside the cantonment. Even with a household staff of six, there was plenty of work for both Mary and Elizabeth. Mary was still not sure they were going to a permanent assignment in the Sublime Porte, so she had the staff divide the household goods into material for storage in their current quarters and goods to be sent by train and steamship to Constantinople. It was a busy time.

On the last day of January, Mary and Elizabeth Bankroft received instructions to visit the western headquarters of the Indian military intelligence service on the following Monday. Mary prepared Elizabeth for her first formal interview with the local commander of the service, Colonel Gareth Winslow-Heath. Elizabeth had met the colonel in the past in social events, but that was long before she was an ensign in the service. Mary provided brief background on the colonel, how he managed his meetings and what he would expect from them both.

It was during these preparations and over tea on that Sunday before the meeting that Mary finally asked Elizabeth details about the events in Bombay in October. Her daughter had offered little insight into how she felt after their last discussion. Mary wanted to know how Elizabeth was coping with the loss of an agent. It was especially important before they met with the colonel, who might ask his own questions about those same events. She started the discussion with a gentle probe by saying, "You already said the last assignment was difficult. Would you like to share?"

Elizabeth nearly choked on her tea. Except for the brief

discussion earlier in the holiday, she had not spoken to anyone about the events in Bombay except in dispatches. In those dispatches, she had been careful in editing information that she felt should not go into permanent files, nor be read by managers in Rawalpindi. Elizabeth could only assume her mother had some other network that provided hints at her real actions in Bombay.

Once confronted, Elizabeth decided to reveal all. "Mother, I already said that I lost Z-1 during the last meeting. He was murdered by a sailor, perhaps from the Royal Navy or perhaps one of the British merchantmen that visit the port. There was a German involved as well." She paused to calm herself. Reliving the event was harder than she had expected. "They beat Z-1 to death, Mother. He did not give up any secrets. He was loyal until the end. It was terrible."

Mary needed to give Elizabeth the chance to tell as much of the story as she wanted. She nodded her head and said, "It is always a terrible thing to lose a colleague. The managers of our cases in headquarters call them agents or assets, but we know them as real people, brave souls, and we know them as our friends."

Elizabeth could feel tears welling up in her eyes. She tasted the saltiness as the first of them started to run down her cheeks. "Mother, I killed a man that night. I was so angry. I know it is not right to kill when you can do otherwise. I know it would have been better to interrogate him. I couldn't help myself."

Mary said, "It is the ladder of consequences."

Elizabeth nodded. In her mind, she still did not know how she killed the sailor. She said, "I know, but I did something terrible. I still don't know how I did it."

Mary said, "What did you do … exactly."

Elizabeth described the events in detail from her carriage ride to the churchyard through to her hunt for the second man who escaped by way of some sort of undersea craft. She closed by saying, "I was so angry. I wanted to crush the man. Suddenly, he was crushed. I never touched him. It was just what I thought and then, it was true. Mother, have I gone mad?"

Mary thought about what Naismith had told her and what Elizabeth said earlier about the events. Clearly, in a moment of anger, Elizabeth had extended her *chi* outside her body. Over the years, Mary heard of martial arts masters who could break bricks and wooden planks this same way. Not through any strike with fist or foot, but just by sheer force of will. It was not something Mary ever thought possible. She always assumed it was some magician's trick. Now, her daughter said she had done so in a moment of anger. Naismith had confirmed indeed she had done so.

This was a very dangerous skill. Elizabeth needed to learn to control it and Mary wasn't certain that she could help. She would have to ask Guru Naismith. Mary said, "Afterwards, did you have time to meditate on your actions?"

Elizabeth shook her head. "Mother, I focused my attention on finding the second man. I followed him using ... what do we call it? The illusory body. I watched as the man got away on some new machine. It was a type of flying warship. Not like the airships we use, though certainly the same size. It didn't exactly float on the water, it seemed to be able to move just above the waves. One thing for certain, it was an enormous vessel. I still don't understand that machinery. It smelled like it was running on some type of gasoline engine. After that, I walked back to my hotel and tried to calm myself. I was not successful. I didn't sleep that night."

Mary watched as Elizabeth focused once more on her actions against the sailor. Elizabeth's face showed real pain and her aura turned bright yellow. She concluded, "Once I returned to my body, I saw what I had done. It was so terrible. That night, I couldn't wash the image out of my head. I see it in my dreams. Not every night and often not exactly as it happened. It wakes me up. I am sweating and crying. How do I make the memories go away?"

"Elizabeth, my love. The memories will never go away. Meditation will allow you to understand what happened and accept what happened. The ladder of consequences is something that effects both the victim and the survivor. That night, you were the survivor. You need to accept what you did and learn from the events. After all, if you hadn't been as quick as you were, you would have been the victim not the survivor. I will help you, but you need to face this yourself. It is the nature of our trade. We are almost always alone when this happens. We can share the story afterwards. It makes it easier to understand. But you need to know that we face the consequences of our actions alone. It is the hardest part of our trade."

"Mother, have you killed a man?"

"Yes, dear." Mary looked down at her teacup and then into her daughter's eyes. Elizabeth deserved the truth. "More times than I wish to say. As a woman in this trade, there will always be men who climb the ladder of consequences assuming we will be the victims. Our gender makes us appear vulnerable, though we both know we are not."

Elizabeth nodded. She pulled a handkerchief from a pocket from her shalwar trousers. She wiped her eyes and blew her nose and then reached out for her mother's hand. She said, "Mother, please help."

Mary was quiet for a full minute as she thought about the fact that she and Francis had put their daughter on this track. She was certain that this was the right profession for her daughter, but it did mean that she was responsible for any consequences of sending her teenaged daughter into harm's way. Finally, she said, "I promise, dear."

On 2 February, Mary and Elizabeth entered the red brick building that served as home to the Indian Army Northwest Frontier Command. From this location, British leaders designed strategy for maintaining order and good discipline throughout the borders between the Raj, the tribes of Afghanistan, and the emirates to the north which were Russian colonies. On the third floor of this brick building was the home of the Western Command of the Indian Army Intelligence Bureau and it was to this office where they were headed. Dressed as might be expected of proper English ladies, they went unnoticed by the officers passing from office to office in service to the Raj. Elizabeth did her best to mask her excitement on her first arrival into the western headquarters of Indian intelligence. Previously, her taskings and debriefings had been with junior officers in map rooms either inside the Navy lines in Bombay or the main public library in Rawalpindi. The junior officers were kind enough, but they did not offer the level of respect that she thought she deserved. After all, she was the one out on the streets, meeting sources, and writing the reports. Well, now she was joining her mother on a secret mission issued by the commander in Western Command Headquarters. She almost wished they were wearing an Army uniform so that she could shock the young officers walking past. Elizabeth knew it was childish, but it was hard to be a secret agent and not be able to brag about her status.

Colonel Winslow-Heath sat at his desk drinking a mug of tea. When his adjutant reported that his guests had arrived, the colonel stood up and walked to the door of his office. "Welcome, ladies. I am so pleased you could come." As he allowed them to pass, Winslow-Heath used his parade ground voice to call out, "Jones, a pot of tea and some biscuits, if you please. That's a good chap."

A Sound like Distant Thunder

This was Elizabeth's first time visiting Winslow-Heath's inner sanctum. She glanced around the room. While it was clearly a room for serious work, it also seemed to Elizabeth it had the look of a proper men's club. Large windows offered an excellent view of the parade ground outside. On one side of the room was a ten-foot-high bookshelf filled with leather volumes. The top shelves were accessed using a polished oak ladder that looked almost as old as the occupant of the room. The spines of the books showed heavy wear. They were not for show, they were for reading. In front of the shelves were four oversized leather chairs and a low coffee table with a glass top. To her left, Elizabeth saw an eight-foot-long teakwood table covered with overlapping layers of Ordnance Survey maps of India. Next to the table was a large globe contained within a carved teak frame. The only sign that this was the headquarters of regional espionage was the teak desk. Trays marked IN and OUT were on opposite sides of the desk. Both were filled with papers, all marked SECRET or MOST SECRET.

A senior sergeant delivered the tea service. He served tea, pouring cups for the two Bankrofts and then walking over to the teak desk, pouring nearly the rest of the pot into the colonel's large mug. He turned to the colonel and said, "Sir, more tea on its way."

"Good man, Jones. I suspect it will be a three-pot conference. Please bring the next pot as soon as you can." Winslow-Heath's aide left the office at a quick march.

Once seated, Winslow-Heath spent the next few minutes asking questions more common to an uncle than a regional commander. Elizabeth watched the colonel as he asked about their holidays. He was old. Well, not quite as old as her grandfather, but old. Perhaps weathered would be a better description. The colonel was over six feet tall, with skin the colour of highly polished oak. He had an enormous white mustache. He was wearing an Army khaki uniform and highly polished riding boots. On his chest were three rows of colourful ribbons which Elizabeth knew designated campaigns and service to the Crown. On the top of those three rows was a single ribbon. It was the only one she recognized: the blue and red stripes of the Distinguished Service Order. As she observed the colonel's uniform, she thought to herself, "If I am going to serve the Crown, I need to know more about Army uniforms and Army awards. I am an ensign, Conrad is a lieutenant, and Mother and Father are majors. What would we look like if we were all wearing uniforms?"

Elizabeth's daydream came to a rapid halt as the colonel finished interrogating Mary and Elizabeth on the family Christmas and tales from Conrad's time on the Bolan Pass. Sergeant Jones arrived with a second pot of tea. He placed it on the table and departed, closing the door behind him.

"A good man, Jones. He has been with me for nearly my entire career. Honestly, I don't know how I would have survived the death of my family in Bombay if it wasn't for him." The colonel took a long drink of his tea. "Now that we are free from interruptions and I have heard from my favourite family, it's time to start the meeting. Is that satisfactory?"

Elizabeth wasn't sure how to respond. She had her cup in one hand and a tea biscuit headed toward her mouth. Very much like Winslow-Heath, Elizabeth was an avid tea drinker and could not avoid the temptation of shortbread. She turned to her mother, hoping that Mary would take over so she could eat her biscuit. Mary smiled and said, "Sir, absolutely. We are at your disposal."

"Excellent. I suspect you are wondering why you are both here. To be honest, I am taking full advantage of the fact that you are the only mother-daughter team in the entire British Intelligence service. It is most definitely an advantage. Most definitely." Winslow-Heath nodded and Elizabeth noticed the intensity of the colonel's blue eyes set in a tanned and wrinkled face. The colonel was smiling but Elizabeth could see from his aura of red-orange surrounding his face that he was troubled. Troubled by what would become clearer as the briefing continued.

"Let us start with the reporting that has come from Elizabeth. In the fall, Z-1 reported German travelers mucking about Bombay. In December, one of our assets in Aden, M25, reported the Germans were strolling near the Royal Navy docks observing one of our older cruisers taking on coal and supplies. I received a note recently from the station commander in Hong Kong that Germans are spending time near the Navy lines in the Crown colony. As you well know, Mary, I don't believe in coincidences. I suspect these Germans are conducting a reconnaissance in advance of some unknown operation." Winslow-Heath stopped to refill his mug and pour out the little remaining tea into the china cups used by Mary and Elizabeth.

Once refilled, he continued, "I want to know more about these men. It appears that there are two pairs traveling back and forth on our flagged liners. I had our men check the White Star and P&O manifests for the past year. Two pairs of Germans have travelled from Cairo to Hong Kong and back again four times in the last eighteen months. They stop at Singapore, Bombay and Aden along the way. It makes me nervous. Worse still, it makes the Admiralty nervous. I don't like to be nervous and I definitely do not like it when the Admiralty is nervous."

Elizabeth finally decided she needed to be part of the conversation. She said, "Sir, why would the Germans be conducting reconnaissance?"

The colonel looked Elizabeth in the eye. It was the first time he focused on her and it made her nervous. His eyes seemed to drill into her mind. He said in a direct tone of voice, "Elizabeth, they are conducting reconnaissance because they are preparing for war with our country."

Mary Bankroft was surprised at how blunt the intelligence chief was with her daughter. There were always adversaries out there, but war? She said, "Sir, I don't mean to question your statement, but I have not heard anything that argues the Germans have any notion of war with Britain. The Kaiser is, after all, a relative of both the King and the Russian Tsar."

"Mary, we live many miles away from a Europe already aflame with ethnic, social and political conflicts. The telegraphic reports I have been reading suggest that at the very least, the Admiralty believes the single greatest threat to our navy will be Germany. If not this month or this year, certainly in the next few years. Consider if you will the facts. Just three years ago, the Germans, the French and our fleet almost started shooting at each other over the Moroccan coast of Agadir. The Germans already have the strongest army in Europe. They have established themselves as the protector of the Ottoman Empire. In that regard, they have had multiple dustups with the Russians in the Balkans where it could have come to war. Now, we are not exactly allies with the Russians, but the French are and that could mean trouble for us." Another long sip of tea kept the colonel silent for a moment.

He continued, "They are building a great fleet of warships including battleships and heavy cruisers. Their battleships are meant to rival our best, including *HMS Dreadnaught*. They are also building a fleet of submarine torpedo boats known as *Untersee Boots* or, as the Admiralty calls them, U-boats. At present they don't have as many as our Navy, but it is only a matter of time. They are also building different sorts of airships. Some are based on the Zeppelin design like our own. Some are true aeroplanes designed as scouts and bombers. Then there are also experimental craft. They are new designs that are neither ship nor aeroplane. It was one of those Elizabeth reported seeing in Bombay in October. The Royal Navy calls them "sea skimmers." Then there are new German engineering developments. The boffins here call them fuel cell engines and say they are powered by the same gas we use in our airships. I am a simple artilleryman. I can calculate ranges and the necessary elevation and explosives to place steel on target. These discussions baffle me completely other than making it clear that they are all dangerous new inventions; in the case of their torpedo boats and perhaps that sea skimmer that Elizabeth observed, perfect for warfare in the restricted waters of the Red Sea and the Arabian Sea." Winslow-Heath paused to refill his tea mug. He reached to the honey pot and spooned a dollop into the tea.

Refreshed with another sip of tea, the colonel said, "Our leaders, bless them, prefer, as would any sane man, to avoid conflict on the continent. I have seen real war in Afghanistan and in South Africa. It is not like our Indian frontier butcher-and-bolt operations. It is horrible. It is beastly. Not in the least bit honorable as the war correspondents write. Of course, we should all prefer peace over war. Most especially those of us who have lived it." He stopped to drink more tea. Elizabeth wasn't entirely certain the pause was just for tea or for theatric effect.

Either way, Winslow-Heath continued by pointing his mug at them both, "But, the secret to avoiding war is to confront your adversary so that they know the threat of losing a war is real. Whitehall does not seem to think it is time to confront the Germans. I know the Admiralty does and I do as well. In fact, I fear it is almost too late. The Germans and the government of the Sublime Porte seem the think it is time to confront the Russians in the Black Sea and in the Balkans and Russians seem foolish enough to allow themselves to be goaded. They have threatened to attack Constantinople and have approached Whitehall with a mad plan to carve up the Ottoman Empire with the Tsar controlling the seat of the Orthodox Church in Constantinople." Winslow-Heath shook his head. "They are working secretly to build some sort of pan-Slav alliance that would rival the alliance among the Germans, the Austrians, and the Young Turks. It will be very hard to avoid war if a conflict starts in Eastern Europe. I think the Germans, specifically the Germans based in Constantinople and the German fleet, are preparing for war and focusing their attention on India."

There was another pause while the colonel drank his tea. Elizabeth thought about what sort of horrors would be possible in a world war. The modern world was filled with wonders, but she had seen examples of how these modern wonders might turn into nightmares. What if airships were used to bomb troops or even to bomb cities? What if the aeroplanes were used to bomb Royal Navy ships in harbor? The Bombay harbor was filled with Royal Navy warships passing through the Indian Ocean and heading into the Arabian Sea. The guns looked like they could launch shells inland for miles.

And what about the soldiers? Modern weapons were far deadlier than the sword and the musket used by the Afghans. It was hard to imagine why any government would choose to begin this sort of worldwide destruction. If war arrived, would Conrad and his troops head to battle? If so, where? Afghanistan? Or, perhaps, Mesopotamia where her mother had worked this past year? It was frightful.

Winslow-Heath looked at the two women. He knew he was sending them into danger. Still, it was his duty and theirs to protect the Crown. If they were successful, they might even prevent a war. Finally, he nodded and said, "We are in the business of gathering intelligence so that our leaders know the next threat and precisely when it might arrive."

He paused again for tea. "Now, on to your mission. I believe these Germans travellers are intelligence officers conducting reconnaissance at the expense of our Navy. They can't visit our Navy bases in Britain, but they can visit our Navy lines in the colonies and in our coaling and refit stations. They can observe our ships, our logistics systems, and even talk to our sailors. If they have a strong navy, what will stop the Kaiser from using it if he has good intelligence?"

He looked at Mary and said, "Mary, added to this growth in new warcraft, you collected information on the theft of the analytic engine. This could mean a rival fleet might have exceptionally accurate naval gunfire and torpedoes and the German army could use the analytic engine for long-range artillery, perhaps even artillery mounted on railroad cars. The Admiralty and the War Office are both worried."

Elizabeth couldn't help herself. She asked, "Analytic engine? Someone has built an analytic engine based on Mr. Babbage's Difference Engine?"

Winslow-Heath chuckled over his tea. He said, "I wonder how many people in India or even in England would know what an analytic engine is much less that it is based on a design by Charles Babbage. Elizabeth, one of the greatest secrets of the Admiralty was their prototype of the analytic engine. It is a high-speed calculating machine powered by electricity coming from ship's generators. I have been told that it will significantly improve navigation and naval gunfire because..."

Elizabeth completed his sentence, "Because a calculating machine would speed the process of matching the location of the ship, its speed, the distance to the target and any meteorological data. At The Viceroy's College, we studied calculus computations using examples of artillery-firing tables. I always wondered how in the world the Royal Navy calculated gunfire given the additional factors of a ship underway such as the pitch and roll at sea. It would be easy enough to calculate one ..."

Mary Bankroft interrupted Elizabeth's monologue which she knew might go on for some time. She said, "Elizabeth, we now know that you understand the basics. The colonel is trying to focus our attention on a new mission."

Elizabeth blushed and said, "My apologies, sir."

Winslow-Heath laughed and said, "No apologies necessary, Elizabeth. I heard you were top of your class in tradecraft at The Viceroy's College. I had not heard that you received top marks in mathematics."

Mary said, "I believe Elizabeth finds mathematic puzzles engaging."

Winslow-Heath stood up, mug of tea in his hand, and walked over to the map table. "Here is a puzzle that you both need to engage."

The Next Mission

February 1914 — Baghdad

JAMES AND MICHAEL O'CONNELL STOOD IN FRONT OF THE MASSIVE OAK desk separating them from Colonel Manfred von Trier. They knew von Trier had a new mission for them, but it was not clear what that mission might be.

The meeting began without any social niceties. The colonel said, "Master O'Connell, I want to commend you for your recent trip to Jerablus. Your reporting was precise and timely. Honestly, I was not expecting you to gain information so quickly. It is clear your father has taught you well."

Michael did his best not to smile. He had completed the task nearly three weeks ago, but he knew that the Germans would not have appreciated his report if he delivered it too early. Years ago, he read a brief story about magicians, especially the great Hungarian Erik Weisz who used the stage name Harry Houdini. Houdini told his colleagues that no matter how easy the trick or the illusion, magicians had to make the trick look difficult, perhaps death defying. One way to do so was to "delay the reveal." Michael decided that if he delayed the report, it would appear to have been harder work than it was. This would encourage the Germans to believe he was exceptionally good at the job while not revealing how easy it was to accomplish their tasking. Michael knew that his response had to appear diplomatic and properly humble. He bowed his head and said, "It was my honour to serve."

The colonel huffed into his mustache. He said, "And now, I need you both to take on a new mission."

Michael couldn't help himself. He said, "Sir, are we going to chase the British into southern Palestine?"

The colonel clearly did not enjoy being interrupted, but he forgave the young man for his enthusiasm to pursue the enemy. This was precisely the sort of action he might have suggested in his days as a junior officer in the Imperial Hussars. Scouts find the enemy and then pursue the enemy, sabers drawn. He paused for a second and fingered the scar on his cheek. It was not always the best plan, but it was the most glorious. "No, Master O'Connell. We have others already in place to report on the Englishmen in southern Palestine. We have a much more important mission that requires the skills of both O'Connell the younger and O'Connell the elder." He smiled at his use of the English phrase. He was proud of his language skills learned while on assignment in London at the German Embassy.

James O'Connell decided to enter the conversation before his son interrupted the colonel again. He said, "Sir, we are ready to receive the assignment." He looked at his son and using telepathy sent the message, "Patience, son. We need to hear him out before we determine what part of the assignment we will perform." Michael nodded ever so slightly to acknowledge his father's instruction.

The colonel stood up from his desk and walked over to the large wall map. He waved for the O'Connells to join him. He started slowly. "As you know, we are working with the

Ottoman government to ensure they remain our allies in any future conflict with the Russians. The Tsar is determined to control the Slavs of Europe and to capture the Ottoman Empire. We know that the Tsar has already sent messages to London stating that he would be happy to divide the Ottoman lands with the British as well as share the oil reserves of Persia and Mesopotamia with the British. The Royal Navy would have unlimited fuel for their capital ships. At the same time, the Tsar's representatives to the Sublime Porte are offering an alliance to the new government in an effort to undermine our relationship with the Turks. We are all playing a complicated game." He nodded to the O'Connells to see if they understood.

James O'Connell decided to speak for them both by saying, "Colonel, we understand full well that we need to keep the Ottoman Empire intact and allied with Berlin. As you know, we have both worked hard to provide you with insights into the failings of our allies when it comes to the Arabs and their weaknesses regarding the Persian court. Michael is a Russian speaker as well as an Arabist, so he is well versed in the actions of the Russians in Central Asia. It should be easy enough to disrupt the Tsar's plans."

The colonel nodded and said, "O'Connell, what we need is to disrupt the relationship between your English colleagues and the Arabs. That is the mission that you will take on for me."

This time it was Michael who answered, "Sir, we are at your command."

The colonel nodded assent. He said, "Our senior scholar in Berlin, Max Von Oppenheim, has provided me with detailed reporting on the nature of the relationship between the various Ottoman governates and the Arab tribes. As one might expect, the tribes have little interest in who claims to govern them since they believe they are independent. They live as nomads in the desert and respect no authority but the authority of their tribal chiefs. And, according to Von Oppenheim, they barely respect them."

James said, "With the exception of the Arabs who live in cities like Baghdad or Damascus."

Von Trier said, "Precisely, Herr O'Connell. And this is where you will begin your work. Our sources in Damascus report that there is growing unrest among the Arabs who are working for the Ottoman pashas in Damascus. These are educated men; many are officers in the Ottoman army. The Ottoman pashas are convinced these groups pose a far greater danger to the Sublime Porte than any of the nomads that live in the deserts of Arabia. The pashas are all Turks. They believe any educated Arab poses a threat to the regime. We want an independent look at this so-called threat. I need to know if there is rebellion in Damascus and, if so, I need to know the leaders of these rebellious groups, where they meet and what they are planning. If they are truly a threat to the government, then we need to eliminate that threat. I need a man with your skills to infiltrate these groups, determine if they are truly a threat and then deliver that information to my men in Damascus. We will do the rest."

Michael assumed his most erect stance and said, "We are ready, sir."

The colonel smiled and said, "Ah, Master O'Connell. I do admire your aggressive way. I think you would have made a good hussar if only you were born in Germany. However, you are not going to be working with your father yet. We have another mission for you. You have proven yourself adept at disguise. I need a man to travel into the tribal areas, into the desert. We have reporting of British officers traveling into the Nejd and meeting with two of the most dangerous tribes, the families of al-Rashid and al-Saud. The al-Saud are the most dangerous because of their commitment to a very conservative sect of Islam ..."

Michael interjected, "The Wahhabis."

"Just so, O'Connell. Now, the Ottoman government worries very little about these nomads. They are mostly bandits and, often, they busy themselves raiding and killing each other. But we have reporting of British in the area. There have been two British officers, one named Shakespear and another named Leachman who have traveled among these tribes. There is even a report of a female adventurer named Gertrude Bell who has travelled among them. My instructions from Berlin are clear: We are to determine why the British are spending time in the Nejd. Our Ottoman ..." Michael noticed the colonel caught himself before he said something too unkind. "Our Ottoman colleagues are dismissive of the tribals as you would expect educated men to be. According to Doctor Von Oppenheim, we must not dismiss the threat to the Ottoman Empire from these nomads. Especially when we are working so hard to use similar tactics against the British in Egypt and in India."

The colonel paused for a moment and concluded, "So, the English have been guests of the tribal leaders and are working to build political ties with them. It is not clear to me why we care about the desert nomads, but I have my orders and now, so do you. We have reports that the British consul in Bushire, or shall we call him what he is, the most senior British spy in the region, is building greater ties with the Persians. That means access to the Persian oil fields for the British Navy. I need a man who can report in detail on their actions in the desert and in Persia. I need a man who can travel with the Arabs, but is a European who will produce reliable reports on the actions of these nomads and their British contacts. We need to know what is really going on. We need reports that are not filtered by prejudices created by the Turkish pashas who are supposedly in charge. That, young O'Connell, is your mission."

Michael had hoped to work with his father in Damascus. Damascus was a city with a long history of culture and sophistication. It would have meant living in an apartment with good food and servants to take care of the smallest of his needs. Instead, the German was asking him to assume his Arab persona and live among the nomads. His experiences in Afghanistan, traveling on horseback, and his brief time in Jerablus had been more than enough hardship for him. He knew he could not refuse the order, but he needed to make that order less onerous. When he spoke, he used just a small bit of his mesmerism voice. He said, "Sir, in my previous assignment, I was able to work against the British by playing the role of an orphan. Among the nomads, an orphan is not going to have the access nor the mobility to deliver your requirement. May I suggest an alternative strategy?"

Von Trier smiled. He could see the boy was very uncomfortable with the idea of days and nights living in a saddle and sleeping in the black tents of the nomads. He did understand the boy's point: the nomads would treat an orphan outsider as little more than a slave. That would be a waste of his skills and most probably not result in success. Still, it was not proper for a young man to be so blunt to a senior German Army officer. His reply was curt, "Continue."

"Sir, would it be possible to introduce me as part of a small German contingent. Perhaps as part of a military team that is giving modern rifles to the nomads? If I was an officer, a junior officer, who had the power to deliver weapons to the tribal chiefs, I would have access to their tents and to their plans, their intentions, even their thoughts. I believe that would work to accomplish the mission."

The colonel thought for a moment. He was wrong about the boy. He wasn't worried about being uncomfortable. He was worrying about his access to the tribal leaders. He nodded and said, "I think we can make this work. Of course, you are too young to be a senior officer, but you would be a perfect young hussar to serve as the translator for a captain who delivers the weapons. While the captain and some of his men are training the Arabs, you could spend your time with the tribal leaders or, at least, their trusted confidants. Would that be satisfactory?"

Michael could see from the colonel's aura and from his tone that this would be the best he could expect. There would always be a time in the future when he might have to use his skills on a less experienced junior officer to accomplish the mission while minimizing the discomfort. He said, "It is precisely what I was thinking, sir."

The colonel nodded. He said, "Then you are dismissed. My staff have prepared briefing books for you to read in preparation for your missions. Master O'Connell, I will arrange the proper uniform and equipment to be issued and for you to meet the team. There must be no delay. We need to have these reports before the summer heat. I need those reports by April at the latest."

James and Michael O'Connell bowed, turned on their heels and left the office. Michael said to his father, "I will work hard to get this mission accomplished. I will be in Damascus soon."

"Son, you may find this mission far more complicated than you think. I fear you may not be able to provide the colonel with the detailed reporting he desires."

Michael smirked. He said, "Father, the colonel will get his reporting. One way or the other, he will get his reports."

Guests of the Royal Navy

March 1914 — Karachi to Bombay

As Elizabeth and her mother traveled by rail south to Karachi harbor, they talked in detail about their mission. Winslow-Heath wanted the two of them to travel from India to Egypt via the same liner that the Germans were using. If the Germans left the ship, they were to do so as well. If they could elicit information from the Germans while on board, so much the better. Clearly this involved timing their departure to match the arrival of a liner carrying the Germans. Winslow-Heath tasked his entire network to ensure that occurred. The current reports showed two Germans were traveling from Hong Kong, Singapore, and Bombay, passing through the Suez and ending their travel in Cairo. Winslow-Heath dispatched Elizabeth and Mary by rail to Karachi Harbor. There, they would board a Royal Navy light cruiser bound for Bombay. The cruiser was returning from a patrol in the Arabian Sea. The colonel told them that the Intelligence Service representative who replaced Elizabeth in Bombay, Jeremy Haraday, already had their tickets purchased for the liner that would dock in Bombay, so all they had to do on arrival was to transfer from the Navy docks to their ship, the *Medina*, which was returning to London via the Suez Canal.

"Mother, is it true that His Majesty took the P&O ship, the *Medina* to Bombay for the Delhi Durbar?"

"Yes, dear. Of course, the Peninsular & Oriental Steam Navigation Company has carried dignitaries and the Royal Mail ever since its creation. Still, I'm sure the company was thrilled to have the entire ship chartered by the navy to carry the Royal Party to India." Mary smiled and continued, "I suspect you won't see any royalty on this trip."

"I just hope we see the Germans that the colonel is certain are conducting military reconnaissance against our Navy."

"If I know the colonel, he will have made all the arrangement to make sure we have that opportunity."

While the Royal Navy captain on *HMS Fox* thought taking on two women on his ship was "irregular," he accepted the tasking with grace once he read the dispatch from Rear Admiral Sir Richard Peirse, commander in chief, Royal Navy East Indies and Egypt Station. The Rear Admiral made it clear to Captain Francis Wade Caulfield that his two passengers were critical to Royal Navy success in the Arabian Sea. While the captain could not imagine how that could be, he was not about to question instructions from the CIC. He politely asked Mary and Elizabeth to stay in a spare officer's cabin for the duration. He would have their meals delivered to the cabin. He explained, "There is some salty language used in the officers' mess and I would not want to embarrass you ladies."

Elizabeth was about to make a "salty" remark when Mary intervened and said, "Thank you, Captain. We shall endeavor to avoid causing difficulties on our brief stay on your ship." Elizabeth noticed that her mother used "just a touch" of her mesmerism voice to calm the captain and gain his trust.

Later she said, "I thought we were to avoid using our skills on other Britons."

Mary laughed and said, "I could see the captain could be difficult. We don't need any problems this early in the trip. I just smoothed the waters."

Elizabeth looked around the steel walls of the small cabin. No portholes and no access to fresh air. She said, "I hope we have smooth waters for this part of our trip. Otherwise, this could be uncomfortable."

"Relax, dear. I checked with the meteorological office in Karachi. We should have an easy voyage on this portion of our trip. It is only two days. I am sure we can find something to do."

Elizabeth knew that tone of her mother's voice. It was the same tone she always used when about to instruct her children or give them a household chore to accomplish. Elizabeth accepted it would be a useful lesson if not necessarily easy.

HMS Fox was a fast ship and the transit from Karachi to Bombay was uneventful even if it felt to Elizabeth like she was in a prison cell. On her previous travels by steamship to England, Elizabeth had enjoyed a regular promenade on the deck. It gave her a chance to see the ocean, enjoy the breezes and, when the ship was close to shore, to observe the sea birds. This time, there was only the murmur of the engines to remind her that they were underway. As promised, the captain had their meals delivered twice a day as well as tea in the afternoon. That was the only time that the door to the cabin opened and, unfortunately for Elizabeth, closed.

Mary knew that even in a two day voyage her daughter would crave some entertainment. She had packed two books, one by Mr. H.G. Wells and another by Mr. Conan Doyle. In both cases, she chose books which, though fiction, discussed what she considered modern natural philosophy. In the former, the book was Well's *The Island of Doctor Moreau* and in the latter, Doyle's book *The Lost World*. Elizabeth devoured Doyle's book though she scoffed at the character Professor Challenger.

"How could a man like Challenger ever get anything done with his irascible constitution? And, really, Mother. Jurassic creatures in the Amazon. It is too much for anyone to believe."

"Dear, I think that is what novelists would call a plot technique."

"To what purpose? I found Challenger hard to believe."

Mary was not about to start a discussion of natural history with her daughter, so she changed the subject. "You do know it is actually based on the adventures of a British explorer, no? Did you not see the connection?"

"Challenger is a real character?"

"Well, no more so than Doyle's detective Sherlock Holmes. But, Doyle's friend, Percy Fawcett, had many adventures in the Amazon. He also happens to be part of our Service."

"An explorer and an intelligence officer? Now I am more interested in the book."

"Well, Doyle doesn't reveal any of his friend's ties to the Service, but you can imagine how easy it would be to explain travels in distant lands if one was a scientist of one type or another."

"An archaeologist or paleontologist for example?"

"Or a botanist if you follow through on your education."

"Plant espionage?"

"Elizabeth, the Crown has sent botanists around the world to acquire plants by whatever means necessary. Tea for example."

"Tea?"

"The Chinese controlled the tea market for centuries. They did not allow foreigners to see their tea plantations.

They only sold harvested tea leaves to foreigners in controlled markets on the South China Sea coast. It wasn't until British agents of the Crown ventured into central China to acquire tea plants — at great risk to their lives — that we ended up with tea plantations in India. Your colleagues from Kew may have seemed to be eccentric scientists, but they come from an organization that has collected plants, including trees, for economic benefit of the Empire."

"Have you done this sort of work, mother?"

"Dear, our job is with *military* intelligence. You can imagine that acquiring tea plants is not part of that job."

"Still, exploration might be part of the mission."

"Of course. Early on, military intelligence missions were the same as geographic missions. The goal was to observe the land, reporting on roads, bridges, tribal villages, and generally supporting the Army in advance of war. As the colonel said, our job is to collect the information before the war and we hope with the information our leaders may prevent war. There are precious few locations that haven't been mapped. Now, we collect on what is in the minds of our adversaries, not on where they live."

Elizabeth was quiet for a time as she sat on her bunk facing her mother. She decided to ask a question that had puzzled her for over a year. She said, "Mother, I saw a portrait of you and father at The Viceroy's College in a hall with other honored alumni. What action did you both complete to receive such an honor?"

Mary pondered how to respond. On the one hand, the events associated with the award were still considered secret. On the other hand, her daughter had already proven her own skills in the trade. She decided to offer an abridged tale. Completely true, just not truly complete.

She started, "Since we have time on our hands, I will tell the story. Of course, like all good stories, it begins with once upon a time. So, once upon a time, your father and I were tasked to provide security for the King."

"The King?"

"Well, at the time we thought it might be the King. We ended up protecting a member of the royal family."

"Who? When? How?"

"If you will be patient, I will tell you."

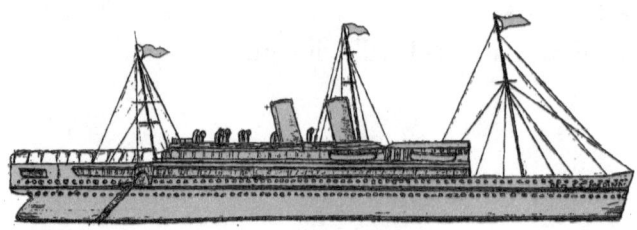

The Juggernaut

MARY STARTED WITH A SIMPLE QUESTION. "ELIZABETH, WHAT DO YOU KNOW about the princely state of Hyderabad?"

Elizabeth had settled in for a story. Now she realized that this was going to be more training and less adventure story. She responded, "The princely state of Hyderabad is one of the semi-independent states of the Raj. It is ruled by a *nizam*, I believe. It is an enormous area in central India. Far larger in square miles than the United Kingdom. It is a wealthy state, or should I say, he is a wealthy *nizam*?"

"Indeed, he is a wealthy man, perhaps the wealthiest man in the world. My story is about the previous ruler of Hyderabad, Mir Mahbub Ali Khan. The current ruler, Osman Ali Khan, is his son."

Elizabeth noticed her mother stopped for a moment in what appeared to be a reflection though it might have been simply an effort to recall the story in the level of detail that her mother knew she would demand. Either way, after a few minutes of silence, Mary continued.

"Mir Mahbub Ali Khan was a strong ally of the Raj. He and his son are both modern rulers who are determined to make Hyderabad a model of what could and should be India. The *nizams* of Hyderabad have been allies of the Crown going back to the days of the East India Company. They have also taken grave risks in their allegiance to the Raj. During the revolt in 1857, the personal security forces of the *nizam* fought alongside British troops to protect the residency in Hyderabad City and in Secunderabad. This support and the *nizam's* affiliation with the Barelvi sect of Islam, a moderate sect of Sunni Islam which is tolerant of Sufi mystics, made him a target. He was hated by both conservative Muslim and Hindu religious leaders as well as members of the Indian independence movement."

Mary paused for a sip of tea. She said, "Your father and I were invited to attend a Ramadan end-of-fast feast known as an *iftar* meal in the last week of December 1902 by the assistant resident of Hyderabad, Captain William Jardine."

Elizabeth said, "I remember you and father leaving on a business trip right after Christmas that year. Conrad and I were most disappointed."

"My dear, you will learn in this trade that often work will intrude on family life. It seems as if fate always chooses holidays. In truth, it is bad actors who often choose holidays — Christian, Muslim, and Hindu — to do their worst. It is another part of the nature of the trade."

Until this moment with her mother, Elizabeth had not thought of how many times either her mother or her father, or both, had missed holidays or birthdays. It was something that she needed to ponder.

Mary continued, "We were invited to attend the *iftar* meal because both the Indian police special branch and the military intelligence bureau were very concerned about the threat to the Duke of Connaught during the Delhi Durbar in January of '03."

"I remember the excitement! The papers were filled with the details of the arrival in Bombay of the brother of the King, the train travel to Delhi and then the photos of the royal encampment at the new city outside Delhi. It was amazing."

"Our work helped to make that visit as splendid as it appeared in the papers."

"Mother, you must tell the story. I want to know."

"Curiosity is one of your most endearing traits, dear."

If Elizabeth had been a few years younger, she might have stood up and stamped her foot to express her displeasure at her mother's comment. Instead, she stayed silent and looked directly at her mother. Mary realized after all the work that Elizabeth had endured over the past three years, she deserved more of the tale, so she continued.

"The *nizam* used some of his great wealth to create a railroad line that linked the Bombay line to the old city of Delhi as well as what he knew would become the new capital of India, New Delhi. Prior to the passage of the royal train, the *nizam* would take his own train to Delhi to await the festivities. The Viceroy expected each of the leaders of the Princely states to build their own tented compound. Mir Mahbub Ali Khan was the most senior of the Princely rulers and his compound needed to be the most beautiful. We were sent to Hyderabad to determine if there were any threats to either the *nizam's* train or the royal train."

"And there was?"

"Elizabeth, if you will be patient, I will explain." Elizabeth did her best not to pout as Mary continued, "We used the *iftar* dinner to meet with a number of the entourage of the Hyderabad household. After all, if there was a threat to either train, it would require knowledge of the train schedules. Only the household would know those schedules. We used the meal as a start point and your father and I used our best elicitation skills as well as some of our mesmerism skills to gain additional information."

"Father has those skills?"

"Elizabeth, your father would be the first to admit he would rather use a fist or a pistol to solve problems. But, yes, he does have both mesmerism and telepathic skills. They are just not as developed as yours or mine. He just doesn't practice those skills. Still, at that point, we were only a dozen years from our own time in The Viceroy's College, so we were both adept at the necessary means to gain information from willing and, sometimes, unwilling subjects. We found that the *nizam's* household had been penetrated by both Muslim and Hindu extremists determined to disrupt the Delhi *durbar* and, perhaps, kill the *nizam* or the duke. I focused on the Hindu extremist network and your father focused on the Muslims."

"Why?"

"Dear, there will be times you will face prejudice. You must accept that as a woman, even a modern woman like yourself, there will be barriers that you cannot defeat. One of those barriers you must have already realized is that Muslim extremists do not reveal their secrets to any women — even their own wives. On the other hand, the Hindu extremists regularly include women in their conspiracies. In truth, Hindu extremist movements include both men and women. Your father's skills in disguise and language made it possible for him to infiltrate the Muslim groups. My own skills allowed me to do the same. We simply divided our work to ensure success."

Mary lifted the tea cozy on the tea pot. She said, "The tea has gone cold. Elizabeth, please ring for more tea."

Elizabeth knew her mother was teasing her. Her mother was saying she would have to wait until she had a new pot of tea. Of course, this was not a cruise ship. It was a Royal Navy cruiser. They couldn't just "ring" for more tea. Elizabeth said, "Mother, I do not intend to wait until 4 o'clock when the steward brings us more tea. Please do continue."

Mary smiled and said, "Very well. But it is a tale that has many twists and turns."

"Twist and turn away, Mother. I am ready."

In the next ten minutes, Mary outlined the various steps that she and Francis Bankroft took to infiltrate the extremist communities. They had only a few days because the *nizam's* train would depart before the new year and the royal train would pass through Hyderabad in the early morning hours of New Year's Day. The advantage they had was the extremists hated each other as much as they hated the Crown, so they did not coordinate their efforts and they spent as much time collecting information on each other as they did on plotting villainous action.

Elizabeth listened carefully as her mother explained her methods to gain information from the Hindu extremists. Finally, Mary said, "The most important point I found was that the Hindu leaders were more interested in killing the *nizam* than disrupting the royal train. That meant that they were plotting an assassination when the *nizam* travelled from his palace to the train station. I uncovered the plotters' names and then turned that over to our contact, Captain Jardine. I did find out one other thing that was curious and helped your father's efforts."

"Mother, please do not do this to me. Your pauses are painful."

"Another question for you, dear. What do you know about the Hindu ceremony of *Jagannath Rathyatyra?*

Elizabeth thought for a moment and said, "It is Sanskrit for … chariot festival?"

"Indeed. The festival is celebrated throughout the Hindu communities and is a festival focusing on the chariot of Lord Vishnu, known as *Jagannath* or Lord of the World. Communities build these enormous chariots, sometimes two and three stories tall and pull them through the streets. It is also the origin of our word, juggernaut."

"An object of immense power."

"Exactly. I found out that multiple Hindu craftsmen had been hired to create one of these chariots. It was the wrong time of the year for the festival, which is a summer festival. At the same time, your father in his typical hunt for danger, learned of Muslim extremists who had stolen a small steam engine from a local mill. When we compared our two stories, we realized that the extremist leadership among the Muslims intended to use the chariot to attack the royal train. They hoped the government would blame the Hindus. It would undermine the ruler of Hyderabad and force the Crown to hunt their Hindu rivals."

"But, how did you prevent the juggernaut?"

"I rode on the royal train as one of the undercover guards in case there were other assassins on board. Your father disguised himself as a committed extremist who had nothing to offer but a strong back. He lived with the extremists for days as they prepared the juggernaut. They needed his strong back, among many others, to pull the chariot up a hill near the train tracks. Their plan was to use the steam engine to accelerate the chariot as it ran down the hill and crashed into the royal train. Of course, your father disrupted their plot." Mary smiled as she said the last sentence.

This time, Elizabeth did stand up and did stamp her foot. "Mother, this last portion of the story was not satisfactory. It was not complete."

Mary laughed and said, "So, you now intend to demand an answer?"

Elizabeth thought for a moment and then laughed as well. "Perhaps, request would be more polite?"

"I should say so."

"Please?"

"Elizabeth, I do not know the specific details of your father's actions up to the moment when the train arrived. I was not there. I will offer you my version of the events."

Mary smiled at her daughter and asked politely, "Will that be satisfactory?"

Elizabeth smiled as well as she said, "For now."

Mary relented. "It would appear your father was able to insinuate himself into the group that was on the hillside waiting for the royal train. They had the steam engine running and ready to engage when they saw the train approaching. I saw the chariot at the top of the hill. It was easily three stories tall with six wheels as tall as a man. It was painted bright red with a blue icon of the Hindu God Vishnu. There was steam rising from a stack. I watched with binoculars as one of the zealots mounted the chariot and stood behind a great wheel like the wheel on a ship. As we approached, the attackers released the wheels and the chariot raced down the hill. I watched as your father jumped on the back of the chariot just as it started down the hill. I was at wits end. There was nothing I could do at that point but hope your father stopped the juggernaut and survived. I was in awe of your father as he climbed to the top, disabled the driver and then wrecked the chariot by spinning the wheel so that the chariot tumbled on its side and crashed well before our train passed in front of it."

Elizabeth had held her breath as her mother finished the story. "Was Father hurt?"

"He did suffer a broken arm. You must remember his time in early 1903 with his arm in a sling."

"He told Conrad and I that he fell from a horse."

"Elizabeth, that was close to the truth. Not a living horse. A steam-powered horse. Most of his bumps and bruises were caused by his escape from the zealots as they chased him for miles. Your father had his partner Pundit Mirza Khan hiding in a gulley, called a *nullah* in the Punjab. They held off the attackers with their rifles until they could escape." Mary paused and said, "Elizabeth, you must remember, everything we tell our loved ones and those outside the trade is usually completely true, just not truly complete."

"Did you receive any thanks?"

"Indeed, Elizabeth. Months after the Durbar, you probably remember we traveled to Simla. During that trip, Viceroy awarded us medals for saving the duke. Your father received the Distinguished Service Order that day."

"A DSO? And what did you receive?"

"My work was less dangerous and less dramatic, dear. However, I did receive the Indian Order of Merit — Military Division. I was the first woman to receive this award. Of course, it was possible because it was a secret ceremony with just the Viceroy, the colonel, your father and yours truly. None of the senior military leadership who are hostile to women in service knew of the award." Mary smiled again.

"So, mother. Is that the entire story?"

Mary's response was interrupted by a knock on the door. A steward in mess whites had arrived with afternoon tea. Mary said, "Thank you so much. You arrived just in time!"

A Spot of Tea and a Bit of Training

AFTER TEA, MARY DECIDED TO CHANGE THE SUBJECT AND, PERHAPS, PROVIDE her daughter additional training. She pulled out a small, hinged box and spilled chess pieces out of the box onto a small writing table. Mary turned the box over and the top and bottom served as the chess board. She started to place the pieces on the board. It took no time at all before Elizabeth joined her and the board was set.

Mary sat in front of the white chess pieces and Elizabeth behind the black pieces. She said, "Are you ready to begin?"

Elizabeth nodded enthusiastically. Mary spent a moment looking down at the board. Then without touching the chess pieces, the queen's pawn moved forward two squares.

"How did you do that?"

"You know full well how. You told me you disarmed that villain in Bombay without ever touching him. You have the skills, you just haven't practiced the skills."

Elizabeth looked down at the pieces in front of her. She concentrated. She imagined her own queen's pawn moving forward. She imagined how it might move, imagined relieving the friction between the piece and the board. After a very long minute, the pawn fell over. Elizabeth laughed. "It would appear that my chessmen do not want to bend to my will."

"Nonsense. You simply were trying too hard. Just relax. Close your eyes. Focus your breathing. Now move that piece in your mind."

Elizabeth did as she was told. She knew Guru Marian at the school had always told her to stop trying and instead focus on doing. She emptied her mind of desire and control. Once she could feel her mind clearing, she just imagined the piece standing back up and moving to the square she desired. When she opened her eyes, the piece had moved.

Mary nodded and said, "Now, we can begin again."

Elizabeth lost the game as she almost always did when she played against her mother or her father. What she did find satisfying was that by the end of the game, she could move the pieces without difficulty.

But she had not expected her mother to be a master of the skill that Guru Naismith called telekinesis.

During her last weeks at The Viceroy's College, Naismith told Elizabeth that the first evidence of the skill was described in the Indian epic, *The Mahabharata*. He told Elizabeth that in the modern era, a Russian named Aksakov and a Swede named Swedenborg experimented with the concept. Naismith said they had focused on what they thought were individuals with special powers. Sadly, that led them down the path of charlatans and mountebanks. Naismith insisted the power to affect objects with the mind was in every human. It simply needed to be unleashed by emptying the mind of assumptions of what was normal or possible. He demonstrated the skill to Elizabeth as had Guru Marian when she moved items around her training room during their one-on-one sessions.

Elizabeth had little time to begin her practice before she was called upon to join the Ravens and save her mother and father from capture in Afghanistan.

Since graduating from The Viceroy's College, she practiced few of her special mental skills as she took on her role as an agent handler in Bombay. Now, here she was inside a Royal Navy cruiser learning the skills from her mother. It was both surprising and slightly terrifying.

Unexpected Company

March 1914 — Constantinople

FRANCIS BANKROFT WAS SITTING IN HIS SUITE IN THE PERA PALACE HOTEL
on a hillside in the Pera section of the city, overlooking the
Golden Horn. It was early morning and Francis sipped
from a glass teacup nestled in its engraved silver keeper. He
was dressed in a thick wool Turkish dressing gown in deep
indigo over his white cotton Indian pajamas. He was wearing
a pair of leather soled Persian slippers with slightly turned
up toes. There was a small coal fire in the fireplace, but he
was still not used to the cold and the damp of a late Turkish
winter. He was drinking tea and looking out the glass of the
French doors that opened on a small balcony. The balcony
overlooked the city, bathed in the last of the winter sun. The
windows in his room offered a view of the ancient streets
and some of the complex stone buildings including a local
mosque, a hammam bath house — partially hidden by trees
—, and the Spice Bazaar.

Francis found the Turkish mint tea, flavoured and

sweetened with a healthy serving of hot apple juice, far more complex in both aroma and flavour than the black tea of India. He had a tray with a tea pot and bowl of dried fruit brought to his room just before dawn each day. He savoured this after his morning exercise ritual and before he would start his day. Eventually, he would dress and visit the dining room for a real breakfast, but he enjoyed the early morning quiet. Francis decided he could get used to the aromas and flavours of this city that served as the link between East and West. After years of living rough with the Pashtun tribes, he decided that he would enjoy his time in civilization no matter how short it might be.

He had yet to find a suitable house for his family, though the challenges of that job at times seemed to rival his official mission in the city. The opulent and very European style of the Pera Palace was not necessarily to his taste, but it was comfortable and near enough to everything and everyone that he was happy to use it as his temporary base of operations. Permanence was not something any military officer expected. Francis expected this assignment would last just until White-hall in London and, more importantly, the Viceroy in India decided that the complexity of relations with the Ottoman Empire was less important than the rivalry between the great powers of Europe.

Francis was not immune to the romance of living in one of the oldest cities in Western civilization, but he had jobs to accomplish. He hoped to be out of the hotel in the next month and find a small bungalow on the Bosporus, perhaps one of the beach cottages favored by the wealthy *s'tanboulis* — as the citizens of this ancient city called themselves. These beach cottages, known as *yalis,* were built right on the water. Usually, a small garden faced west allowing maximum sun-light for growing both flowers and herbs. Bankroft used a local who worked at the consulate to help him find a place. At first, he feared he might be unable to communicate with the owners of the various houses. He was pleasantly surprised to find that most owners spoke either English or French, sometimes both, as well as Persian and Turkish. Some even added Russian to their languages.

The residents of Constantinople were cosmopolitan people. At one point, over tea, one local made it clear where he considered his home. He stated categorically that Bankroft needed to remain on the west side of the Bosporus. When he asked why, the local sighed over his cup of apple tea. He said, "After all, Major. This is Europe." He pointed across the Bosporus, "That is Asia." Francis was not worried about living in Asia, but he did realize living on the other side of the Bosporus might limit his ability to complete his other mission — collecting intelligence on the Ottoman government and the relationship between that government and both Germany and Russia.

But what was his intelligence mission? Francis Bankroft initially chafed at the level of diplomatic protocols and niceties that he had to follow when he arrived at the British mission to the Sublime Porte. He was one of several military officers assigned to the British mission's office of the military attaché. The senior officer was a Royal Navy admiral, Admiral Arthur Limpus. The admiral focused exclusively on the mission of building a relationship with the Ottoman Navy. The British government sold two dreadnoughts to the Ottoman Empire in 1913, to be delivered later in 1914. The two ships were far more complex than anything else in the Ottoman Navy. To pay for the ships, the Ottoman government raised money from the wealthy of Constantinople. These ships would be the pride of the Turkish Navy and Limpus hoped they would cement a relationship with Great Britain.

As an Army officer and, worse still, an *Indian* Army officer, Francis was given the least interesting work. Limpus knew that Bankroft had his own intelligence mission to accomplish, but the admiral made it clear that he didn't intend to accept the risks involved in such a mission. Francis was certain that, if need be, he could force Limpus to accept the mission. It would only take a simple message to Winslow-Heath and there would be messages from the Viceroy and from the Royal Navy sent to the admiral. But Francis had been in service long enough to know that pulling rank on a senior flag-grade officer could do as much harm as good. So, along with his efforts to find a house and his early efforts to build a network of informants in the city, he regularly served as the attaché responsible for handling the formal receptions of Ambassador Sir Lewis Mallet. These were receptions that Limpus and his Navy officers thought were a waste of time. In his bright red tunic, navy blue trousers and highly shined riding boots along with the rows of obscure medals on his chest, and his ability to speak Persian and Russian, Francis quickly became the favourite consort to the ambassador.

At first, the admiral found it amusing, but to his annoyance, the ambassador began to ask the admiral if Bankroft could travel with him on a regular basis. Francis was happy to accommodate the ambassador, especially if it would give him access to members of the Ottoman bureaucracy as he arranged official visits. Limpus made it clear to Francis that he was merely the ambassador's military escort and any contacts with military seniors in the Ottoman government were his responsibility, not Bankroft's responsibility. Francis followed the admiral's orders to the letter. After all, his job was to recruit spies inside the Ottoman government. Francis had been an intelligence officer long enough to know very senior members of any organization made terrible spies. They often didn't know all that much and were never willing to follow instructions. Francis intended to target junior officers and the numerous civil servants who worked in the new government. He would leave the seniors to the admiral.

His intelligence mission was complicated by the layers of Ottoman bureaucracy. After less than a month in

Constantinople, Francis realized why the term "byzantine" — derived from the original name of the city — had come to denote outrageous complexity. When he first arrived, Francis sat down with members of the military attaché office and received a briefing on the twists and turns of politics and war in the Sublime Porte. In fact, the current government had only received something resembling formal status in January. The ambassador and his senior officers, including members of the intelligence service under the cover of the Levant Consular Service, struggled to understand the intricacies of the ruling Committee for Union and Progress (CUP). This "committee" was a trio of oligarchs running the empire. Embassy staff called these oligarchs the "Young Turks." Each individual had his own fiefdom: Djemal Bey served as the military governor of Constantinople, Talat Bey was the interior minister and Enver Pasha the minister for war. Not surprisingly, Enver Pasha was of greatest interest to the Admiralty and the War Department in London.

After some investigation, Francis understood Enver Pasha had a close and continuing relationship with the German military delegation. The German delegation under General Liman Sanders was delivering arms and training to the Ottoman Army. The Germans and Enver Pasha were working hard to create a modern Ottoman land army out of a weak collection of regional militias. Like many of the Young Turks, Enver Pasha was an avid nationalist, secularist and modernizer. He made it clear that the defeat of the Ottoman Army during the Balkan Wars and the ongoing threat of Russian expansion in Eastern Anatolia were symptomatic of an empire in decline. He expressed strong support for the Kaiser's efforts to build the railroad from Berlin to Baghdad and he was exceptionally proud of his relationship with the Germans. He even assumed a German-style military uniform as his day-to-day wear and affected a German military moustache.

Francis could well understand the Ottoman fear of the Tsar's expansionist policies. After all, he had spent most of his career collecting on and, at times, preventing Russian expansion in Central Asia and Afghanistan. Francis could imagine the Russian Navy felt trapped inside the Black Sea due to the Ottoman control of the Bosporus and the Dardanelles. And, the Russians had a religious tie to the Eastern Orthodox church which dated to the dawn of Christianity. The Orthodox Church had its center in Byzantium and remained in modern day Constantinople. Of all the Russian dreams for a greater role in world affairs, their interests in the European remnants of the Ottoman Empire and its capital seemed most realistic to Francis. Before he left Rawalpindi, he read dispatches from Whitehall that the Tsar's representatives in London had offered to share the remnants of the Ottoman Empire with the Crown when the Russians decided to invade Thrace to capture Constantinople. Francis had laughed out loud when he read the end of the report which said the mandarins of Whitehall had ... demurred. Francis was a soldier and an intelligence collector who had no interest in the niceties of diplomacy. He could not see any possible time when he might *demure* when dealing with Russians. Also, he could not see a time when the Russians might be allies with Britain.

The light taps on the door surprised Francis. He looked down at the silver hunter watch sitting next to his tea. It was 0620hrs. Hardly time for any intrusion by the hotel staff. They never recovered the tea service until after they saw him enter the dining room. "One moment, please," was all he said.

Francis stood up and walked over to the armoire in the corner of the bedroom. He reached for the handle of his leather briefcase that sat on the top shelf. He placed the briefcase on the bed, set the lock combination on the case and opened the top. Inside were many of the tools of his trade. A set of lockpicks. A magnifying glass. A pair of throwing knives in sheaths that would attach to his forearms. Finally, his pair of well-oiled Colt revolvers and a small Browning automatic pistol resting in a thin leather holster shaped to fit into the pocket of his overcoat. Francis pulled the automatic out from its holster. It had gold engraving along the slide and had ivory grips. Beautiful as well as deadly. He worked the slide so that a round was fed into the chamber and engaged the external safety. For years, Francis had sneered at Mary's use of thin automatics with what he saw as anemic cartridges. Still, for close work in tight spaces, he realized there was something quite useful about this new design: hammerless so it could not snag on a pocket or a holster. He placed the pistol in the right pocket of his robe and headed for the door.

Another tap on the door. "Yes, yes, I'm coming," was all Francis said when shards of wood exploded from the power of an axe crashing into the door. Both from habit and training, Francis had chocked the door top and bottom with a pair of steel triangles. The intruder had assumed the axe blow to the lock would result in the door flying open. Instead, the heavy wood door swayed under the pressure of the shoulder applied to the lock side of the door, but it did not give way. Francis stepped away from the door. It was too late to return for his revolvers. He would have seven rounds in the Browning before he had to fight hand to hand. He intended to make every round count. He stepped to one side of the door frame and hoped for the best.

This time an axe struck on the hinge side of the door. Splinters flew past Francis. No matter how strong the steel chocks were, this was enough for the door to finally give way with the first assailant struggling to keep his balance as he shouldered his way into the hotel suite. He was a broad-shouldered man dressed in ill-fitting European clothes and wearing a burgundy fez. In his right hand was an ancient axe and in his left was a Persian dagger from the last century. He had the misfortune of passing within an arm's length of

Francis. Bankroft used a blade hand thrust into the man's neck. He fell dead with a broken neck. The axe and dagger clattered along the wood floor and skidded under the table with Francis' tea service.

The second assailant came into the room waving a wicked -looking curved sword with a Damascus steel blade. Unlike his colleague, he was wearing a gray and white striped Arab robe, a brown wool cloak, and a black-and-white checked Arab head covering known as a *gutra*. He had the scarf pulled over his face revealing only his bloodshot eyes. The curved blade glinted in the early morning sunbeam from the windows as he waved the sword. Francis had seen some of these in ceremonial use when he traveled to Topkapi Palace with the ambassador. Unlike the ceremonial version, this one showed nicks in the blade from hard use. This was neither a weapon nor a fighter he intended to face unarmed. Francis pulled his automatic from his dressing gown pocket and fired three rounds. He carefully fired two rounds into the chest and one into the assailant's forehead. It was all that was needed.

As Francis turned to look toward the doorframe, he realized a third assailant had decided this was not his day to draw an assassin's pay. All Francis saw was the tail of his striped Arab robes as he turned to run away. Before Francis could start his pursuit, he heard a groan from the hallway. Francis was still not clear how many assassins were involved, so he carefully peered around the now splintered doorframe into the hallway. What he saw was a tall man in a floor-length navy-blue wool coat bent over the third man. He was pulling a curved dagger from the chest of the third man. The cloaked stranger wiped his blade on the clothes of the assassin and looked up. The thin, pale face smiled and said, "Francis, I see that you are incapable of even a peaceful stay in a hotel!"

"Naglieff!?"

"Please, after all we have been through, can't we use our Christian names?"

Bankroft thought of the years in Afghanistan where he had avoided Naglieff's efforts to kill him. That included a recent one where Naglieff captured both Mary and himself. They were saved just in time by their daughter and the service commandos known as the Ravens. It would appear that Naglieff was willing to work together for now. Perhaps Francis might even trust him … a bit. He said, "Sasha, what are you doing here?"

"I was wondering the same thing of you, my friend." Naglieff offered a mirthless smile and continued, "I will be happy to explain over breakfast in the dining room. But first, I think we need to clean up a bit. I don't know how you are going to explain your doorframe, but I suggest we dispose of these *gromila* first."

Francis chuckled. Naglieff knew he spoke barracks Russian, so he had offered the Russian slang for hoodlum. "Indeed, Sasha. There is a stairway at the end of the hall that ends in an alley. Pera is a dangerous part of the city and the Ottoman authorities will be happy to accept any sort of explanation that does not include residents of this fine hotel."

Naglieff shouldered the assailant in the hallway and said, "Then, let us begin. And, by the way, I do think you should get dressed first."

They took care of the bodies and returned to Bankroft's room. Naglieff manufactured evidence of a ransacked room while Francis changed clothes. Before they left, they scanned the room to see if there was any evidence of death. Seeing none, they left for the dining room with Francis carrying his briefcase with his weapons and tools.

After their first cup of Turkish coffee and the arrival of their breakfast of pastries, eggs, and Turkish "hunters' sausage" known as *sujuk*, Naglieff started his explanation.

"Francis, it is just good fortune that I was coming down to breakfast when I saw the three malefactors heading down the hallway. It is too early in the season for the Pera rooms to be full. I thought I was the only one staying in our hallway. When they took an axe to your door, I decided whoever their target was, he might need some help. It turns out I was right. I believe our respective roles in the tournament of shadows have morphed into an alliance of sorts."

Francis did not for a minute believe Naglieff. Still, it was a reasonable story and one they could both live with for the time being. What was most interesting was that a senior in the Russian intelligence service who was an expert in Central Asia and Persia might be in Constantinople. Instead of arguing about Naglieff's story, Francis said, "And I was lucky to have an officer of the Tsar's army at my side."

Naglieff smirked. He said, "It turns out that I was the lucky one back in Afghanistan. When I returned to Moscow, I thought for certain I was going to be demoted based on the events at the Amu Darya when you were saved by your airship and your special services team. Instead, I found out that our two governments had signed an agreement to cooperate. Kidnapping you would have been ..." Naglieff paused to sip his coffee. "Well, shall we say an embarrassment? But, my report on the German activity was considered a brilliant stroke of intelligence collection. I ended up receiving a small medal and reassignment to Constantinople to determine what the Germans are doing here. Good fortune, no?"

Francis nodded. It seemed to him that at least some of the tale was credible. He said, "*Kismet.*"

Naglieff nodded. "*Kismet* or luck or whatever you wish to call it. Our two sovereigns have legitimate reasons to limit the role of Germany in the area where our two empires meet. I am assigned as a member of our embassy to the Sublime Porte. I suspect you are here under the same guise. While we did not have time to determine who your attackers were, I would expect they were paid in German gold."

This was not the first time that Francis had faced assassins paid with German gold and he suspected it would not be the last. He was not yet willing to reveal his full mission, so he decided to turn the tables on his sometimes adversary, now apparent ally, Colonel Alexander Naglieff. Francis was not as adept in the skills of mesmerism as his wife or, for that matter, his daughter, but he had enough skill to make it difficult for a target of his intentions to avoid his questions. That was if he made them indirectly. He started slowly while he looked across the dining room table and into the eyes of the Russian. "Sasha, you are right on both counts. I think we all are wondering what the larger German plan is in the Ottoman Empire. You already know the German purpose against my country given our previous encounter with them in Afghanistan, but what threat do the Germans pose to the Tsar?"

Naglieff's tone of voice started to show evidence of the light touch of mesmerism. He spoke slowly and gently and, Francis hoped, without guile. "The Germans are using their ties to the Ottomans to create Muslim unrest in Daghestan. We have fought the extremists there for years. You have certainly heard of bandit *Shamyl*. In your country, I think his image is one like your Robin Hood. In fact, he was a zealot who fought against the Empire, committing atrocities along the way. He was captured but only after a brutal war."

Bankroft could see that his mesmerism efforts were weakening. He decided to keep the conversational thread intact by adding, "As you know, we have our own extremist mullahs in India. I have heard of *Shamyl*. But his story is from the last century, no?"

"Francis, you should know by now that tribal memory is long and feuds last forever. If the Germans and the Ottomans are looking for embers to fan into flames, they will find them in the Caucasus. But they are doing more than this. They are also encouraging links among Armenian and Circassian socialists and Russian dissidents. You may not have heard of Pyotr Kropotkin or Vladimir Lenin or Leon Trotsky. They consider themselves professional revolutionaries determined to destroy my country. Lenin was sentenced to internal exile for years near the Islamic emirates and Trotsky has been sentenced to Siberia — twice." Naglieff shook his head. "Now, they are traveling in Eastern Europe with the support of the Germans. Dangerous business." Naglieff continued after another sip of coffee, "And, these Young Turks have a long reach. Even the Emir of Bukhara has faced an uprising from a group who call themselves the young Bukharans."

Francis paused to think about the level of commitment the Germans might have in manufacturing unrest in Russia and Central Asia. Under his spell, Naglieff would not lie. That said, what he believed deeply might not be the truth. Francis had a dozen questions he needed to ask and was about to push for more detail when the concierge of the hotel walked up to the table.

"Major Bankroft. Something terrible has happened."

Francis looked up at the concierge with the most innocent face his could manufacture. He smiled and said, "Konstantos, what has happened. You had trouble matching the sheets and the towels? Your service is most agreeable and I do not care if the colours match."

"No, sir. Your room, it has been destroyed?"

"Destroyed?"

"The door is off its frame. It looks as if it was attacked by an axe. Your belongings are strewn across the whole suite. Robbers, sir. Robbers. We are most embarrassed."

"Konstantos, please calm down. Let us see what has happened." Francis stood up, picked up his briefcase and turned to his Russian partner and said, "It would appear there is some difficulty with my room. Please excuse me."

Naglieff had a coffee cup in his left hand. He waved his right hand and said, "Major, please take care of whatever needs to be done. I will see you again." He smiled as he nodded.

Bankroft turned to the concierge and said, "Now, Konstantos. Let us consider this difficulty." The concierge in his frockcoat and Bankroft in his newly tailored suit walked out of the dining room and toward the grand staircase.

A Cruise in the Arabian Sea

April 1914 — Bombay-Aden

THE TRANSFER FROM THE ROYAL NAVY CRUISER TO THE *MEDINA* WAS
without drama. Elizabeth was very helpful because she was
familiar with the city of Bombay. After all, she had been running agents and observing the city for the past year. Also, her
replacement, Ensign Jeremy Haraday, had arranged a horse-
drawn carriage waiting for them inside the Royal Navy dock-
yard. The carriage took them on the circuitous but fastest
route to the P&O dock on the north end of the port. For
the first time in her life, Elizabeth had the chance to talk
about a city that she knew better than either of her parents.
The crowded streets of carriages, horse-drawn goods haulers,
the occasional automobile, bicycles, and people made what
should have been a short trip nearly an hour long. During
the hour, Elizabeth offered a running commentary about the
cosmopolitan nature of the city and the wonderous architecture. The sounds and smells of Bombay spoke for themselves. Mary let her daughter serve as a tour guide. She did

not reveal that she had run agents in the port long before Elizabeth was born.

The *Medina* had docked the same day and most of the passengers had left the ship for an excursion around the shopping areas, the Taj Hotel Sea Lounge and, for those with more lurid tastes, Lal Bazaar. The stewards on the gangway welcomed Mary and Elizabeth and guided them to their stateroom. Again, the intelligence bureau had been most kind and provided them with a large stateroom with two beds. The stateroom was placed in what colonial travelers fondly called *posh* — portside outbound, starboard homeward bound. Both Mary and Elizabeth had travelled on steamships before, but the *Medina* was a modern ship and their stateroom was first-class accommodation. They were pleased with their new, albeit temporary home.

After unpacking their steamer trunks and ordering a light lunch and tea served at the small table near one of the port-holes in their cabin, Mary began outlining her plan. "We should have at least two allies on board. I know the colonel has reached out by telegraph to the P&O staff in Hong Kong. The captain and his first officer will know our mission is to engage the two Germans on board. It should be easy for them to place two unaccompanied women at a table with two unaccompanied men. We will need to keep our wits about us because we will be most popular with all single men traveling on the *Medina*. Our focus has to be on the Germans."

Elizabeth nodded. She waited until she had finished the last bite of shortbread before she said, "Mother, as luxurious as these accommodations are, I understand we are on a work trip. I promise I will not be distracted by other ... men."

Mary said, "Perhaps so, but other men will definitely be distracted by you. You are quite a beautiful young lady and the frocks we have brought with us are designed to make us pleasing to the eye. We can only hope that the Germans will have accomplished their missions at this point and are simply heading home. That will make them relaxed and willing to spend a pleasant set of evenings with us."

"And how exactly do we get them to talk about their work?"

Mary smiled, "I suspect you know well how we will accomplish this. We will use mesmerism to eliminate their defenses and then simply ask them. We will need to separate them so that we each have time one-on-one. If that doesn't work to our satisfaction, then we will engage in a bit of burglary and search their possessions. While I doubt they will leave their notes out for anyone to see, I think you will have no problem finding their hiding places."

"Me?"

"Yes, dear. You. After all, if it comes to that, I suspect I will have greater success engaging both men. You will simply have a headache or wish to return to our cabin to write letters or … whatever excuse you prefer to use. I will use telepathy to warn you when they tire of me."

"Mother, I suspect they will not tire of your company."

"One never knows, dear. In our trade, one never knows."

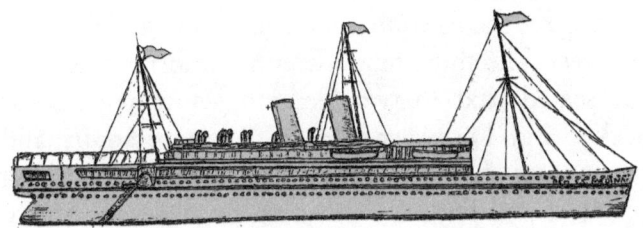

The Game Begins

THE NEXT AFTERNOON, THE *MEDINA* PULLED AWAY FROM THE BOMBAY harbor and set sail for its next port of call, Aden, at the south end of the Red Sea. From there, it would make its way to the Suez Canal and Alexandria. Once there, passengers would travel on the *Medina* to England or transfer to other passenger liners heading for other ports on the Mediterranean Sea. Alexandria would be where Mary and Elizabeth Bankroft would transfer to an Ottoman passenger ferry headed to Constantinople.

Elizabeth was on the observation deck as the ship pulled out of the harbor, traveled past the Royal Navy docks, rounded the southern tip of the island and headed out to sea. This was the first time Elizabeth had seen the city from the sea. She knew that the city served as an important port for both commerce and for the Royal Navy, and the protected nature of the harbor was especially obvious as they sailed away. Mary joined Elizabeth on deck as the ship's steam turbines increased pitch and the liner knifed through the still waters of a warm spring evening. The Indian Coast receded quickly until it was just a green line on the horizon. Mother and daughter stayed on deck long enough to see the sun set over the water but before the night air turned chill.

Mary Bankroft said, "Elizabeth, we have work to do tonight, so it is time to return to the cabin and dress for dinner. Dining on the *Medina* is a formal affair, and we need to look our best. The ship's first officer has informed me that we will be seated next to two German gentlemen named Elbert Becker and Dieter von Hertl. Their passports and papers report that they are German businessmen working for Krupp Steel and they are returning from a sales trip to Japan."

"Mother, do we believe any part of that story?"

"Dear, that is precisely our job tonight. What do you know about the Krupp company?"

"Precious little, mother."

"Well then, you need to be ever so interested in learning tonight."

"It will be a pleasure."

"And, Elizabeth, please no use of mesmerism tonight. Just simple conversation with a small bit of elicitation. We are seated at a table for six tonight. We will share our table with Josiah Berkliff and his wife, Janet. They are returning to England after a five-year assignment working for the P&O offices in Hong Kong. They should be interesting partners in our game, don't you think?"

"Particularly if our German colleagues have spent time in Hong Kong."

"We need to guide the conversation in a way that provides us with the best possible understanding of our German colleagues and where one or the other of the Berkliffs ask the hard questions."

Elizabeth nodded. Before she joined the intelligence world, she had always assumed her parents were natural conversationalists, able to entertain with ease. Dinner parties inside the Rawalpindi cantonment were relatively dull affairs made up of officers and their wives. She and Conrad were rarely included, and they were happy to avoid those dinners. However, when they were traveling "up the country" as her mother called it, they often attended parties that included senior officials working for the princes of the independent Indian states. It was in these parties she had noted how successful her parents were in keeping the conversation alive and engaging the officials in a way so that they offered interesting vignettes on palace life.

Now, she saw the world through a different set of eyes. Natural conversation must have been guided to their advantage as intelligence officers. The conversation was designed to either elicit information or to begin the process of gaining collaboration. She now resided in that same shadow world of misdirection and deception. Elizabeth wasn't entirely sure it was a moral world, but she knew that her efforts were in direct support of the Crown. For now, that was enough.

To Elizabeth's eyes, the first-class dining room for the *Medina* looked like one of the luxurious restaurants in London. The wood-framed doors and windows were highly polished, the carpet exceptionally thick, and the tables and chairs of oak. White linen table clothes and napkins framed crystal goblets and porcelain china. It hardly looked like it belonged in a ship. Elizabeth understood now precisely why the Royal Navy had chartered this vessel to serve as the royal conveyance to India.

She and her mother were dressed in long white gowns with pearl-white slippers. Her mother was wearing a string of pearls around her neck and a second string as a bracelet around her right wrist. In the cabin before they went to dinner, Mary provided Elizabeth with a small broach of four emeralds set in silver and platinum. "A gift from your grandmother, dear. It was hers and then mine and now yours." Elizabeth had never been much for what she dismissed as high society, but her mother had insisted that this was just as truly a uniform as was the Ravens' uniform she had worn the previous year when she saved her parents in Afghanistan. "We have to look the part of two innocent women, Elizabeth. That is the only way we are going to get close to the Germans."

Now, as they entered the dining room, it was clear that her mother was correct. As they entered, Elizabeth could hear a trio playing chamber music. There were white-uniformed servers delivering cocktails and appetizers on silver trays. The men were in formal evening attire and the few women who were in attendance were in pastel-coloured silk gowns. Most of the women were older than her mother, and were wearing clothes that would no longer be considered in style in London. The gowns were of high-necked design more common from the Victorian era. Elizabeth suspected these women had purchased their clothes a decade ago in London and used them sparingly as they served as wives of government or commercial officials in Asia. Now, they were celebrating their return to England and each night, they would be living in this fantasy world.

The maître d'salon greeted them by name and guided them to their table. The others at the table were sharing a cocktail before the dinner service began. The three men stood up and the two Germans assisted Mary and Elizabeth as they sat down. Elizabeth sat to the left of Berkliff and Mary sat to his right. Almost immediately, a waiter arrived to take their drinks. Mary ordered a glass of German Riesling for both of them. The waiter nodded and, Elizabeth noted in wonder, was gone before she even noticed her mother had ordered. As the eldest gentleman at the table, Josiah Berkliff offered the introductions. "Mrs. Mary Bankroft and Miss Elizabeth Bankroft, may I introduce you to my lovely wife, Janet." Berkliff pointed to his wife across the table from him. "And, our two dinner companions, Elbert Becker and Dieter von Hertl." Becker was to Elizabeth's left and Mary sat next to von Hertl.

Elizabeth thought to herself, "The board is now set. Let the game begin."

Mary smiled and said, "It is our pleasure to join you tonight. We are traveling back to England. My husband and son are in military service, and we will be spending the summer away from the burning heat of India."

Janet Berkliff nodded and said, "I often wish we had been closer to England so that we could travel more often. I'm afraid our only travels were associated with Josiah's exploration of possible new routes for the P&O. So, Singapore and Darwin were our excursions. Well, now we are returning home for good. Josiah will be a senior executive in P&O in London." Elizabeth noted the blue-green colour of Janet Berkliff's aura. She was most definitely pleased as well as proud of her husband.

Josiah Berkliff offered the expected level of English modesty and said, "Janet is too kind. I will be a simple bureaucrat in the larger P&O system."

"Surely not, Mr. Berkliff." Mary's comment was designed to keep the conversation going and it worked. She continued, "What did you do for the line in Hong Kong?"

"I was the managing director of the office in the Crown Colony. I was also responsible for our offices in Singapore and now Darwin."

"Then you will be going back to a senior position?"

"It is a large company."

Again, Mrs. Berkliff interjected, "He is too modest. Josiah is going to be a senior director of logistics for the entire line."

As the waiter delivered the two glasses of chilled Reisling wine to Mary and Elizabeth, Becker raised his glass and said, "Then congratulations and best of luck to you, Herr Berkliff."

"My thanks to you all."

Becker's gesture and his voice reminded Elizabeth of something, though she couldn't capture what. While she puzzled over what that memory might be, her mother engaged the two Germans, using a gentle voice with just a touch of mesmerism.

"Mr. Becker, what brings you to the *Medina*?"

"Frau Bankroft, my colleague and I are returning from a business trip to Japan."

Elizabeth jumped in and said, "Japan, how exciting. I have seen none of the Far East. The four of you must have seen so many wonderous things."

And so, the conversation went through dinner. Gently, but diligently, Elizabeth and Mary used the Berkliffs to ask the hard questions while they engaged in what would have appeared to anyone as light conversation with their tablemates. Elizabeth noted that the two Germans were reluctant to reveal anything of their business dealings. They were polite, but vague in their replies. As dinner progressed, Mary used her telepathic skills to reach out to Elizabeth. She said, "We are not going to get anything from them tonight. We will need to arrange some one-on-one time with them over the next few days and use our special skills to get direct answers to our questions. Patience, dear."

Elizabeth did nothing more than a shallow nod to let her mother know that she received her directions. Patience was a hard thing to Elizabeth to accept, but in this case, she knew that patience was the only answer.

After dessert and coffee were served, Berkliff turned to the two Germans and said, "Gentlemen, would you consider a cigar on the promenade deck?"

Before they could respond, Mary said, "I think it is time

for Elizabeth and I to retire for the evening. We have had a long journey already and an early night will do us good. Would it be too much of an imposition to ask if we could share a table again tomorrow?"

Von Hertl had already stood up and he helped Mary with her chair. He said, "It would be our pleasure. Perhaps tomorrow we can all share a good bottle of German sparkling wine before dinner. I checked earlier and the *Medina* has some excellent choices."

Janet Berkliff absolutely beamed and said, "That would be wonderful." She turned to Elizabeth and Mary and said, "Perhaps tomorrow we can meet for tea on the promenade deck?"

Mary nodded and said, "Both ideas are splendid. Now, for tonight, we bid you pleasant dreams. Thank you for a wonderful evening."

Once they were in their cabin and had taken off their formal attire, Mary said to Elizabeth, "How tired are you, dear?"

"Not at all, mother. I just assumed you wanted to leave early."

"Indeed. I wanted to leave early so that you could do some exploring using the illusory body."

"I will try, Mother. Where do I need to go?"

"I think a small bit of eavesdropping on the promenade deck. I would very much like to know what the Germans are discussing with Mr. Berkliff."

"You think there is intrigue along with cigars on the deck?"

"My dear, only you will be able to find out. Please do your best."

Elizabeth sat down on the heavy carpeted floor of their cabin. She assumed a full lotus position, closed her eyes, and began a relaxation technique involving what her gurus called "counting breath." A count of five to inhale, another count of five holding her breath, a count of ten to exhale and five more on an empty set of lungs. As Elizabeth relaxed, Mary watched as her daughter began to levitate slightly off the floor. A few inches at first and eventually a full foot. As she reached the necessary transcendental state, Mary observed Elizabeth's breathing slowed to a mere four breaths per minute. Along with the levitation, it was the only sign that her daughter was now projecting her illusory body.

Elizabeth seemed to be a spectator as she left her body in the cabin, passed through the walls of the first-class deck and then up and out onto the promenade deck. Elizabeth felt a shock of wind as she came through the walls and out onto the promenade deck. It was one of the three walking decks, covered by a working deck that included the required dozen lifeboats. It was the best deck for avoiding the exhaust from the two smokestacks that belched black soot as the ship continued its full-steam passage. Elizabeth was not sure where her targets were located on the deck, so she focused her mind and began her search in an anti-clockwise direction heading forward. She could feel her senses stretch out as she moved along the deck. Nothing seen on her first turn, she headed back along the port side of the ship. Finally, near the end of the promenade deck where it opened to the sea, she saw the three men standing next to a small funnel. While she knew she would be invisible to them, Elizabeth still took great care as she floated near them. She realized she was observing the end of a conversation.

Von Hertl was speaking. "Herr Berkliff, the opportunity for you is enormous. Our firm is more than willing to provide you with substantial ... compensation. All we wish from you is a listing of your ships and their routes before the same details are made public. It will help our firm greatly because we will be able to book first class cabins on your ships well before the general public and, perhaps, use your ships to deliver small cargo containers. It is quite a simple thing since you will be aware of these events as you plan both maintenance and coaling stops."

Berkliff seemed torn by the offer. Elizabeth could see his aura shift from green to orange and back to green.

Becker spoke quietly. "It would be a great favor for us. And, I think it would mean a great deal for you in the future as you look toward retirement. After all, we can imagine the line will provide a small pension for you, but hardly enough to ensure you have a lifestyle appropriate for a man of your status and culture."

Berkliff said, "I believe we shall be happy, but it will be a change for Janet."

Von Hertl said, "And, why should your wife suffer because of your retirement? After all, you have been in service to P&O for …"

Berkliff said, "For twenty-seven years next month."

Becker sensed the time had come to push for closure. "Herr Berkliff, we are offering to match your current salary for the next three years and then match your pension so that there will be no changes for your wife. She will have a life as she deserves. And, we are asking little more than we did in our meetings in Hong Kong. Simple details that are available to anyone who is interested, though perhaps revealed slightly earlier than to the public. No great imposition for the level of compensation, no?"

Von Hertl added, "As a sign of your previous assistance, we would like to offer two tokens of what an honor it has been to work with you in Hong Kong this past year." Elizabeth observed Becker open his hands and two small packaged appeared. No magician had ever prepared his audience better for the revelation of the two packages.

Berkliff took the two packages saying, "You are too kind.

I have done so very little for you this past year. After all, I simply offered services that were little more than what I would offer to any colleague."

"Ach, Herr Berkliff. You are the one who has been too kind. You have treated us to insights into the Crown Colony, to Singapore and even to Darwin that would have been outside our reach. Our work in Japan was enhanced by these insights. Please, open the gifts."

In the dim light, Elizabeth had to concentrate to see anything beyond the shadows of the three men. When Berkliff opened the first package, he sighed. "Ah, a beautiful watch."

Becker said, "Not just any watch, the world's thinnest watch. It is known as the LeCoultre Caliber 145. Only 1.38mm thick. A perfect watch for a gentleman of your stature. Now, please open the second parcel. It is for your wife."

Berkliff opened the second box. Elizabeth could barely see what was inside. She moved closer to the three men. Resting on a silk pillow were three jade bracelets. The jade in each bracelet was protected by gold sleeves with intricate carving.

Suddenly, von Hertl said, "I feel chill in the night air. I think it is time for us to return to our cabins. Please keep our gifts, Herr Berkliff. I recommend you save your wife's gift until you reach Southhampton. Consider it an arrival present for her return to Britain."

Elizabeth noted Berkliff was captured by the gifts and the praise he received from the two Germans. His aura was a brilliant blue. Elizabeth moved back away from the three men. The Germans had bright blue-green auras. They were all in agreement. Berkliff may not have realized it, but now he was an agent for the German Empire.

As they walked away, Elizabeth heard von Hertl ask his colleague, "*Hast du die kalte gespurt?*"

"*Nein, kollege.*"

"*Ich dachte, jemand beobachtet uns.*"

"Du solltest dich entspannen, kollege."

As they walked away, even though her German was hardly proficient, she realized she had not been quite as invisible as she thought.

After Elizabeth returned to the cabin and reported back to her mother, they sat for a moment in silence. Finally, Mary said, "At least we know now we are on the right track."

This comment puzzled Elizabeth. "Mother, didn't we know from the beginning that we are on the right track?"

"Elizabeth, in our trade, we often start a project based on an assessment. An assessment is often based on what someone thinks rather than what they know. I fully expect we would not have been sent on this mission if the colonel had not been confident of the analysis from his team. Still, I am never confident until I have data. Now we know for certain that the analysis was correct. And, sadly, we also know of at least one Englishman who is inside the German network."

"Berkliff."

"Indeed, dear. Imagine how useful it would be to have a senior member of a shipping company available to answer questions. The German Navy and, perhaps, the entire German government would want the information that Berkliff would provide."

"He is a spy for the Germans?"

"Based on what you just heard, he is not a spy, at least not yet. He may not even be a witting collaborator. He might believe ... or wish to believe ... that his German colleagues are simply providing him some compensation for small gestures of kindness. Elizabeth, you are early in your career. You will see over time that men, and it is almost always men because they have access to secrets, become intelligence assets along a very slippery slope. First a favor. Then, an easy request coupled with compensation. Then, a more difficult request with greater compensation. The target may deceive himself that this is just "normal business," or the target may decide it is reasonable compensation from an outsider because his own company or his own government does not recognize his value. Sometimes, we let the target believe whatever he wants to believe. Sometimes, we decide he needs to know with whom he is working. That all depends. But, eventually, the target knows what he is doing is improper. By that time, it is too late."

Elizabeth had not been exposed to this part of the trade in her training. She had not debriefed anyone who wasn't a witting and patriotic collaborator. This was an entirely different part of her work. She asked, "Mother, have you had to do this type of work? I imagine it is not easy."

Mary thought for a moment before answering. Easy? Hardly. How much did she want to tell her daughter at this point? She decided the answer was ... nothing. "Dear, there are many aspects to the trade. Your father and I have worked with people who support the Crown. Our job has always been to protect India from outside threats." It was the truth, but again, not the complete truth.

Elizabeth noted the abrupt change in her mother's aura from green to orange. She decided her question had generated a memory that her mother wished to forget. There would be another time and place to ask hard questions. This was not that time or that place. Instead, they needed to accomplish the mission at hand. Her loyalty to her parents, to the colonel and to the trade demanded it. She said, "Mother, have you ever met a person and thought you had met or seen them before?"

Mary was taken aback by the question. "You have met one of our Germans before?"

"I don't know. It was a vague feeling. Like an itch that I cannot scratch. I just wondered."

"Do not dismiss this feeling, Elizabeth. Our subconscious mind often works faster than our conscious one. As we work on these two men, you may eventually determine that either you have seen them before or something about them reminds you of another person you know or have seen. All I can say for certain is that this may be a warning from your subconscious. It may save us."

Elizabeth thought her mother's comment was too complicated to consider at present. She came back to the problem at hand. "What are our next steps with the Germans?"

"We hope to meet them tomorrow night before dinner. I suspect they may be hoping for a meeting. Of course, for an entirely different reason. They are men, after all."

Elizabeth blushed. "Oh, mother."

"I just have a feeling. Let us see what happens tomorrow. Our only mission for tomorrow is to enjoy the promenade deck. If we see them, then we need to work to either separate them so we can use our mesmerism skills, or one of us will need to visit their cabin while the other holds their attention. For tonight, we have accomplished much and need our rest. It is time to get ready for bed."

A Little Bit of Burglary

AFTER A FULL ENGLISH BREAKFAST IN THEIR CABIN, SLIGHTLY BEFORE NOON Mary and Elizabeth Bankroft left for the promenade deck. They were dressed in long wool coats and felt hats, for while the Arabian Sea might be considered the tropics, in early April and on a deck of a ship underway, the air was chill. The coats also provided a place to hide tools that they might need before teatime with Janet Berkliff.

In less than an hour and after only one complete traversal of the promenade deck, Mary and Elizabeth came upon the two Germans. Mary said, "What a pleasant surprise!"

Becker replied, "It is a bit of good fortune to be sure to have a chance to stroll with two beautiful women."

Elizabeth blushed and Mary said, "You are too kind, Herr Becker."

In a few minutes, von Hertl and Becker seemed captured by Mary. Elizabeth was not entirely sure if it was because of her mother's good looks and charm or some subtle mesmerism magic that her mother used on the two men.

Elizabeth was aware of her mother's beauty. Mary Bankroft was in her mid 40s but looked ten years younger. She was tall, nearly six feet tall in her stockings. She had chestnut hair cut in a modern style that captured her natural curls. Her athletic body coupled with well-tailored clothes always made her a woman that caught men's eyes. Of course, her father was also an exceptionally good-looking man. Nearly six and a half feet tall with broad shoulders and thin waist, Elizabeth loved how her father looked in a uniform. Some might say he had a prominent nose, but that was easily overcome by his nearly emerald, green eyes under his dark eyebrows. When Francis and Mary walked arm-in-arm into a room, men and women stopped to look at them. Men were stunned by her mother, women were envious.

Elizabeth knew she had a blend of her parents' looks. Her hair was dark brown, closer to her father's colour than her mother's. She had her mother's blue eyes. She was tall like her mother but was not quite as "shapely." Not the boyish body of her earlier years, but with few of her mother's curves that seemed to draw men's attention. While Elizabeth might have been dismayed at the lack of male attention, in this case, she was more than happy that the Germans were interested in her mother. It meant she would be the one to engage in a little bit of burglary. She waited until her mother sent a tele-pathic message, "Go now."

Elizabeth turned to the two Germans and said, "Gen-tlemen, I apologize but I need to return to our cabin. I need to rest."

Becker spoke for the two Germans and said, "Of course, Miss Bankroft. Of course." Elizabeth quietly turned and headed to the cabins as she heard her mother laughing at some joke offered by von Hertl. Perhaps the joke was at her expense. Elizabeth thought so much the better.

Elizabeth went directly to the Germans' cabin. It was on the same deck and same corridor as her own. At this time of day, the corridors were empty. The staff had already cleaned the rooms and the passengers on this deck were either in their rooms enjoying a quiet time before lunch service or were out on the promenade deck. Elizabeth pulled out a small lock-pick set from one of the hidden pockets in her coat. It took no time at all to defeat the lock. After all, who would steal anything from a cabin on a ship at sea when it would take little time to find the culprit during a search of the ship.

As Elizabeth walked into the room and closed the door behind her, she stopped and closed her eyes. She concentrated on the remnants of the auras of the Germans. They had been busy over the last few days and their auras would show her where they were hiding their documents. There were precious few places in a cabin on a luxury liner like the *Medina* where papers could be hidden, so she went first to the luggage. Elizabeth smiled as she found the first "tell-tale" left by the Germans to determine if their room had been searched. A small hair left on the door to the closet. That was easy, but it meant that the Germans were careful about their room. Elizabeth knew that when she was done with her search, the luggage and clothing must be left precisely as she found them. Again, before she made another move, Elizabeth spent time studying the closet, the distances between the hangers, the order of the clothes and the precise location of the briefcase in the back of the closet with a small crest. Elizabeth knew that the "von" of von Hertl implied some sort of German royalty. She attacked the briefcase first.

Her selection proved correct. It took her a minute of pondering to determine the release for the false bottom of the briefcase. Once that was accomplished, the latch offered no resistance. The results of her search did surprise her.

A Dream in the Desert

April 1914 — Camp of the al-Rashidis, the Arabian Nejd

MICHAEL O'CONNELL WOKE. HIS SLEEP HAD BEEN REGULARLY INTERRUPTED by the sounds of the desert and the occasional snake or camel spider that crawled on him while he slept wrapped in a woolen blanket and then covered with a camel skin bag. He hated the desert. He hated being thirsty and dirty and he hated everyone around him. The German officers and sergeants were intolerant of the "young lieutenant" who served as their translator. They barely acknowledged that without him, they would have accomplished nothing in their trek into the central desert of Arabia. The desert Arabs were nothing like the Arabs of Baghdad or Jerablus or any other city. They were taciturn. They were xenophobic. They had no interest in anything related to the Ottomans, the Germans or anyone else on the planet. They lived in an isolated world of sand dunes and oases where manhood and family profit were based on raiding other nomads or, better still, raiding the villages at the edge of the desert. Michael had to give them credit for their mental map of this world. Any miscalculation as they headed from one oasis to another meant certain death. They were a hard folk and Michael found them hard subjects for intelligence collection. Even when he tried his mesmerism skills, it was as if they had no subconscious to control.

As his mind wandered, he considered the results of his trip. He had made some progress with two young sons of the al-Rashidi leader, Abd-ul Aziz Al-Rashid. Merely boys, they had yet to participate in the raids that served as the economy of the desert tribes and the measure of manhood. Michael thought they had yet to develop the desert crust that covered exposed stones and exposed personalities. They still had some curiosity about the world. More important, they were exceptionally interested in the German Mauser rifles. He used that curiosity as leverage to gain some insight into their world. While the al-Rashidi men were out receiving German firearms training — training that Michael knew they needed about as much as they needed bowties — he took his issued weapons and took the boys out for a brief ride in the opposite direction. Once he was certain they were out of earshot of the camp, he allowed the boys to shoot his Mauser Karabiner 98a rifle and his Luger P08. Almost immediately, they were entranced with the experience of modern firearms. That made it easy to guide the conversation into discussions of tribal politics and, most important to his mission, the British.

The boys spent some time talking about the 1904 war where the al-Rashidis and the Ottomans were unsuccessful in wresting control of the entire Nejd from the Wahhabis of al-Saud. They were children when that conflict took place and they had little to say about why the al-Saud tribals were not defeated. While not as conservative as the Wahhabi sect of Islam, the young men were more than willing to fall back on the simple explanation that it was the will of God.

Michael held his tongue. He was unwilling to accept a

fatalistic view of the world. He was convinced a man made his own luck and God in his heaven cared little about the actions of men. He had seen too much in the way of fatalism in both the Muslim and Hindu populations of India. It was that fatalism that their English overseers manipulated, along with their sectarian and tribal differences, to enable a small number of Englishmen to maintain control over an entire subcontinent.

The boys also talked in detail about strange British visitors. First, they talked about a woman traveler who came to their camps the previous year. They called her *Tabiba* Beyel. She puzzled them immensely as she spent time traveling alone and then spent days in the harem of the tribal sheikhs. They could not imagine why a woman would do such a thing. Michael had already read German reports of the travels of the female adventurer and scholar, Gertrude Bell. He was just as puzzled as his Arab colleagues on why she wanted to travel in this desert hell, especially alone with only her caravan handlers. Still, Michael learned long ago in India that British travelers often made the most dangerous choices imaginable when outside their safe little island.

The boys also spoke of a visit by a British officer they called *Sheikh* Spear and his connections to both al-Saud and the Kuwaiti emir Mubarak. They said this English sheikh intended to deliver English weapons and money to the al-Sauds, and if he did there were would be another tribal war. The two boys were pleased with the arrival of the German weapons because they knew their own bravery and the will of God would result in final victory. In fact, they looked forward to the conflict. Conflict was, after all, the only way they would be judged men. They had not seen this sheikh, but they heard that he was an expert in their language and that he traveled in the desert as they did, on horse or camel and with only God to help him find the next oasis. Michael could imagine a compass and perhaps a sextant was more likely the reason Shakespear did not die in the desert. Again, he offered no comment.

The two boys did know of another Britisher traveling in the desert. This time, they had seen the man who they called an *aljawal*, a vagrant traveler. He had arrived unannounced and left the same way. They said he made great efforts to engage their father and the tribal elders. They noted that he was accepted as one accepts all travelers, his offers of British support for the tribe were dismissed as idle ramblings of a wandering madman. Eventually, he found someone who could tell him the English name of this *aljawal*. He was named Gerard Leachman. Michael had found another British spy operating in the desert.

Before the day was out, Michael decided to use his mesmerism skills on the boys, as much for practice as for any practical purpose. Over tea, he put the two boys into a light trance and delivered a mesmerism suggestion that he knew they would not remember but might act upon if and when they had a chance. In a quiet voice, Michael said to the two young men, "In your future, if fate allows, you must prevent the British agents from succeeding in their effort to capture your lands. They are your enemy, and you must fight them. They will try to bribe your tribe or some other tribe. When that happens, you must argue against this. They are not to be trusted. They are like snakes and camel spiders. They come quietly and do harm before you even know they are in your tent."

He smiled as he thought what might happen the next time Shakespear or Leachman would try to talk to a member of the al-Rashidis. He asked the two boys to repeat his tasking. They did so in the sleepy tone of one under a mesmerism spell. Michael was not sure if they would act on his guidance or not, but he reckoned that it could only do harm to the British if they did so. He woke them from his spell and said it was time to return to camp before they were missed. The two boys scrambled to mount their camels. They raced back to camp with Michael far behind.

Later that evening, Michael reviewed what the boys had said. While hardly the sort of intelligence that Michael desired, he decided at that moment that it was probably as good as he could expect. At the least, it would let the Germans in Baghdad know the nature of the tribal conflict and how the British were doing their best to weaken the Ottoman control of the Nejd. He might embellish the story slightly to make the British threat more credible. After all, who would know the difference?

Very much like the colonel, Michael could see no reason for the Ottomans or the Germans to care about these nomads, but he had his report about the English and that would be enough. He would spend the rest of the trip working exclusively as the translator to speed the German contingents' return to Baghdad. He might even hear something useful in the exchanges between the senior German officers and the tribal leaders. Anything might help to refine and even ornament his notes. That would further demonstrate to the Germans that he was doing his best to serve their requirements.

As he finished his writing, Michael leaned against the camel saddle and carpet that served as his pillow. He did his best to write by candlelight, but eventually the flickering light had defeated even his young eye. He put away his notebook, blew out the candle and settled in for what he hoped would be an uninterrupted sleep. It took only a few minutes for Michael to realize he was going to get very little sleep that night. Michael looked at the radium-painted dial of his pocket watch. It was just after midnight. He started to doze when he seemed to dream of a specter. It was flying around a ship in the ocean. Michael awoke with a start. A specter in the ocean? He sat up, crossed his legs into a full lotus position and started the breathing technique that they taught him at

The Viceroy's College. He let his mind clear of the latest work with the Arabs. He had used this technique several times since he left the school to join his father.

Now he stretched his mind out. He was experiencing the illusory body taught by Tibetan mystics. Time and space were of no consequence to the illusory body. He could travel around the world if he wanted to do so. But, for now, he wanted to know the nature of the specter in the ocean. "Where and why?" were questions he wanted answered.

The only person he knew who had these same skills was his former classmate, Elizabeth Bankroft. At one point, he had thought they might become lovers. Instead, she had been treacherous in school and treacherous again in Afghanistan. He and his father had barely avoided the withering Maxim gun fire from an airship guided by Elizabeth Bankroft. The defeat at the hands of this old rival stung.

But was this specter Elizabeth? And, if so, was she threatening him again? He closed his eyes and willed his illusory body to travel quickly to see the specter wherever it might be. He found the ghost in the middle of the Arabian Sea. He recognized Elizabeth's shadow as it circled around a passenger liner. Whatever was she doing? Michael controlled his own shadow so that Elizabeth did not notice. She was always so arrogant, so convinced of her own skills. She had not even considered there might be another watching her as she watched her targets. But who were her targets?

Michael concentrated. He could just barely hear the conversations on the ship. Eventually, he heard the discussion. It was a pair of Germans who were obviously recruiting an Englishman to support the German Kaiser. He realized there could be only one reason for Elizabeth to observe this meeting. Wherever she was, she intended to disrupt this effort. Michael backed away and began to search the ship to determine who these Germans were. As he passed through the decks and through the walls of the passenger cabins, he searched for any sign of the Germans. Finally, he came upon their cabin. They had made little effort to hide their work and what effort they made had little success against Michael's illusory body.

Once he found their hidden material, he knew that he had to prevent Elizabeth's efforts to disrupt the German mission. They were on a mission to destroy the Raj. After years of the target of prejudice as an "Anglo-Indian," Michael would do everything possible to ensure the Germans' success.

When Michael finally willed his illusory body back to the desert, he rested for some hours. The concentration was exhausting. As soon as he had recovered, he knew there was only one thing to do. He had to warn the Germans on that ship. To do so, he had to use another of his mystic skills, telepathy. He had to send a message to his father in Damascus. From Damascus, the German consulate would be able to send a message to their spies on the ship. Complicated to be sure, but there was no time to lose if he was going to defeat his enemy, Elizabeth Bankroft.

ᛏhe Revelation

ELIZABETH WAITED IN HER CABIN UNTIL HER MOTHER RETURNED. SHE SPENT the time thinking about what the information she saw meant and how she would explain it to her mother. Her first decision was to write down everything she could remember before the details receded from her memory. In her last days before graduation at The Viceroy's College, one of the skills her mentor Guru Marian taught her was how to memorize documents. The skill was based on visualization of the actual document and keeping that image in what Marian called her memory castle. Once in the memory castle, the image might recede from her active memory, but she could recover it through her already advanced meditation skills. Elizabeth was good at this technique, but she also knew her limitations. Even with practice, she could only hold the information for just so long before fine details would disappear.

When Mary entered the room, she saw Elizabeth writing feverously using a pencil and paper from her traveling notebooks. She was sitting at the small table located next to their porthole on the starboard side of the cabin and a sunbeam from the porthole was casting light directly on the table. Mary could see that Elizabeth was concentrating on the document, so she simply watched as Elizabeth wrote page after page. When her daughter finally looked up from her work, Mary smiled and said, "Successful?"

Elizabeth shook her head and said, "Yes, successful. But the information is far more terrifying than simply a collection of details on Royal Navy facilities in the Far East and in India."

Mary had spent over twenty years of her life debriefing willing collaborators and unwilling targets. She knew the best way to proceed was to simply allow Elizabeth to start from the beginning and continue to talk without interruption until she was finished. She said in a calm voice, "Tell me everything you know."

Elizabeth started with her entrance into of the Germans' cabin. She walked through the details of her search and finally to her identification of the concealed documents in von Hertl's briefcase. Mary encouraged her daughter with a periodic nod and when she described opening the concealment, Mary simply said "Bravo!"

Elizabeth said, "I was pleased as well. What I did not expect were two different sorts of documents. First, there were the expected reports on Royal Navy facilities in Singapore, Hong Kong, Darwin, and Bombay. I suspect the Darwin report is based on some sort of debriefing of Mr. Berkliff because that report was far less detailed and had no associated drawings."

"So, the colonel was absolutely correct in the Germans' mission."

"Not exactly, mother. In fact, not at all. I think those reports were secondary to their actual mission."

"Which is?"

"I found documents identifying lists of locals in Hong

Kong, Singapore and Bombay that the Germans have identified as collaborators when/if Germany goes to war with the Empire. These individuals have agreed to work against the Empire. They are ... revolutionaries. They are part of a network across Asia designed to destroy the Raj. In each case, the individuals signed a ledger certifying that pledge. The Germans have noted how much money they advanced to these individuals and what they might do in the future. A few appear to be reporting sources. Most agreed to take up arms against the government. The latter are all members of different independence movements that are also identified in the ledger."

Elizabeth paused and did her best to compose herself. Finally, she said, "Mother, I think I now know why I recognized Becker. I believe he was the second man in the churchyard when Z-1 was murdered! The ledger showed that Becker was in Bombay at that time." Elizabeth did her best to stifle a sob, but in the end, she could not control herself.

She said, "Mother, Becker needs to pay for that crime."

Mary decided to focus first on the conspiracy that her daughter had uncovered. "Do you have the names of those men who signed the ledger?"

"Men and women, Mother. Over a dozen in each location. The notes do not offer any details on how many others are involved. After all, the names on the lists may be individuals or representatives of groups willing to overthrow the Crown. I never knew there were so many angry subjects of the Crown."

Mary repeated her question. "But do you have the names?"

"Mother, they are all on the list I have in front of me. I wanted to capture the memory on paper before I lost it."

Mary needed her daughter to calm down so that she could push ahead in the debriefing. This meant addressing her daughter's concern over the sheer number of Indians on the list. She said, "Elizabeth, do you know the population of India?"

"Mother, I fear I do not."

"Our 1911 census identified over 310 million people in India. It is only logical that some of those people would be dissatisfied with the government of India. That is particularly the case when nearly all the most powerful people in India are either British or those called Anglo-Indian, meaning people who are the children of a British citizen and an Indian native. I suspect one of the reasons why your former colleague Michael O'Connell is working with the Germans is because he was treated so badly as an Anglo-Indian."

Elizabeth thought for a moment about Michael. She had not ever considered him anything but a friend. At one point during her time at The Viceroy's College, she thought they might be ... what? Lovers? Perhaps a schoolgirl's crush, but she did like him at the time. Now, she was not so sure. She hadn't thought he would face any prejudice.

As she considered that point, she said, "But Mother, India is a wealthy part of the empire. We have roads, trains, ports, a system of law."

"And all of those developments came at the expense of original Indian political and economic systems."

"Mother, please do not tell me you agree with these ... traitors."

"Elizabeth, just because I do not agree with anyone who is hostile to the Crown does not mean I can ignore why they are hostile to the Crown. In fact, if you are going to be successful at our trade, you must understand why people are hostile to the Crown. Remember the story of the attack on the Duke of Connaught. We needed to understand how these men thought so that we could defeat them. Not everyone in the government understands why the Crown has enemies. It is our job to find out why, and do our best to disrupt plots against the government." Mary paused and said, "Ideally without causing further hatred of the Crown."

"It seems to me these men and women have been convinced of a fantasy of independence when, in fact, the Germans are just trying to weaken Britain so they can take over control of the region."

"I agree with you completely. The Germans are using frustration and anger to create their own revolution inside the colonies. But, can you dismiss easily the revolutionaries' demand for independence? Their demands for more say in how they are governed? It is important that you consider this as we move to prevent a revolt. It would appear you have uncovered a plot of grave importance and one that should make our leaders consider what can be done to prevent a revolution."

Elizabeth had trouble capturing the larger consequences of her discovery. She decided to return to something more comfortable: the individuals on the ship. "What are we going to do about Becker and von Hertl?"

Mary was entirely serious when she said, "Elizabeth, do you intend to throw them overboard?"

"I could."

"I know you could, dear. I asked if you intended to do so."

Elizabeth thought for a moment. This was the first time she had been forced to weigh her own desires against the likely needs of the service, the needs of the Crown. She relented and said, "I think not."

Mary said, "Good. Then we need to consider how we can disrupt the Germans' plan and, ideally, how we might make their failure result in a professional and, perhaps, personal loss."

Elizabeth smiled and said, "Like throwing them overboard?"

Mary said, "Not at this precise time, dear."

Mary worked for another hour to calm Elizabeth down and then prepare her for tea with Mrs. Berkliff and, eventually, dinner with the Berkliffs, von Hertl and Becker. The first meeting was simple enough since Elizabeth held no animosity for the elderly lady. The second meeting required greater concentration and a commitment to avoid revealing their knowledge of the conspiracy that Berkliff, von Hertl and Becker shared.

As they were dressing for dinner, Mary reviewed with Elizabeth the necessary requirements for dinner. She started by saying, "We are only one day out from Aden. There is no reason to confront anyone tonight. We will disembark when we get to Aden and report. The colonel can decide what must be done with the Germans. Dear, it is important to remember that the colonel may want to let the Germans proceed. After all, he will have the names of the Indian conspirators. They are subject to the Crown while the Germans are not. That will be the colonel's decision, not our own. If need be, we may allow the Germans to proceed to Alexandria on their own and we will travel by another ship to Constantinople. I don't know, but I think we need to be certain that we do not reveal to the Germans that we know their mission. Elizabeth, can you do that? I know you want to punish Becker, but I need to know if you can remain calm tonight no matter what happens at dinner."

"Mother, are you expecting something to happen tonight?"

Mary smiled a humourless smile and said, "Dear, you never know what might happen when you get spies and traitors sharing a meal. I need to know that you will follow my lead no matter what."

Elizabeth smirked and said, "Mother, I am not a child! I will be civil and do my best not to send a fork flying across the table."

A Far Less Sociable Dinner

ELIZABETH WATCHED AT DINNER AS HER MOTHER MANIPULATED THEIR FELLOW diners. She watched for changes in their auras that might have been the first warning of some suspicion. Nothing changed over the meal. While Elizabeth had been polite through dinner, she did her best to keep silent at the table. She was well and truly afraid that the revelation of German intrigue and Berkliff's treachery might somehow leak out in a careless comment. Luckily for Elizabeth, there was no sign that the Germans realized that the Bankroft ladies knew of their clandestine lives. Just after desserts were delivered to the table, a porter arrived with a telegram for von Hertl. That telegram changed everything.

Von Hertl maintained his composure as he read the telegram, but Elizabeth noted a dramatic change in his aura. It went from a calm, even jovial blue to an orange-red when he finished reading the telegram. He carefully folded the telegram and put it in the breast pocket of his dinner jacket. He looked at his German partner and spoke a few sentences in

German. The only part Elizabeth recognized was the German, "*Nicht so gut.*" Elizabeth wondered what was not so good.

Becker nodded and said, "My friends, it would appear we have a slight difficulty with the contracts that we signed in Japan. Herr von Hertl and I will have to work tonight on preparing a response so that we can send a dispatch both to Krupp headquarters and to our Japanese clients. We will dock at Aden tomorrow and we need to have the material ready. I do apologize but we will have to start work immediately on our responses. It has been lovely evening, but we have to go back to our cabin now."

Mrs. Berkliff was surprised and, at least as near as Elizabeth could tell from her aura, more than a little annoyed. She said, "Gentlemen, please stay and finish dessert and coffee. After all, nothing could be that time sensitive."

Von Hertl was already standing. He bowed to Mrs. Berkliff and said, "Madam, when our company tells us it is urgent, they mean us to treat it as urgent. As my colleague said, we do apologize." As he finished his sentence, he turned on his heel and walked out of the dining room with Becker following.

Mrs. Berkliff was the first to speak. "Well, I never! I mean, really, to leave us just like that. It is just not done in polite society." Elizabeth had read descriptions in novels of women who were "in a huff." She had never seen someone demonstrate what that term meant, but now she could see that Mrs. Berkliff was on her way to being angry, most definitely in a huff.

Josiah Berkliff did his best to calm his wife. He said, "Dear, they are German after all."

Elizabeth almost laughed out loud as his comment. Mary prevented her from doing so by reaching across the table toward the glass decanter of port. She asked, "Mrs. Berkliff, would you care for another glass of port to go with your chocolate mousse?"

Elizabeth sensed her mother was at least as impatient as she was about the niceties around the table, but it made sense for them to appear at least as puzzled as Mrs. Berkliff. Janet Berkliff had decided she had been insulted and she could not return to normal conversation. She turned to her husband and said, "Josiah, I do believe I am coming down with a headache. Would you please take me to our cabin?"

Berkliff could respond in only one way. He stood up, helped his wife up as he said, "Of course, dear." He turned to the Bankroft ladies and said, "I apologize for the way the meal ended. There will be many more meals between here and Alexandria. I hope you will continue to dine with us."

Mary smiled her most unctuous smile and said, "It will be a pleasure." She turned to Janet Berkliff and said, "My dear, will you be all right? I do have some sleeping powders if you need something for the headache."

Janet Berkliff looked down at the two ladies from India. She had no reason to be irritated with them, but she simply couldn't cope with the insult from the Germans, an insult that had embarrassed her in front of these two women. All she could say was, "Thank you, but I will be all right. Goodnight."

After the Berkliffs left, Mary looked at Elizabeth and said, "Well, that wasn't precisely how I thought the meal would end."

"Nor I, mother. What do you think the telegram said?"

"I suppose we need to find out, don't you think?"

"The radio room?"

"The radio room."

While Mary could have engaged the captain and they might have shared the message ... eventually, she recommended Elizabeth take a little stroll in the illusory body to the radio room and check the files. It would be quicker and would certainly be invisible to the crew. When they returned to their cabin, Elizabeth did as requested. As with any of her newly established mystic skills, the more she practiced them, the easier they were. This was relatively easy because she had studied the ship's plan on arrival. The radio room was one deck above them and just forward of the captain's quarters. It was not a complicated search.

When she returned from the foray, she looked up at her mother. Elizabeth said, "Mother, I think we have a little problem."

"Problem? Couldn't you see the file copy?"

"Oh, yes. The file copy was there. The problem is I didn't understand what it meant."

"Please tell me what you saw."

Elizabeth closed her eyes and visualized the telegram she saw in the received box in the radio room. She said, "The telegram said: To: von Hertl. Local problem. Immediate action required. 0230. Confirm. MVO. After he left the table, von Hertl sent a reply because the radio operator was sending out in morse code as I watched. The reply said: To: VO. Confirm RV at 0230. VH."

Mary had her own idea what that meant, but she wanted to see what Elizabeth thought. She said, "Well done, dear. What do you think it means?"

Elizabeth thought for a moment and said, "I think they are going to do something tonight. 0230 is probably half past two in the morning." She looked across the room at the wall clock. "That means in three hours. But I don't know what MVO means or RV. Mother, do you?"

"Well, there is only one MVO that I know of in the German intelligence community. His name is Max Von Oppenheim. He is what is called an orientalist, an expert in Arabia and India. It would make sense that von Hertl and Becker work for him, especially given what we know they have been doing in India. As to RV, I can only guess it means rendezvous."

"A rendezvous in the middle of the night and in the middle of the Arabian Sea?"

"Elizabeth, think about how easy it was for you and the Ravens to save us in the middle of Northern Afghanistan. If a service is concerned for the safety of their agents, they will do anything to protect them."

Elizabeth pondered her mother's comment. "A rendezvous while the *Medina* was underway? And a clandestine rendezvous? Hardly something one could do with an airship or a warship. The watch standers on the *Medina* would certainly notice."

"Elizabeth, remember what we heard from the colonel. The Germans could have submarines in the Arabian Sea. A night rendezvous just might work with such a craft."

"So, how do we stop them?"

"Elizabeth, the real question is do we want to stop them?"

Elizabeth puzzled over her mother's comment.

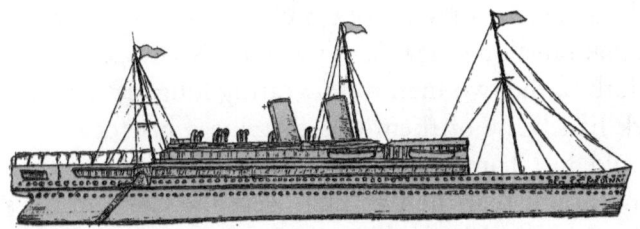

A Rendezvous at Sea

of the *Medina*. It was a moonless night and they were wrapped
in their heavy wool coats and slouch hats against the cold. At
0215hrs, they had left their cabin and climbed the stairs to
the upper deck and then walked over to the railing that overlooked the gangway that ran down the port side of the ship.
Not the formal gangway used when passengers disembarked,
but the working gangway that allowed port inspectors and
port pilots to come aboard. Elizabeth looked down at the
radium-dialed wristwatch issued during her brief sojourn
with the Ravens. The hands of the watch crept slowly across
the dial as she shivered in the cold. At 0225hrs, Mary whispered to Elizabeth, "There is movement on the deck below. I
think our Germans are heading to the gangway."

Elizabeth looked out at sea trying to see anything that
might look like a ship approaching the *Medina*. All she could
see was the silver wake caused by the P&O liner. She said,

"Mother, is it possible they are going to use some sort of floatation devices and wait for their ship?"

Mary shook her head, "The Arabian Sea would be very cold this time of year. I doubt anyone would choose to risk it. We need to be patient."

They watched two men work their way down the metal staircase that ran along the side of the liner. No longer dressed in fine clothes, the two men were wearing long leather coats and black hats. One of them was carrying a briefcase. Elizabeth could just barely make out their features, but there seemed no doubt that the two men were the German spies. Mary whispered in Elizabeth's ear, "Look toward the aft of the liner. What do you see?"

Elizabeth strained to see anything. Then, as she grew accustomed to the dark waves and the silvery wake, she finally saw something. It looked like a black fin rising out of the water, creating its own silvery wake. There was no sound and nothing like the smell of the coal-fired exhaust of the *Medina*. In fact, there didn't seem to be any exhaust at all. As she watched, the fin rose out of the water. A black deck appeared. At first, no more than five yards across, then six, then eight. Elizabeth could see now that the fin she watched was a tower with three separate tubes rising out from the tower. The tower had a small interior deck. On that deck were two men dressed in navy blue coats and formal military caps. As the deck appeared, she noticed a deck gun behind the tower. Elizabeth was stunned at the skill of the submarine commander. They were sailing directly alongside the *Medina*, closing the gap between the two craft while approaching closer and closer to the gangway. Throughout this maneuver, Elizabeth noted there were no engine noises coming from the submarine. While she understood the noise from the *Medina's* boilers would overshadow the submarine's engine noises, she could hear none. The scientist in Elizabeth found that more than a bit curious.

Finally, the submarine pulled up to within a single yard of the liner and matched the speed. A hatch opened on the deck and two sailors appeared carrying a long steel rod with a hook at one end. They carefully captured the end of the gangway and pulled it to the submarine. As soon as they completed that effort, the two Germans crawled down the last stage of the gangway and stepped onto the submarine. In seconds, they were below deck, the hatch closed and the submarine slowed and the liner pulled way. Mary said, "That was amazing. They transferred the passengers while underway as if they did this every day. Elizabeth, what did you think?" Mary turned to her daughter and realized she was gone.

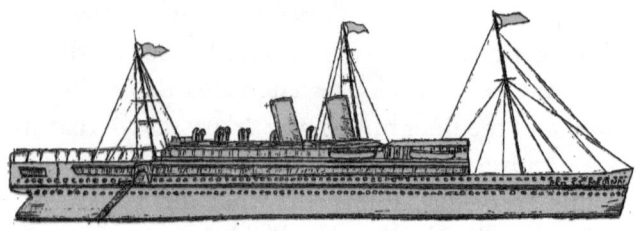

ᛏhe Importance of Control

AFTER MARY CARRIED HER DAUGHTER BACK TO THEIR CABIN AND REVIVED her with a cool washcloth, she spent a few minutes using her own telepathic skills to determine what had happened. The images she captured from her daughter were like reflections in a broken mirror. Nothing made any sense. She realized at that point that only through a carefully structured, gentle debriefing would she, and perhaps Elizabeth, understand what happened. She also knew that she was one of the causes of her daughter's collapse. Since they arrived on the *Medina,* she had been treating her daughter as a peer and as an experienced master of the mystic arts. None of these assumptions were correct. The young lady in front of her was a newly minted intelligence officer and a person with mystic skills who still did not have them under control.

She knew from her own experiences that control over your emotions was the most important part of controlling these mental and physical skills. Learning to wall off emotion from action and learning the importance of control was something that came with maturity and practice. She had pushed her daughter too often in the last few days. As Elizabeth returned to consciousness, Mary used her most calming voice and said, "Elizabeth, just tell me what you remember. It doesn't have to make sense, just tell me what you remember."

"Mother, as I watched their movements down the gangway, I grew more and more angry. I just couldn't imagine that they would make good their escape. These were men who were working against the Crown and one of them was responsible for the death of my friend in Bombay! One minute, I was watching them close the hatch in that submarine and then ..." Elizabeth paused to take a breath. She continued, "I just felt like jumping off the ship and grabbing these two men before they ended up in Germany. I remember the leap over the railing and landing on the deck of the submarine. Mother, did I do that?"

"No, dear. You didn't. Tell me what you felt next and what you saw next."

Elizabeth took another long, deep breath. She wondered at that point whether she was losing her mind. Now that she knew her memories were false, she really didn't know what to believe. Her mother handed her a glass of cold water and she took a long, deep drink. Elizabeth continued, "I landed on the deck and then seemed to melt through the deck into the submarine proper. The interior was bathed in electric light. It smelled terrible. It reminded me of a trip I made one time with grandfather to a farm on the Scottish border. The smell of sweat and, honestly, the smell of urine. It was hard to concentrate. I suppose I stood dazed for a moment as men ran back and forth. They ran over me, no ... through me, to get to their stations. A klaxon sounded. There were orders given in German. I didn't understand them at all."

Mary decided that the only way she could help her daughter understand what she had accomplished was to put her in a light mesmeric trance. She placed one hand on Elizabeth's temple and a second flat on Elizabeth's chest. She looked directly into Elizabeth's eyes and matched her breathing with her daughter's breathing. When Elizabeth's breathing slowed and her eyes lost focus, Mary said, "Elizabeth, what did you do? Did you try to find the Germans?"

Elizabeth responded slowly in what Mary learned long ago was the waking dream voice: "I was so confused, I just turned and walked down the corridor. I suppose I must have been walking aft in this undersea ship, though there was no way for me to know for sure. The corridor had many different doors opening to rooms with different functions. I noticed one room had a chart table with charts rolled up on the side. There were men dressed in sweaters, wool pants and rubber shoes. The air in that room was cold, but fresh. I suppose there must have been a hatch still open there. As I looked in the cabin, I saw an analytic engine! It was clattering away making calculations for ..." Elizabeth thought for a moment and said, "Well, I suppose for the navigator."

Mary could see why her previous efforts to understand her daughter's mind was unsuccessful. The memories were fragmented. Elizabeth's inquisitive nature was captured by a new environment and her illusory body had wandered without direction. Mary said, "What happened next?"

"I seem to have wandered along that corridor for a time. I finally reached a narrow part of the corridor. I watched as sailors squeezed past a metal frame. As I looked over the frame, I saw a pair of piston engines turning two shafts, the propeller shafts. What I couldn't understand was what made the pistons work. There was no noise. It was as if the pistons were turning by electricity, but what was generating the electricity?"

Mary offered no comment. She said, "What did you see?"

"I was at the end of the ship. There was a small compartment with the spinning drive shafts that passed through a sleeve and out through the ship's hull. I turned back. I walked past the pistons and then looked into the first compartment forward of the pistons. It was amazing."

"What was amazing, Elizabeth?"

"The room had a cabinet with dozens of tubes running between a dozen larger glass vials. Attached to the vials were wires that passed from the vials to large black carbon blocks. A long time ago, I read about Dr. Emil Baur and his students attempting to create what they called fuel cells. They generated electricity. I think the German engineers created fuel cells for their submarines, or, at least for this submarine."

"Did you smell anything?"

"No. I expected to smell some sort of gas leakage, but there was none."

"Go ahead, dear. Tell me what else you saw."

"I saw another, smaller version of the analytic engine operating under electric power. I think the Germans were using the computing power of the engine to manage the power creation in the fuel cells as well as the distribution of the power. It was amazing to see an analytic engine actually clattering away as it calculated faster than any man. I suppose the submarine power supply might not work without the analytic engine. In that same room, there was a small engine. I don't know if it was gasoline or diesel, but it was running quietly alongside the analytic engine. Perhaps to run the electrical current?"

Mary smiled at her daughter's insight. Even when she was hunting an enemy, she could find pleasure in science. She said, "When did you decide to come home?"

"I passed through the compartments looking for von Hertl and Becker. I did not find them. In the chart room, I heard the captain instruct the navigator to set a course for Africa and to dive to 20 meters. I could feel the ship deck slowly dip under my feet and the air pressure changed. The fresh air I felt earlier was gone. I felt trapped. Mother, I was afraid that I might not be able to return. I didn't know what to do. The next thing I remember, I was in the cabin with you."

Mary watched as Elizabeth's eyes filled with tears. She could feel her daughter's fear. It was time to break the trance and calm Elizabeth's mind. She moved her hands from her daughter's temple and chest and put her index fingers inside the flat portion of her daughter's ears just behind the ear canal. She gently pushed on the flat portion while saying, "Elizabeth, you are safe. You are back." In a few seconds, she saw Elizabeth's eyes clear and colour return to her cheeks. Her daughter had recovered.

"Mother, how did this happen to me? What did I do?"

Mary thought for a second as she leaned back into her chair. Her knees were still touching her daughter's knees. She said quietly, "Dear, you have deep links into a mystic sphere. Right now, you have not mastered your skills and so those skills are not under your control. The mystic sphere is not necessarily a safe place until you have mastered your own mind and body. I pushed you hard these last few days and you have done well. Now, we need to return to our normal world and consider what we are going to do next. You need to write down some of your memories. Do not expect them to be complete or even to make sense. What you told me about the fuel cells and the analytic engine are so important. As to the rest, we need to consider what we are going to do. I don't know for sure, but we have until we dock in Aden to consider our next steps. For now, after you write your report, you need to rest."

As a young girl, Elizabeth always grumbled when her mother said it was time to rest. It seemed as if she was drawing a line between what children could do and what adults could do. This time Elizabeth was ready to follow instructions. She was exhausted.

Michael O'Connell woke well before dawn. It was the last day of the German team's work with the al-Rashidis. There would be hard work to break camp before the sun rose. He had a number of reports that he would deliver once they returned to Baghdad. Last evening, he had received a brief telepathic message from his father. His father simply said, "Your warning was received by the Germans. They escaped."

Michael cared little for the Germans or their efforts against the British Raj. What pleased him was he had countered the work of Elizabeth Bankroft. He was convinced it would not be the last time he would face his nemesis. This small effort meant he would be able to defeat her anytime she used her powers. He did not have the time or the energy to follow every action of Elizabeth Bankroft, but when she worked inside the mystic sphere, he was confident he could defeat her. After all, she was just a girl. Michael smiled at the thought of her trying to accomplish great things for British Intelligence and being blocked at every turn. The pleasure of his success followed him through the tedium of the day as he worked to load camels and horses and then mounted up for the multiple-day trip back to civilization.

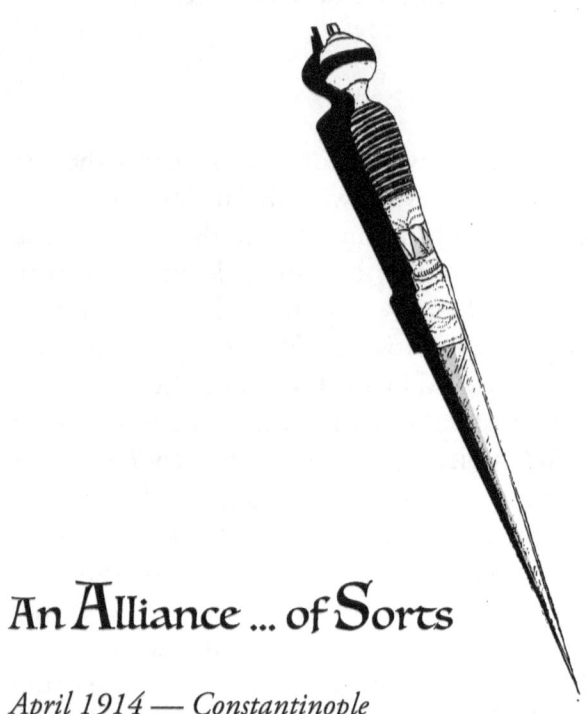

An Alliance ... of Sorts

April 1914 — Constantinople

FRANCIS BANKROFT SAT IN HIS ROOM AT THE PERA PALACE AND LOOKED AT the early morning sun beginning to throw light on the streets below. He started each day with a series of exercises, a quick wash and then tea at his writing desk. He wrote down the events of the previous day on plain sheets of paper, collecting his thoughts, writing and re-writing his reports. Once he was satisfied with the report, he transformed the completed document into a cipher message which he would take to the British delegation at the Sublime Porte. Francis burned his draft notes, dressed for the day, and went down for breakfast.

On arrival at the British Mission, Francis would visit the telegraph room at the Embassy. Every day, the room would transmit messages to Whitehall in London, to Field Marshall Herbert Kitchener, the Consul-General in Egypt, and Lord Harding, the British Indian Viceroy. Later in the day, the telegraph room worked on military reports sent to the Admiralty, the War Department and, in the case of Bankroft's reporting, to the Military Intelligence Bureau in India. The telegraph clerk at the embassy would send the ciphered message to Rawalpindi. A telegraph clerk in Rawalpindi would deliver this message to Colonel Winslow-Heath's office where a trusted aide would use a code book to decipher the message and deliver it to the colonel. To date, Francis' reporting focused on the actions of the "Young Turks" and most especially Enver Pasha with regards to his work with the Germans and his involvement in Ottoman military affairs in Arabia and Mesopotamia. Francis found what he might have called "standard intelligence work" hardly exciting, but he did understand its importance the more he saw how deeply involved the Germans were in virtually everything that Enver Pasha did for the Ottoman government.

One of the interesting things about working in Constantinople was the diversity of cultures that he might meet on the street and in the Ottoman government. The current government might be run by the Young Turks of the Committee for Union and Progress, but the Empire had many locales reaching far outside Macedonia and Anatolia in the Eastern Mediterranean. The Ottoman Empire spanned two continents, Europe and Asia and ran on multiple languages including Turkish, Arabic as well as the twin official languages of government, Persian and French. Along with a diversity of languages, the empire had a diversity of cultures and religions. Sunni Islam was the formal religion of the Ottoman Empire with the Ottoman caliph claiming the religious title of leader of the faithful. His rule extended across the two holiest sites of Sunni Islam, Mecca and Jerusalem, and the Shia holy city of Karbala. But Constantinople was also the center of Eastern Orthodox Christianity, and Jerusalem was the acknowledged center of the Jewish and the Christian faithful. Christians and Jews and Arabs from both the Levant and the Arabian Peninsula all served in the Ottoman bureaucracy.

The cultures of the Ottoman Empire included Turks,

Greeks, Armenians, Arabs, Druze and Kurds as well as dozens of smaller ethnic groups. This blend of cultures and languages in Constantinople might perplex even the most seasoned traveler, but for Francis, it was an excellent starting point for espionage. After all, in a mixed society transitioning from traditional Ottoman rule to some sort of "modern" government based on elections and political parties, there were always going to be winners and losers and those who worried that today's stability might translate into tomorrow's unrest. That was the ideal target set for a representative from the most stable empire in the world, the British Empire. British sovereigns offered by Francis to these targets served as the insurance policy needed in a less-than-secure world.

Francis' first recruits were two Arab officers in the Ottoman Army. Born in Damascus in the previous century, both were mid-level officers who saw their future promotions limited by the new "pan-Turkic" policies of the CUP. They feared a near-term purge of Arabs as Enver Pasha became more enthralled in the military culture of his German colleagues. They watched as Enver Pasha led the Ottoman Army into unsuccessful conflict in Greece and Romania and committed troops to a completely absurd effort in Tripolitania. On the administrative front, they observed long-established military governors in the Levant and in Mesopotamia replaced by Enver's select cadre of Turkish speaking, German-trained administrators. These men had direct access to the Ministry of War and were willing to offer Francis their personal views on the nature of the Ottoman military as well as documents supporting their concerns. They might be loyal to the Caliph and to the concept of the Ottoman Empire, but they were also realists who saw the CUP government creating a state where they would have no place in service to the Caliph. A gentle nudge was all it took for Francis to gain their willingness to report on these changes and what it meant to the capabilities of the Ottoman Army.

Francis was pondering the value of his work over a cup of semi-sweet Turkish coffee, waiting for his breakfast to arrive, when his musings were interrupted by Sasha Naglieff. While he and the Russian officer had similar missions for their respective governments, Francis was always careful about what he should and should not say to a man who only a few years ago tried to have him assassinated. While Naglieff was good company, Francis preferred some quiet this morning. He realized it was not going to happen when Naglieff sat down.

"Francis, it is good to see you this fine spring morning! You have been noticeably absent the past week. Early starts?"

Francis suspected Naglieff had at least one surveillance team watching the British mission compound, so a complete lie about early meetings at the embassy would not be enough to stop Naglieff from a less-than-subtle interrogation. Instead, Francis decided to follow a rule offered at The Viceroy's College. That rule was "If you don't have to lie, don't lie. Just don't tell the complete truth." He smiled at his Russian colleague and said, "Sasha, you know as well as I do, I periodically have to meet people for breakfast. I am more than confident you have your own early starts for the very same reason. I do know that your men following me have been disappointed in their efforts."

Naglieff grinned. This was the sort of gamesmanship he enjoyed with his British colleague. He admitted, "They report that you have the ability to disappear in the most unlikely locations."

"It is just luck, I am sure."

"Just as I am sure these were skills taught at your Viceroy's College."

Francis did his best not to show his surprise that Naglieff knew of the college. He smiled at his Russian adversary-cum-colleague. He said, "I would love to take you to visit my alma mater someday. Though it would require a blindfold much like the one you put on me when you took me to your headquarters in Mazar-e-Sharif."

"My friend, I hope you still do not hold a grudge. After all, I had no intention of hurting you or your wife. It was just part of the game."

"Understood, Sasha. Now, why not join me for breakfast?" Just as he said the word breakfast, a waiter in immaculate white jacket and black trousers arrived with two plates. Each had the same servings of eggs, sausage, flat bread and a side dish of yogurt and fresh figs. A second waiter arrived with fresh coffee in a silver pot and a silver pot filled with tea and a small glass in a silver holder. Francis and Sasha both nodded and said "*Shukran*." The waiters disappeared.

There were a few moments of silence as the two spies from two different empires started their meal. After a few bites, Naglieff said, "I thought you might want to hear what I have uncovered about the men who tried to kill you."

Francis had been busy enough over the past week that he had not spent any time wondering who might have wanted him dead. After years in the espionage trade, he had enough enemies, including the man across the table from him, that he rarely questioned the motives. He said, "I always thought it was you, Sasha."

"Very droll, Francis. Seriously, I had some time on my hands recently because some of my … contacts have been out of town. So, I thought it might be useful to determine who sent the *gromila*. In the long run, it was very useful." He stopped to pull apart a piece of warm Turkish flatbread and use it to push some scrambled eggs onto his spoon.

Francis laughed and said, "I don't want to stop you from enjoying your breakfast, Sasha. But I do hope you intend to tell me what you learned."

"Yes, my friend. First, it is important for you to know that we were both supposed to die that morning. The men we killed intended to attack you first and then come down the hall to attack me. How they expected to do that is beyond my understanding." Naglieff poured tea from the silver teapot and added two lumps of brown sugar. Francis watched as Naglieff stirred his tea and listened as the spoon clinked against the glass cup. He watched Naglieff carefully. He expected there would be lies mixed with truth. Francis hoped that Naglieff's actions, his breathing, and the dilation of his eyes might reveal the difference. So far, there appeared to be no evidence of deceit.

Naglieff continued, "I have a number of sources on the streets in Constantinople. You see, my mission includes both strategic collection, like your own," Naglieff smiled over his tea, "and identifying exiles in opposition to the Tsar. It turns out the assassins were hired by Russian anarchists living in Constantinople. My contacts have identified where the anarchists live."

Naglieff took a sip of tea and continued, "I think it might be useful to visit them before your family arrives. We can finish this problem and, if we are lucky, might even determine where the money came from that paid the assassins. After all, my experience with anarchists is they are usually talk and little more. When they decide to act, it is usually a bomb thrown from a distance. The men who attacked us were used to close, bloody work. Even in Constantinople, those men are expensive."

Francis used the moment to fill his coffee cup to delay his response. As near as he could tell, Naglieff was telling the truth, or at least reporting what he thought to be the truth. Francis had spent no time or effort on building a street network, so he did not have any evidence to determine if Naglieff's tale of Russian anarchists made sense or not. One thing rang true: he did want to solve this puzzle before Mary and Elizabeth arrived in Constantinople. He took a sip of the Turkish coffee and said one word, "When?"

"Ah, now that is the Francis Bankroft I know. A man who

thinks for a moment and then decides. Excellent. I am free tonight. Are you?"

Francis nodded. He said, "Shall we have dinner, make our plans and then visit the home of our anarchist friends after midnight?"

"Indeed, we shall."

Francis and Sasha walked along the back streets of Constantinople near *Misir Carsisi*, the Egyptian Bazaar known among the locals simply as the Spice Bazaar. As they approached the bazaar, even with the doors closed, they could smell the redolent odors of spices from throughout the Ottoman Empire. Francis often used the Egyptian Bazaar as one of his stops along a route designed to determine if he was being followed and by whom. He was certain that on more than one occasion the followers he identified were paid by his current companion. Still, Francis was as confident as any man can be that his former adversary was now his ally. After this evening, he should be relatively certain of that fact.

Both men were dressed for the night's work. Long, dark coats covered their equally dark clothes. They both wore peaked karakul hats died black. They had black silk scarves wrapped around their necks. They walked along on what might at first be assumed to be tall black riding boots. However, the boots were of well-oiled leather, supple and with silent tread. Beneath their coats, they carried their weapons.

In the case of Naglieff, that meant a long, Cossack dagger and a heavy Smith and Wesson Number 3 revolver more commonly known as a Smith and Wesson Russian due to the large number sold to the Tsar's household and Imperial Guards. Chambered in a heavy .44 caliber cartridge, the single-action revolver was a long-barreled, heavy weapon more fitting for a cavalry officer on horseback than a man about to conduct violent action on foot. Francis watched in some amusement at the strides of his colleague as Naglieff addressed the weight hanging from the right side of his belt. The few people who they passed at this late hour would not have noticed Naglieff's strange, rolling gait, but anyone experienced in violent action would have known Naglieff was armed.

Francis believed he was far less obvious in his effort to disguise the night's purpose. The advantage of paired shoulder holsters was they kept his two Colts balanced just below his armpits. Along with his pistols, Francis was carrying a recently acquired dagger of Damascus steel. Five inches of razor-sharp blade sat in a sheath that he had across his chest. In the left pocket of his coat were several lockpick tools and, in the right pocket, a small steel pry bar, just in case they needed to enter unnoticed. He might have brought too many weapons to this gathering, but Francis knew that too many guns always was far better than too few.

When they left the Para Palace, Naglieff recommended that they speak in Persian to disguise their nationality in this most international of all cities. Like the Ottoman empire, the Persian empire had its own mix of Central Asians and even remnants of a Greek community in Georgia. With scarves pulled over their faces, they could be nearly anyone. Francis agreed, with the caveat that his Persian was best described as barracks Persian rather than the more sophisticated Persian Naglieff used. Naglieff smiled and said, "Francis, given how dangerous you look in that coat, hat and scarf, I doubt anyone is going to assume you are a Persian dignitary. Barracks Persian it shall be. And, if you can keep it up as we face our targets tonight, we might even carry the disguise a bit further after the fact. Of course, that assumes any of our adversaries will be left alive after our ... visit."

When Naglieff smiled, his pale complexion, long thin nose and ice-blue eyes reminded Francis of the description of

Count Dracula in Bram Stoker's novel. While Mary and Elizabeth generally preferred more sophisticated reading, Francis found modern novels like *Dracula* to be fine entertainment for long hours on a ship or waiting in a barracks for action to begin. Since they were walking along deserted streets near midnight on a mission that most certainly would include spilling blood, Francis thought the comparison a reasonable one.

As they turned away from the spice market and toward the quay on the left side of the Galatea Bridge, Naglieff offered commentary on what to expect when they arrived at the second-floor apartment. "My sources identified the four anarchists. Two are Russian exiles and two are German agent provocateurs. The sources could not offer any precise reason for the attack on us, but they said the anarchists were only testing their capabilities when they sent their foot soldiers to kill us. They have bragged that they are after far more serious prey — your naval contingent working with the Ottoman Navy and, perhaps, my ambassador. They intend to use several bombs to do their work."

"So, other than the four, how many do we expect to see tonight?"

"I have no idea. Clearly the four anarchists are living in the apartment. If we interrupt a meeting, it could be many more. Are you worried about the numbers, Francis?"

"Not worried, just trying to calculate the odds on whether we can capture one of them alive. If there are too many, it may be bloody."

"Francis, after what they intended to do to us, rest assured, it will be bloody." Again, the wolf-like sneer.

As they approached the target building, Francis offered, "Let's walk around the building. I want to see how many ways to enter." Naglieff nodded and followed Francis as they walked around the block. Minutes later, they had covered the distance and identified only one entrance on the back of the building away from the quay. Francis also noted a small balcony that opened onto the quay street. As they came to that balcony, Francis noted there were still lights on in the target apartment. Stealth would be required if they intended to surprise the anarchists.

Francis turned to Naglieff. He said, "If you take the entrance, I will gain entry through the balcony."

Naglieff shook his head. "Francis, I know you are fit, but that balcony is at least 10 meters above the street."

Francis nodded and smiled as he pulled his scarf up over his mouth and nose. "Sasha, please keep watch for a moment. When you see me on the balcony, enter the building from the front. Climb the stairs and count to ten and begin knocking on the door. When you hear me enter, break down the door and join me."

"How will I know you have entered?"

Francis was already walking toward the balcony. He turned his head. This time it was Francis who sneered. "My friend, I am certain you will know."

As Francis walked under the balcony railing, he stopped and composed himself. He was not as skilled in the mystic arts as his wife or daughter, but he had long ago mastered the Tibetan guru skill of *lung gom pa*. Francis looked up at the balcony railing and willed himself to be on the balcony. To Naglieff's surprise, it did not appear as if his British counterpart had leapt upward. Rather, it looked as if he simply floated up to the balcony. The only noise had been a slight flapping of the long tails of Bankroft's black coat and a slight creak as he landed on the iron grates of the balcony. In the gloom of the night, Naglieff would have sworn that Bankroft disappeared against the wall of the building. Finally, he saw a gloved hand wave him on. It was his turn for action.

Like Bankroft, Naglieff had a lock pick set that he used to open the locked door at the street. He quietly climbed the stairs making sure he stayed against the left side of the stairs both to avoid making any noise on the old wooden stairs and to ensure his right hand would be free if he met anyone concerned about an intruder. Nothing of the sort happened and he arrived at the only door in the long hallway where light was creeping under the doorway. It played with the shadows in the hallway just enough to make Naglieff invisible as well. He pulled up a blood red scarf over his nose and mouth and counted to five. When he reached five, he used the flat of his left hand to pound on the door. He demanded entrance in barracks Persian, the language he and Bankroft had agreed to use in the attack. Seconds later, he heard a several loud crashes. Francis was in the room, and it was time for him to do the same.

Naglieff put a shoulder to the door and entered into the room in a crouch. He was surprised to find four men on the floor with Francis already using copper wire to bind the hands and feet of two of the men. Bankroft looked up and said in his best Persian, "Agha, I asked for 10 seconds, not five. Either way, you have arrived just in time."

Naglieff nodded. The less they spoke, the better it would be for everyone. He finally asked, "How many are alive?"

"Two. I fear I killed two." Francis pointed to the one nearest the window. "That one chose a knife fight."

"And the other dead man?"

"Let us just say he died of fright."

Naglieff shook his head at the mystery upon mysteries that he had witnessed that night. He composed himself and walked over to the first bound man.

The Russian grabbed the man by the collar and slapped the man's face until he finally recovered from whatever technique Bankroft used to render him unconscious. The man woke to face a very sharp Cossack dagger less than an inch from his throat. Naglieff snarled in Persian, "Who are you?"

The man's eyes bulged as Naglieff placed the point of the dagger even closer to his throat. He spoke in Russian, "*Ya ne ponimayu.*" Francis looked at the man's aura. It was not clear whether he did or did not understand Persian. What was clear was the man was terrified.

Naglieff pushed the point of the dagger just enough to break the skin. This time he spoke in a heavily accented Russian. "Who are you, son of a snake?"

Bankroft was amused at the role play. Naglieff might not be a master of any of the mystic arts, but he was a good actor. He had heard the accent before on one of his forays into Central Asia. It was not the perfect Russian of Sasha Naglieff. It was the Russian dialect of a Turkmen who traded with Russians. Bankroft decided to add to the act. He said in Persian, "Agha, this one plays for time. The other one will want to live."

This time the man spoke in Persian sprinkled with a Russian accent. "I will talk. I will talk!"

Naglieff replied in Persian, "Then talk, fool. Who are you and what were your plans in this city?" Naglieff added a small bit more pressure to emphasize his point. Drops of blood mixed with the man's sweat and started to roll down his neck.

"We have nothing to do with the Persian Empire. I am Russian. My Russian partner lies dead through some Persian magic. The other two are Germans. Our only job is to harm the Russians and the British. Certainly, you can see no fault in that? They are both enemies of your Shah."

"Why do you want to harm them? And why do it in Constantinople?"

"We work for pay, agha." The man continued to sweat. He hoped by calling Naglieff agha — the Persian honorific for sir — that he might survive the night. Bankroft could see in Naglieff's eyes that the anarchist's hope would not come to fruition if he did not stop his Russian colleague soon. Using his mesmerism voice on both Naglieff and the anarchist, Francis said, "Agha, we need not harm this one if he tells us who pays him."

Francis watched as Naglieff's face changed from one of blood lust to the more controlled face of an interrogator. Mesmerism was hard in any language, but it was especially hard in a language where you have a limited vocabulary. Still, it appeared to have worked. Naglieff said, "What are you doing here? Why is a Russian in Constantinople? Are you a thief? An assassin for hire?"

The man's words flooded out. "Agha, I am an exile. I am member of a community who call themselves Bolsheviki. We believe in a future Russia where all men will be equal and all men will be rich. There will be no tsar, people will govern themselves. I fled for my life from a Siberian *katorga*."

Francis had no idea what the Russian word meant, but he was concerned that Naglieff might reveal his nationality by accepting the word. He said, "Worm, speak Persian or die!"

The man began to shake. He said, "It was a prison labor camp. I was exiled, but I escaped. I have been in Constantinople for the last five years. I needed money. The Germans offered money."

Francis knew he was walking a fine line with his Russian colleague. He walked over and touched Naglieff's shoulder. He whispered in his ear using the best Russian he had, "I know you want to kill him. I think we should use him as an agent. We can always kill him later if he does not comply. We need to talk to the German." Naglieff nodded. Whether he agreed or not was not clear, but at least he stopped pushing the dagger into the Bolshevik's throat. He let go of the collar of the Russian and the man's head dropped to the floor with a thud. Francis walked over to their other prisoner. Again, using his barracks Persian, he said as he kicked the German in the ribs, "Wake up, worm! My commander wishes to talk to you."

Naglieff clearly enjoyed being the senior in the room. He stepped over the Russian and put a boot over the German's groin. He applied gentle pressure until he heard a groan from the German. "Who are you and what are you doing here?"

The German was still dazed from the pressure hold that Francis had used. As his head cleared, he saw the muzzle of Francis' Colt. It was only an inch from his forehead. "Worm, the commander asks a question."

The German answered in Russian, "*Ya ne ponimayu.*"

Bankroft never knew for sure whether Naglieff was furious or whether it was an act. Either way, before Francis could do anything, the Cossack dagger had drawn blood. The German screamed and then was silent. Naglieff used his Turkmen accented Russian again. He said, "Now, you need to speak, or I will do more harm than a small slice of your rather hefty waistline."

"I am also a Bolsheviki. I was arrested and sent to prison in Berlin. The Kaiser's men released me and sent me here to cause trouble between the Russians and the British. I can do what I please so long as the Russians or the British do not gain control over the Ottomans. If it means a killing here or a bombing there, it is all the same to me. The Germans pay me to cause trouble between these two enemies of Germany."

Naglieff grabbed Bankroft's elbow and they walked to the opposite side of the room. Naglieff whispered, "What do we do with them?"

Francis whispered, "I think we get them to report on their master's wishes. We need to know the full network. These slobs must not be the only group in Constantinople. If we kill them, we will never know the larger game the Germans are playing."

"You just don't want to kill them."

"Sasha, I've already killed two men tonight, I think that is enough. We turn these two into our spies, they report to us and we start to build out the details of our adversary's network."

"How do you get them to do what you wish?"

Francis smiled. "Sasha, it is what I do. It is my trade." He walked over to the German and grabbed him by the collar and dragged him next to his dead colleague. He said in Persian, "Stay." He applied just the right amount of pressure on the man's neck. The German collapsed into unconsciousness. Next, he walked over to the remaining Russian. He grabbed his collar and pulled him into a seated position. Francis extended his left hand along the man's neck putting pressure with his thumb on the right carotid artery and three fingers along the mastoid process behind the man's right ear. He intoned in his best mesmerism voice and his best Russian, "You will work for us. We are in the Persian secret service and we need to know what you are doing against the Russians and the British. You need to know we will be watching you. You know we will be able to come for you anytime we wish. Death will be silent and unexpected if you do not obey. Do you understand?"

The Russian nodded. His eyes were glazed both from the violence he witnessed and the pressure on his mind. He was living in what the master gurus called the waking dream.

Francis continued, "When you awake, you will believe that the two dead men here tonight killed each other. You don't know why they argued, but they did. You are angry with your German colleague that this happened. You do not trust him. You will not trust him ever again. But, you like his money, so you will agree to do what he asks. Before you act again, you will speak to us. Do you understand?"

Again, the nod.

Francis continued, "You will leave a message at the Russian tearoom in Karakoi. Leave the message for Agha Khorasani."

The Russian responded in a dazed voice, "As you say."

Francis applied more pressure on the Russian's carotid artery and he collapsed to the floor. He walked over to the

German and brought him to a level of consciousness that allowed mesmeric control. He said to the German, "You will not remember our time here tonight. You will only remember the fight that took place between your colleague and the two Russians. There was death here tonight. Your colleague was killed by one of the Russians. You will be afraid, but you will not tell anyone what happened here tonight. You think the Russian who survived was innocent. He has a knife wound as you do. You will continue your work for the Kaiser, but you will not tell them about what you saw tonight when your colleagues fought. You will be careful, but you will share everything you know with your Russian companion. If you do not follow these instructions, you will die. Do you understand?"

A nod from the German. Bankroft applied pressure on the German's neck and he collapsed. Francis turned to Naglieff and said, "We will search all four of them and then untie these two. The Russian will be our spy and the German will never know what to believe."

This was not the first time Naglieff had seen Francis Bankroft's magic, but he still was not sure what to believe. He said, "How long will your spell last?"

This time, it was Francis who offered a wolfish smile. "Until we no longer need them."

The Reality of Treason

April 1914 — Aden

WHEN THE *MEDINA* DOCKED IN ADEN, MARY WENT ASHORE. SHE DELIVERED a set of lengthy hand-written dispatches to the Intelligence Bureau counterpart in the British outpost. Her counterpart in Aden, Major William Carpenter, had been most helpful. In his small office, they reviewed the documents and prioritized them into categories of critical, most urgent, urgent and routine. They agreed that the report regarding the German submarine in the Arabian Sea fell into the critical category. The report would outline the German submarine and flying boat activity in the Arabian Sea and posit a likely sea-base somewhere on the coast of German East Africa. Carpenter immediately opened his code book and prepared a cipher cable to the Royal Navy offices in Cairo and to Bombay. While it was most certain that the Consul General in Cairo and the Viceroy in Calcutta would wish to see that information, the truth was it was "actionable" intelligence that the Navy needed immediately. Mary was aware of the tensions that existed between the Indian Intelligence Bureau and military intelligence affiliated with the Egyptian Consul General, Field Marshall Kitchener. These sorts of battles over jurisdiction were of no interest to Mary. From her perspective, she was working for the Crown. She was not about to allow petty bureaucratic arguments delay important intelligence.

The rest of the reporting was prepared into three intelligence pouches — one for the Intelligence Bureau in India, one for the military intelligence officer assigned to the Egyptian Consul General's staff, and a final report summarizing the entire collection effort, which would be sent to the Director of Military Intelligence in London. While they were preparing the documents, they shared their views on the fate of Carpenter's predecessor, Lieutenant Commander James O'Connell. While neither officer could imagine what would force a man respected in the service to switch sides at this critical time in world affairs, they both acknowledged that indeed O'Connell was a traitor to the Crown. Carpenter was particularly shaken by this because he had been O'Connell's deputy for six months before his disappearance into Mesopotamia. Carpenter said he already had received some reporting from his counterpart in Damascus that O'Connell was working with the Germans there. As Mary finished her tea, she watched Carpenter shake his head in sadness. Mary knew Carpenter was one of the standard military intelligence officers inside the bureau. He was not a graduate of The Viceroy's College. Instead, he had worked his way into his current position by diligence and hard study of Arabic language.

Mary knew that any graduate of The Viceroy's College would be less surprised by treachery. The gurus at the school spent hours talking to their charges about the nature of treachery and how easy it was to identify vulnerabilities in any person and then use those vulnerabilities to gently move the targeted individual into a position where they decided to switch sides. Mary suspected there was something in James

O'Connell's biography that would reveal why he decided to work for the Germans. It would take some time and research, but she was convinced it was not as surprising as Carpenter made it seem. Mary realized that Carpenter might be a good observer in the role of a traditional intelligence officer sent out to "go spy the land." If he was trained in the arts of recruiting and handling spies, he would know that the potential for treachery was in the soul of most men.

Elizabeth remained on board the *Medina*, guarding their cabin from any unwanted attention that might come from other, as yet unidentified, adversaries on the ship. During the quiet day as the ship took on coal, Elizabeth puzzled over what she had witnessed and what she had collected during the voyage so far. She remained frustrated that she was unable to bring Becker to justice for killing her friend in Bombay. Her mother underscored the fact that there had been nothing that Elizabeth could have done in those moments while she was on the German submarine. The risks were too great that she might have been lost at sea as her illusory body traveled underwater with the Germans and moved farther and farther away from her corporeal body. Her mother said that not all crimes could be avenged and sometimes in the trade strategic benefits could emerge from tactical losses. Mary pointed out that if the Germans thought their work in India was a success, the Indian Army and the Government of India Special Branch would be more successful in defeating the potential insurrection. Elizabeth had spent the previous night tossing and turning as she considered her mother's advice. It still hurt that the Germans escaped.

Elizabeth's natural curiosity and interest in the sciences caused her to consider the technology that she had seen in both the German submarine and the massive flying boat she saw months ago. She pondered the use of chemical batteries in the submarine. Clearly, the German engineers were far more advanced than anything she had read about in her science publications. Dry cell batteries were relatively new and they seemed of little use in a submarine since they would have to be charged regularly by some other electrical source and their chemicals created a deadly gas that would have to be vented or the crew would die. Her science journals described the batteries in use in the electric automobiles as meager.

The fuel cells seemed capable. Elizabeth was not quite sure how. Of course, it was possible that there was some other engine in the submarine that she had not observed.

Of greater interest to Elizabeth was the analytic engine she saw on the submarine. Given its placement in the chart room, Elizabeth imagined it was used for navigation. Would it also serve as a helpful tool in firing the submarine's deck gun? Elizabeth knew nothing about the new designs of torpedoes and how submarines might use these weapons. What calculations were needed to make the torpedoes hit their target? Surely, the speed of the target, the currents, the temperature of the sea and a host of issues related to the torpedo itself would have to be addressed if you wanted to hit whatever target you identified. It was a puzzlement.

Elizabeth's sleepless night caught up with her just before tea arrived at 1600 hours. She started to doze in the wicker chair placed next to the porthole in her cabin. At first, it was a gentle, relaxing transition into a deep slumber. That transition did not last for long. The face of Z-1 appeared in her dream. He looked at her with his fading eyesight. He said repeatedly, "Why didn't you avenge me?" His face morphed into the faces of Becker and von Hertl in the submarine. They were drinking a glass of wine with the captain of the ship, toasting their success. It was a hurtful scene and Elizabeth's emotions flooded into the dream: anger, fear, disappointment at her helplessness. The flat electric light in the submarine created shadows in her dream. She became one of those shadows. Suddenly, another shadow appeared.

"Elizabeth. Do you remember me, Elizabeth?" A grinning skull appeared. The skull did not appear to be attached to a body. Just a floating, pale image like a mask in the darkness. "Elizabeth, you thought you could defeat me. Now you know differently."

In her dream state, Elizabeth was terrified. She mumbled, "Who are you? What power? What do you mean?"

The skull looked at her. The image morphed into an unrecognizable head. The face showed disappointment that one might expect from an adult speaking to a recalcitrant child. "You don't know what you are doing, do you? It is all emotion and action with no control. Ah, Elizabeth, you are not worth the effort to destroy you. Still, I will destroy you if you continue to trouble me. You are just powerful enough to be dangerous to yourself and your family. Remember this and, perhaps, you will survive." The face morphed once again into a skull. The skull sneered and disappeared.

Elizabeth jolted awake. She was soaked in her own sweat. As the dream faded, she could not remember much of it other than the threat and the gleaming white skull that spoke to her. She wondered if she was losing her mind. She took a piece of paper and a pencil from the writing desk and started to write down what she could remember from her dream. She needed to capture the details before they disappeared, leaving behind only the sick feeling in the pit of her stomach. She knew enough about anatomy to know that the feeling was a chemical creation of the limbic system centered in her brain, not her stomach. That understanding did not help in the least.

Mary came into her cabin to find Elizabeth in her pajamas stretched out on the carpeted floor of the bedroom. Elizabeth was posed in a yoga position known as the pose of the child. She heard her daughter mumbling a mantra taught at The Viceroy's College designed to calm the nerves and cleanse disturbing thoughts. Mary had used the pose more than once, but only when she was coping with the aftermath of violence — usually violence she had been forced to perpetrate on an attacker. That memory alone worried Mary. What in the world had happened to her daughter in the few hours she had been away?

Mary understood she had to let her daughter complete the meditation. She quietly closed the door of the cabin and sat down in the front studio of their cabin and waited. Eventually, her daughter worked through two more positions — the rabbit pose followed by the thunderbolt pose. Elizabeth stood and completed her routine with a standing forward bend. It was after she completed her routine that Elizabeth finally noticed her mother in the studio. She looked slightly embarrassed. She smiled and said, "Success on shore?"

Mary knew her daughter well enough to know that Elizabeth would eventually reveal what was troubling her, so she played along with Elizabeth's false bravado. "Yes, dear. Very successful. You will be pleased to know that our reporting will be delivered to both the Consul General in Cairo and the Viceroy in Calcutta. Plus, the detailed reporting on the German submarine is going to Royal Navy offices in Egypt and India. A summary is also headed to Whitehall. So, your work will be well read by very senior people soon enough."

"Our work, Mother."

"Mostly your work, Elizabeth."

At this comment, Elizabeth blushed. She sat down in a

leather-wrapped club chair across from her mother and said, "I have something I want to tell you."

"I suspected as much when I saw your meditation."

"It is well and truly an odd thing, Mother. Not at all normal."

Mary smiled and said, "And our life on board the *Medina* has been ever so normal." She was pleased to see her daughter smile. "Please just tell me what is troubling you."

Elizabeth started to describe her dream. The more she described it, the more worried Mary became.

A Sound like Distant Thunder

April 1914 — Natiaghali

GURU NAISMITH WAS IN HIS OFFICE IN THE VICEROY'S COLLEGE. HE WAS reviewing the reports from his instructors on the new classes. The first-termers that started in January were moving from the basic classes to more advanced learning of mathematics, science, and language as well as their training in martial arts. This group had been the largest to start the program, with a total of 18 young men and women. Now, four months into the program, there were only six left. In his review of the evaluations from his instructor cadre, Naismith noticed that the students upon entering the program had been younger and less fit than previous classes. It would be a challenge to explain the attrition rate to the Intelligence Bureau. As the world became more dangerous and threats from new and old adversaries loomed on the horizon, the Intelligence Bureau wanted more officers trained at the school. He understood their needs, but he also knew that even the best graduates would face challenges that would test everything they had in body and mind. He would not, could not, allow a student to graduate from the school if they were not ready.

As he stared at his cup of ginger tea and thought about how he would frame his report, he noticed the *phurba* spirit knife on his desk begin to move on its own. Normally, the three-sided ceremonial dagger sat point down in a bowl of black sand. It served him as a focus for his daily meditation as well as a tool as he practiced his own mystic arts. Now, it was moving inside the bowl outside of his control. First the knife rose up so that only the point was in the sand. After a few moments it began to spin. Finally, it seemed to jump out of the bowl on its own and fly across the room. At first, Naismith was amused, but as the *phurba* circled the room at a greater speed, he realized that something more than his own subconscious thoughts was affecting the spirit knife.

Naismith stood up from his desk and moved to the center of the room. He half closed his eyes and began his standard meditation practice, counting breaths and focusing his mental energy inward rather than to the outside world. He began to move through a basic set of slow floor exercises that helped him concentrate. In the deep blue-black of his meditative state, he saw a ghoulish head floating in front of him. The head was not attached to a body. It floated in front of him like a silver-gray balloon.

Naismith uttered the name, "Chodak."

"Yes, soldier. Chodak."

Naismith thought about the last time he had seen Chodak. It was in a cave in the foothills of the Himalayas. Chodak was a young Tibetan monk who was convinced that killing an English soldier would give him the power necessary to destroy the Raj. Instead, Naismith killed him in that cave. He had not expected Chodak's spirit to survive in the mystic sphere. Naismith knew enough about Tibetan religion to know they worshiped many different spirit gods and feared many more that were malevolent forces. He had believed the spirits were simply metaphors to understand the dangers of living in the high mountains where the Pamirs and the Himalayas met. He no longer thought it was an explanation for the reality of the world as it was. The arrival of Chodak meant there really was a spirit world where evil and good did battle.

Naismith had no need to speak. He simply thought, "You do not frighten me, Chodak. There is no such thing as the spirit world. You are simply a figment of my imagination."

"Pathetic soldier. You think that because you can accomplish some parlor tricks that you understand the nature of the mystic sphere. There are many manifestations of the *chi*, your puny body is only one of them. Do you really think there is only this sphere where you act out your little games? Well, I have no interest in frightening you. Call it pride, call it whatever you like. I wanted to let you know I have found another who will serve me. And, I have found one who serves you who is afraid of the mystic sphere. It amuses me to let you know this."

The shaved head of the long-dead monk smiled and seemed to float just outside Naismith's reach. Chodak continued, "It also amuses me to let you know what I know of the future. Do you hear it? I suspect you do not. It is a sound like distant thunder. Soon, your world will descend into conflict. It will destroy your little circus that you call the Raj. It will destroy the European powers' hold over Asia. There will be so much death. Most of your students will die. And, many more of your students will turn to me rather than follow your straight path. This is the most amusing thing of all: you are training students who you think will do honorable service. Instead, they will decide to follow a dark path. Do you find that amusing or terrifying, soldier? I warned you back in Nepal that you had not seen the last of me. Now you know that to be true. Farewell."

Naismith collapsed on the carpet in front of his desk. The spirit knife fell by his side. When he recovered, Naismith realized he now faced an adversary from beyond the grave. An adversary who existed only in a spirit world he did not understand. What could he do to fight someone, something that was the embodiment of evil? And how could he possibly report to the Intelligence Bureau that there was a world war on the horizon?

A Family Reunion

May 1914 — Constantinople

FRANCIS MET MARY AND ELIZBETH ON THE GALATA DOCKS WHEN THEIR Ottoman-flagged ferry arrived. Even after a long sea voyage, Francis was surprised how bedraggled his family looked at they walked down the gangway. Still, the reunion after months apart was joyful and their carriage ride to their new quarters was without drama.

Francis acquired the yali in the village of Beylikduzu on the Sea of Marmara, a property previously owned by generations of Ottoman traders who had lost their fortune in the recent Balkan war. The aging house needed restoration, and Mary and Elizabeth entered through scaffolding, as workers passed to and fro, covered in wood shavings and paint dust. Francis took them immediately through the house and out on the veranda overlooking the Sea of Marmara. He said, "We may be slightly inconvenienced while the workers finish the repairs, but I could not turn down an opportunity to live right on the water. We even have our own sailboat!"

Mary could easily see what had charmed her husband. The house was a mix of old plastered walls framed by polished wood wainscoting. The only finished room in the main floor was the room that accessed the veranda through oak French doors. The room was furnished in an Ottoman style of wooden sofas with extravagant red brocade upholstery. Two large Turkish rugs covered the polished plank floors. It might not be a permanent home, but it certainly would be a good resting place while they served the Crown. Mary smiled and said, "Francis, it is wonderful."

Francis blushed at his wife's praise. He had been worried about the construction which he had left to the new head of his household staff, an Albanian exile named Ibrahim Bektashi, who had been working as a gardener and sweeper at the British mission. Francis conducted his own investigation of this exile using some of his established sources on the streets of Constantinople. In short order, he decided Bektashi was just the man for the job. During his first interview, Bektashi admitted he was in Constantinople because of a blood feud with a distant cousin which had ended badly. Francis opted against viewing the scars that Bektashi offered to show him. Francis immediately paid for a new set of clothes and presented an antique ceremonial dagger on the first day of work. Bektashi had worn the dagger ever since on a hand-tooled leather belt. Woe be it to any of the staff or the local tradesmen who crossed Bektashi. Francis was amused with how quickly Bektashi took on the role of "commander of the house."

However, he did have to remind Bektashi that the dagger should not draw blood in the house. A disappointed Bektashi then purchased a walking stick of polished olive wood which he used to point out work that needed to be accomplished and, periodically, as a prod to encourage the rest of the household staff to do the needful for his master. Francis was reminded of his time working with Pathans. Time on the frontier taught him that loyalty was paid with loyalty. He also knew all too well that loyalty was something that could be purchased if the price was right. He made certain that Bektashi was paid properly both in English sovereigns and in the respect that he would offer to any of his men on the Frontier. In exchange, Bektashi made it clear that he intended to fight to the death to protect the household. Francis countered that he did not expect any fights to the death, but he would be pleased to have Bektashi at his side if such a battle were to occur. The Albanian beamed at that response.

Elizabeth stayed on the veranda for a long time as her parents wandered their new quarters. She was mesmerized by the Sea of Marmara. After a long travel to Constantinople and working against the Germans on board the *Medina*, Elizabeth was glad for this brief opportunity to do nothing but gaze on calm waters and watch shorebirds fishing in the shallows. Farther out to sea were the various ships anchored awaiting access to the Galata docks. Elizabeth heard the workers moving their trunks into the different rooms on the second floor, but she decided to use this quiet moment to collect her thoughts. After all, she would eventually have to tell her father the full story of the trip and the Germans. That thought intruded on the calm of the sea and the shorebirds. Suddenly, she felt the presence of someone watching her. She turned to see the household majordomo, the Albanian her father called Bektashi Bey, standing at the French doors. He seemed distracted, almost as if in a trance.

She said in her best Persian hoping he would understand, "Bektashi Bey, is there something I can do for you?"

Bektashi responded in broken English. "Daughter of the Master, you have aura. My grandmother had aura. She was a leader of women in my clan. Outside the clan, they thought she was a djinn. Are you a djinn, miss?" Bektashi seemed embarrassed by the question, but also determined to know the answer.

Elizabeth was taken aback. Here was a man from the countryside who could see auras and perhaps had other skills that he rarely revealed or even knew he possessed. She smiled and answered carefully in English. "Bektashi Bey, I am no djinn. But I am surprised. You see auras?"

"My grandmother taught me somethings and I have some skills. Do not be frightened. I will protect your secret with my life. You are now my family."

Elizabeth's response was interrupted by a call from her mother to climb the stairs and begin to unpack. She turned to Bektashi and said, "Bektashi Bey, I must answer my mother's call. We can speak of these things later. Now, with your permission, I must go."

Bektashi bowed so deep that Elizabeth thought his wool tarboosh might fall from his head. Elizabeth walked past this new figure in her life. She thought about what it meant to have a member of the household staff who knew of the mystic arts. She decided to raise the question with her parents as soon as she could do so.

The next few days were filled with work-related stories. Francis related his work as a singleton building a network of sources to report on the military plans and intentions of the CUP. He described the strange tension among the Ottoman Navy which was excited with the upcoming arrival of two British-made battleships, and the Ottoman Army, which had internal conflicts between the new Turkish military leadership and senior officers who came from the Arab world or the Armenian or Kurdish Christian communities. The Army also faced challenges as their German advisors delivered new

German weapons and tried, mostly unsuccessfully, to transform the Ottoman Army into one more consistent with the Prussian culture pervasive in the Kaiser's Army.

Winslow-Heath and the Indian Army Intelligence Bureau tasked Francis to focus his attention on conflicts between the Turkish leadership and the Arab commanders. It made good sense given the importance of the Arab world to the Raj. The Indian Army was made up of what British leadership called the "warrior races." Except for the Sikh and Gurkha regiments, these warrior races were Muslim. The Intelligence Bureau expressed concern that the CUP might try to use their own Sunni Muslim leadership to pull the Indian Muslim community away from the British Empire. Also, the key oil fields in Mesopotamia and Persia were vital to the success of the Royal Navy. If the Turks were able to shut off the spigots of those oil deliveries, it would be deadly for the Royal Navy.

One evening at the dinner table, Francis provided Elizabeth with a narrow, waxed envelope with a red wax-seal closure. The seal carried the insignia of the Indian Viceroy. Francis handed it to Elizabeth and said, "I received this at my desk this morning. It is addressed to you. I have been curious about its contents all day, but somehow avoided temptation." Francis looked over at Mary and winked.

Elizabeth received the envelope as she might any letter from a friend. It wasn't until she looked carefully at the note that she realized her name was handwritten on a formal envelope from the Military Intelligence Bureau Headquarters in Calcutta. She broke open the seal and red wax fell on the table. Inside was a two-line letter from the Military Intelligence Bureau headquarters stating that Ensign Elizabeth Bankroft had been mentioned in dispatches sent to the Military Intelligence Department in London on 15 April, 1914. Attached to the formal letter was a handwritten note from Colonel Winslow-Heath. In this letter written in forest green ink, Winslow-Heath stated that Elizabeth's most recent reporting had transformed the Bureau's understanding of the internal threat to the Raj. At the end of the letter, Winslow-Heath said how proud he was of Elizabeth's work and how her reporting was precisely why the Raj created The Viceroy's College. He closed by stating that it was his privilege to promote her to the rank of lieutenant, effective immediately.

For some time afterwards, Elizabeth remained stunned at the importance placed in her efforts. Finally, Mary said, "Dear, this is why we make the effort. A single person in the intelligence service can change the outcome of world events. You should expect more to come as you continue your hard work."

Elizabeth blushed and eventually found the words to accept her mother's praise. She said, "This was mostly your work, not mine."

"Nonsense, dear. All I did was distract the Germans. You did the hard work. Take the credit and be pleased. So often, our work is in the shadows and we never know whether our efforts make any difference at all."

Francis smiled. "Congratulations, Lieutenant Bankroft! You are making an early entrance into the world of the intelligence mandarins in India and in Whitehall. I heard from Winslow-Heath that it changed the way the service is looking at internal threats. The Bureau is using your reporting as a start point for a series of investigations which should uncover more German activities." Francis paused and offered a more serious warning, "Just remember that they are a fickle breed who do not understand how we conduct our trade."

Elizabeth was puzzled by this comment from her father. Mary shook her head and said, "Francis, let Elizabeth enjoy the moment. Just because we have had our troubles with Military Intelligence in London, it certainly doesn't mean the same will happen to her."

This time it was Francis' turn to blush. A bit of pink skin

showed above his collar. He nodded and said, "My apologies, Elizabeth. It is truly an honour to be mentioned in dispatches. I just wanted you to know that we are only judged by our most current actions. And, right now, that means we will be judged by what we do here in Constantinople."

Mary said, "Hardly a necessary comment, Francis. We all know that."

The pink began to climb up Francis' neck. Elizabeth decided to relieve her father from pointed remarks of her mother. She smiled and said, "Father, I understand your point. We need to get to work here."

Francis exhaled slowly and the pink around his jawline began to recede. He smiled and said, "We do have to get to work. But, tomorrow, we will focus on playing a different role. We will be hosting a British traveler. I think you will find her a very engaging dinner companion."

Elizabeth was puzzled by the dramatic pause. She said, "Father, who will be coming to dinner?"

"Elizabeth, we will be hosting Miss Gertrude Bell tomorrow night. She has just returned from a long adventure in Arabia and is recovering in Constantinople before returning home. I hope you will find her at least slightly interesting." He turned to Mary, and Elizabeth was certain this time she saw her father wink.

Dinner with a Lady Adventurer

THE DAY PASSED SLOWLY FOR ELIZABETH. SHE FELT A BIT LIKE A CHILD waiting for Christmas Day. She was about to have dinner with a woman she had admired for as long as she could read. For Elizabeth, this was a dream come true. Here was a woman who had a first in Oxford. An archaeologist. A translator of Persian classics. A woman who had travelled throughout the Middle East and had written about her travels. She was everything that Elizabeth hoped to be. Elizabeth thought about all the questions she wanted to ask and how to ask them without seeming like the adolescent that she knew she was. For an hour, she sat at her desk writing out questions and sorting them into one list that might generate amusing stories, and another aimed at coaxing Miss Bell to share information that Elizabeth was hungry to know.

Even after writing and revising her lists, the hours until dinner seemed to crawl along. Of course, she had more than enough work to do. She had to unpack her things, continue her studies in Russian and Persian, and design a plan for her own intelligence-collection work. Her father had received guidance from the Intelligence Bureau on how each of the Bankrofts would proceed. Francis would continue to work on developing sources in the Ottoman Army. He would be the only one who would have an official title and office at the embassy. Mary and Elizabeth would work from the yali. Mary was tasked to build a new reporting network inside the community of shopkeepers in the bazaars of Constantinople. The goals were to determine the level of support inside the conservative Muslim community for the more cosmopolitan CUP leadership and, equally important, determine the level of hostility against the British presence in Egypt, Mesopotamia and Persia. Elizabeth's mission focused on the Russian, Kurdish and Armenian exile communities in the Sublime Porte. The Intelligence Bureau and the Military Intelligence Department in Whitehall had vague reporting of unrest on the northern and eastern borders of the Ottoman Empire. They wanted any information available on the origins of this unrest and how it might influence Indian revolutionaries.

Elizabeth tasked her father to find any books in the embassy library on the Ottoman Empire's eastern provinces and the ethnic groups located there. He promised to do so. He also offered to introduce Elizabeth to one of his contacts who might have some insight into her tasking. The way her father spoke about his "contact" made Elizabeth wonder if her father was joking or serious. Since there was no way to begin until she had some books to study, Elizabeth spent the last part of the day sorting clothes and trying to decide what she would wear for dinner. She wanted to appear mature, but also did not want to appear too fashionable. After all, their guest was a woman who had spent the last few months deep in the Arabian desert. Elizabeth was sitting on the edge of her bed reviewing three different dress options when her mother came in to check on her.

"Elizabeth, what are you doing, dear? I need your help downstairs working with the staff for dinner tonight."

"Mother, I'm sorry. I forgot about the time. I was trying to decide what to wear tonight."

"Elizabeth, you should wear something comfortable. Francis said he told Miss Bell to be relaxed. He emphasized we were not going to dress for dinner. He meant no dinner jacket and he meant Miss Bell could wear any frock she chose. After all, we have no idea what she has available in Constantinople. Her belongings were shipped from Damascus directly to Alexandria and then home, so the only things she has are a leather portmanteau and a fabric Gladstone bag. Francis reminded her we were from India where a well-dressed woman dines in shalwar kamiz. In fact, that is what I am going to wear and I recommend you do as well."

Elizabeth let out a long sigh of relief. She had not even considered wearing a shalwar kamiz, basically pajama trousers and a long-tailed shirt. She had several in various colours. Better still, it would allow her to wear the cream-coloured dupatta scarf with the three stitched lines issued when she graduated from The Viceroy's College.

Mary smiled at her daughter. Clearly, she was anticipating an evening with a famous personage and she had overthought the event. It was time to take her mind off the anticipation. "Elizabeth, for now, you need to come with me. We have a dinner to arrange!"

The evening finally arrived. The dining room was set and candles lighted; white-linen tablecloth and napkins set out with simple china and silverware arranged for four. The menu was classic Eastern Mediterranean fare starting with salads and flat bread followed by grilled fish, lamb kabobs, and grilled vegetables. Francis was not sure if Miss Bell was a teatotaler or not, so he had water glasses at the table with the wine glasses and chilled Greek white wine strategically positioned in the kitchen. They expected their guest to arrive by the embassy motor launch, so they arranged torch lights on their dock and along the sidewalk to the French doors that opened directly into the dining room. Elizabeth had seen a fair number of dinner parties while growing up in the military cantonment in Rawalpindi, but this was the first time she had helped to set up a formal meal in embassy quarters. She tried to remain focused on the arrival of her guest, but she had to admit to herself, she was already enchanted.

Francis waited down at the dock. He was wearing black wool trousers, an open necked white shirt and an embroidered emerald-coloured vest. As the evening sunset turned from oranges to deep red into mauve, Elizabeth thought he looked the part of the master of an Eastern household. Elizabeth looked at her mother. As promised, she was wearing shalwar kamiz in white silk with her Viceroy's College dupatta. The only colour on her mother's trousseau was a pair of sapphire Persian slippers. In the end, Elizabeth had chosen a turquoise-coloured silk shalwar kamiz with matching Persian slippers. She realized that her cream-coloured dupatta might not be a good match, but she was not about to miss the opportunity to wear her Viceroy's College scarf.

The embassy motor launch pulled up to the dock and Francis helped Gertrude Bell out of the launch, up the sidewalk and through the garden to the house. Two members of the Royal Marine contingent from the embassy stayed on the boat. Francis shouted to them, "Fret not, gents. I will be sending the staff down with a full dinner for you both. And, I suppose some ale might work with that, eh?"

The senior marine already knew that Francis might be friendly in this venue, but he was a lieutenant colonel at the embassy. He replied, "Very kind, sir."

Elizabeth was not disappointed as she watched her idol

approach. Miss Bell was wearing a white wool caftan over dark brown wool trousers. Over that, Bell wore a blood red shawl known in the Arab world as an abaya. She wore a large felt hat wrapped in red flowers hiding an abundance of auburn hair. Elizabeth noticed that Gertrude Bell walked with a purposeful stride and had no trouble at all with her father's pace. Here was a woman comfortable in her own shoes. And, Elizabeth noted, those shoes were well worn, mid-calf lace-up boots. Bell walked up to Mary, greeted her as if they had been friends for years. They embraced and kissed each other on both cheeks.

Bell then turned to Elizabeth. She took Elizabeth's hand in a two-hand grip and shook it three times. She said, "Ah, Elizabeth. I have heard about you. I understand you are a natural philosopher and have your first discovery of a Himalayan orchid. The botanists at Kew must be green with envy. And, your father tells me you are a foot soldier in the Great Game! Actions in Afghanistan and in Bombay. What a record for one so young." She pointed to the three stripes on Elizabeth's dupatta. "Tonight, you will have to reveal what you plan to do next!" Elizabeth was speechless. She mumbled something about how pleased she was to meet the woman adventurer.

Bell looked at Elizabeth for a moment. She was not sure if the young lady was offering praise or criticism. Finally, she decided neither — just a statement of fact. Based on that understanding, Bell broke out into a long and loud laugh. She wrapped her arm around Elizabeth's shoulders and headed toward the French doors. As they reached the doors, Gertrude Bell whispered in Elizabeth's ear, "We have much to say to each other tonight. But first, we need to eat!"

Greetings completed on the patio, they sat at the dining room table and started dinner. Elizabeth noticed that her idol was painfully thin. She suspected months in the desert on horseback and eating whatever was available was the cause. During the meal, Francis and Mary did their best to elicit tales from the latest travels, and Gertrude offered one story after another about her recent trip deep into the Arabian desert. Like many who have faced hardship, she avoided discussing difficulties. Instead, she offered amusing tales of misadventure when she came upon one desert camp after another with her guides not certain that they were coming upon allies, enemies, or simply desert villains.

As the meal went on, Bell focused on her time in the Qasr, or fortress, in Hayyil, the headquarters of the al Rashidi tribal emir. She said, "I do my best to spend time with Bedu men because they are in charge and they treat their women as beasts of burden. The women rarely have anything inter-esting to say and if I tried to engage them, I would spend all my time in some black goat hair tent." Bell looked around the table. Finally, she said, "Would there be a bit of wine somewhere in this house?"

Francis smiled and said, "Ah, I wasn't sure after months in the desert whether you had lost your taste for the grape."

Bell responded with a quote from Rumi. She said, "Saki! The wine that is life's elixir, bring; so that, my dusty body, the fountain of immortality thou mayest make." Elizabeth smiled and resisted the temptation to complete the couplet. She remembered that Bell was a Persian scholar and it would not do to show off.

After the wine was poured and she had taken a healthy sip, Bell continued. "I was proven wrong in Hayyil. Of course, when I arrived at the fortress of the al-Rashidi emir, I tried to break free from enforced purdah, but had little luck. What I found in the harem was a fascinating woman named Turki-yyeh. A Circassian woman given to the emir by the Ottoman Sultan. Her insights into the palace intrigues of the al-Rashidi taught me that I was wrong in assuming that all women in the Arab world were of little interest. In the harem of the emir, I also met his mother, Mudi, and his grandmother, Fatima. I found it most amusing the treasury of the al-Rashidi was in the capable and penny-pinching hands of Fatima. The Bedu pretend to be tyrants over their women and, to some degree they are. But clever women can have the last laugh." Gertrude let out her long laugh.

When coffee arrived, Bell asked if it would be impolite to smoke. When Mary said it was acceptable, Francis went to a corner of the room and brought out a silver box filled with Turkish tobacco cigarettes. Bell reached in, took two, and waited while Francis used a long match to light her cigarette. Elizabeth had never seen a woman show such delight in tobacco. When in London, her grandmother and her tutor Mrs. Edwards had made it clear this was something that women in polite society did not do. Neither her father nor her mother indulged, so Elizabeth had never considered smoking. Watching Gertrude Bell smoke was different. Smoking for Gertrude Bell seemed a natural part of her personality. She smoked the first cigarette in minutes and then lingered over the second. Eventually, Elizabeth considered this to be like her observations regarding Colonel Winslow-Heath. She could no more imagine the colonel without tea than a tree without leaves. And this appeared to be the way with Gertrude Bell and tobacco.

After dinner, they settled in the small library while the staff cleared the table. Francis offered more coffee and a brandy or whisky. Gertrude simply asked for more coffee and another two of the Turkish cigarettes. Now that they had a bit of privacy, the conversation turned more toward what the Bankroft family often called "the Trade." Elizabeth finally realized that along with public recognition as an archaeologist, linguist, and adventurer, Gertrude Bell was also a British intelligence officer.

Bell began by asking a very direct question to Mary. "Did you ever find out what happened with James and Michael O'Connell? Even after some months and a long distance, there are still Arabs talking about how a Baluch tribal woman bested two men on the al-Kut docks. I always assumed it was you, dear."

Mary blushed and said, "They climbed the ladder of consequences on their own. It is dangerous at the top of that ladder no matter how frail a tribal woman might seem." She paused to take a sip of the Turkish coffee and said, "As to the O'Connells we can only speculate that they are now collaborating with the Germans."

Bell shook her head, obscured in a cloud of Turkish tobacco smoke. "I know for certain they are working for the Germans. James is in Damascus working with the German advisor to the Ottoman governor. Michael was seen earlier this year with a German flying column heading to an al-Rashidi camp." She smiled and said, "And, I think Michael met with Hogarth and Lawrence at Carchemish. Michael may have thought he was successful in his disguise as an Arab boy. Indeed, he probably fooled that young imp Lawrence who is very smart but also very arrogant. If Michael had stayed longer, I suspect Hogarth would have seen through the disguise." Bell took a long drag from her cigarette and said, "No matter how good your language skills, the locals will always know. They will just know."

Francis asked Gertrude what else she had heard of the German efforts in the Arabian desert. She began by detailing her observations in Damascus and Baghdad. In both cities, the Ottoman Army had small contingents of German advisors. She noted that some of the Ottoman officers had sprouted German-style mustaches, waxed so that the mustache pointed straight up. She had begun her report on German activities among the Bedu, including the activities of Michael O'Connell, when the sound of broken china came from the kitchen. Francis and Mary stood up at the same time. Gertrude offered a puzzled look to Elizabeth. Elizabeth could only shrug. She said to Gertrude, "Normally, the staff are exceptionally careful with the china."

As Elizabeth looked toward the kitchen, she saw Bektashi backing into the room engaged in a knife fight with a blue-robed figure. Behind those two, four more villains, in blue robes and with dark blue headscarves pulled across their faces, pushed through the kitchen door. Each held a long, curved sword. They flooded into the dining room pushing Bektashi and his assailant against the dining room table. Bektashi and his adversary were locked in mortal combat as they fell to the floor. By the time the attackers reached the library, Francis was on one side of the door and Mary at the other. As the first two attackers entered, the two Bankrofts grabbed the sword arms of the intruders. At first, the attackers smiled at the thought of the ease at which they would dispatch the foreigners. An unarmed man and woman. An easy way to earn their assassins pay. Of course, they could not know they were mistaken.

In the swirl that followed on either side of the door, Francis focused his attention first on shattering the shoulder of his adversary's sword arm. The sword clattered to the ground while Francis shifted behind the blue-robed man. He wrapped his right arm around the man's neck and used his left hand to grab the bearded chin beneath the scarf. Once he had the right purchase, he gave the head a twist. A broken neck and a quick death.

Mary was far less powerful than her husband, but she had the advantage of an attacker who was over-confident. Rather than fight her control over his sword arm, the intruder closed inside arms-length of Mary to grab at her scarf. Mary used one of the martial arts techniques taught at The Viceroy's College to bend the sword arm in a way that no wrist joint could handle. The crack of the broken wrist sounded across the room along with the attacker's cry. Before he could recover his senses, Mary went on the attack. She had pulled his right arm straight out with her left hand. Then, she used her right hand to punch into the attacker's armpit. Mary knew the nerve ganglia in the armpit was tied to key muscles in the arm and diaphragm. The man dropped to his knees, unable to breathe. Mary knelt down and grabbed the man by the throat, extending her hands along the attacker's skull just behind the mastoid processes. She applied just enough pressure to render him unconscious. Slightly more pressure and he would die.

The remaining two attackers forged into the library determined to kill a mature woman and a young girl. Again, they misunderstood their adversaries. Elizabeth stood before the first attacker as he lunged for her. She reached out with both hands in what must have seemed to the attacker as a plea for mercy. It was his last thought on Earth. Elizabeth had extended her chi through her upraised hands. The power she transmitted from her body threw the man across the room. When he landed on his back, he was dead. The bones in his chest were broken and one of his broken ribs had punctured his heart. Elizabeth turned to face the second attacker only to find him dead with the bone hilt of a dagger sticking out of his chest.

Gertrude Bell looked at Elizabeth and said, "You really think I travel anywhere without some weapon? I think this is the first time that Damascus blade has tasted blood, but I can't be sure. It is a gift from one of the Bedu sheikhs I met back in Syria in 1905. It fits quite nicely in a boot."

With that, Gertrude put her left boot on the man's chest and pulled out the dagger with her right hand. She wiped the blood on the blue robe and placed the knife back into her boot. She straightened and walked toward Francis Bankroft.

Francis looked at the wreckage of the room. Chairs in both the dining room and the library were upside down. The table with the coffee cups and the ashtray was against the far wall. Bits and pieces of china and glass covered the Turkish carpets in the library and the dining room. He noted thankfully that Bektashi looked no worse for wear. His attacker was dead at his feet — Bektashi's Damascus blade in his chest. He turned toward Elizabeth and Gertrude and noted their two attackers were most definitely dead. Finally, he noticed Mary crouched over her assailant. He said, "Alive?"

Mary nodded and said, "For now. I want to have a conversation with him."

"As do I. Shall you go first while I work with Bektashi to clean up the mess?"

"Please do, Francis. This may take a little time."

Gertrude walked up to Mary and said, "If it is all right by you, I think I will return to my embassy quarters. It would seem you have some work to do."

Mary looked up from her immobilized attacker. She said, "Elizabeth, why don't you take Gertrude back to the dock. I think she has a motor launch and escort waiting there."

Elizabeth caught her breath and said in a voice she hoped sounded as calm as her mother's voice, "Absolutely, Mother." She pointed toward the French doors in the dining room now adrift in upended chairs and tables. "Miss Bell, if you will follow me."

Gertrude Bell smiled and walked into the dining room to recover her abaya and felt hat. That done, she said, "After you, Miss Bankroft."

As they walked through the garden toward the dock, Gertrude said to Elizabeth, "Do you speak Arabic?"

"Sadly, no. I have good Russian and Persian and, of course, Hindustani. Arabic has not been possible."

"Persian, eh? Perhaps I need to introduce you to some of my Persian-speaking colleagues." Bell smiled. She continued, "I think they may have some use for a Persian-speaking, female adventurer in the months to come."

Elizabeth paused for a moment. She understood the joke, but wasn't sure how to answer. Finally, she said, "I do have my orders already."

"I know, Elizabeth. But tracking exiles in Constantinople

will be of little importance when the world goes to war. I know men in the Indian Intelligence Bureau and seniors in Whitehall that would be most pleased to have a sorceress who speaks Persian."

"Sorceress?"

"I don't have any other way to explain what you did tonight. Probably not exactly magic, though it would certainly appear as magic to those who are not initiated in the mystic arts."

"You knew?"

"Dear, there are many things the world does not know about Gertrude Bell. One of them is that I had my own gurus in the mystic arts when I first traveled into the desert."

Bell opened the palm of her right hand and a small blue flame appeared out of nowhere. Little more than a candle flame, but sapphire blue. Gertrude said, "One of a few tricks I learned in Persia from Zoroastrian mystics." She smiled and pointed to Elizabeth's dupatta. "Perhaps not so different from the Tibetan ways they taught you at The Viceroy's College. Just not as formal. After all, how else could a woman travel in the desert with no fear?"

Bell laughed again and then coughed.

"You were not harmed tonight? No wound or injury?"

"None at all, dear. Simply too many cigarettes followed by a bit of rough exercise."

They had reached the dock and the launch with two Royal Marines waiting patiently. They could hear the slow rumble of the steam engine as it waited to be engaged. Gertrude Bell reached out and gave Elizabeth a hug and a kiss on both cheeks. She reached into an interior pocket of her abaya and pulled out a small leather strap with a bright blue ceramic amulet. Inside the amulet were three small ceramic circles, one white, one yellow and the last black. It looked almost like a yellow eye looking out from the blue disk. Bell reached up and tied the strap around Elizabeth's neck so that the amulet sat just below her collar. "In Arabic, it is called a *nazar*. It protects from the evil eye. Arabs, Turks and Persians all believe in the power of the *nazar*. I think you will need it soon. If the amulet breaks, the Arabs say that is because it has served its purpose and protected you from the evil eye."

She smiled and then leaned over to whisper in Elizabeth's ear, "We shall meet again, dear Elizabeth. Let us hope it is not in the middle of a world war, but I fear it will be so. In the meantime, please take care. Tonight is only the beginning of the dangers facing family Bankroft."

She stood back and shook Elizabeth's hand and said, "Farewell, dear Elizabeth." She turned, adjusted her broadbrimmed hat, pulled her cloak close to her chest and walked toward the motor launch. The adventurer who had just survived a knife fight assumed the guise of a frail Victorian woman. Elizabeth heard her said, "Gentleman, if you please. I need to return to the embassy. I am a bit fatigued."

While one of the marines helped her onto the launch, the second engaged the engine and backed the steam launch away from the dock and out into the Sea of Marmara. Elizabeth stood for a long while, watching the boat disappear into the night. Clearly this was one night she would never forget.

By the time Elizabeth returned to her new home, it had returned to normal. The furniture was back in place, damaged china had been swept up, carpets washed of any spilled coffee and ashes, and a small spot of blood cleaned from the dining room floor. None of the bodies of the attackers remained. It was not exactly magic, but close enough to make Elizabeth wonder for a moment if she had imagined the attack. Her mother and father were sitting at the dining room table. In front of them were small glasses of whisky served neat. A third glass was waiting for her.

As Elizabeth walked through the French doors, Mary said, "Have a seat, dear. And have a bit of medicinal whisky. It can do no harm and just might do a bit of good. After we have a quick discussion, we will all need to spend some time in meditation washing out the terror of this evening."

Elizabeth had rarely drunk whisky, but she took the glass offered and sat down. She said, "Did the attack really happen? I see no evidence to suggest it was anything but a dream."

Francis smiled at his daughter and said, "More of a nightmare than a dream, but yes it did happen. I have charged our man Bektashi to handle the grim task of delivering the bodies to the depths of the Sea of Marmara."

"When I left, one of the men was still alive."

Mary lowered her eyes and said, "I'm afraid that I did more damage than expected. He died shortly after you and Gertrude left."

"Before he could tell us anything?"

Francis took over the discussion. "Yes. We did search their bodies to see if there was anything we could determine about who they were or why they attacked. They were not Turks or any ethnic group we could identify. I will have to check the embassy library to determine if there was anything distinctive about their dress or the swords they were carrying." Francis put his hand over the table and dropped a series of gold coins. "All minted in Germany. Now, I know we can't jump to any conclusions just because they were paid in German gold, but it is consistent with what we already know."

Elizabeth was completely puzzled. "Why exactly are we such a threat to the Germans? What have we done to make them want to kill us?"

Mary said, "I think you already know we have frustrated a number of German plots over the last few years, but I also think you must consider another possibility. They may have been sent to kill Gertrude. She has made no secret of her dislike of the German intrusion into Arabia and, unlike us, she is considered a civilian." Mary paused for a moment before adding, "Even though she is also a member of the Trade."

"The Germans would kill for such a small thing? We are not at war with the Germans."

Francis shook his head. He said, "Not yet, dear."

After they finished their whisky, the family headed to their bedrooms. Mary said to Elizabeth, "Spend some time tonight focusing your meditation on the threats we faced and the actions you took which saved our lives. Tonight, we did not start the fight. We only finished it. It was, as the gurus say, a result of the ladder of consequences. Wash out those negative thoughts as best you can. We can talk more in the morning."

Later, in the master bedroom Francis asked Mary, "Do you think she accepted your statement that we did not have a chance to interrogate your man?"

"I think for now she is willing to accept the fiction. I don't think she wants to imagine what sort of interrogation we conducted. But she also knows that our world is filled with things that are not what they seem."

"It was necessary, dear. We needed to know why they attacked."

"Just because it was necessary does not make it any less gruesome."

"Now that we know the Germans have contacts with the tribals in Tripolitania, it makes the tale so much more complicated. The mercenary told us they have contacts with the Senussi leadership and even deeper into the Sahara with the Tuaregs. I knew some of the Young Turks worked with the Senussi against the Italians when they lost the province of Tripolitania. Still, I had assumed they accepted the Treaty of Ouchy. It appears they have not accepted the treaty and the Germans are willing to help them recover what they see as lost Ottoman lands. So not only does the CUP threaten our oil supplies in the Gulf, but they also threaten Egypt and, by extension, the Suez."

Mary touched her husband's arm and said quietly, "Remember to distinguish what we know from what we think. We know the men were Tuareg. The man we interrogated was a follower of one of the Senussi Sufis. We know they were paid in German gold. That is all we know since that was all he said before he died."

"He died because he fought against your interrogation. He was a strong one, I'll give him that."

"He was already dying. I did not lie to Elizabeth about the fact that I hit him too hard. I tried to save him by putting him in the waking dream. It didn't work. Still, I don't think he had any more to tell us. He was a paid assassin and his Senussi sheikh instructed him to follow German orders."

"Do you think Elizabeth believes Gertrude was the target?"

"Not at all, dear. I think Elizabeth knows full well that the Bankrofts are at war with the Germans."

"Mary, this is the third time we have evidence that the Germans intend us harm. I think it is time we consider whether we can continue to do our mission here under these circumstances."

"Francis, this is not the first time we have faced danger and it is unlikely to be the last. I know you are worried about Elizabeth, but she can take care of herself. I am certain of that."

Francis shook his head. Francis still did not understand what Elizabeth did tonight to the assassin. She didn't touch him, but suddenly he was dead. Finally, he said, "I intend to follow your instructions and do some meditation. I will go into the side bedroom for a bit."

Mary reached out and touched her husband on the cheek. "Be sure to return. Do not let the meditation keep you away from your wife. She needs your embrace as well as meditation to carry her through the evening." Francis smiled as he continued to the side bedroom for a quiet bit of meditation.

Elizabeth used a series of floor exercises to wash out the last of the adrenaline caused by the attack. She could feel her heart slowing as she sat on the floor and began to count breaths. The counting would help clear her mind so that she could focus on her actions of the evening. Once again, she had killed a man. And, once again, the killing had been easy. This raised the question: Could she control this beast within her? It seemed as if a threat and her anger unleashed a power that had no limits. If she could learn to control this power, it would be less worrisome, but that sort of control seemed just out of reach. The counting breaths and meditation helped her as she tried to understand her new power.

Just as she began to slowly wash away the terror, she heard a voice.

"Elizabeth." It repeated her name three times.

She continued to count breaths, but now instead of focusing on the evening's action, she focused on the sound of the voice.

Another three calls of her name. "Elizabeth."

Finally she recognized the voice of Guru Naismith. In her mind, she answered, "Master Guru."

"Elizabeth, you need to return."

"Master Guru, I have a mission."

"Elizabeth, I am calling the Ravens. You must return."

"Master Guru, my orders."

"Tomorrow, you will receive new orders. You need to know they are coming from me. I am assembling the Ravens. You must come quickly."

"Master Guru, I will come."

"Elizabeth, I know you have faced dangers this year. There

are more dangers to be faced. We must have all the Ravens. Come quickly. Come quickly. Come quickly." The voice faded and Elizabeth was left to her thoughts. The Ravens? What could possibly be so critical that all the Ravens would be assembled again? The last time was when the Ravens saved her parents. The mission must be another matter of life or death. She focused her breathing and thought hard about her introduction to the Ravens and what that meant for her future.

Just before she fell asleep, Elizabeth's mind was filled with the image of a bone-white skull. Its empty eye sockets seemed to be staring at her. She tried to continue her meditation, but the skull just floated on the edge of her consciousness.

Finally, it spoke to her. In a high-pitched voice, almost a whine, she heard the skull say, "Girl, you did well tonight. It is good to see that you realize you have the power of life and death in your hands. Enjoy that power, girl. Do not be afraid to use it!" With that, the skull disappeared. Elizabeth was left soaked in sweat. She wasn't sure whether this was a dream or some sort of astral image. What she did know for certain was the only person who might explain it would be Guru Naismith.

Preparing for a Long Journey

THE NEXT MORNING, ELIZABETH TOLD HER PARENTS OF THE MESSAGE FROM Guru Naismith. She told them she was expected to return to India. She also told them the Ravens were being assembled.

Both of her parents listened without interrupting her. When she was finished, her father said, "Elizabeth, do nothing until you hear from me. If there is a dispatch, it will come through the embassy. I will return home once I have decoded the message. Remember, we already have orders from the colonel. Still, we all know that Naismith can make a special request at any time. Thankfully so, given our previous predicament in Afghanistan."

Elizabeth thought for a moment and added, "Miss Bell told me she thought I should be working in Persia and she intended to do something about my assignment here."

Mary said, "My dear, Gertrude is a fine person and most certainly a senior member of the Trade. But she is also an Arabist with more contacts in Whitehall than in India. Her loyalties are to a different command. I am not saying she doesn't have influence, but I don't think that influence extends to Guru Naismith. Whatever she might think about your serving in Persia, for now, I suspect the Ravens' mission is far closer to Calcutta than it is to Tehran."

Francis nodded. He stood up from the table. He looked at Elizabeth and said, "I will make haste and see what is waiting at the embassy. In the meantime, you both need to assemble your thoughts about last night. We need to prepare a dispatch to the colonel about the incident and I need to let the admiral know as well. As you might suspect, the report to the admiral will be far less complete than the one we send the colonel." He smiled, drank the last of his coffee, placed the cup on the table and walked out of the room.

Mary said, "We need to talk about this new assignment. I suspect you won't know details until you arrive, but please be careful. The Ravens are only called for when there is a secret battle."

"Mother, I know. It must be important for Guru Naismith to reach out to me. Even traveling by Royal Navy cruiser, I doubt I can make it to India in less than a week."

Mary smiled and said, "Elizabeth, I suspect you will be there sooner than that."

As expected, Francis Bankroft returned that afternoon with a message from the Intelligence Bureau addressed to Elizabeth. She was to pack immediately and travel back to India. The only remark that helped explain the instructions was that it was based on her previous reporting. Mary and Elizabeth assumed it was about the Indian revolutionaries.

Her route was something she hadn't expected. Her father had instructions to deliver Elizabeth to a spot 10 nautical miles in the Aegean outside the mouth of the Dardanelles.

There, she would be picked up by a Royal Navy floatplane. Elizabeth had not heard of such an aeroplane. Francis said he had asked the admiral who reported that the Royal Navy was experimenting with floatplanes and flying boats. Floatplanes could be carried on the aft deck of a cruiser. Flying boats had hulls like ships and operated exclusively on the water. Elizabeth commented that she had seen a German version of a flying boat in the Arabian Sea. It was that craft that allowed the German provocateur to escape Bombay.

Francis continued that the plane would take her from the Aegean across the Red Sea, stopping at Port Sudan and then on to Aden. In Aden, she would be picked up by a Royal Navy light cruiser which would deliver her to Karachi. From Karachi, she would take an airship to The Viceroy's College. Mary looked at Elizabeth. She smiled and said, "Pack light!"

Francis said, "I have taken the liberty of having a local tailor assemble an appropriate flying suit as well as a skirt, tunic and headgear that will allow you to wear your lieutenant insignia with Intelligence Service crest. I had no idea what sort of hat you might need, so I had the tailor make you a leather flying helmet as well as a felt campaign hat like the one Gertrude Bell wore." Francis smiled and said, "Of course, without the flowers. I will return this evening with the results. We can only hope that the tailor follows my instructions!"

Elizabeth nodded and retreated to her room. She pulled out the leather Gladstone bag she carried with her when she came to Constantinople. The first addition to the bag was her carefully folded night uniform worn by the Ravens. In daylight, it appeared to be dyed midnight blue with a sheen that almost looked forest green. In the dark, it would be jet black. Next, the associated boots. Mary pondered what she should pack next. Certainly underwear, but what other clothes? She was going back to the subcontinent, so she pulled out a single cotton shalwar kamiz and The Viceroy's College dupatta. That would leave her with just enough room for the uniform her father promised to deliver by the end of the day. As she stood in front of the bag with her hands on her hips, her mother came into her room.

Mary walked in carrying a leather box. Elizabeth thought at first it might be a hat box, but it was too small. Mary opened the box and said, "For now, I think you will need these more than I will. I hope they keep you safe. Elizabeth looked inside. There was a stiff leather belt with a leather holster. In the holster was her mother's Browning automatic. The automatic was blued with gold engravings along the barrel and polished ivory pistol grips. Underneath the pistol was a thin-bladed, Damascus steel dagger in a sheath designed to be worn on the arm.

"Mother, these are yours. I am sure I will be issued weapons when I reach The Viceroy's College!"

"And before you get there?"

"I will be in the capable hands of the Royal Navy."

"Aeroplanes are notoriously unreliable. That is one of the reasons why the Royal Navy focused on airships. If you should have to land in less than hospitable circumstances, you might need them. And, honestly, your father already has an arsenal here. If we need weapons, we have plenty hidden in the bedroom and in the library. Your father has the mate of this Browning. A gift from your grandfather."

"But we didn't use them last night."

"We didn't use them last night because we didn't need them. If the assassins had arrived with guns, they would have been met with guns."

Elizabeth smiled and said, "If you are certain, then I would be honored to carry your weapons into any battle that calls for the Ravens."

Mary walked over to her daughter and embraced her.

Then she held her daughter at arm's length and looked into her eyes. "Please take care, dear. Remember, mission success means you must return alive."

Elizabeth cocked her head slightly. She seemed to remember this guidance from her time at The Viceroy's College but she couldn't quite place when she had heard it. She had heard the French term *déjà vu* used in her study of mesmerism and the mystic arts. Recently, she had felt several times that she had "already seen" or heard events before they happened. As she was pondering this, Mary said, "I see Gertrude gave you a *nazar*. Even if it does not protect you from evil, it will certainly tell any Muslim man or woman that you are one of the protected." Mary reached into her blouse and pulled up silver necklace with a smaller version of the same amulet. "Your father has one as well. As you now know, there are many things about this world which have yet to be explained by science. It never hurts to place a bet on faith."

Elizabeth smiled and said, "Indeed, this is one of the lessons I have learned."

Francis returned late afternoon with a series of wrapped paper parcels. The heaviest of the parcels opened to reveal a belted leather flying suit. Francis said, "I also ordered a leather flying jacket which Bektashi will pick up tonight. I think you will look most dashing during your floatplane adventure!"

Elizabeth said, "What does one wear under a flying suit?"

Mary smiled and said, "Something soft so you don't get a rash."

After Francis stopped laughing, he said "Dear, flyers usually wear their uniform under the flying suit. Since I only had two uniforms made and both have skirts rather than trousers, I recommend you wear riding trousers and a light blouse.

It will be cold in flight, but beastly hot when you land in Arabia. Your riding boots will work in either case."

Next came the pair of parcels that held her two uniforms. Francis said, "I checked with the admiral. He said that the services do have women serving in their headquarters and in the field. They are assigned to the Field Ambulance Nursing Yeomanry founded a few years ago after the Boer War. I copied a print I found in the admiral's Royal Navy journal. It might not be quite correct, but I doubt any Royal Navy officer is going to complain about your kit since you will be on orders from Fleet headquarters."

Elizabeth frowned. "I am not a nurse."

Mary smiled at her daughter and said, "Nor am I dear. But we must make allowances. The army simply doesn't have positions for women, yet here we are working for military intelligence. The FANY serve as our ... shall we say our official unit."

"Mother, it is a rude name. Fannies?"

"An unfortunate acronym to be sure. But well-respected in England and supported by the Crown. And, it is an all-female unit, so it can't be all bad, eh? Now, go try on the uniform so that we can make the necessary adjustments."

Elizabeth raced upstairs and tried on her new clothes. While she had never cared about fashion, Elizabeth grew up in a military cantonment and knew that soldiers were judged by the way they wore their uniform. She was determined to get the uniform correct. When she came downstairs, she was wearing a brown wool skirt and belted brown wool jacket with a khaki blouse and a beret with a metal medallion emblem. The medallion was a cross inside a circle. On the circle was written "Princess Royal's Volunteer Corps." Once she arrived in the living room, both Francis and Mary applauded.

"Elizabeth, your formal passing out parade at The Viceroy's College did not include a proper inspection. We need to sort you out." Francis did a quick circle around his daughter. He said, "Well done. There are only a few adjustments that must be made. First, your lieutenant pips are not properly centered." He pulled the pips off her sleeves and recentered them. "Leave them on this blouse and they will be fine." He looked at his daughter again and said, "I acquired proper, sensible shoes for you. They may not be precisely what is worn by the FANYs in England, but again, they will do. You will wear them with these." He held out two pair of khaki knee socks. "I took the opportunity to have proper service garters made with our service embroidery." Like a magician pulling flowers from his sleeve, Francis revealed a set of elastic garters with the red, yellow and white three stripes of The Viceroy's College. Elizabeth took them with all the ceremony she could muster in her bare feet. "Finally, we have one more addition. Come forward, Lieutenant Bankroft."

Elizabeth took a step closer to her father. He reached into his jacket pocket and revealed a medal as well as a service ribbon. He pinned the service ribbon centered just above the left pocket on Elizabeth's blouse and handed her the medal with its green-and-blue-striped ribbon. On one side of the medal was a likeness of the King. On the reverse side was an image of Attock Fort on the Indus. "I checked with the colonel. He confirmed you have been promoted to lieutenant, so you have two pips on your sleeves. Also, you have already earned the India General Service medal for actions in Afghanistan and in Bombay. While it might confound the Royal Navy, they will be forced to recognize you are not some newly minted officer. Navy protocol will ensure you are treated like the officer, admittedly junior officer, that you are."

Mary added, "You need to realize that we rarely wear uniforms except in situations where a uniform might assist us in our duties. In this case, your father is quite correct that a uniform should help you when you are spending time on the

Royal Navy cruiser. After that, pack the uniform away for some future use. If you end up someplace else, you may have to get another uniform that matches your assignment. For example, your father wears a cavalry uniform at the embassy. Totally authorized, but as we have said before, everything is completely true ..."

Elizabeth smirked and said, "But not always truly complete."

Francis closed the conversation by saying, "Precisely. And, just in case you were wondering, your brother has been promoted recently to captain, so if you should see him in India, be sure to salute him!"

They all had a laugh over what her brother Conrad might think or say if he saw his sister in uniform. They all agreed he would demand a salute. Francis recovered first and said, "Now get out of that uniform so it doesn't get too wrinkled. You only have two and it will be a long sea and air voyage, courtesy of the Royal Navy. You don't want to look too frazzled when you put on your uniform in Aden."

Elizabeth did her best salute and said, "Yes, sir." She did a proper about-face in her bare feet and then raced up the stairs.

Mary grabbed Francis' left hand and said, "Well done, dear."

"It was the best I could do under the circumstances."

"And the results were exceptional." Mary stood on her tiptoes and kissed her husband on the cheek.

By Air, by Sea, and Once Again by Air

May – June 1914

THE NEXT MORNING, THE BANKROFTS DEPARTED FROM THE YALI IN THEIR newly acquired sailboat. All three were dressed for a few days on the water. Francis told Bektashi that they would return sometime later that week after a bit of sailing along the coast. Bektashi smiled and provided his best British salute after he dropped off their bags and a large hamper of food.

They left the Sea of Marmara and headed west through the Dardanelles and into the Aegean. Elizabeth found her second passage through the Dardanelles most interesting because she was on deck the entire time and on a much slower craft than the ferry that took her and Mary from Alexandria to Constantinople. Francis decided to use their trip to confirm reporting he had from one of his Ottoman military sources. As they tacked back and forth through the channel, they looked up at the cliffs. While her father stayed at the wheel, Elizabeth and her mother made careful map notations

226

and sketches of the various gun emplacements being built under the watchful eyes of the German advisers. They noticed the Germans watched with great interest as the small sailboat flying a Royal Navy ensign sailed past their positions.

Once in the Aegean, they caught real wind, and in an hour they were anchored a few miles off the coast, sharing a picnic lunch as they waited to rendezvous with the float-plane for the next stage of Elizabeth's travels. Elizabeth wore her wristwatch issued before her last adventure in Afghanistan. Time seemed to stand still as the boat rocked in the gentle waves of the Aegean. Ten minutes before the rendezvous, Francis said to Elizabeth, "It is time for you to don your flying togs. You don't need to wear the jacket yet, but when the aircraft arrives there will be precious little time to change."

Mary helped Elizabeth into the leather suit and her riding boots. Once she was in her new kit, Mary hugged her daughter. Francis came over and did the same. He whispered, "Be safe. The Ravens are always called to do dangerous duty." He kissed her on both cheeks and said, "Lieutenant, make us proud!"

Almost exactly on the hour, the aircraft appeared on the Western horizon. The aircraft was painted a mix of sky blue on top and grey on the bottom. Below the wings, where there should be wheels, two large pontoons extended along the length of the craft. The aircraft circled the sailboat once and then settled into the water. The pilot cautiously coaxed the left float of the aircraft next to the sailboat and Elizabeth crossed over. The tandem cockpit was something Elizabeth had not seen before, but it did mean that there was ample room behind the two wicker seats for her Gladstone bag. Elizabeth pulled on her new flying helmet and gloves and waved to her mother and father as the plane began to taxi. The pilot looked over at Elizabeth and said, "Lieutenant, it's time you belted in. We are going to take off and this kite jumps out of the water like a flying fish. I would hate to lose you at the beginning of our adventure."

Elizabeth looked down at the seat and saw a pair of belts made of bridle leather attached to her wicker seat. She sat down and tightened the belt just as the plane began to lift off the water.

The pilot spent the next few minutes climbing to an altitude of 2,500 feet. Elizabeth could see the altimeter and compass between them. She leaned over and shouted, "HOW FAST CAN YOU GO?"

The pilot looked over and said, "OFFICIALLY THE SOPWITH TABLOID IS SUPPOSED TO GO 90 MILES PER HOUR. WE HAVE TWEAKED THIS ENGINE, SO WE CAN GO CLOSER TO 120. IT IS STILL GOING TO BE A LONG RIDE, SO RELAX."

His voice was calm but serious when he said, "THIS WILL BE THE LONGEST FLIGHT FOR THIS AIR-CRAFT. WE HAVEN'T TRIED THIS BEFORE. STILL, SHE IS A GREAT BIRD AND THE WEATHER IS SOUND." He pointed his right thumb behind his seat. "I BROUGHT TEA AND SOME FOOD, SO WE WON'T STARVE." His eyes crinkled into a smile behind his flying goggles. "BUT YOU NEED TO KNOW THERE ARE NO FACILITIES ONBOARD." He smiled and looked down at his feet. "IF YOU NEED TO GO, WE WILL PUT DOWN ON THE WATER AND YOU CAN SIT ON ONE OF THE FLOATS."

Elizabeth was not one to be embarrassed, but the pilot's comments made her blush.

The first leg of the ten hours had the Sopwith Tabloid cruising along at 2,500 feet in a direct line toward the Suez Canal.

They crossed over Cyprus and landed briefly at the port facilities at the north end of the canal. The pilot, who finally identified himself as Lieutenant Commander Jack Shearing, arranged for the aircraft to be refueled while Elizabeth visited the facilities in the Suez Port authority. She returned with a wicker basket of food and several bottles of sparkling water and two bottles of beer. Shearing did a quick stop at the same facilities and they were off. The turquoise blue water of the Red Sea was dramatic against the brown sands of the Sinai peninsula. Elizabeth remembered her tutor, Mrs. Edwards, telling her about the intrepid Biblical scholars, Agnes and Margaret Smith, who traveled across the desert to visit St. Catherine's monastery in the Sinai. Now, she was cruising along at a breakneck speed in a modern conveyance that Mrs. Edwards would have found terrifying. The noise from the aircraft was deafening so she and Shearing had agreed to minimize their shouting to critical information rather than conversation. Instead, Elizabeth pulled out a small notebook and began to make observations on the coast and the small ports that she could see along the way. These notes were unlikely to serve as anything resembling intelligence, but Elizabeth could not help herself. It was in her nature to observe, to sketch, and to report.

When they landed at Port Sudan, Shearing docked the floatplane next to a Royal Navy torpedo boat destroyer. While he checked the aircraft and engaged the harbor master, Elizabeth walked to the Navy lines and arranged quarters for the night. She did her best to make it clear to the quartermaster that she was an Indian Army officer traveling by air with a Royal Navy Lieutenant Commander. The quartermaster was not impressed until Shearing arrived. The pilot smiled and said the same things Elizabeth said but the results were quite different. Shearing was given a decent set of quarters and Elizabeth was left with a room just big enough for a small bunk and a table with a washing bowl and water.

Elizabeth looked in the mirror for the first time in ten hours. Her face reminded her of a racoon she had seen in the London Zoo. As she watched strange North American creatures climb the trees in their enclosure, Elizabeth saw what looked like masks over their eyes. Now her face was entirely black from the grease bath except for two large circles around her eyes where the goggles had protected. The exact reverse of the racoons. Elizabeth smiled as she realized that aviators might look dashing when they started a flight, but they looked like chimney sweeps when they landed. In fact, dressed in her flying suit she looked like a sausage roll with a panda face. Hardly dashing at all.

She worked hard to remove the grease and then collapsed in bed well before dinner. When she woke, the radium dial on her watch said 0415 hours. It seemed unlikely that she could return to sleep, so she washed again, donned the leather flying suit and her boots and walked out to the quay where the Tabloid was docked. She was surprised to see Shearing there, walking about the aircraft with a lantern, checking the rigging of the biplane and the engine.

Elizabeth said, "Are we ready to depart, sir?"

"Hardly, Elizabeth. I just couldn't sleep so I figured it wouldn't hurt to check the kite after the long day yesterday and the equally long day ahead. Today we will be flying mostly over water with no safe haven if anything goes wrong. Here is a lesson from a pilot: always check and double check. These aeroplanes may be wonderful machines, but they are fragile. Check and double check and you will return alive."

Elizabeth said, "Sir, is it hard to fly?"

Shearing smiled and said, "Not hard to fly a steady course. Hard to take off and hard to land. If you want to try some stick time once we are airborne, you are most welcome!"

Elizabeth smiled and said, "Sir, I would be most grateful to try some ... stick time."

"Well, Lieutenant, you shall get some stick time today.

First, we need to get some rations down our throats." He walked toward the officer's mess with Elizabeth close behind.

The second day in the aircraft would take them to the Royal Navy coaling station in Aden. The aircraft ride had been smooth, though there had been very little to see as they cruised over the Red Sea with bleak desert coastlines to the east and the west. Somewhere around 1000 hours on her watch, Shearing turned his head to her and said, "ARE YOU READY FOR YOUR FIRST FLYING LESSON?"

Elizabeth nodded. Wrapped in a leather flying suit and a leather coat, with a leather flying helmet and goggles, Elizabeth was comfortable even as the wind howled through the wires of the biplane. That comfort, of course, was based on being a passenger, not a participant in the flying adventure.

Shearing said, "THERE ARE TWO PEDALS ON THE FLOOR. DO YOU SEE THEM?" When Elizabeth nodded, he continued, "PLACE YOUR BOOTS ON THE PEDALS. DON'T PUT ANY PRESSURE ON THE PEDALS. YOU JUST WANT TO FLY STRAIGHT AND LEVEL." Again, Elizabeth nodded. "NOW, TAKE THE STICK IN YOUR HANDS. KEEP IT RIGHT WHERE IT IS. DON'T WORRY. MY STICK AND YOURS ARE LINKED SO YOU CAN'T DO ANYTHING WRONG ... MUCH."

Elizabeth thought about the first time she went riding with her grandfather in Scotland. She had ridden ponies in the past, but this time she was riding what her grandfather called a hunter-jumper mare. The horse was calm, but Elizabeth was nervous. Her grandfather told her something like her pilot. "Just be gentle and keep calm. All will be well."

Shearing took his hands off the stick and stretched. It had been nearly four hours in one position, and he was happy to have a moment when he could release the tension in his shoulders. Elizabeth had not been prepared for the sudden pressure from her stick and for a moment, the aeroplane nosed down. She recovered and pulled gently on the stick until it returned to level flight. She smiled and thought, "Just be gentle and keep calm."

"WELL DONE, LIEUTENANT. KEEP UP THE GOOD WORK AND WE WILL SURVIVE THE DAY AND I WILL WRITE A REPORT YOU HAVE HAD YOUR FIRST FOUR HOURS OF FLIGHT INSTRUCTION!" Shearing smiled and continued, "I AM GOING TO LET YOU FLY FOR A BIT WHILE I STRETCH THE OLD BONES. NOT TO WORRY." He pointed to the compass on the center console. "KEEP US ON THAT HEADING AND DON'T TOUCH THE THROTTLE," he pointed to a level between them. Another calm smile. "ONE OF THE ADVANTAGES OF THE TABLOID IS WE SIT SIDE BY SIDE AND NOT FRONT TO BACK. IT MAKES IT EASIER FOR FLIGHT INSTRUCTION." After another smirk, Shearing stretched again and folded his arms. In short order, he was asleep.

As Elizabeth flew the biplane, she could not help herself in letting her mind wander over the wonders of the Empire in this new, 20th century. After all, maintaining a heading over blue water was not difficult, but it was slightly hypnotic. She thought about what had happened to her since her graduation from The Viceroy's College. So much of what she hoped for had come to pass. She knew that was at the cost of the death of a friend and two more deaths from her own hands. It was a strange world.

Elizabeth thought about the dark side of her trade. She had worked on a simple problem in Bombay and yet her contact was murdered. She thought it would be easy enough to unravel the mysteries of the Germans on the cruise ship *Medina* and yet she had to use her illusory body to accomplish the mission. It all pointed to the fact that she was playing a very dangerous game. While she knew the Germans were up to their stiff necks in intrigue, she could not accept Gertrude Bell's warning that there was a world war on the horizon. Exactly who would choose to fight the most powerful country in the world? It seemed foolish at best. Small wars with Afghans or possibly internal battles with revolutionaries seemed possible, but a world at war?

As she considered the reasons for war, she noticed something in the water that seemed to be a mile ahead. As she stared at the object, she gently leaned forward. What she didn't realize was that by leaning forward, she also pushed the stick forward and the Sopwith responded by nosing down.

The change in orientation woke Shearing from his doze. "WHOA, ELIZABETH! WHAT IS GOING ON?"

Elizabeth recovered from the initial shock of how responsive the aircraft was to small changes in pressure on the stick. She gently pulled back on the stick until the aircraft was level again. She noticed that in just a few seconds, the aircraft's altimeter showed she had dropped 200 feet. She was embarrassed by her momentary loss of control. She shouted, "I'M SORRY, SIR. I JUST SAW THE SHIP OUT THERE AND WHEN I LEANED FORWARD …"

"YES, WHEN YOU LEANED FORWARD YOU PUT PRESSURE ON THE STICK. NO DRAMAS, LIEUTENANT. BUT, WHAT DID YOU SEE?"

Elizabeth pointed out toward the nose of the aircraft. Shearing sat up in his seat and finally identified what she was saw. He said, "WELL, ISN'T THAT INTERESTING. LET'S HAVE A CLOSER LOOK. I WILL TAKE OVER FOR A BIT IF YOU DON'T MIND." With that comment, Shearing took the stick and once again the aircraft nosed over. Elizabeth watched the altimeter dial roll anti-clockwise as the aircraft dropped from 1800 feet down to 1000. Shearing leveled the Sopwith at 1000 feet and throttled the aircraft back. They were approaching their target from the north. The mid-day sun was at their backs. Shearing said, "WITH A LITTLE BIT OF LUCK, THEY WON'T SEE US UNTIL WE ARE JUST OVER THEM. PLEASE TAKE CAREFUL NOTES, LIEUTENANT. THIS IS PRECISELY WHY WE CRUISE THE SKIES. WE ARE ABOUT TO FLY OVER A SUBMARMINE THAT IS NOT SUPPOSED TO BE SAILING IN THE RED SEA." He smiled as he lowered the aircraft another 200 feet.

Elizabeth watched as the black hull of a submarine became easier to identify. It was sailing just barely on the surface, looking from above like a sleek whale swimming in the emerald green water. The deck was flush with the water's surface, with a black fin of a tower above the waterline. The submarine's wake was minimal as the tower cut through the waves. Elizabeth noticed the tower had three tubes rising from inside the tower and there were four men dressed in dark blue standing against the leading edge of the tower. All four were using binoculars, scanning the direction of travel and to the east and west. One of the stacks was billowing exhaust. It didn't look to Elizabeth like smoke from a coal fired boiler. She thought to herself, "Perhaps a gasoline or diesel engine?"

As they approached, they could see the submarine was flying the Imperial German Navy ensign from one of the stacks. Behind the tower, Elizabeth recognized a large deck gun wrapped in canvas. The watch standers in the tower had finally realized they were under observation from the sky. They scrambled to get inside the tower as the submarine began to submerge into the clear Red Sea waters. By the time they were over the submarine, it was completely under water with only the three stacks above the surface.

Shearing said, "WELL, NOW WE KNOW THAT THE ROYAL NAVY IS NOT ALONE HERE. I DOUBT THAT GERMAN CRAFT WILL GO THROUGH THE SUEZ

CANAL, SO WE HAVE TO CONSIDER THE GER-
MANS MUST HAVE SOME BASE IN THE REGION."

Elizabeth couldn't help herself as she said, "THEY HAVE
A BASE SOMEWHERE ON THE AFRICAN COAST OF
THE ARABIAN SEA."

Shearing looked over at his passenger with newfound
interest. "SO, YOU ARE NOT SURPRISED THAT WE
FOUND A GERMAN BOAT IN THE WATER?"

Elizabeth shook her head. She realized she had said more
than she should have under the circumstances. Now, she was
trapped into making a follow-on comment. "IT ISN'T THE
TYPE OF BOAT I WOULD HAVE EXPECTED."

Shearing was not about to let her off that easily. He said,
"HOW MANY GERMAN BOATS HAVE YOU SEEN?"

Elizabeth decided to provide the lieutenant commander
with an edited version of what she knew. "THIS IS THE
SECOND ONE I HAVE SEEN. EARLIER THIS YEAR, I
ALSO SAW A VERY LARGE GERMAN FLYING BOAT
IN THE ARABIAN SEA. I ASSUME THEY MUST HAVE
SOME HARBOR IN AFRICA. THEY CERTAINLY
DON'T HAVE DOCKING PRIVILEDGES IN ANY
BRITISH-OWNED TERRITORIES." Again, completely
true, just not truly complete.

"THIS IS WHY OUR NAVY HAS CRATES LIKE
THESE. WE SERVE AS THE EYES OF THE FLEET. IT
WILL BE AN IMPORTANT REPORT TO FILE WHEN
WE GET TO OUR DESTINATION. IT IS INTER-
ESTING THAT THEY SHOULD BE SO FAR FROM
HOME." Shearing reached into the pocket of his flight suit
and pulled out a large gold hunter-style pocket watch. Eliz-
abeth noticed it was a chronograph that had been keeping
elapsed time on their journey.

After returning the pocket watch to his flight suit, Shearing
pulled out a leather-bound notebook and placed it on his

right leg. He used a pencil to make a few quick calculations, then shouted: "BY MY CALCULATIONS, WE ARE ABOUT ONE HOUR OUT FROM ADEN. THAT IS, OF COURSE, ASSUMING YOU DIDN'T LOSE THE HEADING WHEN YOU SAW THE GERMANS."

Elizabeth looked over at Shearing and shouted back, "SIR, I KNOW HOW TO FOLLOW ORDERS EVEN IN A FLYING MACHINE."

"EXCELLENT, LIEUTENANT." Shearing handed her the notebook and pencil and said, "NOW WRITE DOWN YOUR OBSERVATIONS OF THE GERMAN BOAT. I WILL SUBMIT THE REPORT TO THE SENIOR NAVY OFFICER IN ADEN WHEN WE ARRIVE."

As Elizabeth wrote down her observations, she included her best estimates of the size of the vessel and its deck gun, the type of engines and its likely course. When she handed the book and pencil back to Shearing, he said, "LIEUTENANT, WHAT IN THE WORLD IS SO IMPORTANT THAT YOU NEEDED TO BE FLOWN TO ADEN? I DOUBT THE FLEET EXPECTED US TO FIND A SUBMARINE ON OUR ROUTE, SO WHY FLY TO ADEN? I HAVE MY ORDERS AND IT HAS BEEN A PLEASURE TO TAKE THIS BIRD ON A LONG FLIGHT, BUT WHY?"

Elizabeth shook her head. She knew that the pilot had little reason to ask other than simple curiosity. She understood the principle of need to know. He simply did not need to know. On the other hand, it seemed impolite not to reply in some fashion. She remembered her mother's advice on dealing with people outside the Trade. Tell as much of the truth as you think they need and not one word more. She shouted, "HONESTLY, I DON'T KNOW FOR CERTAIN. I'M SURE YOU KNOW I AM IN INTELLIGENCE."

"NOT HARD TO FIGURE THAT OUT, LIEUTENANT. MY ORDERS CAME FROM NAVAL

INTELLIGENCE THROUGH MY COMMANDER. BUT WHAT IS THE HURRY?"

Elizabeth smiled through her goggles. She said, "THAT IS A QUESTION THAT I HAVE ASKED MYSELF SINCE I RECEIVED MY ORDERS. ALL I KNOW IS I AM TO REPORT TO THE INDIAN INTELLIGENCE BUREAU AS SOON AS POSSIBLE. ONE DAY I WAS WORKING IN CONSTANTINOPLE, AND THE NEXT I WAS TOLD TO RETURN TO INDIA. THE REST IS AS MUCH OF A MYSTERY TO ME AS IT IS TO YOU. YOU KNOW BETTER THAN I THAT WHEN YOU ARE IN UNIFORM, YOU DON'T EXPECT ORDERS TO BE COMPLETE. AS AN ARMY LIEUTENANT, MY ORDERS ARE NEVER COMPLETE."

Shearing laughed. "TOO TRUE, LIEUTENANT. WELL, IT WAS A GOOD RIDE, WE ACCOMPLISHED SOMETHING FOR THE NAVY AND THAT IS PROB-ABLY ALL WE NEED TO KNOW FOR NOW."

Elizabeth was tired of shouting into the wind. She was pleased he was willing to accept her claim of ignorance. What she had said was mostly true because she had no idea what awaited her at The Viceroy's College. She decided to change the subject and let her pilot shout instead. She shouted, "WILL YOU HAVE TO FLY BACK TO THE AEGEAN?"

"I HAVE NO IDEA. THIS CRATE CAN BE STORED ON ANY CRUISER OR BATTLESHIP THAT HAS A CRANE. MY REAL JOB IS TO SERVE AS FLEET RECONAISSANCE WITH AN OBSERVER SEATED IN YOUR POSITION — VERY MUCH LIKE WHAT WE JUST ACCOMPLISHED. IF THEY WANT ME BACK IN THE AEGEAN, THEN I MAY FLY THERE, OR MAY RIDE ON THE NEXT CAPITAL SHIP. OR, I MIGHT SERVE WITH THE FLEET IN THE ARABIAN SEA. THERE AREN'T MANY PILOTS OR SOPWITH

TABLOIDS SO THE ADMIRALS GET TO DECIDE. ALL I KNOW IS I GET TO FLY AND THAT'S SPLENDID." Shearing nodded to himself and then slipped into silence leaving Elizabeth to her thoughts for the rest of the flight.

The transfer from aeroplane to Royal Navy warship was simple enough. Once they landed in Aden, Shearing left Elizabeth at the aircraft and reported to the Royal Navy port commander. Elizabeth learned her lesson at Port Sudan. Female Indian Army lieutenants were rare and had little sway in Royal Navy facilities. As a Royal Navy Lieutenant Commander, Shearing would find out the necessary details and with far less drama. When he returned, he said the commander wanted a more complete debriefing later that evening. He did say that his aircraft would be loaded on what was called a seaplane tender that was on patrol in the Persian Gulf. He was also told that his passenger was scheduled to depart the next day on a fast cruiser headed for India and then to Hong Kong.

When Shearing returned, he was carrying a small bucket of soapy water and two sponges. He put the bucket down and said, "First things first. We both need to get rid of the flight grease on our faces. Then, I will take you over to your new quarters at *HMS New Zealand*. While I know they are expecting you, I thought a Royal Navy lieutenant commander might gain slightly more respect than an Indian Army lieutenant."

As Elizabeth worked to scrub the flight grease off her face, she smiled and said, "And God forbid a female lieutenant."

Shearing laughed and said, "Yes, God forbid. Still, a lieutenant who is a spy and a dab hand at flying an aircraft!"

"Hardly, sir. But I do want to thank you for the chance to fly."

"Lieutenant, there are already women flying these crates. I'm not sure if you are the first one to fly over the Red Sea, but there is no reason why you should be the last to do so."

Once their scrubbing was complete, Shearing reached into the cargo bay of the Sopwith and pulled out their two bags. He opened his and put on his uniform headgear with gold embroidery on the brim designating him as a senior officer in the Royal Navy. He said, "I think the leather flying helmet is not quite appropriate for our arrival at the *New Zealand*. Do you have something else to wear?"

Elizabeth reached into her bag and pulled out the two choices: the wool felt hat and the wool beret with the FANY insignia. She asked, "Which would you recommend?"

Shearing thought for a moment and said, "Given that we both look like sausage rolls in our flying suits, I recommend the beret. It has an insignia that looks official and will confound the seaman. It is bad enough that they have to allow a woman on their ship, but an aviatrix? We have to give them something else to ponder and the FANY insignia will do just that."

Elizabeth beamed at the thought of being an aviatrix. She said, "Right, sir. Please lead me to the cruiser." She assumed an appropriate position as they walked. On Shearing's left and one step behind the senior officer. Elizabeth learned that sort of protocol from the Rawalpindi cantonment. This was the first time she had used it.

Elizabeth's arrival at *HMS New Zealand* created some fuss as she and Shearing walked up the gangway to the ship. After a small discussion between Shearing and the officer of the day and the passage of the Admiralty orders that instructed the *New Zealand* to transport Lieutenant Bankroft to Karachi, Shearing turned to Elizabeth and said, "Right, Lieutenant. I've done my part in delivering you to India. Now, I must find my new commander and determine when, where and how he expects me to support his mission. Fair winds and following seas, Lieutenant Elizabeth Bankroft."

Elizabeth came to the position of attention and rendered her best military salute. Once Shearing returned the salute, he offered her his hand. Elizabeth took the hand and gave it a hearty shake and said, "Thank you again, sir. Your flying instructions were most appreciated, and I hope to continue the instruction at some future time."

"Lieutenant, it was a pleasure. Cheers!" With that, Shearing offered a salute to the officer of the day and then walked down the gangway and back toward his aircraft.

The officer of the day, a Royal Navy lieutenant had heard the exchange. It confused him to no end. Here was a woman who was a member of the armed services and a pilot? Unheard of! Well, the orders stated that she was a lieutenant in the Indian Army. Perhaps they did things differently in India. Either way, he decided it was critical to get this leather wrapped ... woman below decks before something happened on his watch. He shouted for his assistant, a young ensign, and issued formal orders. "Ensign Morrell, if you please, escort Lieutenant Bankroft to her quarters below." The ensign in his duty whites snapped to attention. Before he turned to guide Elizabeth below, the lieutenant said, "Lieutenant Bankroft, please stay in your quarters until further notice."

Elizabeth knew that the rank of lieutenant in the Royal Navy was equivalent to the rank of captain in the army. Confusing at best, but it was the nature of the service rivalries. She came to the position of attention, rendered a salute, and said, "Yes, sir!"

At that point, the ensign led her down a ladder and to her

quarters below decks. The ensign had some difficulty figuring out how he should address a female officer, so he spoke little and quickly departed as soon as Elizabeth was in her room. He was convinced that silence was probably the best practice, given nothing in his training had prepared him for such a challenge.

Elizabeth smiled to herself as she watched the door close. As with her previous voyage, the quarters were cramped with only a small wash basin and toilet, a pair of bunks and a small locker for her kit. Given the size of the ship and the number of men on board, Elizabeth was certain that cramped quarters were shared by everyone and this was likely the only berth available that offered any privacy. She immediately stripped off the flying suit and hung it on the hook on the back of the door. Almost immediately, Elizabeth felt lighter. The suit was heavy and it was also hot. She stripped down to her underwear and used the basin to wash up as best as she could. Once her ablutions were completed, Elizabeth pulled out the first of her two uniforms. First the stockings, then the skirt and finally the khaki blouse. She hung the jacket on a hanger in the locker. If she was going to be alone for what she already knew would be two days in the cabin, there didn't seem to be any reason to wear the jacket.

She carefully unpacked her few belongings from her bag. She hoped simply hanging the second uniform and her Raven uniform would allow them to air out. Now that she was free from the Sopwith Tabloid, she realized that the bag smelled of a mix of engine exhaust and motor oil. Perhaps separating the clothes from her bag would prevent that smell from being impregnated into what few clothes she had. After that was accomplished, Elizabeth sat on the bunk and began to write in her journal. While her hours as an "aviatrix" had been few, she wanted to capture what she learned during those hours.

After two days in her cabin on the fast cruiser, Elizabeth joined *HMFS Scimitar* at Karachi Harbor. She arrived at the loading dock thirty minutes prior to its departure. That was just long enough for her to take a few moments to look at the long silver lozenge that made up the body of the airship. *Scimitar* was the latest of the airships to join Indian service. This was its first flight "up the country" as it was said in India. The crew had ferried the airship from the Vickers manufacturing center in England along a circuitous route across the Mediterranean and Arabian Sea. The airship had undergone a full refit at the Navy Lines in Karachi Harbor and was headed north. Eventually, it would be based in Rawalpindi and serve as one of the three airships that cruised the skies over the restive tribal areas.

Elizabeth arrived carrying her single, now very heavy bag over her shoulder. It was filled with her leather flying suit, one uniform, and her Raven combat uniform. She wore her second FANY uniform with beret and carried her flying jacket over her left arm. Elizabeth was not entirely used to receiving salutes from men, but she got her share of practice as she walked through a group of enlisted men working on the airship. She climbed the loading dock and found a Royal Navy ensign with a clipboard and manifest.

Elizabeth handed the ensign her orders and said, "Lieutenant Bankroft with orders to fly to Fort Burnes."

The ensign was taken aback by a woman claiming military rank. He gave her a very serious inspection of her uniform and found that the rank was correct and she was wearing a campaign ribbon over her left pocket. She was carrying a leather flying jacket as well as what looked to be a very heavy and oil-stained leather bag. Since his arrival in India, he had seen many oddities both human and animal, but he had not been prepared to see women in uniform. He looked at the orders offered by this … lieutenant. They were issued by the Intelligence Department of the Mediterranean Fleet through a Rear Admiral in Constantinople and instructed all Navy personnel to deliver Lieutenant Elizabeth Bankroft by the fastest means necessary to Fort Burnes, Northwest Frontier. He looked down at the manifest issued by the port authority and, indeed, there was a listing of Bankroft, E. Indian Army. He swallowed hard and said, "Lieutenant Bankroft, welcome aboard."

Before she had traveled from Rawalpindi to Constantinople, Elizabeth had not thought twice about what it meant to be a woman in uniform. After her flight with Commander Shearing and her time aboard *HMS New Zealand*, Elizabeth had come to terms with how to cope in a man's world. She would be polite, but she would not be demure. She said, "Ensign, thank you. Is there a specific seat you want me to take or is the seating open? I do not want to intrude on a set of seats reserved for Indian Army or Royal Navy seniors."

"Lieutenant, you are our only passenger until we reach Rawalpindi. Take any seat you wish." In a slightly condescending tone, he said, "I hope you are not prone to sea sickness. I believe airship travel is often compared to sea travel."

Elizabeth couldn't help herself. She said, "Ensign, I just arrived on a fast cruiser and before that flew nearly 20 hours in a Royal Navy floatplane to get here. Also, this is not my first flight on an airship. I believe I will be fine on your airship, thank you." She smiled what she hoped to be a polite but firm smile.

The ensign was not entirely certain what to think about this exchange. Here was a young woman who outranked him who appeared to be most familiar with aircraft. He had yet to fly on an aeroplane and here was a lieutenant who had just flown 20 hours in a floatplane? He could only mumble, "Lieutenant Bankroft, just let me know if there is anything I can do to assist."

"Thank you, Ensign. I only have this one bag and I will stow it next to me on the seat. Please send my regards as your lone passenger to the airship commander." As she walked off the loading dock and into the passenger compartment, Elizabeth hoped she had not appeared sarcastic. Not too sarcastic.

The flight to Rawalpindi was uneventful. Elizabeth tried to stay awake, but the quiet rumble of the engines below deck and the soft rocking of the airship as it cruised along the Indus River valley was simply too hypnotic. She was asleep shortly after the airship left the loading dock.

It was night when Elizabeth woke. The airship headed north in the darkness. By her calculations, she would arrive in Rawalpindi at dawn and, depending the transfer of passengers, cargo and fuel, she should be at Fort Burnes, aka The Viceroy's College, by mid-day. Elizabeth was impressed with this new airship. It was clearly outfitted for military use, with less leather in the seating and fewer brass fittings than the airships on which she had flown to and from The Viceroy's College. There were small electric lights running along the length of the cabin with two sets of lenses. One clear, providing perfect white light, and one with a red filter so that the passengers did not lose their night vision when they departed the craft. Elizabeth expected that if she went down one of the ladders to the rear of the cabin, she would find the same weapons as on the other airships — maxim guns capable of firing hundreds of bullets a minute. Given the low level of engine noise, Elizabeth wondered if the lowest deck of *HMFS Scimitar* housed a gasoline-powered engine rather than small steam engines used in the airships on her previous travels.

The lighted cabin meant that when Elizabeth looked out the porthole next to her seat, she saw only her face reflected in the glass. Despite her actual age, that reflection was of a woman rather than a teenager. Before leaving her cabin in the fast cruiser, Elizabeth had pulled her hair into a severe bun at her neck so that her hair did not fill her beret and create an image of a chef's toque rather than military head-gear. She could see the beginnings of dark circles under her eyes from the nights of restless and interrupted sleep. All this passed before her in the reflection. The deaths of two men at her hands also weighed heavily on Elizabeth. She understood that in each case she had been fighting for her life, but that didn't make the killing any easier. She was sure most of her former classmates from The Viceroy's College had been less challenged in their first years of service to the Crown.

Suddenly, she noticed a second face in the reflection. It was the Ensign who had welcomed her on board. Elizabeth thought for a moment. Ensign …? She realized she had not asked his name.

"The commander sends his compliments, Lieutenant Bankroft. He wondered if you would like to join us on the bridge. It will be dawn soon and we should have a glorious view of the great mountains of India."

Elizabeth did her best to not sound like the thrilled youth that she knew she was. She said, "Ensign …?"

"Danforth, Lieutenant."

"Ensign Danforth, I would be very pleased to join you. I need a moment in whatever comfort station you might have on board."

"Comfort?"

"Sorry, the loo, ensign."

This time the ensign blushed. "Of course. The head is in the rear of this compartment just before the ladder to the lower decks. There is even some running water if you prime the pump with the foot pedal."

"Wait right here, Ensign Danforth. I will be right back."

Elizabeth walked to the rear of the compartment. When

she returned, she looked slightly more put together. She pulled on her leather flying jacket, which had served earlier as her blanket, placed the wool beret on her head at what she had decided was the appropriate military angle, and said, "Ensign, lead on and I will follow."

Danforth walked to the front of the passenger cabin and opened the companionway door. They walked up a short flight of stairs and, suddenly, Elizabeth was on the bridge of the airship. The first thing Elizabeth realized was the entire command cabin was a cathedral of glass panels from floor to ceiling. This allowed the commander and his co-pilot full visibility during flight and, Elizabeth assumed, most importantly when they were docking and departing from military posts. Behind the two leather-wrapped command seats were three other positions, one for the Marconi radio wireless operator, one for the navigator and one serving as the flight engineer's position. The latter allowed for direct control of the airship's engines from this forward compartment. Given the fact that the navigator's seat was empty, Elizabeth assumed Ensign Danforth held that role. Elizabeth arrived just as the sun was beginning to illuminate the great mountain chain of the Himalayas, hundreds of miles to the east, and the Pamir mountains directly to the north.

Ensign Danforth cleared his throat and said, "Lieutenant Bankroft is here, sir."

A tall man stood up from the command seat and walked over to Elizabeth. He offered his hand and said, "Commander Roderick Smythe."

Elizabeth looked at Smythe in his Royal Navy uniform with brass buttons and yellow stripes on his sleeve detailing his rank. He was well over six feet tall with silver grey hair cut short and a silver beard clipped in a style like that worn by the King. His broad shoulders were emphasized by his wool deck coat. He was exactly Elizabeth's image of a Royal Navy officer in command of a warship. Elizabeth shook the offered hand and said, "Sir, it is a rare privilege to meet you and see the bridge of a Royal Navy airship."

Smythe smiled and said, "It is a little breathtaking, no? When I volunteered for the airship service, I hadn't expected much. Most of our airships a few years ago were nothing more than gasbags with a small wicker basket hung beneath. The Royal Navy has decided to test out these monsters in India before deploying them anywhere else in the world. Honestly, few outside the Admiralty and the War Ministry have ever seen one of these warships of the air."

Elizabeth tried to sound as adult as possible, "Sir, it is not anything like I expected. It is well and truly magnificent. A marvel of the Empire."

"I wanted you to see this so that you could measure your experience against your experience with my classmate Shearing and his kite. We were both selected for aviation. After flight school, the Navy decided I was too tall and, honestly, too heavy to fly aeroplanes." He pointed to his large frame housed in the deck coat that ended at his knees. "I ended up in airships and I don't regret it at all. All the challenges of flight plus plenty of room to stretch." Smythe smiled and continued, "Shearing sent a message ahead saying that you and he did a long-range flight from the Eastern Med to Aden. He reckons it is the longest operational flight to date for the Tabloid. And, he said you received some stick time during the flight. Well done!"

Elizabeth swallowed hard. She could have imagined the aviation community in the Royal Navy was small, but she hadn't expected her name to come up. She said, "It was exciting to be sure. Commander Shearing was kind enough to give me a chance to fly."

"He just needed the sleep, the lazy bones. Still, flight time is flight time. Perhaps the Navy will eventually get you fully qualified. Who knows what women can do in this new century! What do you think, Danforth?"

The ensign seemed equally captured by his commander's presence and took a second to respond. Finally, he said, "Why not, sir? Why not?"

Smythe stopped smiling and offered a more serious tone. He said, "I understand we are going to pick up a team in Rawalpindi and then deliver you to Ft. Burnes. After that, the *Scimitar* is going to be involved in what the Navy simply called *special service*." Smythe said the last two words in a manner suggesting both enthusiasm but also caution. "I don't suppose you know what that service will be?"

After a few seconds, Elizabeth realized that Smythe was seriously asking her a question. She offered the only answer she knew, "Sir, I am as much in the dark as you are. As I told Commander Shearing, one day I was working on the Intelligence Bureau mission in Constantinople and the next I received orders to report to Ft. Burnes as soon as possible. I can only say for certain that it must be a special mission for that sort of instruction to arrive."

"Are you familiar with the team?"

"I suspect so, sir. We are ..." Elizabeth didn't know how to translate the Ravens into anything a Navy commander might understand. Finally, she said, "We are a small unit that handles problems that require ... discretion."

Smythe put his hands on his hips and laughed loud and long. "Discretion, eh? Well, I wonder how a combat airship fits into that sort of mission."

Elizabeth offered a simple comment, "Sir, the last mission I attended, a combat airship was essential to mission success."

"Do tell, Lieutenant!"

Elizabeth realized she was on thin ice. Telling a story about the last time she served with the Ravens would likely put her in trouble with both the Ravens and with Guru Naismith. She decided to make a hasty retreat. She used just a small bit of mesmerism voice to ensure the commander would not press her as she said, "Sir, I think you will hear more when we get to Ft. Burnes. Until then, I can only say that the combat airship was essential to our survival in Afghanistan. Other than that, I fear I should not say more."

Smythe looked bemused by this answer, but he decided to let this lieutenant off with a simple response, "So be it, Lieutenant. I will await the discussion at Ft. Burnes. In the meantime, if you would like to stay here on the command deck for a bit, I think you will find the sunrise magnificent and the approach to Rawalpindi worth the time on your feet. Walk down these steps to the observer position. It provides the best view. I will ask you to return to the main cabin before we make our approach to the cantonment. Now, I must return to my duties."

Elizabeth watched the morning sunrise from the lofty perch of the airship. Once the airship crossed over Attock Fort and angled away from the Indus River and toward Rawalpindi in the Punjabi plain, she returned to the passenger deck. She spent the rest of the time as they approached Rawalpindi thinking about the upcoming reunion with her colleagues in the Ravens. The last time she was with them, their focus was on rescuing her parents from both the Russians and Afghans. She assumed her recent work against the Germans had some bearing in the upcoming mission. Still, she knew that she would remain the most junior of the Ravens and, as such, she would have to follow the lead of the more experienced men and women on the team. Elizabeth spent a few minutes meditating as they approached the Rawalpindi airship dock. She wanted to appear calm and deliberate as she met her colleagues. That was not as easy as it sounded given her age and inexperience. As she focused her mind through counting her breaths, she pushed the tensions away into a far corner of her mind. By the time she felt the airship bump against the dock, she was prepared as any teenager could be.

Ensign Danforth came up from the command deck and said, "We are going to take on fuel here. After that is completed, we will welcome the new passengers. Do you want to stay here? The skipper says it is your choice."

Elizabeth was not quite ready for the reunion, so she said, "I will stay here. I have to complete a bit of paperwork and this will give me some quiet time to do so."

"Probably no more than twenty minutes before the rest of the passengers arrive."

Elizabeth looked at the watch on her left wrist. She had changed the time before they departed Karachi airship dock. She wanted to be sure of the time and she was certain a navigator would be able to provide accurate time. She asked, "I make it 0730hrs, correct?"

Danforth pulled out a large brass hunter watch from his jacket pocket. Like Shearing's watch, it was a chronograph with a running second-hand started from an extension on the winder. Unlike most hunters that Elizabeth had seen in India and in England, his watch did not have a white porcelain dial. Instead, it had a black dial with large hands with radium paint. He said, "Precisely 0732hrs if you want to reset your watch."

Elizabeth nodded and said, "Thank you. I fear I lost track when I reset my watch to this time zone."

"Easily done, Lieutenant. That's why we maintain two clocks on board — one for the local time and one for Greenwich and each of us has a hunter as well. If you will excuse me, I have to go down to the dock and file our new manifest and flight plan with the command." He turned and walked over to the door at the rear of the passenger cabin, opened it and walked out onto the dock.

Next, the engineer for the airship came up from the

command deck. He was a burly man in an ill-fitting flight jacket and navy trousers. He was wearing three pips on his sleeve. A lieutenant in Navy parlance, a captain rank in the Army. He nodded to Elizabeth and said, "No time to chat. I must supervise the refueling. If there is one time when these gasbags are at risk, it is while we are refueling."

Elizabeth almost forgot protocol when she said, "Risk?"

The engineer looked over his shoulder as he headed to the door. "Lieutenant, we use highly combustible hydrogen gas to make this ship lighter than air. A spark or two and we have a very dangerous situation. I'm going down to watch as the team pumps the gasoline into our fuel tanks."

Elizabeth had not thought twice about how explosive hydrogen would be in the airships. Suddenly she regretted her flip remark to Danforth that she would stay on board.

Elizabeth watched from the porthole as the engineer supervised the refueling. She was lost in thought when Danforth came through the passenger cabin door and said, "Your colleagues are coming aboard."

Elizabeth stood up, straightened her uniform skirt and waited to see familiar faces. The first to arrive was another woman dressed in military wools. Elizabeth said, "Beverly!"

Beverly Mansfield smiled as she looked at her young colleague. She jokingly said, "Captain Mansfield to you, Lieutenant."

Elizabeth was taken aback until she saw the smile. She walked over to Beverly and offered her hand. "I hope all is well."

"As well as can be expected in Mesopotamia, Elizabeth. I didn't mind the orders to leave the river valley before the mosquitos and heat arrive. Do you know why we are gathering?"

"I don't know. One minute I was working in Constantinople

and the next, I received a message from Guru Naismith. It might have something to do with some of my collection on German activity, but, then again, it might not."

"Germans! We certainly have plenty of them in Mesopotamia."

A new voice entered the conversation. "Elizabeth, it is very good to see you!"

Elizabeth looked over Beverly's shoulder to see another familiar face. This time she was the one to offer faux protocol, "Major, it is very good to see you."

Beverly said, "Don't talk to him like that, he already has a big head since he was promoted."

Alexander Mansfield said, "I only put up with this sort of insubordination from my wife."

Elizabeth said, "I never knew you were married."

Beverly smiled and said, "We weren't the last time we met. Our mutual annoyances in Mesopotamia just led us to the inevitable conclusion that we were meant for each other."

"Something I wonder about every day ... oof."

Alexander would probably have continued but Beverly had offered a sharp elbow to his stomach. Beverly said, "Oh. I'm so sorry, dear. I didn't realize you were so close."

Next on board was Eugenia. She was in civilian clothes that would probably have been more common for a rider in a polo match than for a military traveler. She was carrying a leather flying jacket under one arm and a Gladstone in the other. She dropped the bag and walked over to Elizabeth. She grabbed her by the shoulders and gave her a strong hug. "Elizabeth, it is good to see you!"

"Likewise, Eugenia. Still in Tashkent?"

"Indeed, and I could use another Russian speaker in case you want to change venues after the operation."

"I thought you worked with Christopher on the Afghan side of the border?"

The look on her colleagues' faces made it very clear that

her lighthearted comment had hit a raw nerve. Beverly finally spoke. "Chris died late last year. Cholera."

Elizabeth lowered her head and voice and said, "I'm sorry. I didn't know."

Eugenia said, "Risks we all take, Elizabeth."

The last two Ravens entered the cabin. Jonathan and Martha were both in what could only be described as blended costumes. They wore the long shirts of the shalwar kamiz, but instead of the pajama pants, they wore khaki trousers and very dusty riding boots. Jonathan looked up and said, "Well, that was some trip. Horseback to Assam, carriage to Simla, second-class carriage by train to Rawalpindi. I am ready to rest. Anyone bring tea?"

Martha looked at her colleague and said, "I have had to listen to this since our rendezvous in Assam. You would think all the man can do is moan!"

Danforth closed the cabin door and said, "Ladies and gentlemen, we will be departing soon. Please take your seats. We need to get started on our final leg to Ft. Burnes soon while the winds are favourable."

The team sat on both sides of the airship cabin. They were headed toward an unknown mission in a yet-to-be-identified place. All they knew for sure was the Ravens were assembled.

Conspiracies Uncovered, Mysteries Unsolved

Early June 1914 — Constantinople

FRANCIS AND MARY BANKROFT WERE SITTING IN THE OPULENT TEAROOM IN the Pera Palace overlooking the Golden Horn. Across the table from the two British spies was Count Naglieff of the Tsar's Intelligence Service. On the table was a full tea service and a stacked tray offering a mix of sweet and savoury mid-afternoon delights.

Naglieff said, "I always wondered about the English habit of taking afternoon tea. If this is an example of what that means, I believe I need to introduce this habit to my colleagues in St. Petersburg. Of course, if it truly became a habit, I think we would need to have an afternoon ride as well as afternoon tea if we intended to fit into our uniforms."

Mary smiled as she enjoyed a freshly baked macaroon. She said, "Sasha, you don't need to act like Francis and indulge in everything on the tray."

Francis had his mouth full of a cucumber sandwich, so he couldn't defend himself. Naglieff laughed and said, "Well said and well timed, Mary!"

Francis swallowed and then took a sip of tea. "If you are through using me as the source of your amusement, I would like to call this council of war to order."

Mary nodded and Naglieff smiled. Francis continued, "I found out yesterday afternoon that Sasha was also attacked last week while walking in *petit champ de morts.*"

Mary smiled and offered an ironic comment, "I suppose an assassin's attack was to be expected in a cemetery, no?"

Naglieff understood the irony and said, "It is a quiet and beautiful place for a promenade. The Ottomans often mix gardens with their cemeteries. It isn't like our dreary locations. Especially in the spring, it is awash with colour. Oh, and it is also a quiet place to meet a contact."

Mary nodded. "So, the attack was not a coincidence?"

"If you mean: did I have a planned time to be in the garden? Yes, you are correct. My contact disappeared and I fear his body has been deposited in the Sea of Marmara. That is certainly where I put my attacker."

Mary encouraged the Russian with a smile and said, "Do tell."

"Ever since I helped Francis handle the attack in the hotel, I am armed everywhere I go. I can't take my trusty Smith and Wesson revolvers, they are a bit too conspicuous. But, my great coat has more than enough room in its pockets for a brace of Browning automatics."

"My favourites!"

"So Francis has told me. Well, I was attacked from both front and rear so the ambush was well planned. Again, it was most interesting that these men were not Turks. They were Arabs of some sort given their grooming and their clothes."

"You didn't ask?"

"They didn't give me a chance. There were three of them

and I was a bit busy at the time making sure that they didn't deliver cold steel into my body." Naglieff smiled and continued, "I fired the first round and wounded the man to my front," he shook his head, "making a rather nasty hole in my coat pocket. The other two came at me from behind. I suppose they didn't expect me to dodge their rather violent scimitar thrusts. They must have used their swords like axes on previous victims. More than a few years in the Tsar's service has taught me how to avoid that sort of foolishness."

"Two more rounds then?"

"One was dispatched with another round from the Browning. Unfortunately, the Browning jammed in the pocket. Before I could pull out the second pistol, my last attacker was upon me." Naglieff rolled up the left sleeve of his jacket to reveal a large plaster over a wound that ran from his left wrist to his elbow. "You would be amazed how much blood comes out of a sword wound."

Francis said, "I have some experience."

Mary nodded and said, "As do I."

"Well, the wound did make me angry. I reached out with my right hand and I seemed to have snapped the villain's neck. It wasn't my plan to kill him with that strike. I wanted to question him before I killed him. I suppose my anger got the best of me."

"So, no luck in determining why you were attacked?"

"Mrs. Bankroft, please don't think I am a beserker. The cemetery remained quiet, so I took the time to inspect their clothes. Not that they had anything to help identify them, but I did find nearly 1000 piastres in their pockets and a map showing my expected route to the cemetery. I noticed that the map was very reminiscent of a style common among German military sketch maps. I have some experience in that regard."

Mary smirked and said, "Which I am sure you will be happy to tell us another time?"

"Perhaps," was all Naglieff offered to that comment.

Francis said, "So, assassins are targeting us. Is our work so threatening to the Germans that they intend to risk being confronted by our embassies?"

"I suspect the use of surrogates with no known links to Germany is sufficient ..."

Mary offered, "Disguise?"

"I was about to say distance, but disguise will do. I think they do not like our efforts to uncover their activities with the Young Turks. I also think they are preparing for war and they want to have us out of the way when that day comes."

Francis put down his tea cup. "War? With Germany? How exactly would that happen? Our King, your Tsar, and the Kaiser are all related. They know the importance of the current balance of power. We have our differences to be sure, but those differences are not enough to fight a war. It is difficult to imagine."

Mary shook her head. "Pardon my husband's lack of imagination. I can certainly imagine a world at war if our respective governments are foolish. Some of our alliances are fragile and others are linked to cultural issues that could take over. It would be a calamity to be sure, but I can see how the Germans might be preparing for war. The shadow world we live in is a playground for ambition. If the Germans see us as limiting their regional goals, I can see them using clandestine means to remove us from the gameboard."

Naglieff filled his teacup from the samovar at their table. He put a sugar cube in his mouth, poured himself another cup of strong black tea and took a sip. He said, "I fear you English are too trusting. You don't understand the oriental mind the way we Russians do. After all, we lived under the Tartar yoke."

Mary smiled and said, "Over four hundred years ago."

"It leaves scars on the culture, Mrs. Bankroft. We don't forget. In any case, I suspect the Germans intend to weaken your empire by using the Ottoman ruler's status as the Muslim caliph. That could mean influence in the Muslim population of your empire. I certainly would use that lever if I was working against you."

"As you did in Afghanistan."

Naglieff smiled. "Francis, I never used Islam as a tool against you. Just good, old-fashioned greed."

"So, what is their goal with Russia?"

"I think these new Turkish leaders have their eyes on the Caucasus or perhaps Turkestan. Centuries ago, they were in command of virtually the entire region and they wish to expand their empire again. The Germans are simply interested in using the Ottoman Empire as a place where they can train and dispatch anarchists against my country. We have a loyal population who love the Tsar as their holy father, but there are always going to be dissidents. Over the past decade, those dissidents have been educated by the anarchist Prince Kropotkin, basically, assassination by pistol or bomb. You must know of him since your government allowed him to spend years in exile in London."

Mary was aware that the British legal system tolerated political exiles of many different stripes. It was something that her father railed about during every dinner they shared when on leave from India. She used just a touch of mesmerism to calm Naglieff and to change the subject. "So, Sasha, what do we do about this?"

"I think we have to find the Germans who are fomenting these troubles and ..."

"Yes?"

"Well, the Ottoman Empire is a dangerous place. There are villains everywhere. The attacks on yourselves and on me prove that to be the case. If we can find out with some precision who is making this happen, we need to work together to resolve this problem once and for all."

Francis nodded and said, "And if that resolution involves

some violence, then so be it." He asked, "Do you have a lead to the Germans involved?"

"I believe I do. He is not a member of the German mission here in Constantinople. He is a senior academic and advisor to the Kaiser. Max Von Oppenheim."

Mary nodded and said, "I have heard of Von Oppenheim. He is an expert in oriental studies. He speaks Turkish, Arabic, and I believe Persian. But, Sasha, he is an academic in Berlin."

"With foot soldiers throughout the region. I know your people in Persia have run across Wilhelm Wassmuss."

"Definitely an agent provocateur."

"Well, Wassmuss is in the region. He was in Baghdad last year. And, then there are two men you know only too well." Naglieff stared directly at Mary.

"The O'Connells?"

"Indeed, the O'Connells. They are currently in Damascus working for the Germans. Certainly, you could eliminate them from the gameboard? They are English after all."

"It is not as easy as that, Sasha."

"Perhaps you would prefer if I took that action? Then, in return, you could work against some of my difficult targets."

Francis wasn't quite sure how to answer that offer, so instead he redirected the conversation. "But who precisely is after us? The Caucasus, Damascus and Baghdad are far distant parts of the Ottoman Empire. Problems to be sure, but before we can make that reach, we need to know who is pulling the strings of these assassins." Naglieff took another sip of tea. He shook his head and said, "I agree, but I have yet to find the answer to that question."

Mary said, "I may have a thread we can pull that might unravel this complex carpet of intrigue."

Naglieff laughed and said, "Why am I surprised?"

Francis said to Naglieff, "I haven't heard this, so we are both surprised."

Mary took a small cake from the tray and then filled her

teacup. As she started to eat the cake, Francis put his hand on her arm. "Please, do not leave us in suspense."

Mary finished her bite of cake and said, "As you both know, I am working outside the mission. So, that means that I can travel about with far less scrutiny than you two warriors. I am, after all, only a woman."

Naglieff had taken a sip of tea and choked on that comment. "Hardly just a woman."

"Well, we start by considering the question of who would benefit most from our murders. Of course, it is a difficult question to answer because there are many in the Sublime Porte who might benefit. It is easy to say it is the Germans because all of the attempts have been paid with German gold. However, I know a bit about the German psyche as well as the previous actions of Von Oppenheim and Wassmuss. So far, they have been interested in preparing for war, but they haven't been willing to conduct war in the shadows. That would be *nicht in ordnung*. Not proper." She stopped for another bite of cake and a sip of tea.

"So, I ask myself who might take on the job of eliminating us. My first thought was the O'Connells. I have little doubt that their hatred of our two empires would manifest itself in murder. But, as Francis pointed out, they are far distant. It is the only reason I eliminated them."

Mary paused again for tea. "In the past month, I have established a network of women who are equally invisible in the man's world of the Young Turks. They are the women who clean and cook in the various offices of the CUP. It turns out that late last year, Enver Pasha decided the war department needed a special security enterprise to address various ethnic threats to the Empire. The result was a secret organization called *Tashkilaat-e-mahsusa*."

Naglieff translated from Turkish, "The Special Organization? How special?"

Mary said, "I have yet to determine precisely how special.

What I do know is *Tashkilaat* works with both the war depart-ment and the ministry of interior in eliminating threats to the CUP and to the integrity of the Ottoman Empire. They are aggressively building reporting networks in Eastern Ana-tolia against the Armenians and the Kurds. They see both ethnic groups as likely allies of the Tsar or the Persian shah. They are building networks in the Arab provinces. In Arabia, they see the threat coming from Great Britain. The organi-zation makes extensive use of violent criminals released from Ottoman prisons with the promise of pardons from the Caliph if they serve *Tashkilaat*."

Francis said, "That begins to explain why our erstwhile assassins have been so … poorly prepared."

Naglieff nodded. "It also explains why each of the attempts has been made by individuals who are from different parts of the Empire."

Mary continued, "The head of the organization is a CUP military officer known under the pseudonym as Suleyman Askeri Beg. It seems hard to imagine this would be his true name since *askeri* simply means soldier. I am working on a source who cleans the building where *Tashkilaat* has its head-quarters. I have made only a little progress so far. I may have to find a way into the building myself."

Naglieff smiled. "Hannibal said I will find a way or make one."

Francis rubbed his hands and then reached for another cucumber sandwich. "My thoughts exactly."

Mary took a moment to select a particularly interesting pastry with a half apricot on top. Before popping the pastry into her mouth, she said, "So, we have uncovered a con-spiracy but there are still mysteries before us."

A Lesson to Us All

June 1914 — The Viceroy's College

WHEN THE AIRSHIP ARRIVED, GURU MARIAN WAS WAITING AT THE DOCK TO take the Ravens to their quarters. They were stationed for the time being in a small barracks normally used by one of the Guides companies when they were placed in isolation before an operation. The commander of Ft. Burnes' military contingent took the airship commander and his crew to separate quarters that they would use until mission planning was complete.

The next day, the Ravens and Lieutenant Commander Smythe arrived at Naismith's briefing room precisely at 0900hrs. Smythe looked over at the transformation of his passengers from a mix of civilian and military garb to the uniform of the Ravens: deep-blue blouse and trousers, black boots and no insignia. He said to the assembled team, "I will admit I was not expecting a team of night marauders joining me this morning."

Marian said, "Sir, this is our uniform. We often are night

marauders, but to our commanders we are known as the Ravens."

From the back of the room, a voice said, "And Ravens are often needed when no one else can do the job."

Elizabeth was convinced Guru Naismith appeared out of thin air. Smythe asked the question that was on Elizabeth's mind: "Sir, did you just walk through that wall?"

Naismith smiled and said, "Now Commander Smythe, you know that's just not possible." Naismith walked silently over to Smythe and offered his hand. "Lieutenant Colonel Burgess Naismith at your service. And, if you don't mind, we Ravens are informal, so you can choose Burgess or Naismith. The Ravens simply call me Guru but that's because they were my students years ago."

Smythe took Naismith's hand and looked at the slight figure with the stunning green eyes, shaved head and very tight beard. Dressed in the same blue uniform as the rest of the Ravens, Naismith looked so much like an illustration of a magician from a children's book that Smythe said, "Guru it shall be. After all, I want you to teach me to walk through walls. It would have come in handy in some of the more tedious staff meetings I have attended. You can call me Rod. Most of my colleagues do."

Naismith smiled back at the navy officer, "Rod, we will do our best not to be too tedious. Of course, you won't be able to share all of our secrets." Naismith turned to the assembled Ravens and said, "Let's go to the briefing table and begin our challenge."

They walked over to a large oak map table centered to the far left of Naismith's desk. Spread across the table was an Indian Geographical Survey map of Baluchistan. It detailed the entire coastline from Karachi in Sind Province to the border with Persia. The top of the map depicted the northern Baluchistan-Afghanistan border. The map focused on the geographic features such as deserts and mountain ranges. A small number of villages were identified, with only Quetta and Kalat listed as cities. Naismith stood at the middle of the table looking down at the map from north to south. He said, "Ravens, circle around the table if you please. Rod, I need you next to me."

Once the team encircled the table, Naismith began. "Let me start by setting the context. The Special Branch of the Indian police have focused on both non-violent and violent Indian revolutionary movements for the past dozen years. Most of the violent movements are based outside of India, primarily London, but also in Paris, Tokyo and San Francisco. It is a lesson to us of a growing globalism in our modern world. Indians have emigrated to the four corners of the earth to work for the Empire as well as other countries. Some of those emigres have decided that the only way for India to be governed fairly is through violence. As they traveled the world, they were exposed to the philosophy of anarchism and the importance of the assassin and the bomber."

Naismith paused for a moment to see if any of his audience knew of his Anglo-Indian ancestry or saw the irony in an Anglo-Indian military officer arguing against militancy. There was none, so he continued. "Even in London, the anarchists are active. A few years ago, in 1908, an engineering student from University College in London, Madan Lal Dhingra, assassinated Sir William Curzon Wyllie of the Whitehall Indian Office. After committing the crime, he was captured and hanged. It was at that point the government took notice on the penetration of the ideology of anarchy in the Indian community. The Indian government accepted that these were not small, ineffectual groups of angry young men in coffee shops and pubs across the Empire. These were men willing to kill and, more importantly, willing to die for their beliefs. There are always groups of angry young men who are convinced that the world as they know it is working against them. This is the nature of young men. It doesn't help that the British leadership has been unwilling to expand Indian participation in government of the Raj." Naismith paused again to assess his audience. It was clear that Smythe chafed at the idea that Indian "natives" might have a legitimate cause for frustration. Naismith realized he would need to tread lightly to keep the lieutenant commander on side.

"What our colleague Elizabeth has identified is a plot by the German Empire to exacerbate the militancy by supporting selected groups. In a most recent intelligence operation, Elizabeth uncovered significant details of German intrigues in Singapore, Hong Kong, Calcutta, and Bombay. Dozens of Indian insurrectionists are receiving guidance, money, and even training by the Germans. What the Germans have done is focus anger against the British government. Once they accomplish that, they gather the men in foreign locations where the Indian émigré population is largest. We know this in part from the work of Elizabeth who collected the information from two German agents returning home from a successful effort in East Asia."

Elizabeth nodded but kept silent. Naismith continued. "This is consistent with information that Beverly acquired, that a German intelligence officer named Wilhelm Wassmuss is working against our interests in Mesopotamia and in Persia. Worse still, two of our own, James and Michael O'Connell, are working with the Germans in their nefarious plots."

Smythe had been standing behind Naismith for the briefing, but he could not stay silent at that point. "Traitors! We have to do something about this, Guru."

Naismith nodded and said, "We should always remember that while we are successful in gaining access to secrets by convincing others to commit treason, there are always potential traitors in our midst. My own teachers made it clear that when we investigate the minds of men, we need to remember who we are in our hearts. If we cannot keep on the straight path, we need to stop. Clearly, the O'Connells have chosen a different and dangerous road. I promise you, Rod, there will be retribution."

Elizabeth listened to the venom in Naismith's voice. Even though she no longer held any emotion for her former classmate, she feared what Naismith might do to a traitor.

What Do You Desire?

July 1914 — Damascus

MICHAEL WAS SITTING AT HIS DESK IN THE APARTMENT HE SHARED WITH HIS father. He was finishing a new set of reports for the Germans. The Arab revolutionaries in Damascus were easy to engage and more than willing to tell a young English traveler their plans. They hoped to gain the support of England in their effort to overthrow the Ottoman government in Arabia. They didn't have any real idea how to do that, but they certainly were willing to meet with an Englishman and introduce him to their co-conspirators. Michael thought the entire idea of an Arab revolt would be impossible. The elite of Damascus distrusted their counterparts in Baghdad and both sets of conspirators hated the Bedouin who lived in the desert to the south. Family, clan and tribal feuds would prevent their efforts. Still, the Germans were pleased with his reporting. At the end of the day, that was all that mattered because they had promised that they would help Michael and his father return to Ireland. And, if they returned to Ireland, they could be part of the Irish revolutionary movement to liberate their home from the British. So, Michael provided detailed reports on the feckless conspiracies.

Michael must have dozed for a moment. He woke with a start to see a skull that seemed to float in the air above his desk. Michael had become an adept practitioner of the illusory body over the past year using his own skills to wander invisibly through the coffee houses of Damascus. He automatically assumed that the skull was simply a projection of some other powerful figure. He had seen Elizabeth Bankroft's efforts, but those efforts did not include an image of a skull. So, who?

Michael concentrated and projected his own image into the ether. He faced the skull and said, "Who are you and what do you want?"

The skull asked, "The real question Michael O'Connell is what do you want?"

Michael was not about to share his thoughts with an unknown practitioner of the mystic arts. He asked again, "Who are you?"

"Michael O'Connell, you need to know that a great war is coming. It will mean the beginning of the end of the British Empire. The real question is: when that happens, what will you do to accomplish your desires?"

"Skull, you speak as if you know the future."

"The future, the present, and the past are all creations of your pitiful little mind. What you need to consider is whether you are prepared for the future. Will you profit from the chaos or will you be swallowed up in it?"

"Skull, you are talking riddles."

"Riddles that you need to ponder, young one. Do you have the strength? You will face a choice to kill or be killed. Can you kill, Michael O'Connell?"

Before he could answer, the skull faded into nothingness. Michael was completely puzzled. Who was this specter and why was it asking him questions? He lit a small candle and stared into the flame as he meditated on the questions asked. What were his desires? And what would he be willing to do to accomplish his goals?

Where Do We Go
When the Curtain Falls?

29 June 1914 — Constantinople

FRANCIS AND MARY BANKROFT WERE ENJOYING A LATE AFTERNOON SAIL IN the sea of Marmara. The late spring winds were intermittent and that made for a lazy and enjoyable time on the water. It also allowed the two British agents uninterrupted time to consider the current state of their operations in Constantinople. Those operations were neither lazy nor enjoyable, but they were important.

They dropped their sail in a cove about 5 miles from their home and were watching sailboats and steamers work their way across the Sea of Marmara headed either out the Dardanelles to the Mediterranean or toward the Constantinople docks. As the sun approached the horizon, they opened a bottle of chilled Greek wine and relaxed.

After a few minutes of amiable silence Mary said, "My sources are beginning to provide real information on the nature of the *Tashkila'at* and its goals. There is no doubt that they are using violent criminals as a means of conducting their operations while keeping it completely deniable. The Germans are not in direct contact with Askari, but they make their intentions known to Enver Pasha and he transmits those same intentions to the *Tashkila'at*. My dear, I think it entirely possible that our days may be numbered here in Constantinople."

Francis nodded, "I have similar reporting coming from the Turkish Army. The only element within the Turkish government that supports Britain is the Turkish Navy."

Mary nodded, "And why not? They are being trained by the Royal Navy and this summer take ownership of British-made battleships. They have everything to gain."

"Which is why my admiral regularly criticizes my reporting as too alarmist. He is surrounded by Turkish admirals who do everything they can to encourage the relationship. After all, one of the ships, the *Sultan Osman I,* is a dreadnought-class battleship and the *Resadiye* is a battlecruiser that can match nearly anything the Russians have in their fleet. Between these two, the Ottomans will control the Black Sea or the Eastern Mediterranean. Admiral Limpus is unlikely to see the growing power of the German Army inside the CUP leadership. Sadly, Limpus has greater influence over the ambassador than yours truly. I suppose it is lucky that I don't have to clear my reporting with Limpus or the ambassador before I send it to Winslow-Heath."

"What does Sasha say about all of this?"

"He says we are fools to sell warships to the Young Turks when they are so close to the Germans. He is such a pessimist. He is convinced there will be a world war."

"Russians certainly have a reason to be pessimistic when you look at their history."

"No doubt. But I still have a hard time believing in a modern world at war. Can you imagine the devastation? I am a soldier. I don't expect world peace. There will always be global conflicts and small wars where proxies will fight over colonial terrain. That is what we have been doing for about a century against the Russians in Asia." Francis shook his head, "But, a world conflict? What leader would take that risk?"

"Francis, you are a good man. A kind man who has witnessed death. You are also from a middle-class merchant family. Of course, you can't imagine a world conflict. As the daughter of a general, I have met politicians who have no understanding of what war looks like. They are interested only in their political conflicts in Parliament or in Whitehall. I suspect German politicians and the Tsar's entourage are much the same. They may not be as open in their goals as the Young Turks, but they are just as ambitious. They could make a very bad decision based on political ambition. Trust me, no matter how much I am amused by Sasha's Russian pessimism, I think he is right. And, if he is right, then we have to plan for what might be a dangerous time here in Constantinople."

"It might not be a bad thing to have a sailboat."

"No, it just might be ideal when the curtain falls."

Francis moved away from the tiller and sat close to his wife. She leaned into him as they kissed. On the shoreline a man stood in the shadow of a cypress tree. He watched through heavy, navy-style binoculars as they unfurled the sail and headed back to the yali.

As they approached the small dock below the yali, Francis said to Mary, "There is someone waiting for us."

"Did you bring the telescope?"

"Next to the hamper." Mary pulled out the small telescope, extended it and brought it to her right eye.

"It's Sasha. Didn't we agree not to meet at our residences?"

Francis nodded. Mary noticed his jawline tighten. She had known for years that he was terrible at hiding some of his emotions. Anger was one of them. She hoped to lessen that emotion by saying, "We need to find out why he broke the rules." Mary smiled and continued, "At least before you thrash him."

Francis laughed and said, "That obvious, eh?"

"Dear, we've been married a long time. It is definitely obvious to me."

Francis used a set of oars to pull the sailboat to the dock. Mary tossed the line to Sasha, who secured the bow to the dock. He helped Mary out of the sailboat as Francis wrapped a canvas cover over the sail and the boom. Once tied down, he jumped out and secured the stern.

"Francis, before you berate me for breaking our agreement, you need to know that the world has just turned upside down."

Mary expected her husband to offer a sarcastic remark. She could see their Russian colleague was upset. All she wanted was clarity. So, she offered a subtle wave to her husband that they used in the past. It meant: Let me handle this. Mary said, "Sasha, take a breath and tell me what is going on."

"I was at my embassy when the telegraph message came in. Archduke Franz Ferdinand of the Austrian Empire has just been assassinated in Sarajevo. We know little except the likely suspects were the Black Hand."

Francis walked up to his Russian colleague. He said quietly, "Sasha, what is the Black Hand and why do we care?"

Sasha said, "Francis, let me explain. The Black Hand is a Serbian nationalist organization. Like the CUP, it has infiltrated the highest levels of the Kingdom of Serbia. They want to expand Slavic rule to all of the Balkans. My country does not approve of the Black Hand, but the problem is we have a formal alliance with the Kingdom of Serbia. It could ..."

The rifle bullet hit the Russian in the shoulder. It spun him around and Francis caught him just before he entered the water. The second round missed them both primarily because he had bent over to catch Naglieff. After the second round zipped past them, Mary dropped to the dock. She turned to Francis and said, "This is not exactly how I expected to spend the evening."

"I am afraid our plan for a romantic interlude has been interrupted."

"How are we going to get out of this predicament?"

"Dear, give me a minute to think. If you would like to help, you could help me stop Sasha's bleeding."

Naglieff said, "That would be most appreciated."

The crack of a rifle close to them made both Mary and Francis look toward the house. Standing in the doorway of the yali, Bektashi worked the bolt on Francis' Mauser and fired another round in the direction of the hidden assassin. Each time he worked the Mauser action, Bektashi shouted something in Albanian. Francis knew no Albanian and said to Mary, "I wonder what he is shouting."

Naglieff smiled and said, "He is saying that all Turks are cowards. He is demanding the shooter come out and fight him, man-to-man."

Mary said, "I have always liked Bektashi. When did you show him your Mauser?"

Francis nodded, "When I first hired Bektashi, I decided he would either be trustworthy or I would have to resolve his employment ... permanently. Before you and Elizabeth arrived, I showed him some of the arms in the house."

Naglieff said, "In case you were wondering, I would actually prefer to go inside. It is rather cold out here on the dock."

Francis nodded. He said, "I think Bektashi was successful in convincing the shooter to leave. Let's give it a try." He helped Naglieff up, put Naglieff's good arm over his shoulder and raced to the door of the yali. Mary followed at a run.

When they reached the door, Mary put a hand on Bektashi's shoulder and said, "*Shabash, Agha Bektashi.*"

Bektashi beamed and replied in English, "Madam, it is an honor to defend the house of the Bankrofts." With that comment, he worked the Mauser action and once again fired into the woodline. As Mary looked at him, Bektashi smiled and said, "Madam, there was one round left in the magazine. It seemed a shame not to send one last message into the woods."

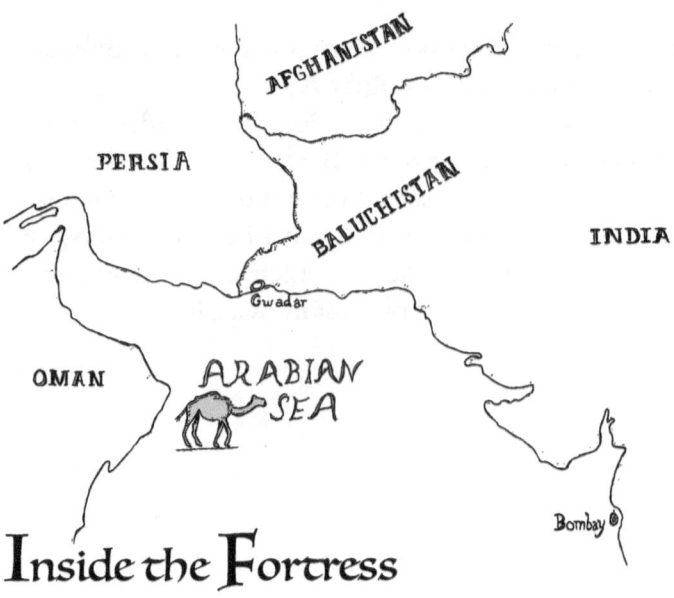

Inside the Fortress

July 1914 — Gwadar

ELIZABETH RODE ON THE CAMEL WITH BEVERLY. THEY WERE PRECEDED BY
Lieutenant Colonel Percy Molesworth Sykes riding a lithe
racing camel, and they were followed by a male camel carrying goods used as Sykes' cover as a copper merchant from
Persia. Sykes was a member of the Indian Intelligence Service in charge of the British mission in Khuzestan, Persia.
He spoke Persian, Arabic and Baluch and had explored the
borderlands between Persia and British India including a
visit to the coastal trading city of Gwadar. While Khuzestan
was on the other side of Persia, the mission was important
enough that he was picked as the only man for the job. On
his previous visit, he travelled as a Persian trader named Sayed
Mohammed Rashti specializing in copper goods. This time,
Sykes/Rashti was traveling with copper goods and his two
wives — Beverly and Elizabeth.

Elizabeth was suffering during the camel ride. It was a less
glamorous and more painful education than any previous

training. A camel saddle sways side-to-side and front-to-back with each stride as the animal walks slowly toward its destination. Left front and rear foot move together, then right front and rear foot. Slowly, tediously working across the desert sands. This was Elizabeth's first ride on a camel, so Beverly was in front of her controlling the camel's pace and direction as Elizabeth rode behind her on the same saddle. It was all to the better. The first day of travel was a nightmare for Elizabeth. She was dressed in proper Persian women's garb and with head covering and an abaya that served as her hejab or face covering as well as covering her shoulders and arms. She had never been seasick or airsick, but hours of the circular motion under a hot desert sun made her queasy. Beverly periodically looked back at her passenger. She understood completely. Luckily, this was definitely not her first time on a camel.

As they slowly approached the walled city of Gwadar, Elizabeth concentrated on the past month as a way to relieve her nausea. That period of time had started simply enough during Naismith's briefing of the overall mission and the parts that each of the Ravens would play.

Naismith stood before the large map of the borderlands between British India and the Persian Empire. The Indian Geographical Survey map showed a bleak desert environment and a rough coastline including a detailed map of a small t-shaped peninsula. He pointed to that peninsula and said, "Gwadar. Gwadar is on caravan trade routes as well as shipping routes for dhows that cross the Arabian Sea. It is also where our targets reside."

Martha queried, "Guru, I realize my work has taken me far to the East, but isn't Baluchistan part of the Indian Empire? Why would we tolerate such an act?"

Smythe interjected, "Gwadar is not part of the Empire. Gwadar is an outpost of the Emir of Muscat. It is the last remnant of the Indian colony of the Kingdom of Muscat. Like their holdings in Mombasa in Africa, Gwadar remains an important trading center for that kingdom. It is considered a freeport. Every pirate, slaver and smuggler in the Arabian Sea knows that Gwadar is the only deep-water port that they can use without fear of the Royal Navy. We wait for them in the open water, but they often escape along the rough coast-line to the west toward Persia or east to the tribal lands of the Makran, Las Bela and the Bugti. That coast is dangerous and the Royal Navy deep water vessels are not suited for the chase. One of the reasons why my craft, the *Scimitar,* has been sent to India is to work with some patrol boats out of Karachi to end the invulnerability of these pirates and slavers."

Naismith nodded and said, "As Rod said, Gwadar is a free-port and the Emir is far distant. His managers in the city are more interested in turning a profit than the rule of law. And, since they are careful in delivering some of that profit to Muscat, the Emir and his wazirs ask no questions."

At this point, each of the Ravens began to pay more atten-tion. Once he had their full attention, Naismith continued, "To be clear, this is important because we know the German government is training Hindu revolutionaries in Gwadar. It is only one of the training centers that the Germans estab-lished, but Gwadar is the largest and the most successful. They conduct the training inside a set of buildings that are supposedly a German commercial trading enterprise. They do work hard to maintain the fiction, buying cargo that fills German flagged trading vessels. What they don't disclose to the Gwadar authorities is that when the German vessels land at the port, they offload weapons and equipment for the Indian revolutionaries."

Alexander said, "Guru, what are we to do? It seems to me that this is more of a job for Royal Marines."

Naismith chuckled and said, "The Royal Marines might storm the city. They would certainly take the city. But, when they were done, they would know nothing more about these German intrigues. After all, we are not at war with Germany..."

Smythe interjected, "Yet."

Naismith continued, "Indeed. Not yet. But in the meantime, if the Royal Marines found Germans in the freeport of Gwadar, what could they do? On the other hand, if raiders came from the sea and the land and attacked a part of the freeport and left with no trace, what could the Emir in Muscat or the Kaiser in Berlin do? They might complain they were attacked by bandits from Baluchistan or from Persia, but they would have no reason to doubt the denials that would come from the courts in England or Persia. As I said from the beginning it is a challenge, but it is a challenge given to the Ravens to resolve."

Smythe shook his head, "Seven men and women?"

Naismith said, "Commander, these are the Ravens." He smiled and said, "Plus, we have the *Scimitar*!"

Smythe nodded and countered, "I am with your colleague who spoke of the Royal Marines. My solution would be to send one of our light cruisers into Gwadar harbor, dispatch an ultimatum, and if the Arab potentates don't comply, we flatten the city piece by piece."

Naismith smiled and said, "Spoken like a proper Royal Navy officer. My friend, there are many problems that should be resolved with shot and shell. However, our masters in India and in the Admiralty are far less audacious. They worry about international trade. They worry about how the Arabs who sell us oil might react. They worry about what might happen if members of the German contingent were killed. They worry night and day." Naismith paused and then said, "And after they worry, they call on the Ravens to accomplish the same mission. If it goes badly, they deny we even exist; if it goes well, they congratulate themselves on their brilliance."

"But what can the Ravens actually do?"

"With the help of *HMFS Scimitar* we can disrupt or, possibly, destroy the German training program in Gwadar. When it is done, no one will be able to complain to the British government because it won't look like the British government had anything to do with it."

Smythe smiled. He said, "So long as the *Scimitar* remains invisible."

"Ah, Lieutenant Commander Smythe, you can trust that your airship will be invisible to our adversaries. How that will be accomplished will be hard to explain."

Smythe shook his head and said, "You actually can walk through walls, can't you!"

Naismith said just above a whisper, "And, so much more, Commander. So much more so long as we have time on our side. And, in this operation, we do have time on our side."

He turned to Beverly and Elizabeth and said, "Now, the first part of the plan involves you two and a member of the Indian Army intelligence service. He is a good man, a brave man, but not trained in any of our skills. He is a member of the old school of intelligence. He is an adventurer willing to go spy the land. We will need his help to get you into Gwadar, but do not expect him to be able to assist in the operation."

After the briefing, Elizabeth and Beverly were dispatched as the lead element in the operation. They travelled for five days in a Royal Flying Corps B.E. 2 aircraft before they linked up with Sykes on the unmarked borderlands between Persia and Baluchistan. The B.E. 2 was a two-seater aircraft, but once Captain Joshua Marshall saw the two intrepid women, he declared that Elizabeth could "fit in" with him. It was hardly a tight squeeze since neither Elizabeth nor Marshall were large. It also gave Marshall a chance to spend time with an English woman, something he had not enjoyed for over a year.

Elizabeth was pleased to use her flying suit again. And, just as important, pleased she had the opportunity to get some stick time in an aircraft. Elizabeth mentioned that her Royal Navy colleague allowed her several hours flying in his Sopwith Tabloid, and Marshall was not going to be outdone by the Royal Navy. He gave Elizabeth his own version of flight instruction over the four days it took to travel from Rawalpindi across the hot plains of the Punjab, the mountains in Baluchistan and, finally, to the Persian border. During that time, he even allowed Elizabeth to try her hand at landing the aircraft and, on the last day, taking off from the Royal Flying Corps provisional airbase in Nushki. Elizabeth's only disappointment was her brother was not around to see her in a flying suit and flying a modern aeroplane.

Elizabeth was proud of herself as she flew straight and level over the Baluch desert. She thought after this mission, she might ask the colonel if it would be possible for her to continue her flying education. It might be useful in the future and it certainly would be fun. She would never forget the look on Sykes' face when they landed outside Turbat and she climbed down from the control seat of the RFC aircraft. Elizabeth was always pleased to force the men in service to consider the accomplishments of women. Her father had never shown any prejudice, but then again, her mother was also in the service proving herself every day. The twentieth century was certain to see more than one success for women. At some point, women might even get the vote!

Her camel stumbled over a rock hidden under the edge of a sand dune and Elizabeth was reminded once again of the discomfort of the camel saddle. She leaned forward and said to

Beverly, "Will we be in Gwadar tonight?" She had tried to make the query sound professional but it came out more like a bleat.

Beverly could understand Elizabeth's impatience. She had travelled by camel, donkey and horse for the better part of five years while serving in Mesopotamia. Camel speed meant that the objects on the horizon never seemed to get any closer. Camels didn't care and apparently neither did their desert Arab masters. They did not use watches or even day-to-day calendars. They lived by the seasons and the moon, and the stars. It took her forever to get used to that pace. After five days of looking at the back of Sykes' head, she was tired of the trip as well. "I doubt it. Gwadar is a walled city on that peninsula. We will have to negotiate the passes that take us off this plateau and down to sea level. We do not want to approach the city gates at night. At best, we would be told to come back at dawn. At worst, the guards would shoot us."

Elizabeth nodded and said, "Do you think this will work?"

"If we keep our wits about us, it should work well. Sykes understands his job is to get us into the fortress. If he sticks to his part of the bargain, then it will be up to us to do the job. Once inside Gwadar, we will be just two Arab women walking the streets of a market town. No one will pay any attention. Sykes will remain with us both for cover and in case we have some difficulties that we can't handle."

Beverly's tone made clear that she was confident she could handle any "difficulty."

Beverly continued, "We know where the German compound is in the town. Sykes identified that the last time he visited Gwadar. It wasn't important then, but he captured the details that will make our work easier." Beverly paused again as the camel seemed to stumble on yet another stone buried in sand. "That's a lesson for you, Elizabeth. You never know when some insignificant detail in one of your reports will be important. Once we can get eyes on the target, it will be up to you to communicate with Guru Naismith. Then, we keep eyes on the target until the rest of the Ravens arrive. After that, it will be up to hard work and luck."

Sykes' camel stopped and went down on its knees. He slid off the saddle and came up to the two female agents. He made a clicking sound and their camel also went down on its knees. He helped Elizabeth off the saddle and was about to do the same with Beverly when she threw a leg over the saddle tree and slid off the camel with the same skill he showed earlier. Sykes said, "I forget that you are used to camel travel in Mesopotamia." He paused and then said, "We are about four hours from the northern gates of Gwadar. We will camp here tonight. We are just far enough away from the city to avoid other caravans waiting to enter, but just close enough that none of the caravans that left Gwadar today will stop here. I will set up camp and we can start a meal."

After five days of travel, Elizabeth was less agile than Beverly in dismounting the camel. Even with Sykes' help, she barely avoided falling face-first into the sand. Elizabeth was convinced that eventually she would look more graceful on a camel. For now, she could only imagine what it must have been like for Gertrude Bell as she crossed the desert wastes in Arabia to visit the sheikhs.

That night they had their final desert meal of tinned meat, tea and the last of the fruit Sykes had purchased in the market in Turbat. Beverly used a small bit of flour and water and baked flatbread on a steel plate that was part of what Sykes called his field kitchen. Elizabeth was left with the tedious chore of finding wood to keep the fire going. She realized that Sykes had planned well. Their location was near a wadi with scrub trees and bushes that offered kindling. Perhaps not as aromatic as it might have been in India, but it burned hot and that was really all that mattered.

When they were finished with the meal and Sykes had "cleaned" their plates with a mix of sand and water, they leaned against their camel saddles for one last review of the mission. Sykes began, "Tomorrow, we will enter Gwadar. The guards may or may not remember me, but the captain of the guards, an African slave from Mombasa who is the senior servant of the city emir, should remember. Last time I came through, I treated him like a potentate, gave him a couple of items from my stock and had tea with him on arrival and on departure. As Arab women, don't expect to be treated better than the three camels. I apologize but that is the nature of the culture here."

Elizabeth worked hard to keep her temper. She realized she was the junior member and needed to listen more and complain less. Still, it was frustrating that Beverly never questioned Sykes on this matter. Sykes noticed Elizabeth fidgeting and said, "Elizabeth, is something wrong?"

"I was just wondering if the Baluch and the Arabs are so different from the Arabs that Gertrude Bell met. She didn't seem to have any problem with her gender."

Elizabeth watched as Beverly's aura flashed orange and Sykes' aura moved back and forth between light blue and yellow. She realized immediately her comment was intemperate. Beverly responded with a remark that bordered on curt. She said, "Elizabeth, Bell traveled as an English woman with a *firman*, a written approval from the Ottoman government. We are traveling as the two wives of a Persian trader. Please remember that our lack of status in Gwadar will be to our advantage, not our disadvantage."

Elizabeth felt chastised and realized that she had lost focus. Their lack of status made them invisible inside the city. That was the point. She bowed her head and said, "Of course. I understand."

Sykes continued. "The last time I was in Gwadar, I was a merchant traveling alone. I stayed in a men's caravansarei. It was a good place to gain the intelligence and I thought it a fair trade for the bedbugs and other vermin that pestered me for the rest of the trip. This time, I will find someplace for a man and his wives. I should be able to find something suitable, though I still won't promise you will enjoy the vermin." He smiled and his white teeth glistened under his large mustache. "The next day, I will make my business rounds and collect as much intelligence as I can from the bazaar. You will need to start your survey immediately if we are going to get this all accomplished before the end of Ramadan. That means we have less than four weeks to accomplish the mission."

Beverly nodded and said, "That is more than enough time to identify our target and make our recommendations."

Sykes said, "How will you get the information out from Gwadar?"

Beverly smiled and said, "Who said we would need to send the information out from the city?"

"Naismith and crew are already in the city?"

"Near enough that we will be able to send our information with little difficulty." Beverly's tone argued that she did not expect Sykes to push for answers. That was not the case. Elizabeth could sense Sykes was used to being in charge. He understood his orders came from seniors inside the office of the Viceroy, but he was not about to risk his life unless he knew more. Especially when he was traveling with two women of unknown skills. Elizabeth watched as Sykes aura changed from yellow to orange.

As he was about to speak, Elizabeth looked across the campfire and said, "You are satisfied that we can accomplish the mission. You will be the hero. You will not ask again."

Sykes nodded in a way that demonstrated he was in the "waking dream" state. He said, "I am satisfied."

Beverly stared for a moment at her young colleague. She practiced mesmerism while serving in Mesopotamia, but when she used this skill, it usually took more time and some sort of direct contact. Elizabeth had just ended the conversation with a quiet voice and staring at Sykes with her jade-coloured eyes. It was both interesting and frightening. In their last adventure together in Afghanistan, she accepted Elizabeth's skills in what Naismith called the illusory body. In this mission, she understood that Elizabeth would communicate with Naismith through telepathy. Still, this was a different level of the mystic arts, and something she would not have expected from a teenager. She said, "Elizabeth, I think our colleague understands."

Elizabeth nodded and released her control over Sykes mind. He shook his head and said, "I'm sorry, I appear to have dozed off. It has been a long day and we have an early start tomorrow. I think we should all get some rest."

Elizabeth smiled what she hoped was her most innocent smile and said, "Absolutely, colonel."

Beverly gave her a hard stare and Elizabeth wondered if she had overplayed her hand. As they set their bedding against the camel saddles, Beverly said, "I would be careful if I were you. We do not want the Ravens to be known as witches as well as fighters."

Elizabeth was not entirely certain if Beverly was serious or playing with her. She cautiously said, "It was simply a means to end what could have been an uncomfortable question we didn't want the colonel to ask."

"Just remember, young one. I don't want to see you use this on one of the Ravens."

"Beverly, that will never happen."

"Then we will stay friends forever!" Beverly's smile and deep blue aura told Elizabeth that she had been joking with her all along.

It was not uncommon to see two Persian women walking together in the busy streets of the trading center. They blended in with dozens of women dressed in the long shalwar kamiz of the Baluch, the robes of Arab women from Muscat, and the coloured wraps denoting slaves from Mombasa. Over the past week, they had made multiple trips to the bazaar buying food and small trinkets and returning each day to the house Sykes had rented. Sykes reported each day on politics in Gwadar and how the local Baluch felt about their Muscat overseers. He noted that the Germans did not appear to have any status or influence other than serving as consular officers protecting German ships visiting the port. The most common answer to his questions on politics was one of indifference. The merchants of the city did not care at all who ran the city so long as they did not demand too many bribes or ask too many questions. After Friday prayers, Sykes returned with news that amazed the two Ravens.

"There is talk in the bazaar of an assassination of some royal in Sarajevo. No one seems to know the name of the assassin or even who was killed. The only concern in the bazaar is how this might disrupt trade with the Ottoman Empire." He paused to drink a small cup of Turkish coffee Elizabeth had made on his return from prayers. Sykes continued, "I know of none of our royals in the region, but that's based on my last set of dispatches before leaving Khuzestan. Before you left Rawalpindi, did you hear of any British government travel in the region?"

Elizabeth had allowed Beverly to handle most of the communications with Sykes so she looked at Beverly to answer this question. Beverly said, "I fear our focus was entirely on this mission. I know of no royalty traveling in Europe though I doubt we would have heard."

Elizabeth added, "When I left Constantinople in May, there was no talk of anyone from the Royal family or from the government traveling this summer."

For a moment, Sykes was taken aback. This young female intelligence officer had been assigned to Constantinople? What in the world could she collect in such a cosmopolitan city? He decided to postpone that question and continued. "Just as I thought. Well, there are plenty of other royal families in Central and Eastern Europe. And it is their nature to be killed for one reason or another. And, as with the Mayerling incident, they are fairly successful at killing themselves."

Elizabeth winced at Sykes attempt at humor. The Mayerling incident, including the suicide of the Crown Prince of Austria and his lover, was something that her tutor Mrs. Edwards had forced her study. It was not in any way charming or humorous. It was just sad. But Elizabeth had learned her lesson from her discussion with Beverly. She smiled and poured him another cup of coffee. Elizabeth realized that Sykes was only trying to be collegial. She asked, "What else is rumbling through the mosque?"

Sykes accepted the question as an opportunity to explain his own work. He started into a long discussion of the intricacies of the Gwadar merchant community. It was a blend of traders, usually Baluch or Persians, and sailors, usually Gulf Arabs. There was what he described as a pirate caste from the Horn of Africa. Gwadar was considered a neutral zone. Close enough to the Raj and to the Persian Empire to benefit from free trade, but far enough from the two empires that laws did not impede profit. As Sykes continued, it seemed to Elizabeth that they were living in a place taken from Sir Richard Burton's translation of the Arabian Nights.

Elizabeth was amazed as Sykes described in detail each of the families, their history and their motivations. By the time he was finished, Elizabeth had an entirely different opinion of Sykes. He might be prejudiced, and he might lack formal training from The Viceroy's College, but he was a very good analyst of tribal and clan subtlety. Elizabeth was not certain it would make a difference for this current mission, but she had to admire his observation skills, his language fluency and his regional knowledge.

The next morning, Beverly and Elizabeth decided it was

time to begin their own collection mission. As they had for each of the previous days, they started by visiting the marketplace to buy whatever foodstuffs were fresh. They stayed well clear of men, keeping their veils and head covering in place as they strolled through the bazaar. Periodically, Beverly would stop and purchase dried fruit, small glass beads and even a small basket for Elizabeth to assist in carrying their items. Elizabeth stayed one step to her left and to her rear as befitting the younger wife. Beverly explained early on that this demure attitude would allow Elizabeth to avoid using her formal Persian which would be noticed in the bazaar where men and women spoke a blend of rural Arabic, Persian, and Baluch. Beverly quickly picked up the proper Arabic accent and Elizabeth did little other than nod and carry whatever Beverly handed to her.

As Beverly had promised, they were truly invisible in the crowd. To avoid the heat and the crowds, they cut through a series of narrow streets. The buildings on both sides of the streets were three and four stories tall and the sun rarely visited the alley. Once they were certain they were alone, Beverly said, "I believe we are on a side street that takes us past the rear of the German compound. Agreed?"

Elizabeth whispered, "Agreed. If we can get next to the wall unobserved and can stop for a minute, I will see what I can see."

"As you walk through walls."

Elizabeth smiled. "Indeed. As I walk through walls."

Ꞁow to Float through Walls

BEVERLY HAD MADE LIGHT OF ELIZABETH'S SKILLS, BUT SHE ALSO KNEW THAT while her young colleague was sending her illusory body into the compound, she would be deep in a meditative state and completely defenseless. It would be up to her to make it seem natural for two veiled women to be sitting propped up against a wall. The only good news was as they approached the wall, she could see the height of the wall mixed with the time of day meant that they would be sitting in deep shadow. It was entirely possible the July sun had never reached the wall or the sand against it. It would be a dangerous place at night, but in late afternoon, it should be relatively safe. At least that was what she hoped. In the back of her mind, she remembered that Naismith once told her "hope is not a plan."

Beverly watched as Elizabeth leaned against the cool wall of the compound. At first, Elizabeth seemed lost in thought. In her black abaya and hijab, Beverly thought that Elizabeth might appear to any onlooker like a pile of black rags thrown against the wall. Beverly decided to sit next to the wall and enjoy the cool as well. Now, two piles of black rags leaned against the wall. One deep in meditation and one tense as she scanned the alley for anyone offering hostile intent. Beverly had no idea how long it would take Elizabeth to do what she needed to do. Beverly only knew about the illusory body. She never tried to project her consciousness outside her physical body. Would this take long? She had no idea.

Suddenly Beverly felt Elizabeth stir. She looked over to see her colleague begin to levitate off the ground. Not any great distance, perhaps six inches, but it was clear that Elizabeth was floating above the sand. Beverly could hear Elizabeth chanting some sort of mantra in a voice far deeper than she expected from a teenager. As she watched, Elizabeth's abaya seemed to move on its own and, in the blink of an eye, the abaya dropped to the ground. There was no evidence that Elizabeth had ever been inside the black cloak.

When she began to meditate to send her body inside the German compound, Elizabeth found it far more difficult than her past efforts to deploy her illusory body. She attributed it to the heat and the mental pressure. After all, the entire Raven mission hung in the balance. She could feel Beverly sit down next to her and as she closed her eyes, she began to relax. As she relaxed, she felt a lightness of being that she had not felt before in what she had decided to describe as remote viewing. It took a few seconds, but she felt herself dissolving into and through the wall and into the compound. She imagined having floated backside-first through the wall, so it took a moment to reorient herself and look across the compound. She saw four buildings arranged in a square with an internal parade ground with the flagpole in the center flying the ensign of the German Empire.

Elizabeth had noted in her previous efforts at remote viewing she had to concentrate to see in a single direction. Otherwise, it seemed to her that she was looking at her target from a great height. As she concentrated on the parade ground and the flagpole, she saw a dozen men dressed in shalwar kamiz. They were barefoot and it was clear they were practicing martial arts routines guided by a European. Each of the participants held a pair of curved Persian daggers. The European was holding two short swords that looked like shortened versions of cavalry sabers.

The European spoke in accented English. "You must keep your blades concealed until the last minute. That way, your target will have no chance to defend himself. Now, follow my moves." The trainer had both of his blades at his side. As he lunged forward, the blade in his right hand slashed across his body at waist height and the blade in his left hand slashed in the opposite direction at what would most probably be shoulder or neck height. The dozen men mimicked the action with varying degrees of success. While Elizabeth was fascinated with this martial arts training, she knew she needed to access the buildings to obtain the best possible information for Naismith and the Ravens.

Elizabeth focused her concentration toward the building that looked most likely to be the headquarters. As she floated up to the windows, she saw five men in shirtsleeves working at desks, filling ledger books with information. She floated into the room to look at the ledgers. Each was filled with names, clearly Indian and Persian names, followed by a location, followed by some sort of code. Elizabeth reached out with what she imagined was her spectral hand to touch the head of one of the clerks. With the help of the clerk's mind, she could understand the code. It was PA for political action, A for attack, and S for support. She realized it would be a treasure of incredible value if the Ravens could capture these ledgers.

Elizabeth moved up another floor to a set of offices. One of the offices looked much like the room Naismith used for briefings. A set of long tables with maps with coloured pins placed on them. The pins on the East Africa coast were blue and all located in port towns. The pins in India were red and located in major cities throughout the Raj. The pins in Persia were green and located in southern cities including Shiraz, Kerman and Bandar Abbas. Elizabeth also noted a set of red pins located at the coaling station of Aden and the Mesopotamian oil depot in Basra. There were too many details for Elizabeth to remember, so she just noted the location of the room inside the building.

A noise from the corridor became a noise at the door of the room. Elizabeth realized that she was invisible to an untrained eye, but she still pushed her body up against a corner of the ceiling and the wall, well away from the map tables below. As she watched, two men walked into the room. The first was a square-shouldered man in a formal German military uniform. The second was a man of much lighter build dressed in what Elizabeth could only imagine as khaki field kit commonly used by miners, engineers, and explorers. Elizabeth did not speak German, so she had no idea what they were saying. The only thing she could make out was their formal addresses to each other. The uniformed one was *Hauptmann* Breslau and one in civilian clothes was identified as *Herr Oberstlieutnant* von Lettow-Vorbeck. It was clear that the man in the civilian clothes outranked the one in uniform. The only other thing Elizabeth could make out was that von Lettow-Vorbeck was going to depart, *gehen* in German, the next day.

Elizabeth was about to move to another building when she was pulled back to her real body in the street. It was not a gentle pull, rather more like a yank. Elizabeth realized that Beverly must be in danger.

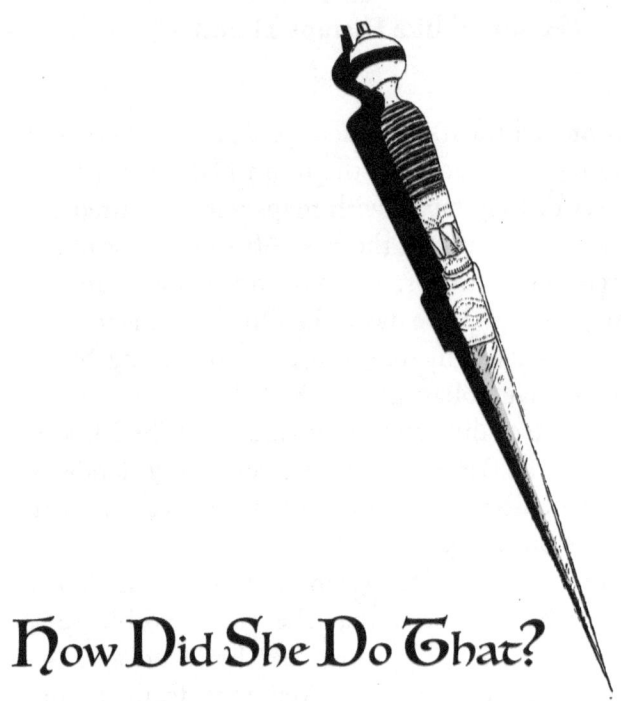

Ꞅow Did She Do Ꞇhat?

ELIZABETH RETURNED TO HER PHYSICAL BODY IN THE ALLEY. IN THE PAST, SHE was exhausted after an excursion in remote viewing, but the first thing she saw when she recovered was her colleague Beverly fighting off three different men. She had two small daggers against men who were at least her height and nearly twice her weight. Elizabeth recovered quickly as adrenaline surged through her body creating a flight or fight response. In this case, it was fight.

Elizabeth stood up and looked at the three men. They were very close to overwhelming Beverly. One had a steely grip on her abaya which prevented her colleague from properly defending herself. A second was trying to accomplish the same on her left side. The third was standing back until the target was defenseless. It was clear that these men fully intended to control both of Beverly's arms, twist them until she dropped her knives. Elizabeth shouted in Persian, "Stop that!"

The man closest to Elizabeth did not understand Persian,

294

but he did realize that another, younger woman had just appeared out of nowhere. When he and his colleagues walked into the alley moments earlier, they had noticed only one woman. A single woman, dressed in full hijab was too tempting a target for the three villains. They intended to rob her and, perhaps, enjoy her body before killing her. It was just another day in their trade as cutthroats in the port town of Gwadar. They normally waited outside the coffee shops and opium dens of the city hoping to capture a full purse from some unwitting merchant. For the time being, they had decided attacking a woman would be a reasonable diversion until dark. Now, there were two women. The new one was younger and smaller. So much the better.

The nearest man dropped his grip on Beverly and headed toward what he believed to be even easier prey. Elizabeth stood her ground. Before the villain could grab Elizabeth, she swept her right hand across her chest from left to right. He had not noticed the thin blade Elizabeth had pulled from her left sleeve. The wound across his throat was mortal. He collapsed in a manner that argued he would not get up. A pool of blood crept out from the body, staining the sand.

Elizabeth turned to the second man trying to push Beverly against the wall so that his partner could steal whatever she might have under her abaya. Elizabeth gently placed her right hand on the top of the man's head and her left arm around his neck. With what appeared to be no effort at all, she snapped the man's neck so thoroughly that his head twisted fully back to front. He dropped to the ground with what could only be described as a shocked look on his face as his eyes glazed over in death.

The third man was not distracted by the movement of his two colleagues. After all, they had not said a word. He was convinced that there would be some profit in this effort. He was wrong. Now that Beverly had a free hand, she reached over and grabbed the man's hand as it probed into her abaya. A vigorous twist and his right arm broke with a loud snap. He looked puzzled as he realized his right arm no longer responded to his commands. He might have realized how painful that injury was, but before that could happen, Beverly had driven a dagger from his neck upward into his skull. He died quickly.

As both women exhaled and recovered from the fight, they realized there was a fourth man farther down the alley hidden in the shadows. Outside of the range of their capabilities, he stood with a brace of large cavalry pistols in his hands. Elizabeth pulled the Browning from a concealed holster under her abaya and prepared to shoot. In a voice they recognized, the shadow figure said, "I thought you might need some assistance. It is clear that was not the case."

Beverly recovered first and said, "Colonel, did you follow us today?"

Sykes nodded and said, "It seemed prudent to do so." He looked down at the three dead men and shook his head. Elizabeth walked past Sykes in what seemed to him to be nothing less than a trance state like that described in the novel by Mr. Bram Stoker. She did not seem at all connected with the outside world. Until that moment, he always assumed the novel was complete fiction. Now, he was not so sure.

Beverly looked down the alley and said, "I think we need to move the bodies so they are not so obviously associated with the German compound."

Sykes nodded. "We can pull them down the alley to the connecting alley. It won't be pretty, but it shouldn't matter too much to any of the locals." Sykes grabbed the first villain's collar and started to drag him down the alley, raising a small cloud of dust that swirled along the alley obscuring their actions. As he passed Beverly, he said, "If it isn't too much trouble, I would very much like to know how Lieutenant Bankroft accomplished what she just did."

A Sound like Distant Thunder

Beverly walked up to Sykes, shook her head and whispered, "So would I." She picked up the woven basket. The day's purchases had spilled across the dirt. She slowly filled the basket and then walked toward the end of the alley and Elizabeth.

Last Days in Constantinople

Late July 1914

Francis and Mary were holding what could only be a family council of war. They were sitting on the veranda of the yali overlooking the Sea of Marmara. It was sundown. The call to prayer was echoing from the neighborhood mosque. It was the first day of Ramadan, a month of fasting and prayer for the devout throughout the Muslim world.

Constantinople was a city of multiple ethnic groups, Sunni and Shia Muslims, non-practicing Muslims, Christians of all denominations, and even a few visitors who probably would admit when questioned that religion played no part in their life as merchants, sailors, diplomats and, of course, spies. The local mullah had woken the neighborhood before dawn as he walked through the streets banging a tin drum calling the faithful to prayer. Mary, always up at that hour, had noticed that the mullah was followed by four Sufis dancing. It wasn't clear if the Sufis were part of the mullah's entourage or were mocking the mullah as he made his rounds. Such was the complexity of the religions of the city that Mary thought it might be both.

Francis had used the first day of Ramadan to make calls on his contacts and Mary had done the same. The streets were quiet, due to the enforcement of Ramadan restrictions. Shopkeepers were not about to lose business, but they did so behind shuttered doors and windows. It was a good time to hold clandestine meetings behind those shuttered doors. When they returned at the end of the day, they were dismayed at what they had heard.

Bektashi met them as they returned to the yali. He remained the ever-practical and ever-vigilant manager of the household. Francis had asked him earlier if he wished to go on holiday to spend time with family during Ramadan, but Bektashi declined the offer.

"Bankroft Bey," the Albanian said, "I have no family that wishes to speak to me, much less spend time with me. And, as to Ramadan, I am a member of the faithful, but no one tells Bektashi when he should eat or drink. Also, who will guard the house while you are at work? You know Ramadan is also the time of mischief makers and mountebanks. They claim to be poor Muslims and then they rob you. No, no, no. I say, no. I will be here guarding the castle."

Mary, for one, was glad to see Bektashi on guard when she returned. He immediately set about to fill a cool bath for her as she changed from her dusty street clothes to something more suitable for an evening with her husband.

Francis arrived just as she finished her bath. He immediately pulled off his military uniform and jumped into the cold bath water. He looked up and said, "This is what I needed. This was a day, I can tell you."

Mary said, "I will have Bektashi open something cold for us to drink. I will meet you on the veranda."

The council of war began after Bektashi delivered a tray of raki, cold water, and mezze that included cheeses, cold meats and pickled vegetables. Francis began by stating, "The Austro-Hungarian Empire declared war on Serbia today."

Mary nodded. "That news was all over the town today. Many of the merchants are afraid that the Empire will be forced to pick sides. They know they will profit at first, but they fear chaos will follow."

"Well, my dear, it certainly looks like they are right. I heard today that London is going to renege on the delivery of the two battleships. They assume that they will be needed if we are plunged into war. The Turks are furious and the admiral is shocked by the Admiralty's decision."

Francis paused to take a sip from his milky anisette drink and continued: "And he was dismayed at how the CUP is responding. Basically, with one decision in London, we have pushed the Turks into the arms of the Germans. Of course, he was not aware that it was Ramadan and that the faithful will be fasting. I tried to explain that as the month continues, even members of the CUP who are Muslims in name only will begin to suffer from the strictures of fasting and sleep deprivation. His response was … not worth repeating."

Mary said, "If Belgrade and Vienna go to war, doesn't that mean Russia will follow?"

Francis nodded, "And Germany, of course. And then what decisions will they make in London?"

Mary noticed that even in the most worrisome of times, Francis' appetite never faltered. He was busy working on the mezze tray. Finally, he continued, "I fear it will be just as Sasha said: A world at war. During my meetings today with the officers in the Ottoman Army, they made it clear that we are no longer welcome here. I don't know if the Ottoman Empire will formally declare war, but they will certainly comply with any bidding from the Kaiser. I sent a message to the colonel today. I told him that our ability to do our work would be severely limited in the very near future. I told him that unless otherwise advised, we would make good our escape in the next ten days."

"By sea or land?"

"I haven't determined which would be best. I think initially by sea, but the Mediterranean may become a very dangerous place. Of course, if the Turks decide to mine the straits, it may be a long land journey back to India."

Mary thought for a moment and said, "It would appear we are not going to see our daughter again in Constantinople."

"Do you know something I don't know?"

Mary smiled and said, "You know Elizabeth and I often link in the astral plain. Of all places, she is in Gwadar!"

"That is a smugglers paradise filled with cutthroats. What in the world is she doing there?"

"It would appear the Ravens are working against the Germans."

Francis sighed. "It makes sense the Germans would have an outpost in Gwadar. Right on the Indian border and a quick sail to Persia. If Elizabeth is with the Ravens, it means she is with Naismith. And, if she is with Naismith, she is safe."

Mary decided to let her husband accept a false premise. If Elizabeth was with the Ravens, it meant she was always in danger. Before she could say anything, Bektashi appeared at the door to the veranda. He coughed just loud enough so that both Mary and Francis looked over to him. "Sir, your Russian colleague is here. Shall I make him wait in the sitting room or bring him out here?"

Francis smiled. "Bektashi Bey, please guide our friend out to the veranda. Also, it would appear that I have eaten most of the mezze. I hope there is more in the kitchen?"

Bektashi smiled and said, "Sir, there are always more mezze in the kitchen. It will take just a moment."

Naglieff strode onto the veranda. He said, "Can you

believe your manservant kept me waiting in the hallway? I fear he has a very different view of the proper place for a servant. In St. Petersburg, we would take that lash to him."

Francis laughed long and loud. "I am the one who trained Bektashi so you will have to take the lash to me," he said. "And Sasha, don't forget he was the one who saved our lives just a few weeks ago."

Naglieff sat down. Bektashi appeared out of thin air and placed a bottle of vodka, a chilled glass, and a new plate of mezze in front of the Russian. He bowed to Francis, and Mary was convinced he winked at her. Mary realized that no matter when or how they left Constantinople, she would insist they take their Albanian manservant along with them.

Naglieff poured himself a glass of vodka and downed it in a single gulp. He poured another and then said to his colleagues, "To the Tsar and to your King." They poured two glasses of raki and joined their Russian colleague in the toast. Naglieff then poured himself another glass of vodka and began to devour the selection of meat and cheeses on the tray. "My household staff are all devout. They refuse to even touch food until sundown. I have eaten nothing more than bread and butter all day."

Francis said, "Another reason why Bektashi is a jewel."

Naglieff nodded as he ate from the tray. To get Naglieff to slow down his drinking and eating, Mary asked, "What news from St. Petersburg?"

"The court is in an uproar. One half of the court, made up of the Minister of War and the Foreign Minister, believes that our only honorable option is to declare war on Vienna. We have a formal defense pact with Serbia and they are Slavs after all. The rest of the court are arguing to temporize to see whether cooler heads will prevail in the Viennese court. The Tsar is pulled to and fro by his trusted advisors. I believe it will be war. We have the largest land army in the world. We will be able to take on the Austrians and even the Germans if they choose war. The real question in my mind is what will England do when we declare war?"

Francis knew that anything he would say would end up in a dispatch tomorrow headed to St. Petersburg. He chose a diplomatic answer though he was certain that London would declare war as well. "Sasha, I don't know what London would do. Remember, we are servants of the Raj as well as the Crown. We have no insight into the minds of the mandarins in Whitehall. I think it would be entirely a function of what the Germans choose to do when Russia and Austria go to war."

Naglieff nodded. He expected his British colleague to say little, but he also knew that Francis' argument was sound. His own sources inside the British Embassy had already told him that Bankroft was an outsider who was rarely consulted by the ambassador or the admiral. The British diplomatic corps and the Royal Navy were both well known in Russia for their closed minds. The Russian Empire was one contiguous whole so some of the prejudices that the British had for their colonial officers did not happen in the Russian Imperial Army. They were all imperial officers regardless of their assignment in the Empire. Naglieff said, "You do realize we need to leave soon."

Mary said, "We were just talking about that when you arrived."

Naglieff said, "I have a recommendation. I know you have your own chain of command that you will need to ask, but I want you to consider taking your boat and sailing into the Black Sea and to Russia. From there, I am sure we can get you to India much quicker than if you tried to sail through the Dardanelles in the Mediterranean."

Mary smiled and said in her perfect Russian, "Of course, it would make your departure easier as well, no?"

Naglieff smiled back at her and responded in Russian, "I never thought of that."

Francis said, "Our diplomatic colleagues might wish to spend the war under lock and key in Constantinople, but I for one want to be of some use to the Crown."

Mary said, "Francis, I think you speak for us all." Mary turned to Naglieff and said, "You do know we will be taking Bektashi with us."

Naglieff smiled for the first time since his arrival. "Given how good he is with a Mauser, I think that would be a good idea."

Enter the Ravens

04-05 August 1914 — Gwadar

ELIZABETH COULD SEE THAT SYKES WAS AN IMPATIENT MAN. TRAINED AS A cavalry officer, experienced in intelligence collection where he was expected to work alone and quickly, Sykes was not used to the complexity of an operation designed to be both invisible and deniable. Beverly had to explain three times why they intended to raid the German compound but only take selected documents and maps. He did not understand why the Ravens would not raid the compound, secure the Germans, arrest the Indians and leave by way of some Royal Navy warship waiting just offshore. Elizabeth was impatient as well, but her impatience was focused on the back-and-forth dialogue that had lasted for over a week. She realized that Sykes was a senior British India officer and they needed to be polite, but it was difficult to imagine why he seemed so determined to be an obstacle to forward progress.

While Beverly and Sykes discussed the plan, Elizabeth had been in telepathic contact with Naismith. She outlined the nature of the German commercial compound, the specific target offices in the buildings and the general lack of security. She told Naismith that the Germans seemed to think a ten-foot-high wall and two guards were sufficient to keep any locals from attempting to break into the compound. Naismith countered by reminding Elizabeth that Sykes' earlier reporting said specifically that the Germans had arranged an entirely different sort of security with the Gwadar emir. Sykes' source from inside the emir's palace stated that one of the emir's own lieutenants told the Germans that any intruders in their compound would be tortured in the city square as a reminder to the various clans operating in this freeport that there were limits to what they could do in their free time. Apparently, it only took one example to terrify this city of thieves, smugglers, and pirates.

In their room later that evening, Beverly confided her frustrations. "Elizabeth, if I have to outline our plan one more time to Sykes, I am going to ask you to put him in a deep trance until this is all over. I know we are not supposed to use mesmerism on our colleagues, but I swear it will be that or I will have to hurt him. We both know striking a senior officer is not wise. It would be much easier to carry a sleeping Sykes to our final linkup than explain why I damaged him."

Elizabeth smiled. For once she was the voice of reason. "I have watched Sykes during your discussions. He is not trying to be difficult. He just can't imagine that our style of operation is even possible, much less offering a hope of success. I can do as you ask, but I think in the long run, Sykes will be the man for the job that Guru Naismith wants him to accomplish."

"Let's hope so, Elizabeth."

It was sunset on 4 August when Sykes stood at one of the

docks as the dhow pulled up. It was time for the *iftar* meal celebrating the end of the fast during the month of Ramadan. During the first week of the Ramadan, *iftar* was little more than an obligation. By the middle of a month of fasting and, most especially, fasting during the heat of the summer, breaking of the fast was essential to the faithful. Sykes had to admit that the leader of the Ravens knew the culture of the desert. The dock was deserted and would remain so for at least several hours while the faithful broke fast and local burglars raided shops.

A man dressed in a deep-blue hooded robe tossed him a line which he made fast to a ring set in the stone dock. In seconds, the dhow emptied. Six men dressed in similar deep-blue robes jumped onto the dock. Their obvious leader, a man with a shaved head and a grey beard, walked up to Sykes and said, "We are ready to follow you."

Sykes walked quickly to the house where Elizabeth and Beverly were waiting. Once inside, the visitors dropped their robes at the entrance. Sykes was surprised to see that the six men were, in fact, three men and three women. They were all dressed in a strange uniform and carried an odd assortment of weapons and equipment. He was surprised they were carrying weapons that looked like they belonged in a museum of the Crusades. Short swords similar to Khyber knives, crossbows, ropes and grappling hooks were all carried in modified harnesses on their back. He was especially surprised by their footgear. They wore boots that looked very supple. Too supple for a long march or even riding. Whatever their design, he noted that even in the house, these Ravens moved silently.

After a short period of greeting, Naismith gathered the team together and reviewed the plan. Sykes was completely baffled by Naismith's plan. It didn't seem possible that these Ravens could accomplish their goals. Still, Sykes was a soldier of the Empire and he had very specific orders: support

Naismith and his people or give up his job as an agent of the Empire and return to serving as a cavalry officer in the Indian Punjab. So, when Naismith gave Sykes his mission, he simply nodded.

Naismith looked at the radium dial on his wristwatch. It was 0200hrs. He walked around the room rousing the Ravens. Sykes was already awake and making tea for the team. After a quick cup of tea, Naismith and the Ravens left by the back door of the house. Sykes watched as they disappeared into the night. He was amazed at how their strange, hooded uniforms in blue-black made them nearly invisible. He finished his cup of tea and donned his own Arab robe. His mission was in the opposite direction.

Elizabeth and Beverly served as the guides for the Ravens as they worked their way along the back alleys of Gwadar. As Naismith expected, the only living creatures in the alleys were cats hunting rats or scrounging in the remains of the *iftar* parties that had run from sunset to well past midnight. The city of Gwadar was now sound asleep. It would awaken well before dawn as local mullahs walked through the streets banging drums and calling the faithful to prepare for the first prayer of the day.

Naismith was sure that sleep deprivation — caused by days of fasting, late night feasting and early rising — would keep the streets empty during the dark hours. If not, he knew the Ravens could handle any unlikely observer.

They arrived in a half hour at the alley where Elizabeth and Beverly conducted their first reconnaissance. Each of the Ravens knew what they would need to accomplish in the next hour. As soon as they finished guiding the Ravens, Elizabeth and Beverly returned to the docks. Sykes might not need assistance, but Naismith had made it clear to them that

Sykes' portion of the plan was essential to the overall mission. Elizabeth was gravely disappointed that she would not be part of the main effort this night, but Naismith's orders, though never phrased as such, served as absolute commands to the Ravens.

Naismith intended to conduct his own reconnaissance of the compound to ensure they would not be interrupted. He walked up to the high wall of the compound and pressed face first against the wall with his arms outstretched. Even Marian, who had seen so much of the mystic arts in her time as a Raven, was astonished as Naismith seemed to melt into the wall and disappear. As he had said to Commander Smythe so many days before, he did have the ability to walk through walls.

Once he was on the other side of the wall, Naismith took a moment to compose his *chi*. Regardless of what the airship commander thought, Naismith knew it took enormous concentration and just a bit of luck to pass through walls. There seemed to be no evidence of guards patrolling the interior courtyard. Naismith extended his consciousness, his *chi*, looking for any sign of the guards. He found only two. Both leaned against the main gate, fast asleep. Once he was certain he would not be interrupted, he turned and leapt to the top of the wall. Ten feet would be an impossible leap for most men, but for Naismith it was nothing more than a simple hop using *lung gom pa*. From the top of the wall, he motioned to Marian and Alexander. They both tossed ropes with grappling hooks up to Naismith. He secured them and then jumped back down into the courtyard.

In less than a minute, five of the Ravens joined Naismith. Silently, they split into two groups. Naismith, Marian, Martha and Jonathan headed toward the building that Elizabeth had described as the headquarters. They were inside the building before the other two headed on their mission at the gate. The headquarters building door was locked, but that was no obstacle to Jonathan who, among other skills, was a master locksmith. Once inside, they split into pairs. Naismith and Martha would climb the stairs to the second floor and capture the maps in the room Elizabeth had identified. Marian and Jonathan would move down the hall on the ground floor and take as many of the ledgers as they could carry.

While their colleagues worked in the headquarters building, Alexander and Eugenia headed toward the sleeping guards. Their single mission was to ensure the guards remained unconscious. If the guards awoke for any reason, the two Ravens would give them no chance to sound the alarm. In the darkness of the compound, they passed like shadows. As they arrived, one of the guards stirred. He turned to his colleague and mumbled something in Baluch. Neither Raven understood Baluch language, but they knew any movement on the part of the guards would put their colleagues in mortal danger. As the guards stood and stretched after their sleep, the two Ravens stalked the two men. As they reached for their cherished German Mauser rifles, they faced two shadowy figures. While Alexander and Eugenia were not as adept in the mystic arts as Naismith, or even Elizabeth, they were well trained in how to disable men with a carefully placed, two fingered strike. Once the two men were unconscious, Alexander and Eugenia whispered in the ears of their victims imparting a false memory that would be the only thing they would remember when they awoke.

Elizabeth and Beverly joined Sykes at the docks in his part of the operation. Naismith was concerned about their escape from Gwadar. It was up to Sykes, Elizabeth, and Beverly to create a distraction at the docks that would allow the Ravens to safely exit the city. Sykes understood the mission, but he wondered how the three of them would make good their own escape after completing their work on the docks. For once, Elizabeth decided to use a slight bit of mesmerism on a fellow officer, just to calm him. She said, "Colonel, do not worry. It will be well." She watched as his aura changed from yellow-orange to blue-green. The mesmerism worked. Sykes was not completely comforted, but he would accept they had a plan to escape. Elizabeth and Beverly knew that he would never believe the plan even if they told him. It would be hard enough to explain to their fellow Ravens, much less someone as practically minded as Sykes.

Naismith stood on the rooftop and looked once again at his wristwatch. It was 0255hrs. The Ravens had been inside the compound for thirty minutes. They had no more than five minutes left to complete their mission. Naismith and Martha had accomplished their tasks. Five different maps were rolled up into leather map tubes they had brought with them. Now, it was up to the rest of the team. His colleagues in the building were supposed to have been on the roof minutes ago. What was the problem?

Two floors below, Jonathan and Marian were collecting the ledgers that Elizabeth had reported listed the enemies of the Raj. Suddenly, the door opened. A man carrying an oil lamp walked into the room. The man was in a German military uniform. He was wearing trousers tucked into his riding boots and a military shirt which normally would have been covered by a dress jacket. The summer heat and late hour meant that his duty dress was less formal. Regardless of how formal, Marian noticed that he was wearing a pistol on his right hip. It was clear he was looking for something. The Ravens hoped that he wasn't looking for them. If he found them, he was certain to raise the alarm and possibly do his best to harm one or both Ravens.

Marian looked at Jonathan and pointed to the corner of the room. Jonathan moved silently to the corner and disappeared in the shadows. Meanwhile, Marian began to stalk the unsuspecting intruder. Marian dropped to the floor and began to work along the bookshelves and desks while watching the boots of her prey move toward her. The only noise in the room was the German's heavy boots, though both Ravens would have admitted that the sound of the blood rushing to their heads might have been just as loud. At the last second, Martha used a yogic technique allowing her to rise from the floor without effort. The appearance of a figure in midnight blue in front of the German was barely reflected in the lamplight. His face turned white from the shock of this specter. Marian raised her right hand and covered the German's mouth and nose. She stared into his eyes and said, "Why are you here?"

In the trance state that Marian had imposed, he answered quietly, "I forgot my notebook. I keep track of my accomplishments each day and then write them into a diary early in the morning. I woke and remembered, I forgot the notebook."

Marian nodded and said in a calm, almost motherly voice, "It is fine. You are done here tonight. You will go back to your barracks and return tomorrow to find your notebook. There is nothing to worry about and you will return to your room and go to sleep. You will feel good about the hard work you accomplished today. You need to turn around and leave the building."

The German was relaxed and compliant in the ways of the waking dream. He turned and left. The lamplight followed him down the stairs and, as Marian watched from the window, out the door and across the compound.

Jonathan said, "That was a near-run thing."

Marian smiled and whispered, "Only if you didn't know

how to control a man's mind. Let's get to the rooftop. We don't want to be late!"

Just after Marian and Jonathan arrived on the roof, Alexander and Eugenia appeared at the stairwell. Naismith used hand signals to send Alexander and Eugenia to the four corners of the roof to create the signal for the *Scimitar*. In their kit bags, they carried with them six small radium-painted balls carefully encased in lead boxes. They configured the boxes in the shape of an arrow pointing toward the Arabian Sea. They looked up to see Naismith give them another hand signal. It was 0300hrs and time to open the boxes, revealing mirrored interior surfaces that reflected the green glow of the radium. These lights would not fail because they were powered by a new, barely understood, atomic science.

After placing the boxes, they joined Naismith and the other Ravens. Marian and Jonathan were wearing heavy backpacks, now laden with the ledgers, and Naismith and Martha were carrying the leather map tubes on slings across their backs. Their mission was accomplished. Naismith looked at his watch. Two events needed to happen in the next two minutes. He hoped they would happen in the right order.

Beverly looked at her watch. It was precisely three. She looked up at Sykes and Elizabeth and nodded. They were sitting on the deck of the dhow that had carried the Ravens to Gwadar. Elizabeth was at the stern, Sykes at the bow. With that nod, they each pulled a lanyard on a chemical fuse. They had five minutes to clear the deck and walk down the quay toward an empty dock. No need to rush, but Elizabeth could tell Sykes was ready to break out into a run. As she joined him and they walked past Beverly, she touched Sykes arm and said, "It will all work as planned, Colonel. I promise." She felt his pulse slow as the three of them walked down the quay.

HMFS Scimitar approached the city in silence. The airship had been hovering nearly a mile away from the northern city wall at five thousand feet. At that distance and altitude, Smythe was certain they were invisible to even the most careful observer. As they closed toward their target, Smythe switched his airship to electric batteries, making their approach silent. Of course, if someone had been looking for the ship, they might have seen the giant grey lozenge shape passing through the fog that rolled in from the Arabian Sea. At 0300hrs on a Ramadan night, no one in Gwadar was awake except street villains and smugglers who were concentrating on their own clandestine work. They would never raise an alarm.

Smythe stood at the forward observer position in the front of the glass bridge. Normally, it would have been one of his two ensigns in this position while he sat in his bridge chair and watched over the navigator and the conning officer steering the ship. This was not a normal night, so he wanted to be the man watching for the signal. Looking through a set of Royal Navy binoculars, he strained his eyes looking for the signal. Suddenly it appeared — a green glowing broadhead arrow. He turned to the officer steering his airship and said, "Conning officer, on my mark. Set course, 188 degrees, full speed."

Ensign Danforth stood at a large oak wheel that would have been more at home in a sailing ship from the previous century. He responded, "Aye, aye, Captain. Course 188, full speed."

He reached down to the four throttle controls that would send the message to the flight engineer: Full speed ahead on all four electric engines. The airship shifted slightly as he steered the new course and as the large propellers increased their rotation. Smythe's airship executive officer, Lieutenant Cooper, watched the various instruments including the compass, airspeed indicators, and battery storage indicator. He stood at the large navigation table and watched as a small calculating machine called an analytic engine clattered away. He fed data into the machine and it was supposed to provide updates using all available information. It was the first time he had seen an analytic engine and he did not trust it completely. He was using his own circular slide rule as a double check. The captain had made it clear; this was not a night to have anything but precision. As executive officer, Cooper was responsible for that precision.

He looked down as the analytic engine delivered its message. He checked his calculations. They were one and the same. He said, "Sir, arrival on target in two, I say again, two minutes."

Smythe looked again through the binoculars and then reached down and looked at the Royal Navy pocket watch hanging from a lanyard around his neck. He was absolutely determined that they would arrive on time. Not only would it matter to Naismith, but it mattered to Smythe that his airship could arrive as requested. "Conning officer, report."

"Captain, we are at full speed, course 188 degrees.

Cooper added, "All systems are at full power, sir."

Smythe said, "Gentlemen, on time delivery is what we must provide tonight. Our colleagues on the ground demand it. We are to hover over the building precisely at 0305hrs. We will make it so." He looked back at Cooper and said, "XO, if you please, go down to the cargo bay and make ready to receive the Ravens."

Cooper had already turned and was headed toward the companionway door. He said over his shoulder, "Aye, aye, Captain." Cooper grabbed the highly polished paired wooden stair rails and slid down them. He arrived in less than a minute at the lowest deck in the three-deck cabin slung below the rigid airship.

Smythe watched as the green arrowhead grew larger. He

said "Conning officer, reduce speed on engines one and two to all slow. Shut down engines three and four. And, if you please, bring us to fifty feet."

Danforth swallowed hard. Fifty feet was hard enough when approaching a formal airship dock. The two forward engines would allow for him to maintain a slow speed, but he wasn't steering toward an airship dock. Instead, he was steering a two-hundred-foot-long gas bag filled with explosive hydrogen among buildings of different sizes with updrafts from each of the rooftops changing every few yards. He said, "Aye, aye, Captain." He watched over Smythe's shoulder as the green broadhead arrow grew larger and larger.

Finally, Smythe said, "All stop."

The conning officer threw the throttles for engines one and two into reverse and then to all stop. He felt rather than heard the propellers on the forward engines stop. The ship stopped moving just above the green glowing arrow. The ensign took a long breath for what seemed his first in several minutes. He looked up at Smythe.

The ship's captain was turned to him. He was smiling as he said, "That wasn't too hard, eh? And right on time. Well done, Danforth."

Down in the cargo bay, Cooper was laying on his stomach looking over the edge of the opening created by the airship's large, clam-shelled cargo doors. Fifty feet below, he could see the green glow of the broadhead arrow and six figures dressed in midnight-blue uniforms. He looked over at his flight engineer and said, "Engineer Mate Jensen, throw the heaving line." The mate tossed a light rope down toward the rooftop. One of the figures grabbed the line and pulled it taught. Cooper said, "Jensen, send down the rope ladders if you please." The mate released two rope ladders. They unraveled along the heaving line toward the ground. As soon as the rope ladders landed, the figures began to climb. As the last figure reached midway along the ladder, Cooper watched as the shadow reached into a bag at his waist. He released five small balls and then continued his climb. As the balls hit the roof, they burst into a white-hot flame, starting a fire that would soon engulf the building.

When the last figure reached the cargo deck, Cooper noticed it was an elderly gentleman with a shaved head and a grey beard. Naismith said, "Please tell the captain it is time to head toward the Gwadar docks."

Cooper nodded. He walked toward the internal command network and typed out a morse code message. It read: "All aboard. Phase two." The internal message responded with three letters: "ACK." Acknowledged.

On the command deck, Smythe turned to his conning officer and said, "All ahead full, if you please. Course, 175 degrees."

"Aye, aye, Captain. All ahead full, 175 degrees."

Smythe was not clear what would happen next. He knew there were three more intelligence officers on the ground. Naismith said he needed to watch for a signal and then steer slightly east of that signal. The team on the ground would do the rest. Given what he had seen so far, he decided to follow his instructions and hope for the best.

Almost as soon as the *Scimitar* began its new course, Smythe saw the "signal." It was an explosion on the docks. One of the dhows moored at the quay was on fire. He turned to the conning officer and said, "Conning officer, steer east of the fire along the quay, if you please."

"Aye, aye, sir."

Naismith arrived on the command deck and said, "Permission to join the captain on the bridge."

Smythe smiled and said, "Permission granted. Welcome aboard, Master Guru. What do we do next?"

Naismith said, "Once you are over the end of quay, if you could come to a full stop, that would be most useful."

Smythe nodded. He motioned for Naismith to join him

in the observation position. They watched as the city of Gwadar passed below them. As soon as they cleared the walls of the city, the quay appeared, illuminated by the fire. Smythe looked at Naismith and said, "Colonel?"

"If you can simply turn east and run along the docks for moment. I think I can see the rest of my team."

Smythe could see nothing at all on the docks, but he motioned for the conning officer to follow Naismith's instructions. Suddenly, Naismith said, "Please stop here for a moment."

"All stop."

"Aye, aye, Captain. All stop."

Naismith reached into one of the cargo pockets in his trousers and pulled out a small knife. Smythe watched in amazement as the knife stood up in the palm of Naismith's hand and began to spin. It seemed to be alive and balancing on its own. Naismith smiled and said, "We won't have to wait long."

Once the dhow exploded, Sykes, Elizabeth and Beverly waited at the end of the quay. The harbor was lighted by the fire. Another fire inside the city back-lighted the fortress walls so they glowed red. Elizabeth looked toward the city wall. Appearing as if a ghost floating over the wall, the grey form of the airship silently approached. It stopped just above them. During their briefing, Naismith told Elizabeth to expect the ship to arrive and then to focus her mind. He instructed her to establish a link between their two minds and then follow his instructions.

Elizabeth heard Naismith say, "It's time. Gather your colleagues and focus on my voice."

Elizabeth nodded to herself and then turned to Beverly

and Sykes. She said, "Please take my hands." Beverly accepted the instruction without question.

Sykes offered his hand but said, "What are we going to do now?"

Elizabeth closed her eyes and focused on enhancing the connection with her master guru. Once she completed, she slowed her breathing and focused on her *chi*.

He repeated his question, "What are we going to do now?"

Sykes never did quite understand the answer to his question. He realized that if he ever told anyone what he thought happened, he would be considered mad. All he knew for certain was one moment he was on the dockyards of Gwadar and the next, he was on the bridge of an airship.

Smythe and his conning officer stood with their mouths wide open as they watched three individuals appear out of thin air.

Naismith smiled at Elizabeth and said, "That was very well done."

As the airship headed out to sea and climbed to a cruising altitude of five thousand feet, the Ravens and Percy Sykes gathered in the passenger compartment to compare notes and review the material they gathered. It was an active conversation with Sykes asking more questions and Master Guru Naismith covering the details he wanted his colleague to know and avoiding discussions that were reserved for the Ravens. Suddenly, one of the senior mates entered the passenger cabin. He said, "Lieutenant Colonel Naismith and Lieutenant Colonel Sykes, the captain wishes your company on the bridge." Both senior officers knew it was not an invitation but an order. They stood up and followed the crewman.

When they arrived on the command deck, it was alive

with action. Crewman were manning various instruments; Lieutenant Cooper was at the navigation table with Ensign Danforth. The analytic engine was clattering away, calculating some future course. Smythe was standing in front of the glass observation position holding a white ceramic mug. He noticed their arrival and said, "Gentlemen, please take tea and then join me here on the observation deck."

Sitting to one side of the command deck was a small oak table with a formal silver tea service and six ceramic mugs. Naismith poured tea for Sykes and then poured himself a mug. Suddenly, Naismith realized that this had been a long night, and strong tea with milk would be most welcome. He looked up and noticed a bright orange line on the eastern horizon. It would soon be dawn. They were flying almost due east over the Arabian Sea.

When Sykes and Naismith joined the captain of the *Scimitar*, they noticed he looked excited and not the least bit tired after nearly 24 hours of flight. Smythe said, "I just received a coded message on the Marconi wireless. We are at war."

Sykes was the first to recover from the shock of Smythe's declaration. He said, "With Russia?"

Smythe shook his head. "With Germany, the Austrians, and, soon enough, with the Turks."

Naismith nodded. It was as Chodak had warned. A world at war. He said, "Captain, I realize the plan was to return to the airship dock in Rawalpindi. Obviously, the plan has changed. What are your orders?"

"I will return you to Bombay and then begin a patrol in the Arabian Sea. It appears the Admiralty believes there are German warships on patrol and we are to find them and sink them if we can. If we cannot sink them, the least we can do is follow them until our warships can engage."

Sykes was not familiar with the capabilities of the Royal Navy airships. He asked, "Captain, how is it possible for you to sink a warship?"

"Lieutenant Colonel Sykes, the *Scimitar* is a scout ship, but we have a weapons deck which includes four machine guns and a few bombs you might call small aerial torpedoes. I expect few ships in the German Navy would be prepared for an air attack, so we would have surprise on our side. If I can engage them, I will."

Naismith said, "We have reporting that the Germans have submarines and flying boats operating between Bombay and German East Africa. I think you will have plenty to hunt as the months go on."

Smythe was about to comment when Danforth walked up to him and said, "Sir, observation deck two has spotted smoke from a warship headed west along our route. It is five miles ahead bearing 080 degrees."

Smythe nodded. He turned to Cooper and said, "Executive officer, calculate an intercept course if you please. We need to determine friend or foe." He then turned to the senior mate serving as the conning officer and said, "Spencer, please sound action stations."

The senior mate smiled and said, "Aye, aye, sir." He pressed a red button next to the throttle levers. Suddenly, alarm bells rang throughout the airship.

"Action stations initiated, sir."

Naismith turned to Smythe and said, "Captain, I suspect we will only get in the way of your operation so Sykes and I will return to the passenger cabin."

Before Smythe could say anything, Sykes asked, "Sir, if possible, could I visit the weapons deck? I would like to observe the mission from that position. I promise I will not be in the way."

Smythe nodded both his dismissal and agreement. In truth, he was already thinking about how he would engage the enemy, assuming there was an enemy out there. No matter the bizarre nature of the early morning events, these intelligence officers were no longer of interest to him.

Naismith climbed down the ladder and into the passenger cabin. The room was alive with conversation as the Ravens shared their actions for the evening and commented on the material that they acquired in the operation. They also wanted to know the reason for the alarm bell and red flashing light.

Naismith spent a moment looking at his team. They were the best of his students and deserved a chance to enjoy the moment. Unfortunately, he needed to interrupt their celebration. It was not something he wished to do, but he needed to do so.

"Attention, Ravens."

The team looked up at their master guru. While he rarely offered a friendly countenance when talking to the team, they realized immediately that he had something serious to discuss. Elizabeth wondered if it was based on some action she completed or failed to complete. As the youngest member of the team, she was always on edge that she wasn't living up to the standard of the Ravens. She shouldn't have worried.

"I come to you with a heavy heart today. We just accomplished a very important mission, and I am so proud of your actions. Once again, the Ravens have conducted a special operation leaving behind no trace of our action, with no enemy wounded and no casualties on our side. We remain the invisible force the Crown needs. Perfect in so many ways. I congratulate you on the success."

Naismith paused to collect his thoughts. He realized that this might be the last time he would see the team together and possibly the last time he would see some of these incredible people alive. He continued.

"I have just come from the bridge of this airship. The Airship Captain Smythe has received a coded message on the

Marconi wireless. Ladies and gentlemen, the British Empire is now at war."

The normally stoic faces of the intelligence officers displayed surprise and concern. Elizabeth gasped and put her hand to her mouth to avoid revealing her dismay. War. That would mean her entire family was now at risk. Her parents were in Constantinople facing a war in the shadows. Her brother's unit would most likely be dispatched to the front lines, wherever that might be. It was too horrible to contemplate.

Naismith continued, "As you well know, Central Europe has been at war for some days, with the Austro-Hungarian Empire and the Russian Empire declaring war based on conflict in the Balkans. Early this morning, German forces conducted a lightning attack through Belgium designed to flank French defenses. Our defense pact with France obliged us to send forces to the continent. We can expect the Crown to request the assistance of the Indian Army and, by extension, our assistance in this fight. For now, the Ottoman Empire remains neutral."

Naismith paused to gather his final thoughts. "As many of you know, the Ottoman government is very close to the German Kaiser, so we can expect the Ottoman Empire to join forces with the Germans and the Austrians. When they do, both India and Egypt will be at risk. Our world is now at war." Naismith paused again. The next statements would be critical. "Ladies and gentlemen, the Crown will expect you to deliver your best efforts to ensure victory. I don't know where you will be dispatched. That is outside my brief, but I have no doubt you will demonstrate your skills on the battlefield the same way you have demonstrated your skills in the shadows. The airship is currently pursuing a target here in the Arabian Sea. When that mission is accomplished, we will be docking in Bombay. We will then take a train to Rawalpindi where we will await instructions from the Intelligence Division."

Naismith took a breath and said, "Our work this morning will be of great importance to our colleagues responsible for the security of India. Whether our work will continue in that line or in support of forces in combat, I cannot say. What I can say is that I have no doubt your future work will be central to the survival of the United Kingdom. I recommend that you try to rest now because we will be very busy in the days and weeks ahead. This may be our last chance to enjoy each other's company. If any of you need help in relaxation meditation, please let me know."

With that, Naismith sat down in one of the passenger benches and stared out the porthole, lost in his own thoughts. The cabin went quiet as each of the Ravens took a seat. Elizabeth saw Beverly and Alexander sit together holding hands. She was jealous of the comfort that they must have felt as they shared thoughts of the dangers ahead. Elizabeth now understood why her parents were so close and had been so successful for so long. The trade, as it was called by her peers, was a lonely one.

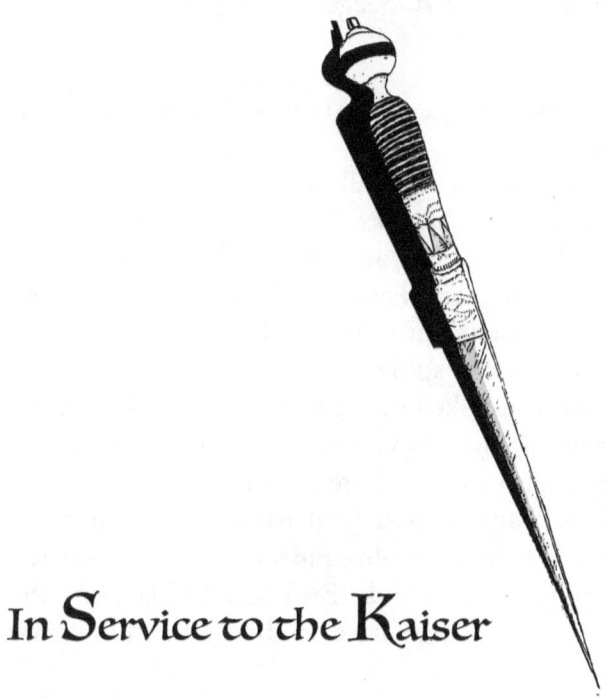

In Service to the Kaiser

06 August 1914 — Damascus

JAMES AND MICHAEL O'CONNELL WERE SHARING A MEAL AT AN INDOOR CAFÉ
in Damascus. It would be dangerous to be seen eating before
iftar even if they were not among the faithful. The most
religious of the Muslim community late in the month of
Ramadan were tired, thirsty and hungry, and anyone having
even coffee at a street café risked being assaulted with fists or
stones. The café owner was a member of the ancient Syrian
Christian community. The community was dwindling as
many Christians left for the more cosmopolitan cities of
Beirut and Alexandria on the Mediterranean coast. The
owner was willing to serve other Christians, but only because
his establishment was frequented by the German officers who
were working with the Turkish military in Damascus. None
of the faithful would risk reprisal from the Germans, but the
owner was still cautious. The O'Connells were seated at the
best table in the darkened café and received the best service.

Unlike the Germans, they spoke Arabic and they treated him with courtesy.

James was staring into his small cup of strong, sweet coffee. He was lost in thought, but his thoughts were not invisible to his son. Michael had long ago surpassed his father in the mystic arts. He saw his father's aura reflected worry as he considered their current situation. Finally, Michael's patience ended and he decided to speak.

"Father, have you talked to the Germans? The Ottomans have stayed neutral, but now Germany and Britain are at war. What do they expect us to do here in Arabia?"

"Michael, we have worked hard to make the Germans more powerful here in the Arabia and we have even gathered information on the actions of the British in Arabia. Now, the world is at war and we may have to choose carefully as we move forward."

"Father, do you trust the Germans to fulfill their promises to us? Will they take us to Ireland?"

"Son, my best guess is that they will fulfill their promise at a time of their choosing. We have demonstrated our skills here and they will use those skills to their advantage. I think we may have to work harder for a time. Once they are confident that we have done all that we can do, they will take us back to Berlin and, eventually, deliver us to the Irish Coast. I just don't know when that will happen. I do know that our activities will be fraught with danger as the war comes to Arabia."

"Who would fight over the land south of Damascus? I understand why the Arabs and the Jews might fight over the coastal plain, but who would fight for a desert?"

"I suspect the Germans care little about the desert, but they care about the oil in southern Mesopotamia and Persia. That is where we will have to go if we intend to help them."

"Then we will fulfill our promises and make sure they fulfill theirs. I will go wherever we need to go so long as we can work together. We will continue our service to the Kaiser so that we can serve ourselves in Ireland."

"Michael, thank you for saying that. I was afraid you would not willingly go back into the desert."

"We have accomplished much as we uncovered the Arab conspiracies in the Ottoman Army. The Turks must know we are able to help them in ways they cannot accomplish. If it means traveling into the desert and toward Basra, then that is our destiny."

James smiled and said, "Son, you have been in the Arab world so long that you speak like an Arab mystic!"

"Father, the mystic arts are shared across Asia. It is the British and the Germans who don't understand."

As Michael looked up from his father's face, he saw the image of a bone white skull floating in the corner of the room. If it was possible for a skull to smile, it seemed as if that visage was smiling. Inside Michael's head he heard a voice whisper, "You understand, boy. This war will be the beginning of the end of the European empires and the rise of the power of Asia." Michael agreed with the sentiment, but he cared little about Asia. All he really cared about was increasing the power of the O'Connells.

Escape from the Sublime Porte

10 August 1914 — Constantinople

FRANCIS BANKROFT LEFT THE BRITISH EMBASSY WITH THE FULL UNDER-standing that he would never return. Earlier that morning, he had a lengthy discussion with both the military attaché, Admiral Limpus, and the ambassador. He pointed out that since His Majesty's government had entered the war, his contacts in the Turkish Army were unwilling to meet with him. He explained to them that because the Turkish Empire was not at war with Great Britain, he had received his instructions from his higher headquarters in Rawalpindi to return to India. The Indian Army was mobilizing to support the war in Europe. While not precisely correct, it was true that the Intelligence Bureau had instructed him to leave as soon as possible.

What he didn't tell either the ambassador or Admiral Limpus was he was convinced the Turks would join the Germans and the Austrians soon and when that happened, everyone in the British Embassy would become well-cared-for prisoners of war for the duration of the war. They had ignored his reporting and remained convinced that the CUP would not be so foolish as to join the Germans. Francis was certain that Enver Pasha and Talat Pasha would carry the day and convince the rest of the CUP leadership that there were good reasons to go to war. They were convinced they could recover lands in the Caucasus lost decades ago to both the Russians and the Persians and perhaps even retake Egypt. Francis thought the idea mad, but all of his sources were convinced that war with the Russians was inevitable and that Enver Pasha was already planning operations across the Suez.

Neither the ambassador nor the admiral argued against his departure, so Francis emptied his office, burned his code books and walked out the main gate. His Russian counterpart, Colonel Naglieff was waiting for him in a carriage bearing the emblem of the Russian Empire. As he climbed into the carriage, the driver snapped his whip, and the carriage shot down the street toward the Bankroft yali on the Sea of Marmara. As the carriage rattled down the broken pavement north of the Golden Horn, Naglieff looked at his colleague and said, "You realize I told you."

"Yes, Sasha. You did and I argued you were wrong. That said, Mary and I made all the necessary arrangements just in case you were right. We are ready to sail into the Black Sea today. I hope you are ready."

"Everything I need is in the trunk attached to the carriage. I have one uniform, my reporting notebooks and my pistols. The rest of my household goods, I have sold or given away. My ambassador is equally blind to the eventual conflict with the Turks. He did give me leave to return to St. Petersburg. He expects me to return. He is mistaken. I am going to war."

When they arrived at the yali, Mary and Bektashi were at the gate. Bektashi picked up Naglieff's trunk and threw it over his shoulder as if it weighed nothing. Naglieff was impressed. "Along with my uniform and notebooks, I have gold, weapons and ammunition in that chest. He must be a massively strong man."

Mary smiled and said, "And most useful as you have already noticed. By the way, we have prepared a final feast at the table. If we are going to sail for some hours, I thought we might need a meal first."

Francis smiled and said, "As always, your planning is impeccable."

Bektashi returned to the dining room and began to serve a mix of cold and warm mezze. He uncorked a bottle of Turkish red wine and stood waiting for orders. Francis gave them. "Bektashi Bey, please join us. We are now in wartime service and we all need to be ready to fight."

Bektashi looked puzzled until Mary said, "Please join us. You are our friend, our comrade in arms. We need each other."

After Mary's comment, Bektashi beamed and said, "I am your honored servant."

Naglieff said, "And a good shot."

"Sir, long before I was a servant, I was a hunter. If I need to hunt men, that is just as good as hunting game in my mountain homeland Albania."

"We may be hunting Turks soon enough."

"Even better!"

As they sat at the dining room table overlooking the Sea of Marmara, Francis looked up and said, "My God! Look what has just entered the port!"

Two slate-gray warships slowly cruised in front of their yali, black smoke trailing from the four stacks and then hovering along the quiet waters of the Sea of Marmara. Francis grabbed a pair of binoculars on a side table. He focused on the ships and said, "They are both flying the German ensign. We have German warships visiting the Sublime Porte."

Naglieff shook his head. "If we needed a sign from heaven to tell us it was time to leave, this is certainly it." He stood up from the table and said to Mary, "With your permission, I will prepare my gear for travel."

Francis said to Bektashi, "It is time to make good our escape."

Bektashi made a deep bow and said, "As you wish, Commander. I fear this city soon will become no place for an Albanian." Bektashi walked into the living room and started rolling up a small, but particularly beautiful Turkish carpet. When he was finished, he threw the carpet over his shoulder and said to Mary, "Madame, there is room on the sailboat. You need to have at least one remembrance of life here in the Sublime Porte."

What Do We Do Now?

15 August 1914 — Rawalpindi

THE RAVENS AND LIEUTENANT COLONEL SYKES SAT AROUND THE LARGE MAP table in the office of the commander of the Intelligence Bureau of the Western Division of the Indian Army. Colonel Winslow-Heath looked over the men and women. All were wearing regulation uniforms, some with rows of campaign medals. This was the first time that Winslow-Heath had assembled the Ravens in his office. He knew each of them from a one-on-one briefing before he dispatched them to the far reaches of the Empire, but he had to admit he was impressed to see them all together and, more importantly, in uniform. Of course, this was by no means a cause for celebration. He had assembled these special-operations troops because the Empire was at war. He wanted to be certain that each of them understood the importance of their recent collective effort as well as the importance that the Crown placed on their future individual efforts on the borders of the Empire.

Winslow-Heath was pleased to see Naismith in uniform. His master guru in The Viceroy's College had an illustrious career in the Gurkha regiment before he took on the role of intelligence collector. He was an "old timer" who shared many campaigns with Winslow-Heath. His rows of campaign medals, including his Distinguished Service Order medal and his Kabul to Kandahar Star, showed his success on the battlefield. Naismith might be a senior instructor, but his background in combat arms with an illustrious regiment, the Gurkhas, made him doubly valuable to India.

He wondered if Naismith would be willing to return to The Viceroy's College with his country at war. Of course, they would need many new intelligence officers, but he wasn't sure the Indian Army would tolerate two years of training when their troops would be in continuous combat. The Viceroy's College might become something far less than it had been all these years. Winslow-Heath understood that you could not mass-produce intelligence officers the way you produced young infantry or cavalry officers. He wasn't sure the leaders of the Indian Army understood.

Another factor would affect Naismith's future. Winslow-Heath had already been approached by the Indian government's Special branch. They had their eyes on Naismith and wanted him to run a counter-revolutionary mission, hunting down the Indians listed on the German rolls just identified by the Ravens' mission. Winslow-Heath thought there would have to be a long, one-on-one discussion with Naismith after this meeting to determine if the old intelligence hand understood why a world war meant that The Viceroy's College would have to close. Luckily, he knew Naismith was fond of a special blend of tea. He had acquired a pound of the best for this future discussion.

In the case of Sykes, Winslow-Heath was pleased to see one of his favourites. Sykes rarely returned to headquarters. He seemed to prefer staying in the borderlands risking his life. For that reason alone, Winslow-Heath admired his officer. He also knew Sykes had a reputation as an independent, headstrong adventurer, intolerant of senior officers who knew less than he did about the subject they were discussing. Apparently, Sykes had either mended his ways or Naismith and his team mended them for him.

Winslow-Heath was pleased that Sykes had succeeded as a member of this special-operations team filled with individuals who Sykes might not have understood or even liked. It mattered little to Winslow-Heath. He already had another assignment for Sykes. Sykes would be travelling in Central Asia to open a listening post on the borderlands between Russia and China. It would require months of hard travel, but that seemed to be just the sort of mission that Sykes relished.

The staff had already laid out a full tea service including sandwiches, pastries, and fresh fruit. One of the few joys for Winslow-Heath of staying in the burning plain of the Punjab during the summer was the ability to enjoy freshly picked mangoes. When alone, he took off his service jacket, wrapped a napkin around his neck and spooned out the luxurious fruit directly from the skin. In this case, the mess staff had chopped up small squares of mango and mixed them with fresh strawberries from the cantonment gardens. He was never able to believe strawberries could grow in the Punjab heat, but apparently the mess sergeant and his Indian staff were determined to deliver a bit of England to the senior staff in Rawalpindi.

Winslow-Heath opened by saying, "Please, I want this to be a celebration rather than a briefing. Take tea, enjoy the food and sit down here in the library. In the future, we will have little time to enjoy together, but for now, there is no reason not to celebrate the recent success of the Ravens!"

Naismith realized that none of his charges would obey the Colonel's instructions unless he did so. As he walked to the table, he said, "Colonel, thank you for your hospitality. We are definitely ready to enjoy a bit of frivolity after the last few days." As Naismith started at the table, the rest of the Ravens followed, with Sykes at the end of the line.

Winslow-Heath said, "I hear that the *Scimitar* intercepted a German submarine in our waters. A first as I understand it. The submarine commander was caught by surprise and regretted his lack of diligence, no?"

Sykes was pouring himself a cup of tea. He looked up and offered, "Sir, the airship commander did a marvelous job and, much to my surprise, was able to sink the boat before the Germans knew what hit them! It is a lesson that we all need to learn. This will be a war on the land, sea and the air."

"Indeed, Sykes. Airships and aeroplanes." The colonel looked directly at Elizabeth and said, "And, I understand that one of the Ravens is on her way to being an aviatrix as well as an experienced intelligence officer. What a world we live in, no?" Winslow-Heath looked over at Elizabeth who almost choked on the scone and marmalade already in her mouth.

Naismith was not in a jocular mood. He had a cup of tea and a small bowl of mango and strawberries. He sat down and said, "Sir, what happens next? Certainly, the Indian Army will be mobilized to support the forces in Europe. But we have already seen the Germans intend to take the war to us here in India. How will you deploy our intelligence officers?"

Winslow-Heath shook his head and said, "Naismith, let us wait to talk grand strategy. Your Ravens need to enjoy their tea, take a day to rest. After that, we can determine what will happen next."

Elizabeth watched the auras of these two giants in her adult life. Both were playing a game that went far beyond her skills. It was clear they were working hard to mislead each other. She could see the colonel would win that battle simply because he outranked her master guru. She decided to change the conversation before there was too much tension in the room. She said, "Sir, what news from my parents in Constantinople?" She watched carefully as the colonel's aura changed from a neutral green to a greenish yellow. She knew he intended to tell a half-truth. Still, Elizabeth listened carefully.

"Elizabeth, your parents are currently making good their escape by way of the Black Sea. They are traveling with a Russian intelligence officer well known to the Ravens, Colonel Alexander Naglieff." Winslow-Heath looked around the room and continued, "Yes, the same Naglieff that you faced in Afghanistan two years ago."

Winslow-Heath stopped to take a long drink of tea from his mug. He shook his head and said, "Of course, the Russians are our allies now, so they have been working together and he has facilitated their escape to Odessa. Once they are in Odessa, I will be sending them new orders to return to India by way of Persia. We need to know what the Germans have been doing in Persia. I suspect it is much the same as what you just uncovered. For certain, they will not be held as prisoners of war in Constantinople and that is a very good thing."

Elizabeth was lost in thought for a moment when Beverly came up to her. She said, "Don't worry, Elizabeth. After all, your parents were conducting operations well before you were born and well before I was in service. They know the trade and will be safe."

Elizabeth was not so certain, but she was pleased her parents were out of Constantinople. She had not revealed to Naismith or the Ravens about the attack in the yali when Gertrude Bell was visiting. Death had been hunting the Bankrofts in Constantinople. Now they were on the run from that threat. An escape to Odessa would be a good thing.

Elizabeth thought for a moment about what this all meant. Just over two years ago, she was a student, a cadet in a school for intelligence officers. Since then, she had seen death and had killed men. She had developed her skills in the mystic arts just when the world was facing the chaos of a world war that would be won by technology, not the mystic arts. Intelligence collection of the sort that she had practiced in the last two years seemed to her to be so artificial, so unimportant. She thought her experience in aeroplanes would be far more useful than working informants. All she knew for certain was her world had turned upside down. And then there was her concern over her parents. It was not clear when she might see them again. At this point, Elizabeth understood that their lives would be changed until peace returned. It was just not clear when that would be.

As the afternoon festivities continued, Elizabeth found herself dozing in one of the colonel's leather armchairs. It wasn't that she didn't enjoy the company of her colleagues; she was simply exhausted. Elizabeth had just fallen into a deep sleep when she heard a voice in her head: merely a whisper, but an emotionless whisper. It intrigued her and terrified her at the same time. Who was this, intruding into her dreams?

"Elizabeth, you will be going to war soon. You will serve your country. You will have adventures. And you will have opportunities to kill. You have already killed. Wasn't it thrilling to have that power? Just give in to that power, Elizabeth. You know great power. Power. Remember. Power."

Naismith approached Elizabeth. He noticed she was daydreaming in the middle of what was supposed to be a celebration. Further, he could see she was terribly uncomfortable. He gently touched her forehead hoping to relieve whatever terror might be racing through the mind of his youngest Raven and to bring her back to the room and her colleagues. As he touched her, broken pieces of blue, white and black glass fell from Elizabeth's neck. He recognized it as a *nazar*, an amulet protecting the wearer from the evil eye.

A well-remembered voice entered his head. "Chodak."

"Yes, Naismith. Chodak. This one will be mine. You wait and see."

"Not if I can help it, Demon."

"But that is the point, Naismith. You can't help her anymore."

Naismith realized Chodak was gone.

And in that moment, Naismith understood that the demon was right about at least one thing: He could not protect his student from herself. It would be up to her.

About the Author

J.R. SEEGER is a Western New York native who served as a U.S. Army paratrooper and as a CIA case officer for a total of 27 years of federal service. In October 2001, Mr. Seeger led a CIA paramilitary team into Afghanistan. He splits his time between Western New York and Central New Mexico.

About the Illustrator

LISE SPARGO has been an archaeologist, an intelligence officer, and the manager of a conservation charity. She is a formally trained botanical illustrator and splits her time between New Mexico and western New York focusing on capturing plant species using graphite and watercolours.

Author's Notes

This book is a work of fiction. By now, it should be clear to the reader that there is more than a bit of history embedded in *A Sound like Distant Thunder.* The description of the clandestine conflict between the British and the German Empires just prior to World War I as well as several of the figures in the book are real.

First, a brief description of the conflict. By 1907, the tensions between Britain and Russia, known as "the Great Game," in England and the "Tournament of Shadows" in Russia, ended with a level of cooperation impossible to imagine in the previous century. Russia, France, and Great Britain entered into a formal agreement known as the "triple entente." While not quite the formal alliance as the Entente Cordial between Great Britain and France, it meant that Russia and Great Britain were no longer involved in a "cold war" on the borders of British India, Afghanistan, and the Russian Empire. In 1911, the German government demonstrated a level of muscular foreign and defense policy that worried the British government in London and the Indian government in Calcutta (soon to be moved to New Delhi). That year, the Germans deployed a gunboat off the Moroccan coastline, threatening French colonial forces. They did so as a means of gaining leverage in Africa for their own expanding colonies. At the same time, the German navy began launching their own version of the super battleships that rivaled the "Dreadnought" class of the Royal Navy. Finally, the construction of the "Berlin to Baghdad" railway established political alliances among the German, the Austrian, and the Ottoman empires. Though never completed before the start of World War I, the British viewed this as threatening the lifeline of the British Empire: the Suez canal. The growing alliance between the German Kaiser and the "Young Turks" of the Ottoman

Committee for Union and Progress (CUP) included substantial German support to modernize the Ottoman Army. To counter that effort, Great Britain dispatched Admiral Limpus and his team to help train the Ottoman Navy in advance of two British-manufactured modern cruisers that would have been far superior to anything in the Russian Black Sea fleet.

Into this geo-political stew, the great powers dispatched intelligence collectors to "go spy the land." In Berlin, the Foreign ministry maintained an "eastern section" managed by the orientalist Max Von Oppenheim. One of Oppenheim's most famous operatives, Wilhelm Wassmuss, conducted operations before and during the Great War in Mesopotamia and in Persia. His primary British adversary during the war was a long serving British Raj intelligence officer and explorer, Lieutenant Colonel Percy Sykes. Deeper in Arabia, the British dispatched an Arabist named William Shakespear. Shakespear was based in Kuwait and used his personal connections with the Kuwaiti emir to travel into the desert and meet with Muhammed Ibn Saud. Two other intrepid adventurers, one official, one unofficial traveled Arabia at the same time and provided detailed reporting on the nature of the Arabian tribes. The first, Lieutenant Colonel Gerald Leachman, spent much of 1913 and 1914 in Arabia. During the war he became one of the most senior intelligence officers operating in the Middle East. The second, Gertrude Bell, was a woman of profound skills and courage. She was an exceptional linguist, a translator of Persian poetry, an archaeologist, a writer, an intrepid desert traveler and, once the war began, a critically important intelligence and political advisor to the British military. Early in the war, she served as a member of the Arab Bureau serving with other British archaeologists, David Hogarth, and T.E. Lawrence and then during the Iraq campaign as the advisor to Percy Cox, the senior British political officer in Basra.

A Small Bibliography

For those interested in further reading on the Great War in the Middle East and/or some of the individuals involved, the following reading list offers a start. There are many others worth reading, but this list should help.

A Peace to End All Peace by David Fromkin. While over thirty years old, the book remains the best possible start point for anyone interested in Middle East history in the first three decades of the 20th century.

Setting the Desert on Fire by James Barr. This work focuses on the Arabia and the desert war made famous by T.E. Lawrence in his two works, *Revolt in the Desert* and *Seven Pillars of Wisdom*.

Gertrude Bell: Queen of the Desert, Shaper of Nations by Georgina Howell. While there are nearly a dozen biographies of Bell, Howell's book in the best start for anyone interested in this brilliant and courageous woman.

Persia in the Great Game: Sir Percy Sykes, explorer, consult, soldier, spy by Anthony Wynn. This is the best single biography of this exceptional British intelligence officer.

The Berlin-Baghdad Express: The Ottoman Empire and Germany's bid for World Power by Sean McMeekin. This book covers both the geo-political and engineering challenges associated with the German-Ottoman alliance prior to the Great War.

The Ottoman Endgame: War, revolution, and the Making of the Modern Middle East, 1908-1923 by Sean McMeekin. This book covers in detail the complexity of the CUP-German relationship and the inner workings of the "Young Turks."

War by Revolution by Donald McKale. This is the most detailed and most readable account of the German operations against the British colonies.

Discussion Points for Teachers and Book Clubs

In this series, I have tried to keep the fantasy tied to the reality of colonial Britain in the first few decades of the 20th century. In that sense, the reader sees the British Raj through the eyes of a young woman who is coming to terms with what her life will be like in this new century as well as what will happen to her world when great powers go to war. Here are a few questions/discussion points.

- How does Elizabeth cope with the role of women in the military? Does she see the limitations she is facing?

- What does Elizabeth know about the structure of the British Indian Empire? She is the daughter and granddaughter of military and intelligence officers who have been in the Indian government for decades before she was born. Does she understand any of the tensions that exist between the governing powers and the governed? How does her mother express these tensions in her stories?

- In both books, we listen to characters who are "Anglo-Indian" talk about their lives. What did it mean to be an Anglo-Indian and what limitations did it put on their lives? How did the Germans use this to their advantage? How does Chodak intend to use this?

- Elizabeth must face death in this book. Both the threat of death and killing. Does she understand what has happened to her because of this? What would it be like to be a teenager who has seen this and who has the powers that Elizabeth demonstrates?

- Control becomes one of the issues related to Elizabeth's mystic powers. Does she understand her powers? How do others see her powers? What are the differences between Elizabeth and Michael O'Connell regarding their powers?

Also by J.R. Seeger

The MIKE4 Series

"Straight from CIA's war zone files, MIKE4 crackles
with authenticity, like a satcom phone in the field."
JASON MATTHEWS, author of The Red Sparrow trilogy

MIKE4
FRIEND OR FOE
THE EXECUTIONER'S BLADE
O'CONNELL'S TREASURE
A GRAVEYARD FOR SPIES
THE SILICON ADDICTION

"If you like good tales of the shadowy, often hard-edged
world of counter-terrorism, read MIKE4!"
GENERAL STANLEY McCHRYSTAL, author of
My Share of the Task: A Memoir and *Team of Teams:
New Rules of Engagement for a Complex World*